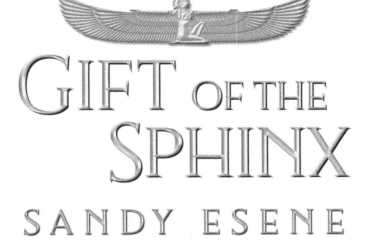

GIFT OF THE SPHINX

SANDY ESENE

BLUE BENU
—PRESS—

Published by Blue Benu Press, Seattle, Wa

Cover design by Mariah Sinclair

E-book: 978-1-7328105-3-2

Paperback 978-1-7328105-4-9

Hardbound 978-1-7328105-5-6

For
Rob
because
everything

CHAPTER ONE

The portal was closing.

Jorge shielded his eyes against the blinding light and jumped. The sharp electric fizz of magic prickled against his skin as he crossed over into the unknown. For a brief moment, or it could have been eons, it was as if he were suspended in limbo between existence and eternity. His upper body was shoved forward, pushing him through the membrane between worlds. He opened his eyes. A surreal and craggy landscape of magenta, red, and orange stretched out before him. As he gazed out in wonder, a final contraction spat him out onto a pile of pointy rocks.

He sat up assessing the damage. A few scrapes and cuts, but nothing broken. Out in the distance, the trio he'd been following hadn't seen him. Jorge hid behind a large orange boulder nearby, waiting for them to get to a safe distance before following.

It was hard to believe it was only a few hours ago that the blue-eyed stranger had told him of the treasure. All he needed to do was follow the Goddess and her two priests. What sort of adventurer worth his salt would pass up such an offer? Now he found himself a stranger in a very strange land.

Jorge leaned up against the rough, porous rock and peered down the slope to the valley below. Cutting through the terrain was a blood-red river. Above, a plateau ran adjacent to the river, similar to the land that borders the Nile. The air around him was still, as if the land were holding its breath. Surrounded by desert, he expected the familiar dusty, dried earth smell he was familiar with, but there was no scent at all. This place seemed not meant for the living.

The alien vista made him wonder if he'd traveled through a wormhole to Mars. Jorge had never been to Mars. Not yet. He was pretty certain this wasn't the Red Planet. If it were he'd be dead already.

Jorge glanced down to check on his quarry. They had discovered a golden boat resting on the riverbank. The old priest and the short, stocky one clambered up into the boat before the Goddess. It was odd that her supplicants didn't guide the Goddess into the boat first. Maybe it was their job to make sure the coast was clear for her Holiness. Jorge chalked it up to yet another strange happening in this alien land. There was something off about the three of them. It was almost as if they were traveling companions and not a sacred hierarchy.

They entered the boat, and it launched itself into the river.

Jorge would need to climb the short distance up to the plateau and follow from there, instead of traversing the uneven land below. It would make for a much better vantage point to stalk them from.

He scrambled up the loose sherbet-colored gravel, creating a sunset-hued cloud of dust. Up ahead, he spotted a giant rock jutting out of the cliffside that would make for an excellent handhold.

Sweaty after he scaled the dust-covered rock, Jorge stared down at the party below. Their slow-moving boat progressed as if it had its own agenda. Neither the Goddess Hathor nor the priests were rowing or steering the craft.

He followed them for quite some time until the boat ran aground on a rocky beach near the mouth of an enormous cavern on the other side of the river. It reminded Jorge of the Benagil sea caves in Portugal he used to explore as a youth while visiting his grandparents.

After climbing down from the plateau, Jorge mustered the courage to cross. The liquid flowing through the valley didn't just resemble blood. It was as if a vein were sliced open from the flesh of the landscape. When he reached the middle of the river, severed heads bobbed up from below and bumped up against him. The warm iron smell of blood wafted up around him as he moved. He did his best to ignore it, knowing if he started vomiting, he might never make it across.

The trek hadn't become easier once he'd made it to the other side. A writhing welcome mat of snakes stretched across the entire face of the cave at a width of seven feet. It was farther than Jorge could jump, which was crucial, as the red, black, and brown living carpet was thick with deadly Egyptian cobras.

This plane of snakes explained why the Goddess and the older priest were carried to the cave by the short and squat one. That priest must have immunity to their venomous bites. Jorge would have to circumvent the slithering mass to get to the cave.

More time lost.

If he lost track of them, he would not only lose the prospect of ever finding the treasure, but he would also lose a way out of this place. Maybe it wasn't the smartest idea to follow them across the Egyptian desert and through the magic portal, but he was inextricably caught up in the chase and tantalized by the treasure the blue-eyed stranger promised. Whether for good or ill, the lure of discovery was Jorge's Achilles' heel.

Jorge resigned himself to the task at hand and carefully circumvented the field of snakes, picking his way around them to the shear wall of rock that framed the cave. He channeled his inner mountain goat as he scrambled for handholds across the stingy cliffside. His tenuous grip threatened to give way with each advance, but the real fear of what lay below was an excellent motivator to push forward.

Dripping with sweat, he arrived at the cave and peeked inside. All hell had broken loose. The Goddess and her companions were scrambling to escape up a magical staircase as hawk-headed mummy creatures pursued them. The old priest trailed behind as he struggled to climb the stairs.

Suddenly the staircase started to fold up on itself. The Goddess and the short priest pulled themselves into a portal in the cavern's ceiling. The structure under the old man collapsed and sent him falling into the waiting arms of the hawk-headed mummies. The creatures grabbed their human treasure and stole off into a distant tunnel.

Jorge tore after them. They held, in their mummy-wrapped arms, the one person who might help him get out of this land with or without the treasure. Once Hathor and her companion escaped through that ceiling hatch to god-knows-where, the old man had become his only hope.

He followed the tunnel the creatures ran through all the way to the mouth of another cave. He glanced back. Luckily, there weren't more of them pursuing him, for now. A terror-filled scream from the old man reverberated through the tunnel.

Jorge hurried to the edge of the cave. If that cry of pain was any indication, those creatures weren't messing around.

At the tunnel's end, he leaned against the wall to stay hidden from sight. His best defense against these creatures might very well be surprise.

Jorge retrieved his water bladder and took a measured sip. Once it was depleted, that would be it. He didn't relish the thought of drinking from the river he had crossed to get to the cave, having no idea what would happen to him if he rallied the courage to drink from it.

In the center of the cave, the old priest was slumped inside a square golden cage.

Jorge had to save him. One of the priests must have created the portal he jumped through. In ancient Egypt, the holy men were known to possess powers of magic. If the old man created it, he should be able to reopen it back to the normal world.

Like the ancient Egyptians, Jorge possessed a fear of dying on foreign soil. The thought of his body slowly decomposing in this alien landscape sparked an aching awareness of his own mortality. Jorge shook it off, not wanting to get stymied by his own anxieties.

He needed to shift into survival mode.

The cavern before him was punctuated with entrances similar in size and shape to the tunnel he occupied. They were spaced about five feet apart and totaled sixteen. Near the golden cage was a large silver tub with an alabaster offering table beside it. Only three of the creatures were visible. *Where had the other ones gotten off to?*

Jorge shivered against the stagnant air that smelled of burnt plastic. Or was it hair? Even aboveground this land had a decidedly stuffy quality to it. It was neither warm nor cold. The overall environment held a peculiar closeness, inflicting a slight but ever-present claustrophobia.

Jorge pulled his binoculars from their custom pocket in his explorer's jacket. Both the public relations team and the stylists on Jorge's weekly television series, *Unearthing Facts of Outer-Space Origins, Recovering the Known,* constantly badgered him to vary his "adventurer's uniform," as they liked to call it. However, they never were required to go deep into the trenches. They never needed to be concerned with the unending dangers of exploration like chasing horrifying beasts to their lairs or emerging in an unknown realm chasing after an ancient Egyptian Goddess and her two priests.

His production crew spent their natural lives in swanky air-conditioned office-pens. Pricey Hollywood real estate that his escapades and personality paid for. Out in the field, all one could expect was the unexpected, and he knew how to dress for it. Adventurers always need to be at least two steps ahead, since preparation is paramount to success. He twisted the binoculars to focus on the figure of the old man, and a wave of revulsion swept over him. On the old man's neck was a raging, red brand. The aroma he smelled was burnt flesh.

Two of the hawk-headed mummies stood over the priest in his gilded jail cell. The largest one held a brightly glowing branding iron. His compatriot guarded the door. Jorge winced at the sight of the glistening, raw flesh. The blood curdling scream the old man made earlier was justified. He was now out cold, probably in shock. The symbol burned onto the priest's neck looked familiar and yet strange at the same time. A third beast poured a milky-white liquid from a jewel-encrusted vessel into the man-sized bowl.

The creature with the branding iron stepped out of the cage. The other latched the door after them, leaving the old man alone. The trio of creatures made their way to the offering table and knelt in unison, with the largest in the middle, creating an odd hawk-headed pyramid. Each raised its arms and then bowed in supplication, palms up, foreheads against the floor.

Jorge slipped the binoculars back into their home. The old man would be dead soon, if the cultural habits of the hawk-headed mummies were anything like those of ancient Earth societies. What he was witnessing highly resembled pre-sacrificial preparations.

To his surprise the hawk-headed creatures were leaving the chamber. He leaned out of the cave and stepped out of concealment. Channeling his inner house cat, he slunk toward the gilded cage. His senses were keen, as if he were investigating a neighbor's yard with an unaccounted for pit bull.

The cage's lock was a simple latch. No security needed in hell, he figured. Jorge pulled the large metal pin. It slipped out of his hand and nicked the cage's edge. A sharp metallic ping echoed through the cave. His ears strained for the heavy footfalls of the mummiod creatures.

Nothing.

The door creaked as he opened it. He entered the small enclosure and knelt beside the old man. He considered scooping up some of the milky substance from the silver tub to splash on the priest's face, but he didn't have a container. The beasts had taken their jewel-encrusted vessel with them.

A hard smack in the face would have to do.

The old priest's face held a serene expression, as if he hadn't a care in the world. Jorge lifted his hand and brought it down with great force. A sharp smack-clap noise of skin against skin cut through the silence.

The man didn't stir.

Double damn. The angry, inflamed brand caught Jorge's eye. He swung his hand hard onto the newly seared flesh.

The old man's eyes flew open. His mouth stretched wide as if to scream. Jorge clamped his hand over the man's mouth. The old man struggled against Jorge's grasp.

"I'm here to help you. Let's get out of here before they return."

The old man stood, then leaned into Jorge for support as they made their way out of the cage.

The cage door clanged shut as the cave suddenly began to shake. Jorge lost his balance and leaned against the golden bars to steady himself as the ground rolled beneath him. Deep, ominous creaks and groans emanated from the rock around them as large stones tumbled down from above. Jorge grabbed the old man just before he was going to topple over and pulled him under the offering table. With each tremor, Jorge's heart thumped against his chest.

A mummy creature emerged from one of the tunnels and ran toward them. Jorge hugged the old man close. The creature closed in on them, its eyes wild with fear. The creature wasn't running toward them, but away from something. Two more hawk-headed creatures quickly loped past, paying no attention to their lost treasure, then disappeared into the tunnel Jorge had emerged from.

Jorge shot out from under the offering table and yanked the old man to standing. "Run!"

CHAPTER TWO

The bland institutional-grey corridor was a perfect match to Alex's mood. If she were a chameleon whose coloring was affected solely by mood, she would have been impossible to see. On top of her general feeling of melancholy, the weight of acting like everything was okay was starting to take a toll. She feared her emotional cracks were starting to show.

Today she decided she would put it all behind her, one way or another. It was the final day to box up the remaining possessions of her mentor, Dr. Charles Buxton, and clear out his office. Her office. She still wasn't comfortable with her newfound authority. The agency promoted her to replace him, or at least to stand in as the interim. By becoming the custodian to the ancients for the Keepers of the Holy and Noble Maat, she was charged with keeping the Gods and their magic safe. She just wasn't sure if she was up to the task, or if she even had the right stuff to fill Buxton's shoes.

Beyond the day-to-day pressures of the new position, what plagued Alex was the abject fear that she would not be able to live up to the memory of one of the agency's most beloved agents, her long-dead father, Phillip. He died while she was a young girl, giving Alex just enough time to firmly establish him as her hero. One day he left to go on yet another archeological excavation in Egypt, never to return. At least that was the story she was told. KHNM and her hereditary connection to the agency was something her mother went to great pains to hide from her. It wasn't until one of the Gods became mad with power and wanted to enslave humanity that Alex learned the truth.

The task of packing Buxton's things had been easy to put off. The emotional impacts of rummaging through his affairs ranged from mind-killing mundane tasks to reliving all over again what she lost in him. But today, she needed to buckle down. She couldn't procrastinate about it any longer. People were depending on her, and she owed it to them to get her head straight.

On the rare occasions when she allowed herself to delve into the positive thoughts that lay deep under her layers of grief, she would find a dust mote–sized hope of finding clues leading her to the books of spells Buxton mentioned when they first met. With the agency on the line and Buxton gone, if there was one thing she could use, it was strong magic.

Down the hallway, Bruce the maintenance man was pressing his formidable weight against her office door. His screwdriver glinted in the bright-white florescent light as he worked to pop Buxton's nameplate off. He was straining to get the proper angle between the door and the old brass plaque. Atop his tools trolley lay a garish and bright new nameplate with *Alex Philothea—Custodian to the Ancients* emblazoned across it in bold Helvetica.

"Usually they come off easier than this." His voice was almost apologetic as he shifted to try another angle of attack.

Alex hated that Buxton's name was cleaved from the door, punctuating the finality of her loss; KHNM's loss.

Bruce pushed hard against the door. "The adhesive really bonded with the wood." With one final shove the nameplate flew off the door and landed with a clank.

Alex mustered a positivity she didn't feel. "I had a feeling you would win."

As if reading her anxiety, Bruce laid his hand on her shoulder. "You'll do just fine. Your dad would be proud." His voice cracked with emotion.

She stood in stunned silence as he collected his tools then headed down the hallway. It continually surprised her that no one really ever spoke of her dad.

"Thank you, Bruce," she called out.

He half turned and saluted her, then continued down the hallway.

Alex swung the door open. Her office was already occupied. Luke was busy putting together the boxes that her assistant Thorne ordered days ago. Alex kicked herself for letting the boxes lay fallow for too long. It gave Luke time to take notice and offer to help. Before she could say thank you but no, he started in about the archival process and how it would be more efficient if he was present, being the agency's head archivist and all.

Alex held no argument against that, since Buxton's possessions were agency property. And ultimately, she didn't really have a beef with Luke. She just felt a tinge of annoyance at what felt like an intrusion. She couldn't put a finger on why, but she held an odd possessiveness when it came to Buxton. She wanted to have the freedom to take care of his belongings as she saw fit and on her own time. She had no real claim on him. He wasn't kin, but his death was a great loss to her. Not only did she lose her mentor, but a close, personal link to her dead father.

Alex cut through the room to Luke. He handed her an empty box.

"Where should we start?" His expression was like an overeager golden retriever who is thrilled at the sight of the dried kibble in their bowl. The two of them would be packing up belongings, records, and books, not exploring unknown worlds, but you'd never know that by how amped Luke was. As an archivist, Luke possessed an overactive attraction to the mundane. However much his job suited him to a tee, Luke was different from most archivists she'd known. It was a common condition of the profession to be as pale as a peeled mushroom, since they are generally forced to exist in hidden, windowless basement work environments. Luke, on the other hand, had a rustic, tanned skin tone and well-earned surfer highlights in his wavy blond hair, proving his more than healthy relationship with the outdoors.

"I'll take care of the desk. Maybe you should start on one of the bookcases." Alex walked over to the mahogany rococo-style desk and set her box down. The leather chair's casters squeaked with age as she sank into its supple embrace. She rubbed her hands over the silky timeworn wooden desktop, remembering how Buxton prized it. In spite of the fact it was in direct aesthetic opposition to his preference for clean, modern lines.

The ornate style was popular in the eighteenth century and was known by its fanciful curved asymmetrical forms and elaborate ornamentation. His attachment may have come from the fact that it was passed down from director to director over the past two and a half centuries. If there was a coded note, or clandestine file or secret drawer, it would be hidden in the massive wooden desk, with all of its delicious nooks and crannies. But she'd not yet found any such thing.

"I can never quite get used to the idea that the old man is really gone." Luke's voice wavered with emotion as he continued to work.

"Me neither." She let the silence drag on between them, deflecting any emotional connection Luke was trying to make. She didn't have it in her to travel down a Buxton-filled memory lane with Luke. One path could lead to another, and she might admit the one thing she hadn't spoken aloud to anyone. Ever since she returned from the Netherworld, she couldn't shake the incongruent feeling that Buxton was still alive.

Alex observed Luke working at his task. How carefully he handled each item, teasing each one from the shelf with a gentle touch, reverently brushing away the dust with his gloved hand, logging and wrapping each object in protective archival paper to be packed away. KHNM couldn't ask for a more thorough and thoughtful archivist.

Although Luke had invaded her office, it was considerate of him to wait for her. She would have been really pissed if he'd plunged forward and started packing up without her. He was a good man, but at the moment his overt concern was mildly annoying. She never could stand being fussed over.

Alex pushed up the bridge of her glasses, ready to work.

The bottom drawer of the desk pulled out easily. Alex thumbed through the folders and pinched out about ten or so, then placed them on the desktop. As she flipped through the humdrum files, her mind wandered to the memory of Buxton's demise. Going over it a thousand times, trying to figure out if there was anything she could have done differently, anything that would have saved him.

She could almost feel the cold, transparent platform pressing against her chest as she lay on it suspended far above the cave. Her arms stretched down through the portal, ready to haul him up as he rushed toward her. Two hawk-headed mummies were close at his heels. Suddenly the portal shrunk. Buxton reached up. His fingertips grazed hers as the stairway collapsed. He fell to the waiting mummiod creatures below.

She wiped away a tear and gazed out beyond the stack of files in front of her to the virtual fortress of boxes Luke constructed. Somehow, she'd managed to miss that Luke had practically filled the room with empty boxes. He must have been waiting for her for quite some time. The sheer number of them was ridiculous. She smiled at the thought of Luke building away at a fort of cardboard boxes like an industrious boy looking to create a realm to rule over. He must be hurting too. He had been very close to Buxton.

Alex longed for someone she could depend on. Someone who could help her navigate through this difficult time, a confidant. Could that person be Luke? After all she'd been through, Alex couldn't fathom letting someone get close again. One thing was clear: it would never be Dr. Roberta Thorne, Buxton's old assistant, who was now assigned to Alex. Thorne held a silent but palpable grudge against her. The frigidly cold shoulder from Thorne seemed linked to the woman's high opinion of Alex's father. It was as if Thorne thought Alex had fallen far from the familial tree and in no way lived up to being a direct descendant of such a great man. They never addressed it, but that shadow always hovered over any interaction between them.

Then there was the question of Niles. She was foolish to have fallen in love with an Immortal. Did he still go by Niles? Or was it Thoth now that the Gods had returned to the Field of Reeds? Did he ever think of her? Or did she repulse him after he shed his earthly form? Was she really just a meaningless mortal fling? His silence spoke volumes.

Even Gormund, the only God to retain his human form, and the one she once counted as a dear friend, was tight lipped about Niles. Alex had called him a few times at his restaurant, Bes's Café, in New Mexico where he was hiding in plain sight, but each time the subject came up he would either clam up or awkwardly change the subject. It was disappointing, especially after all that she and Gormund had been through. Apparently, saving humanity with someone doesn't guarantee a forever friendship.

In moments of desperation, betting that possibly Gormund might be more forthcoming in person, she considered a quick trip to New Mexico under the guise of checking in with her ancestor Meyret. Gormund guarded the priestess while she rested under an enchanted sleep in an ornate tomb located under the café. She had every right to visit Meyret but couldn't bring herself to use her relationship with her just to get dirt on Niles.

Alex pored over the files that contained dull day-to-day minutia of office administration. She hoped to find a folder with a bright yellow tab labeled *Lost Books of Magic* or *Upon My Death Please Read* or *The Secrets to Successfully Running a Supernatural Containment Agency*, but she found only personnel files and fiscal logs. There was absolutely nothing regarding the ancient books of magic or anything with a semblance of interesting information.

The one time Buxton spoke of the books of magic, he said that they were created in the primordial era, before heaven and earth were separated and the Gods of air, water, earth, and sky were created. Atum, the creator God, held the books in his arms as he emerged from the waters of chaos. Now it was anybody's guess where they were.

Alex wished that she'd pressed Buxton for more information instead of assuming she would have years to pick his brain and enjoy his friendship. Once things settled down at KHNM, she would focus on locating them, even if she had to take a leave of absence.

The legend surrounding them told of powerful spells of creation within. It wasn't much of a stretch to think that they could create a portal to the Netherworld. She could return and find Buxton. Maybe they would hold primordial incantations that could allow her to breathe life back into him. Admittedly, it was a little desperate to hope for a miracle, but in the moment, she didn't have much else to hold on to.

She glanced up from the files. Caught, Luke's eyes flashed bright then shifted to the large leather-bound book splayed across his hands like a hymnal. How long had he been watching her?

"Is there something else I should keep an eye out for?" asked Luke, pointedly gazing at the pages in front of him.

"Just pack them up. I can always review your log entries." Her words came out more as a directive to a subordinate than a suggestion. The culture at KHNM never was top-down. The agency prided themselves in their egalitarian values. Alex didn't mean to come off harsh.

Luke's expression hardened. He opened his mouth as if to say something and then closed it.

"Sorry. I'm wound tight. That came out wrong."

"It happens." He rubbed at his eyes, then turned his back to Alex.

"Luke?"

"Yes." He replied to the bookcase facing him.

"Just let me know if you see anything that seems out of place."

"Roger that."

Alex scanned another folder of soul-killing budgetary records. As she reached into the drawer for another, it hit her: Why did Buxton have so many financial records? His work didn't involve the nitty-gritty; his role was more big picture. If he wanted to hide something from prying eyes, would the best place be among a parched desert of budgetary files? She took care to replace them in their original chronological order as she stowed them in the box. "When you take everything down to the archives, leave this one here."

He grabbed a book from the shelf he was working on. "Whatever you say, boss."

Apparently, Alex hadn't managed to change the course of her ship yet.

The door to the office swung open. Thorne entered the room with a self-satisfied look.

Alex slid the box of files under the desk with her foot, out of Thorne's view. "What's up?"

Thorne stiffly handed Alex an official-looking trifold letter. Alex scanned the text, her heart sinking. "The Gods have frozen all KHNM accounts and holdings. Apparently they are suing us?"

Thorne's smile widened. "Read on."

Alex immediately understood why Thorne was so pleased by Alex's discomfort.

Niles was the Gods' legal representation.

CHAPTER THREE

J orge and the old man bolted through the cave and made it aboveground with astonishing speed. Jorge was no expert on earthquakes, since he'd only experienced one years ago in Japan. That event had topped the Richter scale at a 7.0. This one was far more violent. Rocks and large boulders were tumbling down to the valley below. Jorge glanced behind him. Great clouds of sunset-hued sand and dust followed in their wake. Jorge pushed himself to run faster, his feet digging in as the ground rolled beneath him. The movement incongruently helped his forward progress. It was as if the ground waves were propelling him toward the golden boat resting on the rocky riverbank.

The fear of imminent death must have energized the old priest, as he trailed Jorge by only a few yards.

"To the boat!" yelled Jorge as he barreled toward the golden vessel resting against the shoreline. Luckily, they didn't have to maneuver through the carpet of snakes. They must have slithered away to safety during the quake. Jorge hopped into the boat and then heaved the priest up and in.

They both slunk down onto the cold metallic bottom. Neither man spoke as the river slapped violently against the back of the boat while the quaking continued.

The old man's face was dangerously purple-red, and his breathing was labored.

The boat was a safer place to be, but what they really needed to do was launch it into the river. Jorge couldn't see how he and an out-of-breath old man would be able to move a boat made of solid gold anywhere, let alone push it six feet into the river.

He pulled himself up to his knees and peered over the edge to look for inspiration on how to launch the boat. There was a great scratching sound, and the boat moved on its own, sliding over the orange-pebbled banks into the blood-red river.

Jorge sat up and stared dumbfounded at the old man. After all he'd been through, did the priest have enough strength to magically move the boat? He must possess seriously strong magic. Jorge's hopes lifted. Maybe there was a chance he could return home.

"Magic . . . Boat . . . of . . . Re." Gasps punctuated the old man's words.

Jorge rubbed his hand over the smooth gold planks beneath him. He couldn't believe he was actually sitting in the God's boat. "Where will it take us?"

"Don't . . . know."

As soon as they were fully in the river, the earthquake subsided and the water calmed.

"You don't know? Aren't you a high priest of the Great Goddess Hathor, Lady of the Western Mountain?"

The old man's eyes narrowed. A strained laugher struggled to escape between gasps for air. "Priest?"

"You and the little guy traveling with Hathor."

The old man held up his hand and waited to speak until he caught his breath. "No, you are mistaken. I am no priest, and I have no idea where this boat will take us. You saved my life, and I thank you for that. That woman was no God. She is Alex Philothea. A colleague of mine. What made you think she was Hathor?"

Jorge's gaze traveled out past the old man to the towering cliffs downriver, attempting to hide his shock. Why was the old man hiding his priesthood? Was it some sort of cover for the Goddess? Or, was his companion really another human and the blue-eyed stranger was the one who'd lied? Whenever Jorge didn't know who to trust, he reverted to not trusting anyone. It would be best to keep his cards close to his chest and let the man lie until Jorge could catch him in it.

The old man smiled at him weakly and extended his hand. "Forgive me. My name is Buxton, Dr. Charles Buxton. I am an Egyptologist and a professor at the Oriental Institute. Thank you again for saving my life."

"What brought you here? This is a particularly odd place for archaeological research."

"We were searching for a rumored chamber in the Osireion when we stumbled upon the portal. Once we crossed over, we realized our mistake and were looking for a way back to the mortal world. Wherever my colleagues are, I sure hope they found one." Charles craned his neck, looking back at the caves in the distance.

Why was the old man going out of his way to hide why he and his companions were here?

"Well, I've been following all of you since you jumped through that portal. I'd lay good money on the fact that your being here is anything but a mistake. It looked like the three of you were searching with intention for something very specific. So, Charles, why are you really here?"

"Buxton, please. I much prefer it to Charles. I guess the same question could equally be pointed to you. My friends and I had business down here. To my mind you are the interloper."

"Interloper?"

"You were following us uninvited. We never intended for a civilian to be involved with this."

"Civilian?" Jorge could feel his anger start to rise.

"Someone not prepared for the extraordinary."

This man was unbelievable. Unique and extraordinary were Jorge's bread and butter. "Do you have any idea who you are talking to, Buxton? You may be some highfalutin Egyptology prof, but I am—"

"Jorge Trinculo."

Jorge was taken aback. "How do you know who I am?"

The old man paused. "Of course I've seen your show. Who hasn't? You search out connections between humans and aliens. Quite fascinating stuff, really."

Jorge couldn't quite read Buxton's expression. *Was that respect shining in his eyes?* "Well, if you've seen it, then you are well aware that I, in my everyday life, seek out and prove the extraordinary. If I were to guess, I would say that you are the outsider here, sir."

The old man smiled. "I apologize. I misspoke. Maybe you're right, young man. I am tuckered out, but there is no excuse to be rude. Especially to my savior."

For the first time Jorge noticed his warm brown eyes. Maybe

they'd just gotten off on the wrong foot. The man obviously had good taste in entertainment choices. Also, he knew enough to pronounce his name with the Portuguese soft *G* at the beginning.

"You really don't know where this boat will take us?" asked Jorge.

"The ancients didn't write much about the Duat, what we call the afterlife, or even the Netherworld, other than being the place you wanted to end up after you'd died. One thing is clear, in the myths the sun travels through the Duat at night. I think that is where we are. I would surmise that this river might run along the same circuit as the sun each day. Hopefully, the river will bring us back to where we started."

"I can't believe my continuing to exist hinges on *hopefully*." The boat moved with an unnatural smoothness as if running on tracks, like a family-friendly theme park ride set in hell.

"Why did you think my companion Alex was Hathor? What gave you that idea?"

Jorge told him the story of the private party he'd been invited to on a grand private Nile cruise ship. Although he couldn't remember any specific details of the party itself, he woke up on the ship's deck with a strange man leaning over him, telling him of the treasure awaiting him if he just followed Hathor. As he shared the tale out loud, it sounded ludicrous to go off half-cocked on an adventure chasing after a Goddess at the mere suggestion of a stranger. But then again, that was how he earned his keep, following the faint trail of the fantastical.

"What did the man look like who told you to follow her?"

"All I can remember are his deep blue eyes. I could tell the color even though a deep shadow cut across his face."

"Did you happen to notice if there was anything else remark-able about him?"

"Now that you mention it. . . his irises almost looked like they had amber-colored starbursts surrounding them."

The old man's face warmed as if remembering something familiar and pleasant. "I'll be damned. It must have been Niles."

"Niles?"

"He's another colleague of mine. He told you where to find Alex? What made you do it? I mean, other than him telling you she was a Goddess."

"Like I said, he told me she would lead me to great treasure."

The old man burst into laughter. He winced in pain and grabbed his side. "I guess I am a little too bruised for sudden laughter. I am sorry to be the bearer of bad news, but you were sold a very tall tale."

"Why on earth would he send a stranger off on a wild goose chase? What sort of person is this so-called colleague of yours?"

The mirth in the old man's expression faded to concern. His mouth turned down in a soft frown, and his eyes were half-lidded with sorrow. "I can only guess at why. In this case, guessing will do neither of us any good. I just know him, and I have to assume he did it because it mattered greatly. Right now, we should be focusing on how to get out of here. At this point, who cares who broke the eggs—we just need to figure out how to make a decent omelet out of this mess."

Something about this man was vaguely familiar to Jorge. He couldn't put a finger on it, but he could have sworn he knew him from somewhere.

Jorge leaned over and patted Buxton on the shoulder. "Why don't you lie down and have a rest. You look exhausted. There isn't much we can do right now. I'll keep an eye out and wake you if our situation changes."

Buxton doffed an imaginary hat at Jorge and stretched out on

the cold, hard boat floor. His loud snores started almost immediately.

—◞◟—

As Buxton slept, Jorge gazed out at the landscape painted in hues
of orange and red, letting his mind wander as he contemplated
what he'd gotten himself into. Before setting off to search for
Hathor, or rather, this person called Alex, he'd talked himself out
of bringing one of his crew with him. At the time, it was an
interesting lead, but he wasn't sure if it was going to pan out. He
didn't want to involve anyone until he had an idea what was
going on. Now he wasn't certain how wise flying solo was. On
one hand, he didn't like the thought of another person trapped in
this realm; but on the other hand, another hale and healthy
companion with quick wits would be useful.

Aside from the vibrant colors of magenta, orange, and red
that painted the landscape, the surrounding topography was
monotonous, almost lunar in appearance. Everything beyond the
river was a vast sand sea with occasional boulders jutting up
through the grainy ground. Craggy mountain ranges ran parallel
to the river, and massive rock-islands protruded from the blood-
red waters. The current created a horrific froth around the jagged
islets. Only one time did he make the mistake of looking over the
boat's side, once again seeing the severed heads tossing about in
a gruesome flotsam. He quickly sat back down to quell the angry
gods of vomit that were threatening to erupt.

Luckily, he didn't end up having to choose.

The sameness of the landscape lulled Jorge into a half-sleep,
half-trance state. Aside from the drunken snooze on the party
boat, he hadn't gotten much rest in the past forty-eight hours.

His head knocked against the hard side of the boat, waking him. He rubbed the newly formed bruise, wondering how long he'd been out of commission. He breathed in deep, the air sweet and clear for the first time since he'd entered this realm. Jorge shifted up to his knees to peer over the edge of the boat.

They were gaining speed, no longer drifting at a lazy pace. Off in the distance, the scenery was changing. The red and orange faded to a pink blush. He squinted. Further afield the landscape transitioned to white, as if a waterlogged paintbrush was dragged slowly across the landscape until no pigment remained. Jorge pulled out his binoculars. Just beyond the white area was a verdant land mass, very similar in appearance to the Nile valley. Could the river be taking them back to the realm of man? Or was it some sort of mirage?

He shook Buxton awake.

"We've landed?" Buxton rubbed at his eyes.

"There's a change up ahead." Jorge handed the binoculars to Buxton.

Buxton knelt, bracing himself against the side of the boat as he lifted the binoculars.

"Well, I'll be . . ."

"It looks like we made it back." Jorge could barely contain his excitement, but for some reason Buxton's expression remained dour. "Aren't you glad? We've made it."

Buxton shook his head. "If only that were so. I am afraid that place up ahead is not our home. At least not yet."

"What do you mean?"

"I would guess that to be the Field of Reeds of ancient Egyptian lore. Only the dead call it home."

"Do you think we've died?" The words felt surreal as he spoke them. It was odd that he felt so unfazed at the prospect.

Maybe that in itself was evidence to be scored on the side of being dead. Could it be that when you die you primarily feel at peace and are ambivalent to no longer living? Jorge crossed his arms. He felt very much alive. How would the dead feel, anyway? Would they feel at all? Would they have a pulse? Jorge unknit his arms and placed two fingers on his wrist. It was weak, but there. "If we are in the Netherworld, it would make sense that we are dead. Maybe our souls are riding this golden boat to our eternal reward."

"Oh, I doubt that very much," said Buxton.

"But you just said that the Field of Reeds is where the dead reside. Here we are, on a boat, on the river that flows through the Netherworld. What leads you to believe we aren't dead? This river appears to have parallels to the River Styx of Greek myth."

"I take it you've read Joseph Campbell's writings?"

"Great stuff, huh?"

"I have always taken umbrage to his idea that there are parallels between the myths of all cultures that are plainly transferable from one to the other. Personally, I think that diminishes the uniqueness of each society and their belief in their own god system. If you pull far away from any subject, all things can seem similar. Don't all the planets look the same to the naked eye in the night sky? No, this body of water has no partnership in the myths of the Greeks, and you and I are most definitely alive."

"Come on, old man, it's human nature to deny one's own mortality. If either of us should be bummed at the prospect of being dead, it would be me, being far younger than you. You've at least lived out your potential."

Buxton laughed. "Lived out my potential?"

Jorge stared out into the far distance where a string of date palms lay far inland from the river. "Mine is but a short flicker in the shadow of your grand flame."

"Apparently, the idea of your own death has managed to make you wax poetic. No, it's not the ability of humankind to lie to themselves about the inevitable that leads me to believe that we still exist. There are other mitigating factors that are painfully obvious to me."

"We aren't transparent apparitions?"

"I hadn't thought of that, but no, that's not it. Have you any memory of your heart being ripped out and weighed against the scales of truth? Or have you witnessed Osiris's Devourer of Souls, Ammut, at the ready to eliminate you from the annals of existence?"

"No. But maybe that's something you aren't meant to remember. Maybe when you are judged to be true of heart, you are sent to the afterlife as a clean vessel."

"Do you really feel like a clean vessel right now?"

"Well—"

"There are two points which I think prove my point. One, do you or have you ever actively worshiped the Egyptian pantheon of Gods?"

"No, but—"

"Two, putting aside any grand opinions you may hold of yourself, is there anything you've done in your bright, short flame of a life that has either been epically heroic or pharaonic?"

"I saved you from being sacrificed to Re. That was a little heroic."

"However grateful I am about that, I can't see some ancient bard creating a poem about saving an old archaeologist from the grip of death."

"Why does the poem need to be epic?"

"Can't you see your rescuing me is even further proof we are not dead? Do you really think a God would be pleased for his gift to be whisked away at the last minute? If anything, I think it would state an obvious case for you to be sent to the Devourer of Souls and not to the Field of Reeds."

"Then we aren't dead."

"You sound disappointed."

Jorge wasn't disappointed, he just wanted to know where the hell he was. Or in this case, which hell he was in. "Then what are we?"

"I fear we are dreadfully lost." Buxton handed Jorge his binoculars as the boat thumped against the shore.

A massive clutch of golden reeds swayed overhead. They were crowned with green grasslike tendrils that reached up to the vast blue sky.

"I guess this is where we are meant to get off," said Buxton.

"Get off? Shouldn't we ride the boat until we make it back to where the portal is?"

"Since it stopped here, I have to guess we're meant to disembark. I clearly remember the look of shock on your face when you realized it moved on its own. I don't think it is wise to fool ourselves into thinking that we are captains of this craft."

Jorge scanned the shoreline with his binoculars. There was a narrow trail that cut into the dense reeds. "Look over there."

The old man threw a leg over the metal rim of the boat and heaved himself over. Jorge replaced his binoculars safely back into their pocket and followed suit.

They picked their way down the narrow shoreline, walking with great care, neither wanting to dip into the gruesome red-black waters that lapped against the verdant riverbank.

Arriving at the minuscule path, Jorge realized how dense the foliage was. He regretted that he did not have his machete with him. Jorge reached into a large front jacket pocket and pulled out his leather gloves. The gloves he'd wished he'd thought of when he was racing through the tunnel earlier. He winced as he slipped them over his abraded palms. It was a small price to pay for saving a life.

Jorge pushed through the thick growth and trampled the slender stalks to make the way easier for the old man. The trodden greens made him think of the crop circles of Northern England, except in this case they were man-made.

Ahead, the tall reeds thinned, but the small openings in between only gave a hint to what lay ahead. As a seasoned explorer, not having a clear sight line set Jorge on edge.

His foot struck something hard. Pain shot through his big toe. Parting the giant stalks of grass in front of him, he could see the offending object was the granite base of a massive sphinx.

Just above his head, carved on the creature's chest, was a large cartouche. The sphinx's regal, pharaonic head towered over them with a headdress of alternating stripes of gold and deep-blue lapis lazuli of the nemes crown. Around its neck was an electrum-clad pectoral collar adorned with green-blue faience beads framing a large turquoise representation of the cow-eared Goddess Hathor. The depiction was one of her looking forward with her thick hair tucked behind her horns. Hathor was the Egyptian Goddess of love, and aside from Bes, the only one who was ever depicted in profile as well as head-on.

Jorge's treasure-hunting instincts awakened at the sight of the bejeweled necklace. He stepped in close to appraise it, wondering if it was detachable and something he could slip into his explorer's jacket for a little Netherworld memento. His mind went wild trying to contrive a reasonable way to contain and transport the large object. On the open antiquities market, a piece like that could raise a fortune. If he could manage to bring it home, he could break away and produce his show, maybe even create his own network.

"The sphinx that guards the Field of Reeds. Isn't it beautiful?" The old man was pointing at the cartouche on the sphinx's chest with an expression of sheer wonder.

"What does the cartouche say?"

"It tells his name, Horakhty, Horus of the Horizon. And that those who visit this altar shall—"

A great rumbling emanated from the body of the sphinx. "We'd better get out of here," Jorge yelled as he tried to move. It was as if his legs knitted themselves to the sphinx's paw. He jerked his torso from side to side as a burst of adrenaline shot through him. He looked over at Buxton, who was also struggling to move.

"I'm stuck," yelled Buxton.

The sphinx's stone body glowed red. Jorge braced himself for a burning sensation that never came. Specks of gold shone through the red, becoming more and more prolific until they pooled together to cover the sphinx's entire body. The creature stretched its head upward, then from side to side as if cracking its neck. Its bright golden face lowered to gaze down at them. Its mouth pulled up into a sly smile. "M-m-m-m, live ones. It's been far too long."

CHAPTER FOUR

As the mediation center elevator lifted Alex toward the inevitable, her mood sunk to an all-time low. She'd been dreading this meeting ever since she received the letter announcing the lawsuit the Gods were initiating to shut the agency down.

Today was the day KHNM needed to defend its existence to the Gods, or at least to one of them, Niles. Which for Alex was an intense personal complication that made this meeting just about as attractive as diving into a pool of sharks with a very large still-bleeding wound. She couldn't give in to feeling vulnerable. People were depending on her.

Would this be the day she allowed the agency that was entrusted in the care of her family for over two thousand years to end? Would she be the one that let it all break apart? On its own, the lawsuit was extremely problematic. If things didn't go well today, it was possible the agency would have to shut down operations. Not only would good people lose their jobs, but the magic that was re-released into the realm of man when the Gods returned to the Field of Reeds would go unchecked.

That was a surefire recipe for big trouble in the realm of mortals. It wasn't so long ago that Alex, like most humans, was blind to the myth and magic woven into the mortal world.

When KHNM called her to duty to battle Raymond Sol, the Immortal anthropomorphized form of the God Re, it took some doing for her to embrace the outlandish story that the ancient Egyptian Gods banked their powers two millennia ago to walk among humankind.

Over time the Gods became restless. Raymond hatched a plan to kill his immediate family of Gods to become the Aten, or The One True God. It was a quest for power that grew into an unquenchable thirst for complete rule over the mortal world.

Raymond enlisted his daughter Salima, the Immortal form of the Goddess triad of Bastet, Hathor, and Sekhmet. In the end, she helped Alex defeat Re, sending all the Immortals back to the Field of Reeds in their God forms. Alex was never certain where Salima's loyalties landed. Did Raymond put her up to it? Did she join in on his plans wholeheartedly? Or, was she a double agent on the side of KHNM, as Buxton believed? Had he been mistaken?

At the rate things were going, with Buxton dead and her being persona non grata with the Gods, Alex would probably never know. She was left to wonder what, if any sort of punishment, Raymond and Salima had paid for what they'd done. Did the Gods just brush it all under the magic carpet and forgive their family their trespasses? As far as Alex knew, Raymond had never been even reprimanded by either his Immortal family or KHNM for killing her father all those years ago. He'd admitted killing him to her before he'd left her to die in an abandoned tomb. Apparently, Immortals were above human laws and proprieties.

Alex was flanked by Luke and Thorne. Luke, on her right, was cool as a cucumber. Thorne, on the other hand, bristled with a sharp anger. Alex had no idea why Thorne took issue with the suggestion that Luke join them during mediation. Was his presence somehow an affront to her? Did it go against her self-perceived hierarchy of KHNM? Whatever the reason might be, it didn't matter. As the director, Alex's word was final.

Over the past few days, Alex found it somewhat entertaining to try to throw Thorne off her game. It was vaguely humorous to see her anticipated reactions to Alex's suggestions and ideas, curated specifically to entice a frown, furrowed brow, or the very special pinch-faced rotten-egg-smell expression Thorne was so adept at.

Humor always was a survival technique for Alex. If she could find something even vaguely funny, she could get over almost any hurdle. With all she'd been through lately, she would take vaguely funny whenever it was available.

Between taking the reins of the agency and worrying about its future, Alex hadn't had a good night's sleep. Last night was no different. Her mind kept running through varying tracks of trouble that would come if things didn't go right today.

One thing that kept trying to creep into her sleepless thoughts was Niles. Every time the Niles door opened, she immediately slammed it shut. She didn't enjoy the double burn of foolishness and hindsight that turned her insides out. If simply thinking about him sent her into a mental tailspin, what would it be like to be face to face with him?

What an easy mark she must have been for his finely honed Immortal charms. Alex didn't find it easy to trust, and the one time she let her guard down, she got burned. Big time. Maybe Salima was right all along, and Alex was only a plaything for Niles to kill time with while he embodied his earthly Immortal form.

The elevator doors slid open, revealing the intentionally muted decor of the mediation center. The reception area was all smooth lines and frosted glass. Something about it reminded her of all the treatment centers her mother was admitted to over the years. That association was not exactly a comforting portent of what was to come.

By the looks of it, a lot of money was spent making the space feel peaceful and at the same time oddly corporate. Rubicon Mediation Center was a safe harbor for hire in the moneyed world of dispute resolution. Alex guessed a lot of high-dollar dirty laundry was wrung out in this facility. It was a little unsettling that the Gods held an account here. Which got her wondering—how much did Rubicon know about their supernatural client? Were they completely in on it? Or, were they in the dark, like 99.9 percent of humankind?

Alex stepped onto the beige carpeting woven in patterns to look like raked sand, bringing to mind a Zen garden. Across the room, water cascaded down a large freestanding waterfall, its calming flow intended to work parasympathetic magic on the mood of those waiting.

The receptionist looked up. Her eyes were bright and youthful. She was most likely a college intern from one of those Ivy League lawyer factories.

Alex's mouth went dry. It was go time. "We have a ten o'clock with—"

A pink flush crept up the receptionist's creamy complexion. "You must be meeting with Mr. Greene." Her sugar-sweet tone spoke volumes. Niles must have worked his charms on the poor girl. "He and his assistant are in the Waterloo conference room. It's the second-biggest room, next to the Teutoburg room." Her eyes stared longingly down the hallway, as if hoping to catch sight of the ridiculously handsome and debonair Mr. Greene.

Luke scrolled his hands dramatically toward the hallway. "My lady."

Alex led the way. Each door they passed displayed a large placard noting the conference room's name. It amused Alex that, for all the calming environmental strategies this facility incorporated, the rooms were named after serious historical battles. She chuckled as they passed by the Kadesh boardroom, wondering why Niles hadn't secured that one.

Alex slid the conference room door open and immediately spied Niles at the far end of the room. Alex intended to project a general state of aloofness at seeing him, but her body refused to cooperate. Her heart skittered at the sight of him as her skin came alive with a sharp tingle-fizz of goose bumps at the thought of his touch.

Suddenly, she flashed back to just a few weeks ago at Luxor Temple, looking up into his strange blue eyes, their pent-up longings reaching critical mass as they were drawn into a long and all-encompassing kiss. A kiss that made Alex feel like an entire universe opened up as they collapsed into each other. That night their desires flew like a pair of caged birds that were finally able to take to the sky.

Being together in that sacred space under the full moon felt right, so natural, as if the very ancient ones surrounding them bore witness and blessed their union.

Now he sat at the far end of the table, not even looking up as she walked in.

Niles's head was turned in conversation with a woman who sat next to him. Alex couldn't quite recognize who she was. She was of an advanced age; however, her hair possessed an unnatural gloss as if it were a wig. Then it hit her—Niles's assistant was Akh-Hehet, the seer. A great friend of the agency and of Alex's late father. She credited Phillip with saving her life years ago. Back then, Akh-Hehet had been wandering around the streets of Cairo, lost in her own unfocused powers. He helped her find a place to live and kept a protective eye on her while she was working at honing her gift.

As KHNM's director, Alex had learned a lot more about the old woman. Aside from the data file the agency had on her, she was a beloved fixture within the agencies social circles. Most everyone had a story or two about the seer.

Akh-Hehet lived a semi-immortal life. In her first life, as a mortal, she was a high priestess in ancient Egypt during the accession of Pharaoh Akhenaten. A religious upheaval of the time required that she, as a mortal, take many trips into the Netherworld, thus strengthening her Ba and making it nearly unbreakable. During each lifetime the body she occupied would eventually die. Once released, her Ba would travel the world looking for another appropriate shell. She needed to find someone who was not only a seer, but also stood on the precipice of death. After locating a candidate who fit the bill, the most challenging and hazardous part was yet to come.

She could only take possession of the body at the exact moment the other soul was vacating it. This allowed for the safe crossing over for the original owner and an empty vessel for Akh-Hehet. There was one subject that the seer didn't like to talk about. It had taken her centuries of trial and error to get the soul transfer down to a science. No matter how good she got at it, there was always room for error. In her official file, a note was made by Alex's father that she was constantly haunted by the memories of her botched transitions. Like the current one. When Phillip drew the seer under his protective wing, there were large gaps and misalignments in her consciousness most likely caused by a jumbled transfer into her current body.

Alex counted her as a good friend after the escapades they'd gone through together. Could Alex have misinterpreted her friendship with both Akh-Hehet and Gormund? Alex slipped into the mesh-backed office chair. As in the elevator, Luke and Thorne were on either side of her. Luke slid his chair close so their forearms touched. This small gesture of solidarity buoyed her mood. Which she needed, as it seemed this was going to be nothing like a true mediation. Alex noted the distinct lack of neutral parties in the room.

Niles glanced up. His steely eyes locked with hers ever so briefly, then quickly shifted to the paperwork that lay in front of him. There was a strained expression in that brief connection that Alex couldn't quite read.

Niles tented his fingers in front of him. "As you know, the Gods are suing KHNM." His tone was all business. Now he looked at Alex as if she were a complete stranger to him. "I'll dive in if everyone is ready. I believe we'll all be glad to put this distasteful business behind us."

Alex steeled herself and met his gaze straight on.

Niles picked up the document and slid it over to Alex. "As per this legal brief, the Gods have determined that from this day forth, the organization known as KHNM should be disbanded immediately. As you are all aware, KHNM was established as an overseeing body while the Gods walked among mortals. As that is no longer the case, the Gods assume their authority of oversight and will be shutting down operations forthwith. They have determined that KHNM was negligent in their duties, causing great harm to the Gods. As of midnight tonight, all of the usual funding sources that would normally be sent to the coffers of the agency will be disabled."

"Negligent?" A surge of anger shot through Alex. They had been anything but negligent. The agency had put everything on the line to defeat Re, sacrificing their leader Buxton to right a wrong that was created by the Gods themselves. She was floored at the nonchalant attitude the Gods had toward an agency that served them faithfully for over two thousand years. Her family had paid the ultimate price to keep the Gods content. Alex's father was dead because of them, and her mother, Roxanne, continually grieved as she faded into the shadows of addiction, virtually making Alex an orphan. Only recently, after her mother's last stint in recovery, was Roxanne finally among the living again.

Niles gave a curt nod. "The Gods have a watertight case. Charles Buxton, then agency director, did allow, on his watch, the murder of and acquisition of the immortal powers of the Theban Royal Ones by Raymond Sol, allowing Raymond to attempt for a second time to attain Aten-hood. KHNM is in direct violation of the original founding covenant. All property and assets belonging to the organization will be inventoried. All items will be deaccessioned, dismantled, destroyed, and disarmed." The room was dead silent except for the click-clack of Akh-Hehet's diligent note-taking.

"Disarmed?" asked Luke.

A microflash of annoyance passed over Niles's face as Luke spoke. Alex couldn't guess at what Niles might have against the KHNM archivist. For all she knew, they'd never met.

Niles returned his attention to the documents. "KHNM is in possession of residual magical items in the mortal realm, left-overs from our interactions over the centuries. These items have the potential to be used as weaponry by humans. Artifacts that are determined to be dangerous will be destroyed."

Alex anchored her gaze at Akh-Hehet's glistening wig in hopes she might feel the weight of her stare and make eye contact. It puzzled Alex that such a dear woman, who she thought was her ally, would be on the other side of this table.

"You have thirty days to inventory, pack, and close down. After that time KHNM will no longer exist. The agency is no longer relevant."

Thorne's complexion turned sheet white.

Alex urgently needed to try to convince Niles to keep the agency open. "But what about the magic? Now that magic has been restored into the realm of mortals, wouldn't it serve the Gods to have KHNM stick around to ensure that there are no magical catastrophes? Our agents are already trained and in place. Why not use them? I am certain we could form a new magic containment policy that would ensure the safety and well-being of—"

"Mortals?" Niles snorted. "The future of your kind is not at the forefront of our concerns."

Your kind. The familiar words and the distaste in which they were spoken pricked at Alex's heart.

Akh-Hehet looked up from her typing and directed a deep scowl in Niles's direction.

Undaunted, Alex continued. "If humans can't be trusted with magic, what happens if they annihilate themselves once they discover the ancient magic? What will you all do if there are not humans to speak your names anymore?"

"In the immediate, the Gods are not concerned about that. They want vindication for being forced, by you, to return to a realm that has been neglected for over two thousand years. As you are well aware, as Gods we tend to value immediate retribution."

Alex felt a slow burn working its way up her neck.

"We are used to having power that goes beyond anything you might imagine." He shrugged. "Who knows, maybe we will just create another life form to worship us."

Shocked at his callous attitude, Alex leaned into the table and glared at Niles. "What about the magical artifacts that have been scattered around after all these years? Even if we were able to pack up everything that is currently in our possession in the timeline that we have been given, which I think is impossible, there would still be many magical items hidden or lost in the realm of man. The agency should still be around in order to track all the missing ones down to be destroyed. The Gods should see the sense in keeping the agency going at least through a containment period."

Niles's expression sharpened. "That is something I will have to take back for further negotiation. I am doubtful the Gods will care, though. As I said before, none of us are very pleased to be in the current circumstances in which we find ourselves."

"I thought that the Gods had tired of living in the realm of man," said Alex.

"We can be fickle."

"Someone took their understatement pill today." In her mind it was a mumble, but it came out loud and proud, as if her mouth pushed its override-brain button.

Niles glance up at her, something unreadable in his eyes. He scooped up the documents and shoved them into an accordion file. "You are ordered to start the inventory and packing immediately. I or another will be in touch within the week with further instructions. Until then, I will broach the subject of your counterpoints with the Gods regarding the continuation of KHNM as an active body, at least temporarily. But don't hold your breath."

A minuscule spark of hope lit within Alex. She might be able to save the agency after all. At least for a little while.

"Akh-Hehet, did you get that?" Niles asked.

"Yes sir." Her reply sounded more like a sarcastic dig than an epithet of respect.

From somewhere behind Thorne the soft whirring of a laser printer sounded. Akh-Hehet made her way over to collect the rather long document and placed it along with a pen in front of Alex.

Akh-Hehet squeezed Alex's shoulder. The warmth of the old woman's touch was reassuring. She leaned in and whispered into Alex's ear, "No hurry, dear." Then returned to Niles who was collecting his possessions.

Niles slipped on his raincoat. "As soon as you've had time to read it over, sign and leave it with Lucy at the front desk. She knows how to find me."

An unwanted twinge of jealousy shot through Alex. "What if we don't agree to sign it?"

"KHNM will be closed at midnight tonight. The room is yours for however long you need it." Niles cleared his throat. "Good day."

Alex was dazed as Niles and Akh-Hehet left the room. "Why don't you two head back to the office. I'll catch a cab back to the residence when I'm done. Who knows, maybe I will find a loophole or something. We really don't have a choice but to sign."

"Then why read it?" Thorne's wintry mood was still evident.

"I need to know exactly what we are agreeing to."

"I guess we've been dismissed. Come on, Luke." Thorne shot out of her seat and headed to the door.

Luke stayed behind. "Are you sure you don't want me to stay?" His soft words held a hope for yes. The golden retriever in him always wanted to try and make things better.

"No, I need to take my time with them."

Luke slipped out of his seat. The door softly closed behind him, leaving her all alone.

A small chill ran through her.

This was it. This was the end. The end of many things.

She stared at the printed legal documents that lay before her. Alex grabbed the pen Akh-Hehet placed with them. It was a blue Montblanc pen with an ibis-headed clip. *He must have these made in bulk.*

CHAPTER FIVE

J orge pleaded with the massive golden sphinx that towered over the two of them. "Let us go. You have no use for us."

"Obviously you have no idea how lonely I get lying here day in and day out. I doubt you can imagine what it's like staring off into the same vista year after year."

"Since you can't go anywhere, how would you know any different?" asked Jorge.

"Maybe you'd like to trade places with me, human?" The words were more a growl than anything.

The sphinx's breath warmed Jorge's cheeks and smelled surprisingly of incense. It was incongruent that such a fierce creature had such a pleasant smell. A blend of patchouli, musk, and sandalwood filled his nostrils, reminding him of every metaphysical bookstore he'd ever been to. Over his career Jorge was invited to speak at a number of New Age conferences, so he was quite familiar with this particular scent profile. He inhaled the sphinx's sweet-spicy breath, which he found oddly calming. "So how does this work? You ask us a riddle and then—"

"If you get it wrong, I eat you." Perfect and gleaming pearly whites were revealed by a self-satisfied smile.

Jorge glanced from the very large teeth to the old man. Who would be the first to get eaten if they failed? Jorge guessed the first to go would more than likely be him, since he was far younger and probably tastier. For him there was no room for error to get out of this tangle. "So, it is a riddle, then?"

"Are you suggesting another protocol?" The sphinx hitched up one of his golden eyebrows.

Maybe a suggestion of a new approach could buy them some time. "How about we have a riddle contest. If we can stump you once out of three tries, you'll let us go."

"You expect me to answer riddles?" The sphinx grimaced as if Jorge set a large bucket of stink in front of him.

"No, it just seemed that you were feeling stuck and itching for a change."

"Hmmmm. It might be fun. You have three chances to come up with a riddle I don't know."

"If you'd like." Judging by Buxton's advanced age, Jorge guessed he would have some riddles rolling around in that balding head of his. He glanced over at Buxton. "You know some riddles. Right?"

"Only one. However, I don't know how good it is."

The sphinx's eyes glimmered. "Try me."

The old man cleared his throat. "Many have heard me, but no one has seen me, and I will not speak back until spoken to. What am I?"

The sphinx laughed. "You really couldn't come up with something more original than that? Even that dullard Akhenaten knows that one." The creature leaned down and sniffed the old man's head. "The one nice thing about eating old bones, they have a nice crunch to them. I wonder where I might find some salt?" The creature looked around as if searching for a saltshaker.

Buxton audibly gulped.

"Are you stalling?" Jorge asked.

"Oh Gods, no. I'm just disappointed at how quick this new game is going. I was hoping to drag out the fun a little." His lower lip fell into an exaggerated pout.

Jorge crossed his arms. "Answer, please."

"Echo. That riddle is riddle making 101. I have heard that one probably a thousand times over the centuries. You are going to have to bring up your game." The sphinx tilted his head as if pondering something. "I really do appreciate how you are making this process a little more fun for me. Usually by now I would have devoured you both. I may use this approach in the future. It is so infrequent for me to get edible toys. Especially ones that want to play. In consideration of your considerations, I will do everything I can to ensure your death is relatively painless."

Jorge frantically tried to remember a riddle, but all that ran through his mind like a crazy earworm was that there were only two more chances. Jorge leaned toward Buxton. "Do you know any more?"

Buxton shook his head.

"Mmmm . . . brains." The sphinx said wistfully. "Tastiest part, really. Kind of like a custard, but savory. I usually save it for last, but since I have two here, maybe I will just save one for last." The massive sphinx's head turned and loomed over Jorge, his gold-and-lapis-striped nemes headdress flopping forward. "Another? Or should I just tuck in?"

A fully formed riddle stirred in Jorge's memory. How could he have forgotten it? The riddle was a real eye-roller, one that his father used to whip out whenever Jorge brought home new friends. "No, I got one."

The sphinx's head pulled back.

Buxton exhaled.

"There are three men in a boat with four cigarettes but no matches. How do they manage to smoke?"

"Ohhhh. Now that is rare. A riddle I've never heard before." The sphinx's gaze moved up to the sky in deep concentration.

Could it be that Jorge beat the eternal beast with just two questions? Jorge puffed his chest out. As a celebrity, people were usually hyperbolic in his presence, telling him how intelligent he was, likening him to a genius. In general, he took great pride in his ability to manage all the compliments and kudos, allowing them to slide off him like water off well-oiled gear. But defeating a Netherworld beast made him feel almost godlike. Jorge cleared his throat. "Give up?"

The sphinx squinted his eyes and pursed his lips. If it possessed free use of its hunched-up legs, it probably would have stood and stomped the ground in frustration or kicked a rock or two. "Give me a few more minutes. I know I can figure this one out."

The sphinx in the moment was like a game show host, exuding an all-knowingness while reading what was on the card. Feeling a little more positive about the chances of their survival, Jorge pushed the sphinx. "I think we've been more than fair with the time allotted."

"I just need a few more—"

Buxton wagged his finger at the beast. "We've given you far more time than you gave us to come up with another riddle. Fair is fair. What is your answer?"

"Damn it. I don't know. I just can't figure it out." The sphinx sounded genuinely dumbfounded.

"So you'll let us go?" asked Jorge.

"After you tell me the answer."

"Then we are free?" Buxton's voice was filled with hope.

"If you win, you win."

For a brief moment Jorge took enjoyment in the dour expression on the defeated sphinx's face. "They throw one cigarette overboard and make the boat a cigarette lighter."

The sphinx burst into laughter.

Jorge breathed a sigh of relief at the thought of this corny old thing saving their lives. He tried to move forward, but his leg was still held firmly in place. "You're gonna let us go now, right?"

The sphinx snorted as his chuckles subsided. "Oh, you aren't going anywhere."

"A deal is a deal." Jorge stared at the double-crossing magical creature in disbelief.

"Right you are, tasty morsel. I mean mortal." The sphinx laughed to himself. "Come to think of it, you really qualify as both."

Buxton planted his hands on his hips. "You should set us free. We played your game and you lost. Fair and square. It would be bad form to eat us as a sore loser. Our agreement was that if we could stump you on one out of three riddles, we would be set free."

"In that you are right." The sphinx looked smug.

"So let us go," Jorge demanded.

"I cannot. You didn't win. That was a joke, not a riddle."

"Joke?" asked Jorge.

"In a riddle you have to be able to logically solve it by the words that it contains. Yours contained a punchline, not a solution. Your precious second chance of three is gone."

"You are mistaken. That is a well-known riddle in the realm of man." Jorge wished that his cell phone worked down here. It would just take a Google search to prove the sphinx wrong.

"I say it is a joke, not a riddle. You have one last chance."

"But—"

"One more." The creature's stomach made a loud rumbling noise. "The mere suggestion of eating you both has managed to whet my long-neglected appetite."

Buxton shrugged his shoulders. "Sorry, I've got nothing."

Apparently, it was going to be up to Jorge to save their lives. Was there a blind spot he could exploit to confound the creature? An idea crept up on him slowly, rising like a snake out of a basket, and then it struck him. The old Greek adage, know thyself. One thing that Jorge knew was that in life, it is almost impossible to see oneself in the way others perceive us. "What is like a lion yet lacks in courage, its legs don't hunt but kneel in submission, and possesses the eternity of the pharaohs yet will never rule?"

The sphinx scowled. "A slave. No. Wait. That is not my answer. A slave would not possess eternity. What possesses eternity? A star. No, that can't be it."

"Come on, we need an answer." His plan might just work.

The sphinx gazed in Jorge's direction but not at him as he searched for the answer.

For the first time Jorge noticed the rich coloration of the sphinx's eyes. The irises resembled molten pots of gold with flecks suspended within.

"I give up. What is the answer?"

Jorge flung his arms out as if producing a great reveal. "The sphinx."

The golden eyes of the sphinx now burned like a red-hot forge. A roar concussed the air. Buxton's ashen face went wild with terror as the creature's head stretched down to face them.

"How dare you insult me, mortals!" The ground rumbled as the sphinx spoke. Jorge's hands flew to his ears.

The creature craned its neck then opened wide, filling his mouth with Buxton. The sphinx's cheek brushed against Jorge's elbow. Jorge didn't want to witness the old man being eaten. Before he could close his eyes, a bright object flashed in front of his face. He found himself staring at a gleaming blade that was pricked into the sphinx's outstretched neck.

"Let the old man go, and I will spare you, sphinxcter," said the sword-wielding man who appeared out of nowhere. The pressure of the blade deepened against the sphinx. "Don't mess with me. You know I am good for my word."

"All right, all right," the creature garbled as he pulled his head back, revealing a sphinx spit–coated Buxton.

As Buxton attempted to wipe away the slimy goo with his hands, more cascaded down from the crown of his head, recoating his face once again.

Their savior looked vaguely familiar. Jorge couldn't quite place where he might know him from.

"Akkk." The sphinx made a noise like he was trying to dislodge a giant fur ball. "That sphinxcter thing, not funny. I wish you would let that go."

"Dangerous moments take heavy medicine, my friend. You need to let these two go now. I've got a request from the big house that I take them in. I'll bring you a snack later."

The force that was holding them fell away. Jorge stepped off the creature's paw. Buxton followed in a daze after almost being eaten. They walked toward the man who stood leaning on his huge broadsword.

Buxton swiped more sphinx spit from his face. "I'll be damned." The old man ran toward the man who saved them with his arms outstretched. "Phillip?"

CHAPTER SIX

Alex slunk down the curving mahogany staircase at the KHNM residency, thankful that the carpet runner muffled her footsteps. After signing the paperwork from the mediation, she found it next to impossible to sleep. The last thing she wanted to do was to invite company by waking the others, especially Jeeves. If she woke him, the whole house would be up in short order.

Jeeves, the resident miniature schnauzer, belonged to Luke, but everyone claimed him. Typical of schnauzers, he possessed a mind of his own, and that mind didn't take kindly to being woken up. His approach to voicing his displeasure was loud and drawn out, to the great displeasure of those around him.

The first time she visited the residency, Buxton and Luke entered on tiptoes with hushed voices, making Alex think that Jeeves was a temperamental butler. It wasn't until Luke tripped on his way to his room that Alex knew the truth. She smiled at the memory of the high-pitched yapping parade that followed

Luke to his room as he limped along on his twisted ankle. Jeeves was a lovable crank. His owner Luke wasn't so bad either.

Alex missed Buxton so much, although she'd only known him for a short time. She was instantly drawn to Buxton's warmth and charm. From the first moment she'd spent with him, she felt instantly at ease. She sorely missed the mentor she never knew she needed until he was gone.

Alex's wanderings led her to Buxton's old bedroom. She glanced around to make sure no one was in the hallway. If Luke or Thorne showed up, she would fake going down to the kitchen for a midnight snack. She couldn't put a finger on why she felt an aversion to running into either of them. She wasn't doing anything wrong. Maybe she worried that they would think her too sentimental, hanging out in the old man's room. Or maybe it was after such a hard day, she was feeling antisocial. Either way it felt better to not have any witnesses or questions.

The hallway was clear. Alex turned the knob and stole into the room.

The furnishings suited the house more than Buxton. Alex could pick out a touch here and there of Buxton's modernist aesthetic amid the formal decor. The bedding's primary colors outlined in bold black lines stood out against the turn-of-the-century bed.

She sat down on a chest at the foot of the bed and turned her attention to a drawing that hung over the large fireplace. It was an illustration of a tomb in a gorgeously ornate frame. Alex came in close to study the masterful details carved deep into the golden halo of wood.

The frame's decorative pattern was stylized hieroglyphs. Hieroglyphs were not her specialty, but she was able to pick out a few words. It appeared to have something to do with entering and finding.

Her gaze moved from the frame to the artwork. It looked like a typical Victorian illustration of a tomb interior, but under closer inspection, instead of the usual parade of the Gods on the tomb's wall, the focal point was a plain-looking false door.

Often, illustrations like these were considered part of the archaeological documentation process and not artworks. It was odd that the draftsperson almost completely ignored the sacred texts and found the standard false door more appealing.

Alex wandered over to a bookcase that flanked the fireplace. She gently traced the spines of the old books with her finger, scanning the titles. Her finger stopped dead on one. Why would Buxton have a book in his personal collection by Joseph Campbell? Buxton was not a fan of his theories on ancient myth.

Intrigued, she pulled the book from the shelf. She heard a soft clunk, as if something small fell to the floor. Alex looked down. A tiny key lay on the Oriental carpet. She held it in her hand, inspecting it closely. The key reminded her of one that belonged to a music box from her childhood. Instead of an ornate head with a silky pink tassel looped through, this key was decidedly art deco in design with a pattern of intricately nested rectangles rendered beautifully in miniature relief.

What could the key belong to? Although the key's aesthetic was right up Buxton's alley, he didn't seem to be the type to keep a little locked diary. The thought of him journaling made her chuckle.

Alex glanced back at the illustration. Could it be that simple? She made her way back over to the etching and lifted the key to the false door. A small but bright light glowed from its center. Her hand was drawn closer, as if the illuminated keyhole was made of a rare earth magnet. She slid the key in and gently turned it to the right.

A crashing noise came from the hallway. In the distance Jeeves erupted into barking.

Alex returned the key to the locked position and extracted it, then slipped it into the pocket of her pajama bottoms.

The light on the illustration disappeared as the door to Buxton's room was thrust open. Jeeves ran past Luke and toward Alex, barking up a storm. He flung his outstretched front paws toward the fireplace's mantle, stretching his slender salt-and-pepper body up the wall and toward the illustration.

Alex clapped her hands and called his name, but he just ignored her. She scooped Jeeves up to deflect attention from the artwork and carried him to Luke.

Luke shouted over the barking. "Can't sleep?"

Alex was unsure if his question held concern or curiosity. The dog's tirade stopped as soon as he settled into Luke's arms.

"I was feeling a little restless tonight. Had a hard time shutting my mind off after that meeting." She wanted to confess to Luke that she just wanted to spend some time with the lost specter of Buxton and feel like there was still something of him left in the world that she could latch on to.

Luke's kind gaze warmed her. "Today was a real doozy. I am sure tomorrow will be more of the same. So much to do before our time is up. You should really get some sleep." He lowered Jeeves to the ground.

For a brief moment, she felt a strong tug toward Luke. It was similar to the feeling she experienced on top of skyscrapers, like her body was willing her to jump against her better judgment. Except in this case all she wanted to do was to fall into Luke's arms and cry on his shoulders. Alex shook off the thought.

"You are right. Sometimes when I can't sleep, it helps for me to walk around a bit. Get out of my own head. I guess I was drawn to Buxton's room, missing him a little." Alex looked over at the bookcase. Jeeves was sniffing and growling around the area where the key fell.

"It feels so strange to not have him around anymore." Luke's voice cracked.

Jeeves's small body brushed by Alex's calf. The small mustachioed dog swung his paws up to Luke's calf, his little stub of a tail wagging.

Alex reached out and clasped Luke's forearm. "It must be hard on you."

"I feel like he was the first person in this world who utterly understood me. Really listened to me. It is hard to not have him around. He was my mentor and a great friend."

Alex envieded Luke's relationship with Buxton; at least he had that. "I wish I would have had more time with him. To get to know him better."

Luke leaned in toward Alex. "I know he would have liked that too. Your mother laid down the law that there was to be no contact with you. He did his best to keep an eye on you from afar. I know not being able to be a part of your life was something that really tore at him."

Luke picked Jeeves up. He turned to walk away, then tilted his head back at her. Now both man and dog were looking at her. "Try and get some sleep."

As Alex watched them make their way back to their room, she realized she needed a plan. A plan to get everyone out of the house tomorrow.

She had to find out what that key was for.

CHAPTER SEVEN

After leaving the sphinx to stew about his lack of captives, Phillip took Buxton and Jorge on a long trek to his house through a landscape that looked remarkably like the Nile valley. They passed through a delta-lush patchwork of grasses and crops. Off in the distance lay buff-colored cliffs, much like those that line the city of Thebes, or what is known as Luxor today.

It was obvious that Buxton and Phillip were old colleagues and had a lot to catch up on. From what Jorge could glean, Phillip had been dead for quite some time, hence the earlier joyous reunion.

There was no doubt where they were now. The Egyptian Netherworld, or realm of the dead.

Phillip led them upriver from the sphinx until they came to an ancient Egyptian village complete with the required mud-brick houses, and a small temple, but not a soul to be seen.

Somehow the absence of already-dead-but-living-in-the-afterlife types gave Jorge the creeps.

Phillip's well-appointed house was adjacent to the Nile river. As soon as they arrived, he showed each of them to their own suite of rooms.

In Jorge's experience, high adventure usually ensured the best sleep ever, and his body was bone tired. After he took a long bath to soak his tired muscles in the absurdly large tub, the orange-red dust that accumulated on him swirled down the drain. He tended to his cuts and scrapes and then slipped on the pajamas his host provided for him.

Once he was mended and clean, Jorge climbed into bed and sank into its comforting embrace. He couldn't believe how downy soft it was. He lay there for a moment and closed his eyes, imagining that this would be exactly how it would feel to sleep on a cloud, or a mattress filled with cotton candy, covered with a silken fabric of unimaginable thread count. He let his body relax into its soft support. However, instead of drifting off into a dreamless sleep, he tossed and turned, unable to find sleep for all the treasure in the world. Troubling thoughts about his current situation chased each other around on an endless track in his mind.

The only thing that this land provided was uncertainty. The man who saved them was very familiar to Buxton, but could he be trusted?

On the way to his house, Phillip warned them that they would have to spend a chunk of time in the Netherworld before returning to the realm of man. It was something to do with the moon at its third quarter, which Jorge didn't quite understand. Regardless, if that were the case and if Jorge's calculations were correct, it would be almost ten days away. Did Phillip have a reason to try to keep them there? Could it be a trumped-up excuse to spend time with his old friend Buxton?

Jorge couldn't shake the thought that there was something decidedly strange about Phillip, and it wasn't just that he was dead.

As Jorge lay sleepless, he replayed an earlier scene from the emotional reunion between Phillip and Buxton. The sphinx had lowered his humanesque face down and said snarkily, "Touching isn't it? You know, human, you got me thinking, with that pathetic and insulting riddle of yours . . ." The fragrant breath of the sphinx warmed Jorge's cheek. The creature was so close, too close. It made Jorge wonder if he was going to try to sneak a bite while the others weren't looking. He stepped aside, putting some distance between them.

"Don't run away, we were just having a moment." The sphinx leaned toward Jorge and whispered, "I've got something to tell you. A secret that will make you never want for anything ever again. They can't overhear it, though. Come closer."

"Why would you want to tell it to me?"

"I may be rooted in place, but I know things. And I know things that both of those men wouldn't want you to know. Think of it as a payback. A payback to Phillip, for taking away my toys." The sphinx nudged Jorge in a way that was simultaneously playful and scary.

"Is this a trick? Are you just trying to get me in biting range?"

"Trust me, the last thing I want is that one over there with the sword to be angry at me for snarfing you up, no matter how tempting that might be. I get so few visitors around here, and really, that Phillip has always been a little full of himself. I was created when the Gods emerged from the waters of chaos, eons before he was even an upcoming human footnote in the eternal story of time. I have to find my fun where I can. Come close, so I can whisper it in your ear."

The decision was instinctual and instantaneous as he leaned in to hear what the sphinx said. He was betting that if the beast was going to try and eat him, Phillip would put a stop to it quickly. There was no way Jorge could let an opportunity for treasure pass him by. That instinct put him in a lot of sticky situations, but it also delivered to him many glorious successes.

"Go alone. Seek the resting place of the great one who ruled with a double false beard under the shadowless mountain. Climb to the holy of holies and say its double name doubly loud in honor of the holy triad. There you will find a book of magic. Show it to no one. Keep it hidden until you reach the realm of man."

～⌄～

The next morning Jorge woke up feeling almost hung over from sleeping so hard. The Netherworld seemed to have a slightly different atmospheric makeup than the realm of man. Years ago, he traveled to Machu Picchu and remembered waking up feeling similar to this. In that case it was due to the high altitude. He was certain altitude wasn't a contributing factor deep within the Netherworld.

Jorge retrieved his freshly washed laundry from outside his bedroom door. When they arrived last night, Phillip instructed them to leave the dirties out for his servants, and they would launder them. It took time to retrieve everything from his explorer's jacket before he set it out, but it was totally worth it. He felt renewed when he slipped his clean clothes on. Nothing like a fresh start.

After putting all of the usual suspects in his explorer's jacket, Jorge headed out of his room. Directly across from the door was a railing surrounding an atrium which cut through all three floors of the house. He walked over and looked down. Everything from their arrival the night before was a blur. The top floor appeared to be all sleeping quarters. He wasn't sure what the second floor held. He had the impression that all the common rooms were on the ground floor.

Jorge peered down through the atrium to where Buxton and Phillip were sitting near a large burbling fountain. The water noises were amplified by the open space above, drowning out the possibility of hearing anything they were saying.

At times Jorge forgot Phillip was dead. Every once in a while, when the light would hit just right, there was an odd transparency to his form. Other than that, his appearance wasn't ghostlike in any other way. Once Jorge had bumped into him and was surprised to find his body held a solid form.

The building materials for the house were compressed mud brick and plaster. All of the walls were painted with various Egyptian-themed vignettes that were similar to ones that might have graced the palaces of the ancient pharaohs. Across from Jorge was a lovely marsh scene with all the flora and fauna lovingly depicted. It reminded Jorge of renderings of ancient Egyptian palaces during the Amarna period, when the court artwork deviated from the standard formulas of proportion and subject matter and tended to have a more naturalistic aesthetic.

He walked softly to the staircase and headed down. If at all possible, he would love the opportunity to eavesdrop. It could prove useful for Jorge to grasp what they were saying. Jorge spotted a little niche that was close enough that he should be able to hear what they were saying over the splashing water. He kept to the shadows and skirted the wall. Suddenly he was thrown off balance as his foot dipped into uneven flooring, sending him toppling into a large potted plant. Both men stopped talking and looked up at him.

It was awkward for Jorge to extract himself from a large potted palm whose location was only good for eavesdropping.

Buxton waved at him and motioned to the third stone bench that faced the fountain. "Have a seat. We have a lot to talk about."

As Jorge drew nearer, the scent of rose petals filled the air. A confetti of red, pink, yellow, and white floated atop the fragrant water.

The old man spoke first. "Phillip has been filling me in about our circumstances. I fear what he said last night is true. We can't leave this place for another ten days. Apparently, the only way undead mortals like us can escape is to leave at the moon's third quarter, which puts us in quite a pickle."

"Ten days is quite a lot of time. Are you sure there is no other way?"

Phillip nodded. "It's not an easy thing. Your kind aren't meant to be here. So there aren't a whole lot of options. The moon thing, that is really just a loophole I figured out some time ago. Other than that, as far as I know, you'd be up a creek."

Jorge's stomach rumbled loudly, drawing everyone's attention. "Is the kitchen close? I could use something to eat. I didn't want to dig into any of my reserves."

"Therein lies part of our problem. We can't eat or drink anything from here. If we do, we will never be able to leave. Rules of the Netherworld. And as you know, our bodies can only last a finite time without food and water which would pass well before we are able to leave this place. So in that respect we could end up staying here either way." Buxton suddenly looked older and tired.

Phillip's expression softened. It was evident that he cared for the old man. "I know ten days is an impossibly long time for those who are living to go without both needs. I think the absolute longest someone can go without water is about a week, and I think that is a very generous estimate."

Jorge knew that in reality it was only about three days, especially for an old man like Buxton.

"Being on the upward slope of sixty, I feel that I am already at the outer limits of what my body can take."

"So are you saying that you are going to have a big breakfast and just stay? Give up on going home?"

"Nothing would be further from my mind. I just wanted you to know exactly what we are up against. Phillip has a suggestion on how we might beat this thing. He has learned a lot about this realm in the roughly two decades that he's been here, giving him plenty of time to get a feel for its nuances."

"I have to fill my time with something. When I first arrived, I wondered why I was assigned a house in an empty village. If you haven't noticed, it's a real ghost town around here. But then I realized why I was all alone. If I'd been entombed in a proper burial, this village would be alive with all my funerary ushabtis busy with whatever work I needed done. But as a normal modern human allowed to spend their eternity here, I've got nothing."

Jorge tugged on his explorer's jacket. "But you do have servants, right? Or did you wash our clothes yourself?"

"Over the years I have managed to collect a few servants here and there."

Buxton smiled at his friend. "Knowing you, that is a euphemism for some sort of caper."

"You know me too well, my friend."

"If I ever make it out of here, we could create a second burial for you and stock it full of ushabtis. Hopefully that would make your life here more comfortable," said Buxton.

Jorge piped up. "Trust me, if you are able to get Buxton and me out of here, you will never have to want for a servant or a companion. If you'd like, you could have a ushabti for every hour of the year."

"I think that might be a little overboard, Jorge, but I appreciate the sentiment."

His host was in a receptive mood. If Jorge came at it from the right angle, maybe he could pry out some intel from Phillip about the surrounding landscape, or the mountain the sphinx referred to. "So do you get out much? It sounds like most of your explorations of this realm took place when you first arrived."

"I used to venture out more outside of the village, but after a few run-ins with the Devourer of Souls, I greatly dialed back my excursions. Once he starts in, there is just about no stopping him. I think he liked having something to toy with. I wish I would have remembered at the time that he is only interested in those who haven't transitioned and been accepted into the Netherworld. It would have saved me a lot of stress. I've not seen him around for a while. Maybe there has been an onslaught of naughty people trying to enter the land of the dead, and he has no time for random games of chase. When I first arrived, I used to go down and hang out with the sphinx and play the riddle game. Over time, though, I got tired of being around an insufferable know-it-all. It was actually sheer luck that I ran into you yesterday. I'd decided I needed a little fresh air, or whatever you would call that down here."

"You took your sword with you for some fresh air?" Jorge still couldn't shake the feeling that he should know Phillip somehow. Usually when Jorge had problems placing someone, it turned out to be a person he'd interacted with while researching an episode for his show. He knew that he either had ten days or an eternity to try and figure it out. He hoped for the former.

"Oh, that was for the Devourer. In case I ran into him. That blade is about the only thing that can harm him."

Jorge tucked away that bit of information. It could be very helpful if he ended up hunting down his treasure. "Will it kill Ammut?"

"Oh heavens no. Nothing can kill the Devourer of Souls. Let's just say it can slow him down a bit. If you don't hit him right where it counts, then you are in for what becomes a protracted game of chase."

"How long would he chase you for?" Buxton asked.

"About a day or three. Being dead has some advantages. You never get tired or hungry. In a way these runs were a mixed blessing. It proved to be a great orientation to this realm. I was able to cover a lot of ground with him on my heels."

Buxton laughed. "Silver lining, then?"

"Yeah, I guess you could call it that. One silver lining to your current situation is that the living don't need much to subsist on here. These environs seem to slow down a mortal's metabolism. So it may be that without any assistance you both could survive the next ten days until you are able to depart. But I am not certain, and I don't think it is worth testing it out as a theory."

"So what exactly are you proposing?" asked Jorge.

"There is a cave that I used for storage in the foothills. I can take you there. Once you enter the cave, I can cast a spell to induce a deep sleep. Once asleep, the cold temperature will slow down your body's metabolism even further, allowing you to safely reach the time when the moon is in its third quarter and you are both able to jump through a portal to the realm of man."

The mention of this cave certainly got Jorge's attention. Could this be the same cave that the sphinx spoke of? "So you are saying you will lead us to this cave, make us go to sleep, and that we should rely upon you to wake us up at the proper time?" Jorge shook his head. "It doesn't sound very safe to me."

"There is a gate at the cave's entrance. Once it is secured, it can only be unlocked by me."

"And then we would have to just trust you to wake us at the proper time. Again, I don't like it. It puts us in an extremely compromised position."

"Jorge, I trust this man implicitly. I understand that you don't know him like I do, but he is a man of honor. Regardless of what you do, I think this is my only option. I don't think my battered body can stand the ten-day wait."

"I have some beef jerky and some energy bars, and an almost-full canteen of water that could keep me going until our departure. I think that is the best option for me." Jorge crossed his arms over his chest.

"You are of course free to do as you wish, but if you follow my suggestion, your body will be rested for your travels back to the realm of man."

Jorge knew there was no way he was going into cold storage. With a quick mental inventory of his supplies, he decided he would take a chance on waiting it out. Not only did it seem like the best way forward, but it would also give him some time to treasure hunt. "I think I am good. I am pretty fit. I am betting that I will be fine."

"If you change your mind, I can reopen it at any time and let you in. One thing to keep in mind is that the longer you go without eating and drinking, the harder it will be for you to resist. We don't need to eat, but we dead like to. There are fruits and all sorts of delights around to tempt you. Just remember, one sip of water, one bite of food and you will be here forever. I really think it would be much less of a risk to sleep the time off like Buxton."

"I'll keep that in mind, but risk is my bread and butter." Jorge was pretty certain he would have to deplete all his resources and be down to almost his last breath before he allowed someone to put him to sleep and lock him up.

Phillip stood and faced Buxton. "Although I hate to cut our reunion short, I guess we better get you to that cave as soon as possible."

Buxton got up from the bench and leaned over to shake Jorge's hand. "Well, I guess I'll see you on the other side of the moon."

"Oh, I planned on joining you two. The least I can do is see you safely tucked in." There was no way he was going to miss this guided tour of the Netherworld.

"I guess we should get going, then." Phillip clapped his hands.

Suddenly, a bald man wearing nothing but a white starched kilt and a lot of black eyeliner burst into the courtyard. "Phillip, I must talk to you. Alex is—" The man looked around him as if seeing Buxton and Jorge for the first time. "Oh, I see you have guests. Maybe it'd be best if I stop by later."

Buxton's face went sheet white. "Whatever happens to Alex is of grave concern to me. I won't move from this spot until you tell me everything you know."

The man looked uncertain how to proceed.

"It's all right, Horemheb. Anything you have to say to me can be said in front of these two." He motioned toward Buxton. "This is Charles Buxton. He is a close colleague of Alex, and this man is his traveling companion, Jorge Trinculo."

"Are you certain?"

Jorge witnessed a microflash of annoyance that crossed Phillip's face. "Of course. Tell us what you know. Let's go to my library, and you can fill us in. There are at least more comfortable seats there. I am guessing you may have a lot to tell us." Phillip turned toward a hallway at the far edge of the courtyard.

Buxton fell in step with Phillip, leaving Jorge to walk in tandem with Horemheb. "So you're named after Pharaoh Horemheb?"

The man looked at him askew. "I am Pharaoh Horemheb."

Jorge stopped in his tracks. Of course—it made perfect sense. He was in the Netherworld; the pharaohs of ancient Egypt would be rattling around here. It was crazy to think that he was standing in the presence of the great man who took the reins of government after Tutankhamen died. Oh, how Jorge would love to spend the next ten days peppering him with questions about his life and what it was like to live through the rule of Akhenaten.

"Time's a-wasting, Jorge." Phillip held a grand-looking golden door open.

As Jorge passed through the threshold of the library, it visually surpassed his expectations. Books of all colors and sizes covered almost every inch of the large room. On a far corner there was a floor-to-ceiling wine rack, but instead of bottles it held rolled-up papyri. Oriental-style rugs were scattered about the floor, setting an elegant ground plane for the Victorian furnishings that populated the room. It was a bit of a shock to come from the sparse courtyard into the ornate and jewel-toned library.

It was almost as if Phillip read his thoughts. "You'll find the rooms in this house vary a lot in decor. This library is one of my favorite rooms. It helps me occupy my time here. Since you won't be joining Buxton in the cave, you might find it helpful as well."

Jorge sunk into a chaise lounge, the only choice left, and stretched his legs out. Feeling decidedly awkward in such a lounging position, he swung his feet over the side and sat up.

Phillip sat across from Horemheb, with Jorge and Buxton on either side of him. The way they encircled Horemheb, it was almost like he was the subject of interrogation. "Since I know everyone here, let me do introductions." He indicated the pharaoh. "Horemheb, great and last pharaoh of the eighteenth dynasty, I introduce to you Jorge Trinculo, adventurer extraordinaire." He motioned in Jorge's direction. "And Dr. Charles Buxton, Alex's mentor."

"At KN—"

Phillip spoke over Horemheb. "Dr. Buxton has been a colleague of Alex's for quite some time now."

Was Phillip trying to hide something from Jorge?

Buxton shifted in his seat, anxious for news. "What's going on?"

The pharaoh crossed his legs and pulled at his kilt to cover his knee. "It all started with that shaking the other day. As far as I can tell, that quake was caused by Alex defeating Re at his most recent attempt at Aten-hood," said Horemheb.

"Re tried to become the Aten?" Jorge was beginning to realize that this trip to the Netherworld was turning out to be a downright residency on the actual lives of the Gods of myth. If he survived, it was going to change everything.

Buxton sighed. Jorge noted that an unspoken communication passed between Buxton and Phillip.

Horemheb continued. "Yes, and the Gods are none too happy. For the past two thousand years they have roamed the earth. They became bored with that existence, but it still felt like their choice. Now they have been forced, by Alex, to return to the Field of Reeds, which is in less than perfect shape after being uninhabited for about two thousand years. The energy among them is very dark right now. So dark I hightailed my way down here to warn you, Phillip."

"Warn me? Alex is safely out of the Netherworld, and the Gods are back in their places. All should be good, right?"

"If only. There are big changes coming down from on high. Changes for all of us."

"But why are they mad?" This scenario made no sense whatsoever to Jorge. He couldn't be anything but happy if he was returned to his home.

"All their palaces are in disrepair and their energies are drained, so they are not able to rebuild speedily. They are not being kept in the style to which they had been accustomed to since they were born from Geb and Nut. Two thousand years of dust and disrepair and limited magical powers to make it right. They were all in a dither about how to punish Raymond and Salima for the part they played in this newest of failures, when Raymond managed to, very convincingly, throw all the blame for their situation directly on Alex. Knowing the Gods as you do, I am sure you can imagine just how eager they are to exact revenge on Alex and her mortal flesh."

"They want to kill my daughter?" Phillip shot out of his seat and started pacing the floor. "How dare they? Don't they realize that one of them caused the problem in the first place?"

"You should know better than that. They all place the blame at her feet. They have spun themselves up into an angry froth. The general sentiment is that she is a danger to them and to the realm of man. Basically, they want a scapegoat. Everything in the Field of Reeds has transformed over time from Godly to shabby." He paused and absentmindedly played with the pleats of his kilt. "There is even talk of making the non-God inhabitants of the realm work toward renovating their habitation."

"Having the pharaohs actually doing physical labor?" asked Buxton, his tone incredulous.

The thought of this wowed Jorge. "You mean you will actually be conscripted like farmers were to build your pyramids and tombs?"

Horemheb seemed taken aback by the excitement in Jorge's voice. "Yes. The pharaohs and heroes of the great ancient culture would be put into service as common laborers."

Jorge laughed. "I sincerely doubt the pyramids would still be standing if a bunch of pampered royals had built them."

Phillip stopped pacing. "After two thousand years of having the Field of Reeds to yourselves, I would think you'd be bored out of your minds and looking for a project. But, back to Alex. What sort of trouble is she really in?"

"The Gods determined that Alex is a double threat. Not only has she ventured to the Netherworld and survived, but she has also defeated a God. I am sure you know what that could mean."

"They fear she may attain powers. Powers that she could use against them." Phillip said it so softly, Jorge could just barely make out what he said.

"Niles stepped in and—"

"That damned Niles," Phillip shouted. "I make him promise to protect her, and what does he do? Falls in love with her, gets his judgment clouded, and puts her life in jeopardy. I don't ever want to hear that name uttered in my household. You got that, Hormey?"

Jorge stifled a laugh. Hormey. Now, that was great.

Horemheb stiffened at the nickname. "Okay, have it your way. Thoth stepped in and—"

"I told you I didn't want to hear his name."

"Whether you like it or not, you are going to hear one or the other. You wanted to know what was happening, and I am trying to tell you. Stop interrupting."

Buxton motioned toward the seat next to him. "Stop pacing. We'll figure something out."

Phillip continued to stand, crossing his arms.

Horemheb continued. "There isn't much time. The Gods wanted to send down an immediate force to eliminate your daughter, Alex. Niles stepped in and offered an alternate option. He offered to watch over her to witness if any powers came forward. They made him promise one thing, though."

"What was that?"

The old pharaoh shifted uncomfortably in his seat, then cleared his throat. "That if any powers became evident, he would kill her himself."

CHAPTER EIGHT

lex jumped out of bed. She yearned to investigate the illustration and its seeming magical properties further. Could it be another portal to the Netherworld? If it was, it could make looking for Buxton a whole lot easier. Alex wasn't certain if she could find the original portal she, Buxton, and Gormund used all those months ago to enter the Netherworld and battle Raymond. She didn't even know if it existed any longer.

Alex stepped onto her Central Park–facing balcony. The honey-sweet fragrance of hyacinths blooming in terra-cotta pots filled her with springlike optimism. In the sky above, a large bird swooped and glided in the swells of air created by the urban canyons of concrete and glass.

Since she was a California girl, New York always struck her as entirely romantic and cosmopolitan. Now she was living in a beautiful residence smack-dab in the middle of Manhattan. If her life weren't in shambles, her situation would feel idyllic.

She glanced at her watch. It was time to head down to break-fast to initiate the plan she came up with as she tossed and turned last night. The plan was simple. Fake a migraine and send Thorne and Luke away to start packing up the office, allowing her to explore Buxton's room unobserved.

Although Alex was tired from lack of sleep, she was glad for the time to think things through. Not only had she come up with the plan to get rid of Thorne and Luke, but she worked out a strategy that could potentially put a wrench in the Gods' lawsuit against KHNM.

She hummed a happy tune as she reentered her room and shut the French doors behind her. She paused, knowing she would welcome the fresh-sweet aroma of the blooms when she returned, and reopened them.

Alex padded across the room to the bathroom to stage her plan. Her appearance, although bedraggled, was not quite dramatic enough. Fake-sicking always stressed her out. She was never good at subterfuge. Her crutch for attempting deception lay in the staging. If she put on a mask of sorts, it felt more like trickery than lying and therefore something she could buy into.

She grabbed the container of dry shampoo her hair stylist gave her to pump up the volume of her brunette locks. After six or so puffs of the bergamot-scented powder, she grabbed a towel off its warming station and rubbed at her hair vigorously. Drop-ping the towel to the floor, she looked at her handiwork, satisfied with the chimney-sweep look that she'd achieved.

Now came the part of her dramatic costuming that she least looked forward to. It was something one of her elementary school friends taught her to do for maximum effect. Alex dabbed her finger on the wet hand soap and touched the corner of her eye. It stung like mad, but it caused the desired result. Her eye was sufficiently bloodshot. She steeled herself and took care of her other eye.

All was at the ready. Now it was time for her to go downstairs. Before exiting the room, she shrugged on her bathrobe and slid into slippers, then headed downstairs.

Breakfast was laid out in the dining room buffet style. The salty-smoke aroma of bacon made her stomach grumble.

Both Thorne and Luke sat in silence across from one another. The room was filled with angry energy as if they'd just thrown verbal barbs at one another. More than likely it was Thorne who started it. In Alex's experience, Thorne's flag of superiority rose with the dawn and snapped in the wind over some lucky soul before breakfast ended. This time the victim was Luke. Alex knew him to be laid back and have an easy smile, but he would not allow himself to be steamrolled. In Thorne's world, she was superior to him, and he should defer to whatever she asserted. It piqued her anger when he didn't play along with her delusions.

At the buffet table, Alex poured herself a cup of black coffee, spooned in three heaps of sugar, and topped it off with a generous amount of cream. Neither of them had noticed that she had entered the room as they fumed at each other in cold silence.

Alex sipped her coffee taking a moment to get into character. In attempting a deceit, she always panicked a little about finding the proper tone. One that lay somewhere between pathetic and stoic, always wondering if she nailed it or if her playacting was transparent. She sat down and cleared her throat. "I probably won't be joining you today. I have a horrible migraine. Hopefully, I will feel better in the afternoon and be able to come over."

"That is unfortunate. Do you have any instructions for us?"

Thorne's acidic tone managed to make her question more of an angry statement.

"Luke can start with the packing." Alex rubbed her head for dramatic effect and gazed down at the table as she massaged her temples. "Thorne, I have something I need you to tackle right away. I need you to track down the records regarding the God machine and how it was reconstructed after being moved here from Egypt. When you are done with that, I need you to craft a letter to Niles—I mean the Gods—explaining that we need an extension on our deadline. Dismantling the God machine could be like pulling apart an old piece of furniture or shutting down a nuclear cooling tower. Since it contained the Gods' magical powers for over two thousand years, we will have to treat it with kid gloves. And lastly, track down the original covenant between us and the Gods. I need to have a look at that language."

"What you are asking is impossible. The covenant went missing years ago." Thorne didn't say, "Any fool would know that," but left it to be understood by her tone.

Alex continued to rub her temples, feeling a tinge of an honest-to-goodness migraine coming on. "Do the best you can."

Luke's concerned gaze searched her eyes as he spoke. "Do you think they'll even care about the God machine? Wouldn't they see that as more of a problem for the mortals? Reading the language of the lawsuit, it doesn't seem as if they give two shakes about us."

"All we can do is hope that they will. Channel whatever powers of persuasion you have, Thorne." Alex smirked internally, as she knew her assistant possessed no such powers. Strategically, it made sense for Thorne to hammer out a draft that Alex could flesh out with a softer diplomatic touch.

With marching orders given, she pushed her chair back and walked past them, then stood in the doorway. "If I don't make it in today, we can catch up on what you've found before dinner." She gave a short wave and headed toward the elevator to her room.

~~~

Once in her room, Alex stood on her balcony, rejuvenated by the fresh air and the promise of discovery. From the high perch, she could determine exactly when Thorne and Luke left the building.

It took Luke and Thorne much longer to leave than Alex would have expected. A chill overtook her after standing outside for so long. She longed for a cardigan, but didn't want to miss them leaving. Goose pimples erupted down her arms and up her neck, making her shiver.

Immediately after Thorne and Luke crossed over Fifth Avenue to Central Park and entered the metal staff door leading to the Temple of Dendur exhibit, she headed down to Buxton's room.

Alex stared at the average-looking illustration once again. Standing on her tiptoes, she leaned in to examine it more closely. There was no keyhole to be seen within the false door. It must only appear when the key was brought within the proper range. Alex retrieved the key from her pants pocket and lifted it to the drawing. The small glowing keyhole appeared. She slipped the key into the shaft of light and turned it. Nothing. No sound. No rumble like last night. Had somebody been following her?

The black lines of the illustration pooled into one another and expanded until the drawing disappeared into an opaque surface resembling liquid silver. Waves of the material cascaded over the frame and flowed down to the floor, creating a large rectangle shape on the wall. Unafraid, she touched the cool surface. The substance fogged up at her touch. The mist spread outward until it reached the edges then cleared, revealing a beaded curtain with a depiction of the Pyramids of Giza.

Alex laughed at the absurdity of it. The curtain was something you would find at a novelty store rather than the entryway of a magic portal. She parted it with her hands, the cool painted bamboo beads sliding against her hands.

She stepped into what appeared to be an ancient library. The room was circular and constructed out of creamy beige sandstone with marble accents. The domed ceiling was adorned with a depiction of the night sky similar to the Dendera Zodiac in the Louvre. In this case the constellations of the ancient Egyptians were picked out in ivory and gold against a dark lapis-blue night sky. The entire space was lit by unseen lights that must have been inset around the perimeter of the celestial dome.

Her spirit lifted at the sight of all the documents surrounding her. Libraries of any type usually gave her butterflies. Had she stumbled onto a resource that could answer all the questions she'd been searching for? Did this room contain the owner's manual for dismantling the God machine? Or, dare she hope that hidden in the depths of this vast archive could lay the elusive covenant between KHNM and the Gods?

In the center of the room was a table that looked to be more of a workstation than a desk. As Alex drew near, she recognized it as a place to view or work on artifacts. She was intimately familiar with the tools that lay about its surface. Across the top of the desk was a round magnifying optic on a movable arm. She held its white power button down until the light flickered on.

The continuous and curved wall of this room was filled with

hundreds if not thousands of nooks. Each nook held either an object, book, or papyri. She wondered at her discovery. Was she still in the residency? Did the space she occupied extend out from KHNM's townhome and into the adjacent property? Or did she enter a completely magicked space or a portal to some other location in the world or realm of magic?

The ancient Norse myth of Skidbladnir came to mind. She ran across it in a world myth class during her undergrad years. It was a story that always piqued her interest. The legend was of a boat that when no longer needed could be folded up like a piece of paper and stowed away in a pocket. Was this vast library stowed in a similar fashion within the drawing?

Alex scanned the artifact-filled cubbyholes. There didn't seem to be any rhyme or reason as to where things were and why. She assumed there must be a key or catalog somewhere. She spun around looking for one and spied a doorknob across from her. She made her way over and pulled it open.

The room was as sparse as the other was opulent. It was filled with row upon row of shelving units filled with what appeared to be ordinary cardboard boxes. She wandered through a narrow aisleway between the shelves. At the very end of the corridor of boxes was a massive card catalog. Under initial investigation, it was a straightforward set up with alpha listings on the forward-facing drawer ends.

Could these be the records of everything KHNM had ever done? Or was it more than that? Was it something having to do with the Gods and the natural world? Was this some sort of real-life three-dimensional encyclopedia to the known world?

Excitement ran through her. If this was a repository for the agency, it must contain information about her dad. She could kill two birds with one stone. By searching for information on her father, she could satisfy a personal need and figure out the cataloging system.

She ran her finger over the wooden cabinet and its many small horizontal drawers. Her finger halted on the drawer labeled PH-PL and she pulled it out. The small drawer was stuffed full of cream-colored cards, most of them with grey-aged edges. Only occasionally would she run across a bright white one. She pushed against the tightly packed cards with her finger. Even so, she was barely able to read what was on the card. She pulled one out to read it. PHILOSOPHER'S STONE PHST-01-333-24.

Alex was certainly tempted to hunt this one down; however, she would have to save that for another time, as there were other mysteries to solve at the moment. With a tinge of disappointment, Alex wedged the card back into its proper spot. She continued to pry apart the tiny cards, searching for her father's name. When she caught a glimpse of it, her heart leapt into her throat. After a long string of reference numbers, the card read, PHILLIP PHILOTHEA.

Alex scoured the shelves and found the reference system intuitive. Eventually she located an ordinary box. It wasn't even archival. It looked like a random orphaned shipping box that someone decided to reuse. Her shoulders sagged with disappointment. She assumed her father's personal items would have been given a much more suitable container, something that would honor his memory as a valued KHNM agent. How could it be that all his possessions were left in such a haphazard way? Considering the way Buxton spoke of her father, as if he was the son he never had . . . would someone put their son's last possessions or their material goods in a stupid cardboard box?

As she pulled the container down a flash of red caught her eye. She turned the box sideways and smiled. Yes, it was a plain old box, but it was one that a case of 100 Grand bars came in. Her father was rabid in his love for these candy bars that packed in everything but the proverbial kitchen sink. The affront dissolved like confectioners' sugar in tea with Buxton's irreverent tribute to her father.

Alex grabbed the box and carried it out to the worktable in the domed room. It surprised her how light the box was for its size. Setting the box down, she peeled back the sealing tape that secured it. What would she find in this box? His personal effects? Or boring personnel files? She pulled the flaps back and was surprised at its contents. It appeared to be more or less the stuff her father had on his desk at the time of his death. Not at all what she expected.

There was a picture of the family when they all went to D.C. on vacation. A lightness filled her at the sight of the three of them together caught midlaugh at something off frame. Alex was about six at the time and cherished the memory of how they leisurely explored all the Smithsonian had to offer. It was their only trip together. She smiled at the memory of her dad asking some tall, dark stranger to take a picture for them all as they stood in front of the Washington Monument. Her dad explained how the Egyptian obelisks inspired the great monument and how one day he would bring her to his beloved Egypt and show her the great stones that still stood.

She put the picture back into the box. The few items left behind by her dad may not have been full of pomp but were over-full of memories. She extracted a small black leatherette day planner. Upon opening it, a business card fell to the floor. The name on the card was Albright Knox, from the Beinecke Rare Book and Manuscript Library on the Yale campus. An eleven-digit number was scrawled across the back. She wondered why this of all things would have been kept with his possessions. Was it an oversight? Or, did it have significance? Could it have been the last thing given to him before he headed off on his last assignment in Egypt?

Alex would definitely try to find this Mr. Knox.

As Alex replaced the planner, she noticed a small velvet box hidden in the shadows. The hinges creaked with age as she opened it. A golden ring was tucked into a cleft of the soft crushed material. The ring's face was flat like a signet ring and engraved with a rendition of a false door with many nested rectangles.

Inside the interior lid was a piece of paper that was jammed in. She tugged it loose. Her heart skipped a beat as she unfolded it. The note was written in her dad's handwriting. *Things have changed for the worse. Please make sure Alex gets this if I don't return.* A hot burn of tears stung at her eyes.

Alex slipped the ring over her finger and smiled against the feelings of loss. Would her mother know anything about this ring? Alex would ask her next time they talked. As she gazed at the small number of items left by her dad, she made the decision to take them all back to her room. Luke and his procedures be damned. She had every right to them. She was Phillip's daughter.

Alex returned the empty velvet box to the cardboard container, then tucked it under her arm.

A small whisper of sound made her jump. Her ears pricked up. It sounded like voices that were singing or chanting in the far distance. Could there possibly be someone in that archival work-room? Or was her being overtired making her hear things?

Although the sound stopped, she sensed another psychic presence in the room. There was a soft swooshing sound as if something brushed against an object close at hand. Had somebody followed her? Her heart thumped in her ears. Her senses were on high alert, picking up on a soft rhythmic tapping coming from the storage room. She headed toward the beaded curtain to make her escape.

The noise was following her. Alex glanced back into the room and breathed a sigh of relief. Her pursuer was only Jeeves. She chuckled as she squatted down to pet him. Her palm swept back his bushy silver-grey eyebrows. His little stub wagged hello. "What are you doing here, little guy?"

Jeeves barked, as if he had a solid reason for being there.

"Well, I'll forgive you this time for following me, but—"

As if called by an unseen voice, Jeeves suddenly turned tail and charged back into the storage room.

"Jeeves, come here!" She waited. No Jeeves. Exasperated at the contrary attitude of this funny little dog, Alex walked back to the storage room to retrieve him. In the distance, her eye caught his grey form over by the card catalog. Something near it had his full attention. "Jeeves, come on."

His head popped up. Jeeves held in his mouth what appeared to be a dirty and dust-bunnied white cloth.

She squatted down and patted her knee. "Come on, little guy."

Jeeves leaned down on his front legs with his butt up high in the air, in the stance for play. A spark of mischief burned in his eyes for a second, and then he dashed by her.

Alex only caught a glimpse of the treasure in his jaw. But from what little she did see, it most resembled an ancient mummy finger.

Alex darted after him, chasing him through the beaded curtain and into Buxton's old room. Alex glanced back to the portal. It was closing in on itself, and the illustration was normalizing.

Jeeves was fast. Alex barely kept up with him as he charged out of Buxton's bedroom and to the stairway. Could she catch up to him and entice him into giving up the evidence of her explorations?

CHAPTER NINE

Jorge gave it a day or two after they'd taken Buxton to the sleeping tomb to steal away in search of his treasure. At least he thought it had been that long. It was challenging to find mental purchase with mortal concepts like time in the Netherworld, as they seemed to become a blur of memory and moments spun together in a dream-fog.

His muscles strained as he pulled the barge across the river toward the Netherworld version of the Valley of the Kings. The rough rope burned his palms with each rep. This time across the Nile was much slower going. During the earlier excursion, Phillip pulled the boat across in an effortless manner. In hindsight, it made sense that Phillip didn't suffer rope burns. He was dead.

Jorge's stomach made a long, yawning growl. It was so long since he'd eaten, making him wonder if this journey for treasure was the best idea. Burning calories at such a fast pace could easily empty his tank with disastrous consequences. There was only a small amount of turkey jerky left in his reserves.

The option of joining the sleeping Buxton didn't feel like an option at all. Having a stranger put him to sleep magically in a tomb just didn't appeal to Jorge. Entrusting his life to unknown entities went directly against his adventurer's code of self-reliance.

With the vast desert stretching out before him, Jorge thanked his lucky stars the idea came to him of tagging along with Phillip and Buxton to the sleeping tomb. It was an excellent opportunity to get the lay of the land. That excursion affirmed his suspicion that the area surrounding Phillip's empty village was a Netherworld twin of the Luxor valley in Egypt.

One thing that stymied Jorge about where to find the treasure was the location of the shadowless mountain. There was light all around during the daytime, but it was more of an ambient glow instead of coming from a giant celestial orb like the sun. He was confused as to what the sphinx meant. The shadowless mountain could be any mountain in the Netherworld.

The suite of rooms Phillip gave Jorge included a rooftop retreat. A raised lounging pavilion with curtained netting surrounded by a large planter garden. It was a paradise of miniature fruit and incense trees and a profusion of flowering hibiscus, ranging in color from the palest of pinks to the deepest of reds.

He reclined on the large daybed, propped up on the multitude of pillows and cushions. It afforded a grand view of the valley below. The platform was an homage to the ancient practice of sleeping on the roof when the weather was too hot to bear. He was certain the only practical purpose it served was to rejoice in the surrounding landscape, because in Jorge's experience, the Netherworld was neither hot nor cold.

After dropping off Buxton at the sleeping tomb, Jorge spent a lot of time up there scouring the vast landscape for clues of where his treasure might be hidden. Then the answer hit him. Since the valley below replicated the area around the ancient city of Luxor, the pyramidal-shaped mountain across the Nile must be the sacred place where the ancient pharaohs chose to rest for eternity, the Valley of the Kings. This must be the mountain the sphinx was talking about.

With his path forward illuminated, Jorge jumped from the pavilion lounger and ran down the stairs and into the main house to "borrow" Phillip's broadsword. One thing Phillip was clear about was his warning about Ammut, the crocodile-headed Devourer of Souls. Jorge wondered about this creature and what sort of threat he might be. It was hard to imagine the mythical beast as being very fast. It was known to have forepaws of a lion and a hippo back end. Not exactly aerodynamic. All the same, having the sword would make him feel better.

The sword was hiding in plain sight amongst a number of other objects on a large bookshelf. The fact that it wasn't under lock and key surprised Jorge at first, but then again Phillip did live in an empty village in the Netherworld, so there probably wasn't a very high crime rate.

Something massive bumped against the bottom of the barge, knocking Jorge out of his thoughts. He tightened his grip on the rope as the barge rocked violently, fighting against being tumbled into the water to whatever waited below.

Many years ago, Jorge witnessed a pod of killer whales in the Antarctic. One hunting strategy was for one of them to slap itself up onto the edge of an ice floe and tip the slab of ice up, sliding the tasty seal down to the waiting pod. There couldn't be any orcas in this body of water, but there could be a different dire threat—hippos. For all the fat jokes and disrespect that hippos got, they were the real killers of the Nile. Or at least they used to be, before they were hunted to extinction. Was this river overrun with the departed creatures that no longer swim in the Egyptian Nile?

Suddenly the barge went still. In the near distance large brown bodies breached the water, presumably to catch their breath. Jorge didn't waste any time. Taking advantage of their retreat, he pulled as hard and fast as he could. The shore was tantalizingly close.

The barge bumped onto land. Jorge hopped onto the thin strip of rocky shore. There was barely enough room for him to stand. Papyrus stalks and wild grasses entwined themselves into a thick thatch directly in front of him. A golden frond from a broken stalk of grass tickled his nose. After brushing it away, he slid the broadsword from its sheath. The razor-sharp blade cut through the thick brush. Sweat poured down his back as he thwacked through it. *More calories burned.* He quickly shooed the thought away. Focusing on the negative wasn't what made him who he was, a popular star of an adventure television show. He must focus on the prize.

He emerged from the thick grass and stepped out into the rocky beige desert. It stretched as far as the eye could see. Much like Egypt, in the Netherworld the line between abundant fields and harsh desert was a thin one. Life or death; each only a breath away.

Salty sweat burned his eyes as he marched toward the mountain. His body swayed a little, as a lightheaded feeling overtook him. Jorge pulled out his last stick of jerky. He chewed slowly, savoring its salty meatiness.

The valley was silent. The stark landscape ahead was nothing but rocks, sand, and sky. Absent were the birds that would be soaring in the midday sky in the realm of man. A small breeze whispered against his skin but carried no scent whatsoever.

A tumble of rocks skittered behind him. Jorge spun around to see if he was being followed. He saw nothing, but he couldn't shake the feeling that something was lurking out of sight.

Off in the distance stood a temple surrounded by a high wall. If his memory of the Luxorian valley was correct, and he wasn't suffering from a Netherworld-induced blur of facts, it was most likely Pharaoh Hatshepsut's mortuary temple.

The words of the sphinx echoed through his head. *Seek the resting place of the great one who ruled with a double false beard under the shadowless mountain. Climb to the holy of holies and say its double name doubly loud in honor of the holy triad.*

Jorge stopped in his tracks. The sphinx didn't intend him to go to the Valley of the Kings to search out some generic pharaoh. It was obvious. The treasure place lay right ahead of him, the very special one-of-a-kind mortuary temple, Djeser-Djeseru, built for the female pharaoh who ruled as a man—Hatshepsut.

It surprised him the resemblance didn't occur to him sooner. The Netherworld sphinx's facial features were remarkably similar to one Jorge saw years ago at the Metropolitan Museum of Art. It was commissioned by that great gender-bending ruler. The ancient sphinx statue was memorable, telegraphing kingly power, but with an all-knowing Mona Lisa smile.

Jorge headed toward the temple, reinvigorated. What would he see when he passed between the twin obelisks and the massive pylons that lay ahead? Would the temple and its surroundings reveal themselves to be sand and stone like the ones currently in Egypt, or completely different? In the realm of man, the protective walls had disappeared years ago, leaving the bones of the temple exposed.

The first time he'd ever seen Hatshepsut's temple in Egypt, Jorge was awed by its grand symmetry. It consisted of three levels of colonnades connected by a center ramp that ran through it. The temple's style was vastly different in design from any other pharaoh's mortuary temple, but then again she was a very different pharaoh. Hatshepsut ruled ancient Egypt successfully for more than twenty years. She assumed the trappings of a man, false beard and all. Many of her great deeds lived on, despite the efforts by many to wipe the memory of this powerful ruler from the history books.

On one of the temple's exterior walls, Hatshepsut's royal artists recorded a grand expedition she commissioned to the ancient land of Punt. The great pharaoh charged her emissaries to bring back exotic plants and animals to adorn her temple in the desert. All of the living treasures transplanted in this newly constructed paradise were sustained by irrigation drawn from the great Nile in a feat unparalleled in ancient waterworks. It must have been a wonder in its time.

As Jorge passed through the obelisks toward the opening of the outer wall, he caught a glimpse of what lay beyond the pylons. A vast garden flashed like a jewel with a shocking display of verdant opulence. The colors were so overwhelmingly green his eyes burned at its lush intensity after the sandy beige eternity outside.

Past the massive pylons he strolled into the deep shade from the ancient trees overhead. An unexpected carpet of cool moss softened his footfalls. The serenity of the surrounding garden called him to sink into the welcome cushion below and rest.

Out of nowhere a projectile thunked against his head. Jorge

peered into the fruit-laden branches of the persea tree above him as a blur of brown fur and long tail skittered away. He smiled at the thought of this enchanted garden and its playful beasts. A sense of well-being cascaded through him as he wandered. It wouldn't be the worst thing in the world to stop for a while and let his body recoup for a few minutes. The thought enveloped him like a downy-soft blanket, its pleasant weight drawing him downward.

The spicy-sweet aroma of cloves mingled with oranges filled the air. Jorge closed his eyes and breathed in the heavenly fragrance. A vision of Hatshepsut in a thin linen shift danced in his mind. She beckoned him to her. A whisper carried to him on a breeze, like a dandelion puff lazily floating by. "Breathe deep, my love. Rest. Lay with me, my dear one."

The clear, sweet voice was like honeyed wine. As he knelt down on the grass, the knees of his canvas pants absorbed the cool moisture that clung to the green living carpet.

"Yes, my dear Senmut," she whispered.

A shiver ran through his body. His skin ached for her touch. "I am here. Where are you?"

"Close your eyes, dear one."

When he closed his eyes, he could see her in his mind. She was swaying to the music from unseen musicians. A breeze fluttered through his hair as if the fingers of the wind were her touch.

"Senmut." Her voice spiraled through his mind in slow circles. Feeling familiar and yet foreign . . .

Jorge stood fast, making his head spin. Senmut? Hatshepsut's lover? He bit down hard on his cheek, the salty taste of blood on his tongue. Hatshepsut would have to wait for some other fool. Jorge struggled toward the temple's first ramp, flanked by lion statues. Their bodies turned from stone to animal form. When he passed, they both stood and yawned, displaying their sharp ivory teeth. In a synchronized movement they both spun around and curled up, each one, into a tight ball to sleep. Their purring, deep and loud, resonated through Jorge's body. The low vibrations surrounded him in a comforting hum. Their low voices echoed in his head like the hum of a Buddhist chant. "Stay, dear Senmut. Rest. Hunt. Play. Serve our lady."

Unable to resist, Jorge staggered over to one of the giant sleeping lions and tumbled into its soft downy fur. The purring grew louder and deeper as Jorge sunk into the warm thrum of the noise.

"Yesssssssss, my dear one." Hatshepsut's contented voice cascaded over him as he gave in to the rhythm of the satisfying rattle from the large sleeping cats.

A loud clank broke the spell. His eyes flew open. The silver cup his mother gave him was rolling down the ramp. The vibrations must have loosened it from its pocket. Jorge extracted himself from the lion and retrieved his cup. Continuing on, he struggled with every step to ignore the multitude of enticements that were being used against him.

Walking past the reflecting pools, he made his way to the second and final ramp. It was lined with sphinxes, each with the head of Hatshepsut. They sang to him in high chiming voices, begging him to stop, to rest, to stay. Adding to the cacophony of sound that rang through his head.

Resisting as best he could, Jorge continued to the third level of the temple. As he crossed the threshold of its outer courtyard, he was reinvigorated by the sight of the small holy of holies: the room where high priests would make offerings so that Hatshepsut would have everything she needed in the afterlife.

As he stepped inside, all of the voices calling to him halted. He breathed a sigh of relief. It was time to hunt for treasure.

The interior of the small space was unexpectedly damp, but everything about this temple was unexpected so far. He turned on his headlamp. It shone bright wherever Jorge's gaze landed. As far as he could tell it was completely empty except for a painted depiction of the royal family making offerings to the God Amun. Was this all for naught? Was he wrong and the treasure was really hidden somewhere in the Valley of the Kings?

Closing his eyes, he summoned all of his focus. What was it that the sphinx said? *Climb to the holy of holies and say its double name doubly loud in honor of the holy triad.* Could it be that all he needed to do was say her name?

Jorge breathed in deep and stood stock-still, clearing his mind. He reflected in solemn silence until he was moved to speak. "I honor thee with this respectful offering. Hatshepsut! Hatshepsut! Hatshepsut! May you and your divinity thrive in the Field of Reeds."

He opened his eyes. Nothing changed. The painted faces of the royal family stared lifelessly back at him. He turned to leave the holy of holies, saddened that he would leave Djeser-Djeseru with nothing.

Then it struck him. He laughed out loud at the sphinx's wordplay. The name of the temple was Djeser-Djeseru, the holy of holies, and here he stood in the holy of holies of Djeser-Djeseru. He turned back around and focused once more, closing his eyes. With conviction he yelled, "Djeser-Djeseru! Djeser-Djeseru! Djeser-Djeseru!"

A flash of light played against his eyelids. Jorge opened his eyes. His headlamp caught a glint of gold on the floor. He went over to investigate and saw what could easily be the most beautiful object he'd ever seen. It was a golden book, encrusted with turquoise, about the size of a standard dictionary. He picked it up, finding it surprisingly lightweight given all the metal and precious stones adorning it. The back cover was made of a delicate pattern of filigree shapes and symbols.

Jorge wanted nothing more than to examine the book thoroughly, but he needed to get back to Phillip's before his host started to wonder what he was up to. He stuffed it in his explorer's bag, then headed out of the cave. Now that he knew what was ahead, the way back would be a breeze.

As Jorge trudged through the desert, he still couldn't shake the feeling he was being followed. Every so often he would hear the rustle of the desert scrub in the windless realm. His glances back would only reveal the vast beige landscape that stretched out behind him. After recrossing the Nile, he could have sworn there was a splash among the clusters of papyrus. It didn't make sense. His fatigue must be making him paranoid. But just in case, he gripped the strap of the broadsword.

While he made his way through the endless sea of sand and rocks, a grunt snapped Jorge out of his reverie. He glanced behind him. Charging toward him was the patchwork body of the God Ammut, the Devourer of Souls. The sharp teeth of his crocodile head glinted at Jorge, while its hippo back legs somehow managed to keep up with its graceful and fast lion forelegs.

Jorge ran. His shins screamed as he pounded forward. He'd never fought with a broadsword before, so the idea of stopping and fighting didn't seem like a good strategy. He couldn't chance it. He just kept running, hoping he was closer to the villa than he thought he was. He really didn't have much left in the tank on this involuntary Netherworld cleanse.

Jorge stumbled a little as he chanced a glance behind him. The beast's mouth was wide open, as if ready to scoop him up like an exceptionally large whole chicken. The razor-sharp teeth glinting in the light of day gave Jorge a new burst of energy. He could have sworn that he could feel the hot, moist breath of the beast warming his calves. His legs pumped harder at the thought of being perforated by those pearly whites.

The village was in the near distance. His legs were like rubber and his throat burned as if it were rubbed raw with high-grit sandpaper. The calculus of his survival was feeling less and less optimistic.

In the distance, he spotted a sturdy shrub or young tree that lay beneath the balcony to his room. He might just make it.

He leapt into the bush, and it swayed under his weight as he scrambled up its meager branches. Something soft and oddly granular squished in his hands. Dotting the limbs above him were small golden fruit. It must be a sycamore, the sacred tree of the Goddess Hathor. He hoped it was a good omen.

He grabbed onto a tree branch as the tree shook violently from below, holding on for dear life. He had no desire to be shaken down, like ripe fruit, to the waiting jaws below.

Ammut's odd body was stretched up the tree, pawing the tree like a hungry bear, if a hungry bear possessed lion's claws and the head of a crocodile.

Jorge reached up and tore off a large branch loaded with fruit and tossed it into the gaping maw of the creature. As Ammut turned to hack it out, Jorge summoned all of his strength and kicked hard at its head, then pulled himself up and over the balcony.

His feet slammed down to safety as he steadied himself against the wall of the balcony. The beast glared up into Jorge's eyes and growled in a deep baritone rumble. Its golden irises burned bright. Jorge felt an odd compulsion to climb back down to the waiting beast. It was a sensation not unlike the one people feel when they're up high somewhere and feel a compulsion to leap off. He shook off the thought and broke eye contact.

Jorge laughed at the creature below him. Grabbing more figs from the tree, he tossed them down. "Looks like only vegetarian for you today."

Ammut turned and headed off toward the Nile.

—␥—

Jorge breathed a sigh of relief as he stepped into his suite of rooms. He slid the balcony door closed and locked it.

He slid down onto the floor to rest. His throat and lungs burned from running, and his stomach rebelled against its emptiness. He yearned for a glass of cold, clear water. The temptation to drink liberally from the bathroom sink just across the way was hard to resist.

Once he caught his breath, Jorge pulled himself up to standing and ambled over to the bed. He lifted off the broadsword and set it down. Eventually, he would have to find a convenient way to return it. But for now, he would investigate his newfound treasure.

Jorge lay his explorer's bag on the bed and retrieved the book. Its bejeweled cover glinted in the light. The sphinx said that with this treasure Jorge would never want for anything. Was that a statement purely based on its retail value? Jorge silently hoped that some magic might come along with the treasure to help him in his situation. But for now, it really did just look like a book. A really fancy book, but just a book nonetheless.

Jorge carried the book to the chaise lounge across the room, disheartened with the knowledge that his treasure wasn't going to help him return to the realm of man or provide for his life sustaining needs. He'd soon have to join the sleeping Buxton. His supplies were almost completely tapped.

At least he'd have a few moments alone with his treasure. Of course, Jorge would do his best to hide the book, but he was pretty certain that Phillip would most likely find it while he and the old man slept.

Jorge got comfortable and opened the book. The script swirled around in gorgeous patterns, making him think of the marbled paper in vintage books. He blinked to try to focus, unsure if it was his eyes or the script that was catawampus. He pulled the book closer. The lines and loops were shifting as if searching for their proper forms.

The book in front of him was less like a book meant for reading and more like a hollowed-out book meant for squirreling away secrets. Except in this case, instead of a hollowed-out body, there was one very thick page with markings on its edges to give the illusion of many pages. Dead center on that one page was a burnished gold mirror in the oval shape of a cartouche, framed by a delicate rendering of papyri reeds, their feathery heads twining together at the crest of the mirror.

There was one word on the mirror—*need*.

Jorge scanned the rest of the page for any sort of clue. What was this book? Was this some sort of joke? Was this some sort of Netherworld idea of a self-help book? The sphinx had definitely gotten one last laugh on Jorge. He tossed the book down on the floor. Its gold cover flickered in the light.

He checked his anger. His hunger must be getting the best of him. He knew deep down this wasn't a total loss. He at least would have a one-of-a-kind thing that he could probably sell back home for a pretty penny. He picked it up and inspected the fine work of the book's cover. There was a depiction of two Gods. One was in the form of a man with the head of a frog, and the other was a woman in a linen sheath with the head of a serpent. He wasn't one hundred percent sure, but he thought they might be two of the Egyptian Ogdoad, the original four God-couples that emerged from the primordial chaos of nothingness.

Surrounding the turquoise inlay of the Gods' bodies, were the hieroglyphs for eternity. At the top of the cover, the book's title was now legible. The inlaid turquoise spelled out the word *Abundance*.

He opened the book again. Even in the golden hue cast by the mirror, he looked drawn and tired. Maybe it was time to put the book back in his explorer's bag and ask Phillip to use the sleeping spell on him. He needed to face the reality that their departure was still a long way off.

Looking closely at the finely rendered papyrus stalks circling the mirror, he saw there were tiny words engraved in them. He squinted to read the text. One side said, *abundance spoken*, the other, *abundance received*. Jorge said the words aloud. Suddenly, the mirror face changed to a dark void.

Abundance . . . what could it mean? His stomach growled. He would have given anything to eat from his favorite Friday night haunt back at home, Chaing's Gourmet. The best Chinese food. Ever. He imagined what it would be like to gorge himself on his usual—but before he could finish the thought, a to-go bag with the customary red-lettered *Thank You* appeared in the black void.

He reached in and grabbed it. The bag was heavy with food, and the smell was a heavenly blend of garlic and the mellow spice of those red peppers they put in just about everything. He lifted the bag up and gently laid it on the floor. Jorge dropped the book and scrambled to the bag, tearing it open. Inside, he found five large takeout containers along with a smallish one which would more than likely hold the rice. He popped each container open and marveled at his favorites, pot stickers, duck with ginger, green onion pancakes, green beans with garlic, and almond chicken. The only thing missing was the wonton soup.

He reached over to where the book lay and said the words "abundance spoken." The mirror faded into black once more. He said, "Chaing's Gourmet's wonton soup." He figured since it was not included in the last batch, he should specifically ask for what he wanted. Another takeout bag appeared with a large plastic container.

He placed the container of soup near his bounty of edibles. The green beans with garlic were his favorite. He reached over and grabbed one of their vibrant green, stir-fried bodies, breathing in their savory goodness. There was a knock on the door, halting him from consuming the succulent veggie.

"You okay in there, Jorge?" Phillip was working the knob.

He muffled his tone to sound off-kilter. "I am all right." His mouth was watering at the delightful aroma surrounding him. "I need more rest. Reserving my energy, the best I can. Thanks for checking on me."

"You sound very weak. Are you sure you don't want to join Buxton?"

Jorge peered down at the containers of Chinese food strewn around him. "No, I have a few protein bars and some jerky left. I think I'll be okay."

"If you want some company, I'll be in the library for a while."

"Will do," he said with probably more gusto than he should have. He was so anxious to start eating that he was having a hard time continuing this play-acting of a withering man. If Phillip didn't leave him alone, Jorge might have to use that book of abundance to somehow get rid of him altogether.

"What's that smell?" Phillip's tone sounded bemused. "Could it be garlic?"

"Oh, that." Jorge's mind whirred at top speed—how was he going to account for the decidedly Szechuan smell that was emanating from the room? "I've been chewing on a head of garlic. Always carry some with me. Strengthens the immunity, you know."

"Interesting. I'll be downstairs if you need anything." Jorge heard the footfalls of Phillip's retreat.

Jorge pulled the waiting green bean to his mouth and halted just before biting. Was this okay? Was this considered food from the Netherworld? The food obviously came from Chaing's and was made by human hands in his favorite restaurant in the human realm. There was even a handwritten receipt in Chinese script stapled to the bags. He'd have to remember to pay them for the food when he got back home. He always sensed it would be a bad idea to get on the bad side of the matriarch who ran the place. The last thing Jorge would ever want to do is compromise his future dumplings with an unpaid bill.

He bit into the firm and garlicky-sweet-yet-salty bean. He quickly located the supplied chopsticks and wolfed down chunks of duck and chicken, alternating with the green onion pancake. Then his eye spotted the soup. He peeled the plastic lid off and gulped down the warm and satisfying broth and slurped up a small wonton, delighting in the flavor of the small pork and shrimp ball inside. After he'd inhaled each and every entrée, Jorge pondered the epic pile of empty containers and let out a mammoth burp.

Jorge leaned up against the chaise lounge, satisfied and gorged. His mouth felt slightly puckered from all the salt. Water. That was what he needed—cool, crisp water. He grabbed the book and requested an ice-cold bottle of mineral water. His wish was instantly fulfilled. He downed the bubbly water, then crawled up onto the bed. Propped up by the large square throw pillows behind him, he leaned back, sinking into the delightful comfort. Jorge closed his eyes and found himself drifting into a blissful sleep.

The remaining days consisted of Jorge spending time in the library with Phillip, poring over all the amazing publications his host amassed over time. There were world reference books, and of course a plethora of them were about ancient Egypt, but there also was a huge section dedicated to novels. There were old classics as well as contemporary best sellers. If you had all eternity to spend in a realm, you would want to be sure to have some good reads around. Jorge wondered where Phillip got his books from. Did Amazon deliver to the Netherworld? The thought made him chuckle. During his search of the library, he was disappointed to find that Phillip's collection was not very magical, nor were there any books regarding the Netherworld. He'd hoped to find some writings that might point him in the direction of other magical items that he could bring home with him, but unfortunately there were none to be found. If Phillip owned any such items, they must be hidden away. Jorge filled the remaining days reading some old standards, like Jules Verne, up to some riveting detective novels by Tess Gerritsen.

On the very last night before he and Buxton were to return to the realm of man, Jorge spied Phillip looking very intently at a document. Once finished with it he carefully folded it up and secreted it away somewhere among the books.

Jorge surreptitiously tracked Phillip's movements at the bookcase with his peripheral vision. Jorge waited for what felt like eons for Phillip to finally retire. After waiting a few clicks, Jorge investigated the general location.

He pulled out a hefty old Crock-Pot cookbook. Phillip didn't strike Jorge as much of a one-pot-meal guy, dead or alive. A small piece of paper slipped out and fell to the floor.

Jorge slipped the square of paper into his pants pocket and headed up to his room. Once he unfolded it, he realized he'd struck gold. It was a highly detailed hand-drawn map of the Netherworld with X's marked all over. An X marked the spot where Jorge found the book of magic, proof of the map's usefulness. After returning to the realm of man, maybe he could use this book to return to the Netherworld and do some unscheduled treasure hunting.

Jorge woke up that last morning with a fresh outlook. It was the day to head back to the realm of man. His heart filled with joy at the thought of it. Maybe he and that Buxton character could start a partnership of sorts. The old man knew an awful lot about Ancient Egypt and seemed to be a fan of Jorge's television show. Maybe he would like to be a recurring talking head. Once they made it to the other side, Jorge was going to pop the question. His show could use some new blood.

Jorge grabbed the book to order up some breakfast. He was excited to eventually have some quality time to really experiment with the book. Once he learned its secrets, who knew what he could accomplish. The possibilities were limitless. He could call forth the government files that prove the existence of aliens to be delivered directly to him or a treasure trove of riches to fund his grandest adventures ever.

His stomach growled.

He would be able to dream big and have all he wanted once he made it home. Jorge opened the book to order his food. Before he could place his cosmic order, a clear and vivid vision of Buxton broke his concentration. "I wonder who you are, old man."

A bright light blinded him. Jorge pressed his fingertips against his shut eyes to blot out the spots of light. Memories flooded through him like a flash flood tearing through a dry desert wadi. He opened his eyes knowing he would never see the world the same again.

He knew exactly who Buxton was.

CHAPTER TEN

The office was empty. All of Buxton's personal and professional belongings were gone. A lifetime of service to the agency stripped bare. The highly ornate rococo desk looked ridiculous surrounded by empty bookcases and curio cabinets. The pressure of his legacy weighed heavy on Alex's shoulders. Filling the room would take much more than a simple shopping trip or two. It would take years of hard work to collect the artifacts of success that filled these walls. With the agency's current problems, it was uncertain if she would get the chance to try. It felt like she didn't have a leg to stand on in convincing the Gods of KHNM's usefulness.

She picked up the black old-school receiver from its cradle and dialed the number on the card she found in the archive. Was her hope that Dr. Knox might have some answers a false one? Just because he was a contact of her father, and the director of a library with the largest rare book collection in America, didn't necessarily mean he knew anything about the God containment system or the books of magic Buxton mentioned.

The phone continued to ring unanswered. Maybe he wasn't even alive anymore. She leaned into the receiver resting against her shoulder, listening to its empty ring. It went on into infinity, with no promise of voicemail. It struck her that this phone number might not even be active any longer. The ringing stopped; she drew the phone to her ear.

"Hello?" She could hear breathing on the other end.

"Sorry. I thought I was going to miss your call. Knox here." His voice halted with every word.

Alex shook her head—yet another technology denier, like her mother, still clinging to the time before cellphones and voice-mail. "Dr. Knox, I am Alex Philothea. I believe you knew my father, Phillip. I found your card in my father's belongings with some sort of reference number on the back. Do you know anything about that?"

There was a sharp intake of breath on the other side. "Oh yes. How I have wondered about you over the years. I am so glad you have called, and I think I may have *exactly* what you are looking for."

By not addressing her personally, it was as if Dr. Knox was being intentionally covert, as people are when there are inconvenient ears around to hear what is said. Before Alex could ask, he continued on. "I would love to personally show you those items in the special collection. Since I am leaving for a conference tomorrow, it will have to be today."

"I will check the train schedules, but I think I can make that happen. I'll shoot for around four. Does that work for you?"

"I'm sure I can arrange something, being the keeper of the keys and all. Well, good day, and I look forward to seeing you."

The line went dead. The phone call offered up more questions than answers.

Alex made a reservation for the 1:03 train to New Haven. She had just enough time to inform Luke and Thorne then head to the station. Maybe tonight she would get some answers and talk to someone who could shed some light on the God machine or even the books of magic. Hopefully it wasn't a wild goose chase, but it was the only lead so far.

Even if it turned out to be a dead end, it might do her some good to get out of town and find some space to clear her mind, if only for a few hours. Alex had suffered vivid and peculiar dreams ever since she returned from the Netherworld. Each time she would take the form of a bird. She never knew what type of bird she was. Judging by her sharp talons and bright yellow beak, she assumed her body was that of a bird of prey. The entire dream involved complex and challenging patterns of flight, dipping and darting through the air, soaring to high altitudes, then diving down to earth at breakneck speeds. When she woke, it was as if she'd competed in a triathlon, feeling anything but rested.

Alex headed out of her office to the maze of corridors that led her through the bowels of the museum, the utilitarian underbelly that no one ever saw. The first time she'd come down there was with Buxton—on that late night not so long ago when she found herself following a complete stranger through the deserted halls. At the time, she had no idea what was in store for her. A strange and fantastical reality was revealed to her on that day, and she could never go back. Sometimes she mourned that innocence, but whatever she'd lost, she'd gained twice over in her newfound strength and command.

She pushed open the staff entrance door and stepped into the Medieval Art Galleries, making her way toward the Egyptian collection. More specifically the annex that held the Temple of Dendur. Although she held the keys to this magnificent kingdom of art and treasures, it was still surreal that she could explore it whenever she pleased.

One night, when Alex first took the reins of KHNM, she waited until late in the evening when all the staff from both KHNM and the Met went home, and wandered the halls in the half glow of the security lights, wandering like an errant ghost. She reveled in the wickedly delicious feeling of her unscheduled roaming of the treasure house—alone. As if all the art and artifacts contained within the museum walls were for her eyes only, she could linger wherever she pleased. Her eyes were greedy thieves of the opulent beauty that surrounded her.

That exploration ended with her lying on the granite floor of the Dendur Temple exhibit. She recalled gazing at the stars as they glimmered through the massive glass panels above her, each moment filling her with the most sublime joy.

She felt herself lucky that she wasn't caught during that escapade by a guard or some other museum staff working late. Most likely her wanderings made it into the security video archive, but no one ever said a word to her. She was thankful for that. As the director of KHNM, she had all-hours access, but it was likely the museum would see her wanderings as an abuse of her power. Maybe the museum granted an unspoken hall pass to those who had newly gained full access. Whatever the reason, Alex certainly didn't want to be the one to shatter the relationship between the two organizations.

KHNM wasn't officially a part of the museum but part of a long-standing agreement that allowed the agency a satellite office in close proximity to the God machine housed deep underneath the Met.

The God machine was built with powerful ancient magic after the last Ptolemy, Cleopatra, committed suicide. For hundreds of years prior to her reign, before the time of Alexander the Great, the Gods' powers were in great decline. Many invaders had ruled the red and black lands of Egypt, kings from Libya, Nubia, Persia, and eventually Macedonia. Under the neglectful watch of these usurpers, the sacred language and holy rites of ancient Egypt had been lost long before that great queen ascended to the throne. During this era of foreign rule, the Gods of Egypt suffered greatly, weakened by the scarcity of sacrifice and praise given them.

In the time of Alexander the Great, a prophecy foretold an eventual obsolescence of the Gods. Panicked, the Eternals searched for a remedy, taking the entire Ptolemaic reign to find it: the God machine—a massive relic to contain and preserve what powers still remained, allowing the Gods to walk among humanity as Immortals.

During the mid-twentieth century these Immortals realized that they'd all taken up residency in the United States, drawn to the energy transmitted to them by the American enthusiasm for all things Ancient Egypt. They yearned to have their power containment system in closer proximity.

It took some doing. KHNM agents went undercover to infiltrate the Egyptian government, unseen to mortal eyes. Their patience paid off. Over time, it became obvious that the construction of the Aswan High Dam was a perfect cover to move the God machine. With twenty-two ancient monuments and complexes that needed to find higher ground before they were swallowed up by the newly created Lake Nasser, and with the involvement of missions from five different continents, KHNM was certain there would be plenty enough chaos for a particularly large magical object to be secreted out of the country unnoticed.

The KHNM agents working deep within the Egyptian government made sure that the temple was gifted to the Met, and they oversaw the construction of the exhibition space, along with the containment room that was built underneath.

Now the God machine lay dormant and broken, after Alex sent the Immortals back to the Field of Reeds. And KHNM needed to figure out how to dismantle and dispose of it.

Alex climbed the stairs to the temple and walked past it to the two pylons fronting it. They stood as the ceremonial gateway to the holy precinct. Worshipers of old would pass through, knowing they were now entering another realm, the realm of the Gods. Standing underneath one of the squarish archways, she clasped her newly forged djed pillar pendant, repeating the words of entry in her mind three times, *Khnum, Creator of Man, Lord of the Crocodiles, keep me safe.*

Pinching her eyelids together, Alex braced herself for the flash of light and the peculiar jolt of energy that signaled being transported down to the containment room. The empty, sharp popping noise accompanied by the void-smell of electricity signaled completion. She opened her eyes to the massive workroom where the God machine was housed. Now that the Gods had returned to their realm, the container that held their powers for centuries was dark. It used to resemble an exceptionally large plasma ball floating in space, lit from within by hundreds of delicate lightning bolts. Its deactivated surface reflected the slate-colored rock surrounding it. It possessed a semiopaque appearance that landed somewhere between heavily smoked glass and a mirror. A chill traveled through her. Something about this dead machine gave her the creeps.

Alex scanned the large cavern that stretched out before her. Her eyes caught a slight movement through the murky ball. As she rounded the dark mass, she laughed out loud at what she saw. Luke was lying on his back with his head craned as if he were trying to somehow check for an oil leak. Thorne towered over his prone body as if scrutinizing his technique.

"What are you both doing here? Does this mean you found the instructions for dismantling it?" asked Alex.

Thorne crossed her arms. "No, I just came down wondering where he'd wandered off to."

Luke's voice reverberated strangely against the large magic globe. "Sorry, just needed a little break from the packing."

Thorne towered over Luke with her mummy posture in place, standing stiff as if bound with bitumen-hardened wrappings, her arms crossed tightly over her chest, with a frozen look of disdain on her face. "I don't know why you all are tiptoeing around it like a bunch of timid mice. It was only a container."

Luke pushed out from under the orb and dusted his hands off on his jeans. "Oh, yeah it was just a container. A container that just happened to hold a huge amount of magic in it for . . . oh, I don't know, a couple thousand years. The Hanford nuclear reactor was only around for a couple of decades, and the state of Washington has spent billions of dollars and decades to clean that up. God knows what we are dealing with here."

Alex smiled at Luke. "So, it makes perfect sense to get your brain as close to it as possible." She fully expected him to laugh and was surprised he remained unmoved by her lighthearted sarcasm. He'd been stuck working with Thorne a lot lately. It might be good to mix assignments up, for his sake.

"All I was trying to say is, let sleeping dogs lie. This structure was built around this thing. Why not just let it sit here? Cover it up with sand and move on," said Thorne.

Alex realized she'd crossed her arms, mirroring her adversarial assistant, and uncrossed them. "That approach only works for cat poo and archaeological digs you can't get to until next season." Alex was certain that would break Luke's facade of seriousness, but to no avail. "I completely agree with Luke. We need to try and figure this thing out."

"How do you propose doing that? Everyone who knew about it is long gone, and our search for any leads has run dry."

"Does the name Albright Knox ring a bell for either one of you?"

Thorne cocked her head. "I think he had something to do with the original build-out when the Temple of Dendur was brought to the Met. Although not a KHNM agent, he was good friends with the museum's director at the time. I am guessing this Knox must be pretty ancient."

"I'd found his business card among Buxton's things the other day. He is the head librarian at the Beinecke Rare Book and Manuscript Library."

"Yale?" asked Luke.

"I'm going to meet with him today."

"You are going to drive all the way to Connecticut?" asked Thorne, her eyebrows pinched together in disbelief.

"I've booked a train ticket for this afternoon. I just came down to let you both know. I'm going back to the residency to throw a few things in a bag then head to the station."

Luke threw an exasperated look in Alex's direction. "I'll go with you. Not much more I can do today."

Alex took the clue. "Thorne, could you lock up my office? I didn't think of it before I left." It was a lame thing to make her do, and there wasn't a real need for it, but it would get her out of their hair.

～～

The short walk from the staff exit at the Dendur Temple exhibit across the street to the KHNM residence took almost no time. Luke was surprisingly quiet. His urgent need to leave must have had everything to do with Thorne.

Luke opened the front door and Jeeves shot out and flung his front paws up against Luke's jeans, the dog's stub gyrating with excitement. Luke bent over and ruffed the dog's coat. "Hello, little buddy." His voice warmed at seeing his furry friend.

Jeeves jumped down, dropped a small toy at Luke's feet, and then ran back into the house as if starting a game of chase.

"I wonder what that is all about?" asked Alex as Luke reached down to pick up the toy.

Her breath caught in her throat. The small item was the very mummy finger he stole earlier in the day.

At the top of the stairs, the dog barked again in earnest, calling his master to play. Luke stared at the object, dumbfounded. "A mummy finger? Where on earth?"

Alex feigned surprise. "A mummy finger. What?"

Luke looked at the finger, then Alex. "I think you might have some explaining to do."

CHAPTER ELEVEN

A surge of anger stormed through Jorge as the memories of Buxton and the agency he led flooded over him. How KHNM had, over the years, wiped his memories away with a callous disregard. He was just an unimportant pawn to them. Not a living being. This careless violation of his reality was an unforgivable act of violence. How dare they play God with the lives of others?

At first the memories came in familiar flashes, then grew quicker and brighter until they became a steady, searing light of truth. He was filled with anger and a lust for revenge. It took every molecule of restraint to not go to the tomb where the old man slept and wake him to witness his own death.

A deep sorrow settled like a dead weight. Gwen. Her name rang through his head. Jorge's one true soul mate, the one he was going to marry, until KHNM wiped Jorge's memories. What she must have thought when he never showed up at the altar and then disappeared in full sight by resuming his very public self, ignoring her, snubbing her, forgetting her. He remembered her approaching him at a fan-based convention and causing a scene. At the time he thought she was a rabid fan and called security to drag her away.

A vision flooded his mind. She was standing in the chapel they'd reserved in Vegas, her auburn hair falling in luxurious waves over her handmade violet lace wedding dress, clutching the bright bouquet of cosmos she'd picked out the day before. He imagined the sharp sorrow and hatred that would have darkened her usually bright green eyes as it became clear he would never show.

Gwen.

Buxton be damned. The old man would die today. Jorge charged at the door. As he grabbed the handle, Gwen's face appeared in his mind. Tears streamed down his face. Gwen. The love he'd lost forever, the love who probably thought that he was the greatest devil that ever walked the earth.

He let go of the handle and returned to the chaise lounge, sobbing. A quick death was too good for Buxton. Jorge was going to spend the rest of his life ruining the daily existence of the old man and everyone he cared for. And he would do it in the slowest, most painful way possible.

Nausea churned within him. He had saved that man from certain death.

Now he knew why he struggled with feeling like his life was an incomplete tapestry that he could never mend. He could never shake the feeling that something had been skipped over or fast-forwarded. Normally he chalked it up to déjà vu or just the random faultiness of being human, but now he knew. And Jorge would find a way to get his revenge.

~~~

Jorge followed Phillip back across the Nile and up to the western mountains to retrieve Buxton from the sleeping tomb. Phillip had his broadsword strapped across his back. He never realized that Jorge had taken it. Jorge was glad for that.

As they silently trudged their way through the rocky desert-like hillside, Jorge tried to manage the urge to shove Phillip off the high cliff, to hopefully a second death. Before setting off on their journey to retrieve Buxton, Jorge remembered that Phillip had taken part in the very first of the many memory wipes that KHNM performed on him. In fact, he was the one who initially made the case that wiping his mind of the magical incident he'd witnessed was a more humane action than killing him.

Over his lifetime, Jorge had the misfortune of being at the wrong place at the wrong time when it came to the Gods and KHNM. Each time his memory was wiped, it was as if the remedy was worse than the disease, altering his molecular makeup to be more receptive to the Immortals' energies and turning him into a moon that couldn't help but orbit their celestial bodies.

Jorge didn't quite know how he would take revenge on a dead man, but he'd spend his whole lifetime to figure it out. Didn't Buxton mention Phillip had a daughter?

Phillip fiddled with a large ring of skeleton keys when they arrived at the tomb. Jorge tucked away the knowledge of them. Maybe some of them belonged to locations on the treasure map he'd found.

The small tomb was painted with vivid scenes of a sporting life on the Nile. Figures stood on long rafts, holding spears with a myriad of different-colored fish swimming in the depths below.

The owner of the tomb was also a fan of waterfowl, as there were beautiful renderings of them throughout the air and water. The bright, naturalistic style was like that of the Amarna period of Egyptian art. Who could such a tomb belong to? And who needs a tomb in the afterlife? This Netherworld adventure was certainly a grab bag of mysteries.

They both stood over Buxton, who lay atop a large granite slab. "Sleeping like a baby." Phillip smiled at Jorge.

Jorge flashed his most charming for-the-press smile back at Phillip.

Phillip knelt down and tilted Buxton's chin up, opened his mouth, and poured the antidote into his mouth.

The old man sputtered awake, then propped himself up to sitting.

Phillip stood, placing his hands on his hips. "Did you have any interesting dreams? From what I understand, the living who sleep in the Netherworld can have wild dreams, some even say prophetic."

"No such luck." Something flashed in the old man's expression, making Jorge wonder if the old man was lying and really did see something. Something he didn't want to share with Jorge.

Phillip helped Buxton off the ground. "Well, let's get on with it. We only have a few hours until the door closes for another few weeks. I can't imagine either of you desire more quality Netherworld time."

Buxton and Phillip chatted as they exited the cave. A disturbing thought crept into Jorge's psyche. What if, by eating the food produced by the book, he was stuck here forever? What if he made exactly the wrong choice?

"Where are we headed?" asked Jorge.

"Up to the crest of that mountain." Phillip pointed to the top of the sand-colored pyramidal shape that loomed over them.

They clambered upward. When the terrain leveled off, Jorge could see a path that led all the way up to the mountain peak.

When they reached the top of the mountain, a crescent moon hovered above them. Phillip retrieved a bow and arrow from his pack and a rope ladder. The ladder appeared to have no end as it tumbled out of his bag, yard by yard, like a magician's handkerchief.

Phillip tied a large knot to the top rung on the ladder, then thrust the arrow through it. He nocked the arrow, then aimed at the hollow of the moon. Phillip drew, then fired, letting it fly. The arrow pulled the ladder up into the night sky.

A loud thunk sounded from above.

Phillip pulled out a pair of binoculars to check his handiwork. "It's time."

Buxton looked wistful as he replied, "All those years ago, after you died, Phillip, I regretted never telling you what you meant to me. You were like a son." Tears welled up in the old man's eyes.

Phillip hugged him. "I've missed you too. Take care of my girl."

Phillip walked over to Jorge and shook his hand. "It was a pleasure to meet you. You better head up. It's a long climb to the top."

Jorge looked up at the beige rope that disappeared into the night sky. "What happens if we miss the window of time?"

"I'll be seeing you back here sooner than expected."

"Will you wait for us?" asked Buxton.

"Of course. I will watch you until you disappear into the void, even if I have to fight off Ammut. If I get chased off and you haven't made it out, make your way as quickly as you can back to the house. Then we can figure out a plan B."

"What if we fall?" asked Jorge.

"I wouldn't if I were you."

"Why is that?"

"It is a long way down. If you fall, you will return to the Netherworld, but as a full-time resident."

"Safety not guaranteed," said Buxton.

"When is it ever?" Phillip asked.

Buxton waved in the direction of the ladder. "You'd better go first, you will be faster. I don't want to hold you up."

Jorge grabbed the ladder and climbed.

~~~

Jorge looked down at the old man, who was surprisingly not too far behind him. It was disconcerting to be blindly pulling your-self higher and higher through a black void. He wondered if at some point he would see daylight, but the further up he went, the darkness thickened.

He paused for a minute. A glimmer from above caught his eye. He scrambled toward it. The arrow was pinned into the void that surrounded them. Below, the ladder was tugging and swaying as Buxton tried to catch up.

Jorge yelled down. "Hold up. I think I've reached the top, and I am not sure at all how to proceed. Stay where you are. I don't think a collision would do either of us any good."

"All right." The old man's voice was ragged. He had to be exhausted. Hopefully he wouldn't croak before Jorge had the pleasure of ruining his life.

Jorge freed one of his hands from the top rung and felt

around. Nothing. He placed his hand where the arrow pierced and felt something soft and fuzzy, like a velvet curtain. He leaned into the rope ladder to steady himself and reached around with both of his hands. Jorge pulled and tugged, trying to tear a small hole in the fabric, but no luck. Did they miss the window of time and the portal was closed?

Glancing at the arrow, it appeared to be illuminated from an unseen source. He heaved himself up. A minuscule tear in the fabric shone bright, blinding him. Jorge lowered himself and wrapped his arms around the ladder again and reached into the top pocket of his explorer's jacket. Finding his Swiss Army knife, he opened it to the scissors tool. He tried to cut the fabric but was a hair shy of reach. This was a job for the longest blade. Holding the fabric down with one hand, he cut upward with the other. A wide slit gaped open and light flooded into the void. He tried to blink away the burning sensation as bright floaters passed over his vision.

As his vision slowly cleared, a desert landscape came into focus.

His head was poking out at ground level of the Egyptian desert, like a peculiar human groundhog. He shoved his arms outward and lifted himself up. His feet lost purchase of the rope ladder as he hung, clinging to the land, just barely, by his armpits. Jorge's arms shook with strain as he pushed his body up and forward and wormed his way to stability. Pulling his torso level to the ground, only his legs left dangling in the dark void, he slithered forward, pulling his legs out.

He stood contemplating the tear in the ground plane he just pulled himself from. He reached down with both arms and yelled at Buxton. "The hole is closing. Get up here, now!"

The jerky movement below sent puffs of the stale Netherworld air up to Jorge. The old man was huffing and puffing hard as he labored up the ladder. Jorge fought the instinct to shove the old man off the ladder and let the portal close. That would be too easy for Buxton. What Jorge craved was an up-close-and-personal kind of ruination for the old man, to make him suffer like KHNM made Jorge suffer.

Jorge grabbed hold of the old man and heaved him up and out. The momentum sent Buxton and Jorge in an entwined tumble to the desert floor.

Jorge pushed Buxton off him. The hot noonday sun glared down at him. The old man was gasping for air.

They surfaced somewhere near Lake Nasser. As far as the eye could see there was nothing but desert, rocks, and lake. If he squinted hard, there was a small temple off in the distance. It could serve as a temporary shelter for them. He needed to figure out how to get the old man down there.

Jorge took the time to mark the spot where they passed through from the Netherworld. It would come in handy to know where they were at this moment, if he ever ended up trying to get back. The thought of the treasure map tucked away in his explorer's bag made him smile.

"Are you okay, old man?" Jorge asked as he finished his marker. He was going to make it in the traditional form of an *X*, but then thought it more fun to do something more personalized, so he made it a large *N* for Netherworld out of the small desert rocks that littered the desert floor.

"Hard to say."

Jorge walked over and helped Buxton up to sitting. "Do you think you can make it down there to the temple?" Jorge pointed in the direction of the structure at the bottom of the hill. "It could offer us some shelter from this sun." Buxton didn't answer; he just stared into the far distance. "We could rest there now and travel at night, when it's cooler. I think it is likely a long hike back to civilization."

Finally, Buxton looked up at Jorge with weary eyes. "I don't know if I am going to make it. That climb took everything out of me. I am not a young man anymore. You might be better off leaving me here."

As his driving desire was revenge, Jorge knew he was going to do anything he could to make Buxton survive until he had the pleasure of slowly yanking everything and everyone he held dear away from him.

The route to the temple was pretty much all downhill. If it came to it, Jorge might just roll the old man down. There was no way he could carry his limp, elderly body all the way down there. He held his hand out to Buxton. "Come on. Let's give it a try." Jorge reached into his explorer's pack and pulled out his refillable water bladder. It was about a fifth of the way full. He handed it over.

"Where did you get this?"

"I've just been sipping on it slowly. There is a little bit left. You are welcome to it." Jorge loved the secret of abundance that lay in his explorer's bag. Let Buxton think he was being a hero.

Buxton shook his head. "No, I won't take your last bit of water."

Thinking on his feet, Jorge waved his hand toward the large lake below. "No worries, old man. Once we are down there, we'll have all the water we need."

"Only if you don't mind the diarrhea and vomiting that comes with it." Buxton cracked a wan smile.

"I've got a pocket purifier. Trust me, that water is all yours." The lie slipped off his tongue with ease.

Buxton gulped the water down. "Thank you." He pushed himself up to standing, then rested his hands on his hips. "Let's get down to that temple. I guess if I need to give up, I can always roll down, let gravity do its work."

They slowly picked their way down the rocky hillside in silence. The surrounding landscape was a great expanse of beige and burnt orange sand topping loose scatterings of dark grey rocks, all set against the pale yet intense blue sky of the desert.

Rocks skittered down behind Jorge, making him check back at the trailing Buxton.

"I'm starting to lose my balance. Go on ahead. I'll meet you at the temple."

Jorge went over to Buxton and stood in front of him. "Put your hands on my shoulders."

The pace quickened as Buxton could steady himself against Jorge.

Buxton mumbled something.

"What was that?"

"Dakka Temple. I think that is where we are. It is a Greco-Roman temple dedicated to Thoth."

"You seem to know a lot about ancient Egypt—what sort of organization did you say you ran? I feel a little at a disadvantage. You are familiar with my work, but I don't know what you do."

"The work I do is affiliated with the Oriental Institute of Chicago."

"And what sort of work is that?"

"I used to lecture, but now my role is mainly an administrative one."

"I assumed you were more along the lines of an archaeologist or something with a relatively high adventure level, as you ended up in the Netherworld. Didn't you mention some sort of acronym in relation to your work?" Jorge gave Buxton a few beats to chime in. But no answer came. "It was something like ATUM or ATEN or something like that." Of course, Buxton never said anything of the sort. Jorge was just going on a fishing expedition.

Jorge couldn't see Buxton's face, but his tone was hesitant. "I don't know what you are talking about. The only acronym I might have thrown out there was the DONES, Department of Near Eastern Studies."

Apparently, the old man had no intention of shooting straight with the man who'd saved his life more than once. They made it down to the dirt road that led to the temple. Judging by his state of exhaustion, it was a fair guess that not long after they arrived at their destination, Buxton would be fast asleep. That would give Jorge some alone time to figure out what exactly he was going to do with the old man.

Sweat trickled down Jorge's face as the sun beat down on them. He too was starting to feel the effects of a lack of hydration and was anxious to get into the shade and call forth some delectable mineral water out of sight of the old man.

A bird came out of nowhere and swooped down over Jorge's head and into the temple. If he didn't have his magic book to rely on for survival, he would know to look for a nest in the cool recesses of the temple walls. Searching out a clutch of eggs saved his life more than once. He was thankful he wouldn't have to gulp down any of the salty goop of raw eggs, or worse yet, raw bird. But no matter what, Jorge would suffer whatever he needed to stay alive.

As they passed under the massive pylon, Jorge looked at the weary man next to him. For a brief moment his deep loathing melted away, and he saw only an old man struggling to make his way to the enclosure. He stood in the temple entrance and surveyed the large interior colonnade. "If we stay in this outermost chamber, we'll have the benefit of both the cover and the light coming in through the entryway." He grabbed his headlamp out of his explorer's jacket and turned it on. He crossed to the far end of the room. His skin tightened into goose pimples at the delightful coolness as he moved deeper. He checked the corners for any rats, scorpions, or vipers.

Jorge shut off his headlamp. "It will take a moment for our eyes to adjust, but once they do, I think we will be fine without the light. I think conserving resources wouldn't be a bad strategy."

"You are right. Who knows how long it will take us to get back to civilization."

Jorge slipped his explorer's bag from his shoulder and let it rest on the dirt floor. He pulled off his jacket and rolled it into a tight cylinder and placed it on the floor. "I know it's not much, but you should lie down and rest. My jacket makes a sufficient pillow."

"You should have your jacket." Buxton motioned toward the floor. "I'll just curl up in the corner. I am so tired I could probably sleep standing up."

"I don't need any rest. I feel somehow wound up. I might head down to the lake and get us some water."

Buxton sat on the floor. "Thank you."

Jorge grabbed his explorer's bag and pulled out a protein bar for Buxton, and for a second the book of magic's gold binding winked out from the bag. Had Buxton seen the book? Jorge handed a protein bar he'd called forth earlier, from the special grocery store near his home. "You're going to need to replenish your body after that hike we took."

Buxton pushed it away. "I can't."

"You must. I need you rested and in top form when we leave this place and try to find a way back to civilization. You mentioned earlier that you thought this was Dakka Temple. Do you have any idea how far away we are from anywhere?"

Buxton unwrapped the bar of dried meat and held it up to his nose and breathed in. His eyes closed with pleasure as he chewed. "I think we are about a hundred miles away from Aswan. There is probably not much between here and there." He took another bite of the bar, then pointed it toward the opening of the temple. "There is not much to attract people to live in that."

"Once we both get a chance to rest up, we should head out toward Aswan. But for now, you should lie down and get some sleep."

Jorge slung his explorer's bag over his shoulder and made his way to the entrance. In front of the temple were two massive statues of Horus that cast a great shadow. He figured it would be a good place to camp out and get some thinking done.

Jorge reached into his bag and grabbed the book. The bumpy texture of the inlaid turquoise made it easy to grasp, even with sweaty hands. He brought it close to his face, marveling at the fine craftsmanship.

A feeling of self-satisfaction rolled through him as he thought about how lucky he was that KHNM couldn't wipe away his love of adventure. If he'd gone to sleep in the cave like Buxton, Jorge would still be a stranger to himself. His memories were restored, and he found a book of magic that was going to transform his life. Not a bad haul for one outing.

For a moment he could see into his future. A future where the world opened for him like a treasure box, the book of magic being the key to opening up unknown wonders. Once he made KHNM pay, Jorge could really change the world for the better, in an ever-expanding search for the truth. With unlimited wealth and resources, he could spend his life hunting down tangible evidence that would prove his alien contact theories.

He opened the book and gazed at himself in the mirror inside. There were deep dark circles under his eyes. He needed rest too. Maybe the first thing he should do once they reached Aswan was to sleep for a few days. Using the book, he ordered some chilled mineral water and some regular bottled water. As he chugged the sparkling water, the light effervescence tickled its way down his throat.

Jorge filled the water bladder with the still spring water. Having his thirst sated, he ordered pastrami on rye from Katz Deli in New York. As soon as it appeared, he wolfed it down and bunched up its paper wrapper in a tight ball. Then he ordered a few more protein bars, for appearances sake and Buxton.

CHAPTER TWELVE

Alex wished that she could have put off this conversation with Luke until later, until she'd returned from New Haven with some answers. It just felt tidier to hold her thoughts close to her chest right now. It wasn't that she couldn't trust him. Luke was about as honest and straightforward as they come, but she needed more information about the books before she went public with her ideas about them. The last thing she wanted was to look like a fool. She didn't project a lot of confidence in her role as the interim director and didn't want to compound the feeling. In general, she suffered from impostor syndrome, but this situation magnified that tendency exponentially.

After Jeeves dropped the mummy finger at Luke's feet, the need to chat became apparent. Alex suggested Luke pop up with her while she grabbed some items for her train trip.

They rode in the private elevator to her room in silence.

When she took over as interim director, she thought about

moving to Buxton's suite of rooms, but never quite got around to it. The room she occupied was originally considered the director's suite, but Buxton found the room too posh for his tastes. Alex loved the room and that it possessed its own elevator. She loved the ability to disable it when she pleased, making her feel insulated from disturbances and intrusions.

The elevator doors slid open, revealing her fifth-floor suite. The room included a sitting area by a roaring fireplace, a massive curtained four-poster bed large enough to need a small step stool to climb up, a walk-in closet, a full bath, and a small adjoining office. The one thing that gave her the most joy was the spacious balcony with a commanding view of the Metropolitan Museum of Art across the street and of Central Park.

It was too chilly for them to talk out on the balcony, so Alex motioned Luke toward the loveseat and armchairs near the fireplace. Alex sat in one of the antique tapestry chairs with mahogany scrollwork. She never sat in the chairs when she was alone, as they always felt far too formal. It felt odd to be sitting opposite Luke now, in these chairs, in her room. There was something that felt out of place, and she couldn't quite put a finger on what it was, but it made her a little uncomfortable nonetheless.

Luke broke the silence. "So, when were you going to tell me you found the room?"

"Well, I was going to but . . ."

Luke broke eye contact with Alex. His gaze traveled to the balcony across the room. "Don't you trust me?"

"Of course I do." But truth be told, she doubted him. Lately she'd been doubting everyone. After being duped by Salima, Gormund, and Niles, all of whom pretended to be a friend to her, she just didn't have a lot of trust to give out. She knew she should trust that Buxton thought the world of him, but it was hard to make herself vulnerable again. Alex was at a loss for words as she searched her mind for the perfect thing to say to erase the awkwardness between them, but she could think of nothing. "You deserve to know the truth of it. Instead of racking my brain trying to come up with something that sounds reasonable, I'm just going to tell you the unvarnished truth. I think a part of me didn't want to trust you." Alex could see the hurt in his eyes.

"But why? Ever since I met you, I have gone out of my way to make you feel welcome and comfortable at KHNM. You know how close Buxton and I were. How could you think I have anything but your best interests in mind?"

"You are right in that, Luke; you have always gone out of your way to be kind. I've just been feeling a little gun-shy lately in the trust department. I found that room just yesterday. I meant to ask you about it, but for some reason, I decided to keep it close to my chest. Maybe because it was never mentioned to me. It made me wonder if I happened upon something that I needed to keep secret."

"I should have filled you in on the room. Since Buxton's departure was so unexpected, I think there have been a lot of holes in your orientation to the agency. Also, there is the issue of clearance permissions. It feels like dismantling the God machine and then the lawsuit have made operations extremely abnormal. It had been so long since the agency has seen any real action, and we have all become somewhat complacent. Like never putting in place a procedure for succession to the directorship. In hindsight that seems pretty dumb, especially since Buxton wasn't exactly what you would call a spring chicken." Luke leaned into the armrest and chuckled, his expression warm and affable. "Since we didn't have any real procedures, I figured I would be the one who would tell you about the archives. I kept meaning to do it, but it never boiled up to the top, and you have a lot on your plate right now. So, I owe you an apology as well."

"*Archive*. That sounds much more official than *secret room*." Alex was glad the conversation turned more friendly.

"Yeah, but 'secret room' sounds so much more fun."

"So, let me guess—since you are the archivist, you probably have access to the room as well."

"I certainly do. Where'd you think the beaded curtain came from?" He laughed.

"That was you?"

He beamed at Alex. "One hundred percent. I held off telling you. It seemed you wanted to stay in this room instead of moving to Buxton's quarters. I wanted to give you the time to figure out what your preference was."

Alex took in the sumptuous surroundings. The room did have a certain amount of charm, and Alex always felt safe here. The very first time she'd slept in this room was the night she'd been called to duty by KHNM. She'd just met Salima and Buxton and was too wound up to sleep. She'd been in a strange city, surrounded by admittedly strange people who were telling her amazingly strange things, but she felt safe in this room. Safe enough to sleep like the dead, under the heavy down comforter with the balcony doors open to the crisp fall air. "I'd like to stay in this room, but that is probably impossible, right?"

"What would make you say that?"

"Wouldn't I have to stay in Buxton's room in order to access the archive?"

"Oh no. It is the prerogative of the director to choose any bedroom. All I'll need to do is to hang the illustration. And I guess you'll have to make room for some Joseph Campbell on those shelves over there."

"Whose idea was it to have Campbell be the key?"

"Buxton's, of course. He once told me that every time he used that book to activate the illustration portal, the fact that Joseph Campbell was the key to everything gave him no end in amusement. I have a similar setup in my room. Mine enters into a workroom that is adjacent to the storeroom."

"Well, Luke, I am glad we've cleared the air some. I should get to the train station. I have a librarian to meet." Alex led Luke to the elevator and pushed the down button. She could feel him standing close to her. Tension hung between them like an unspoken intention, similar to the awkward feeling after a date where each person wonders if they are going to kiss. Alex coughed and stepped back, embarrassed at where her mind went. She was his boss.

Feeling awkward, she pressed the elevator button again.

"If you wanted, I could go with you. It might be good to have someone around to help you with any research that might come up." His tone was hopeful.

The elevator doors opened, and Luke stepped in.

The pleasant thought of spending time with Luke blossomed again in her mind like an inappropriate flower. She reached in and blocked the door from closing. "Thank you for offering, but I think it would be best if I go alone."

She removed her hand and the door started to close. Luke's brow furrowed. She shoved her hand in to stop it from completely closing. What a lunkhead she was, not even saying goodbye. "I really am glad we had the chance to sort this all out."

"Me too. I'll get that picture and the book settled while you are gone."

"Thank you, Luke." She retrieved her hand and the doors closed, sending Luke down to the foyer below.

She grabbed her things; she couldn't stop thinking about that silly beaded curtain and how Luke's face lit up when taking credit for it. A change of scenery was probably a good idea.

CHAPTER THIRTEEN

Jorge's eyes flew open at the abrupt sound of flapping wings. Buxton was still sound asleep in the far corner of the temple. What had disturbed the bird? The feeling of being watched overtook him. Were they still alone or did something lurk in the deep temple recesses? He listened, ears pricked and heart racing.

Hearing nothing further, he stood. Jorge's muscles were stiff with the twilight chill inflicted on him by his temple floor accommodations. He grabbed his explorer's bag, which served as his pillow, and walked to the temple entrance and peered outside. A diffuse golden glow of dawn was softening the sharp edges of night. He'd slept too long. Now they would have to wait until dusk to leave their shelter and make their way to Aswan. It wasn't worth it to leave in the short hours of morning only to get caught in the midday sun with nowhere to escape from it.

Jorge gathered the bottles and balled-up wrapper from his feast yesterday. It would be wise to find a place to bury it before

Buxton could see it. Once out of sight, he could have a quick breakfast. Maybe order up an egg sandwich or something. With that thought he happily followed the rock-lined road that led down the slight hill that the temple crested. He looked for a spot where he would be hidden from Buxton's eyes, but all he saw in the immediate area were rocks and sand. Off in the distance was a much smaller temple and what looked like stone sphinxes. The perfect place to get rid of his trash and fill his belly in seclusion.

He looked back at the temple. Maybe he should have left a note for the sleeping Buxton in case he woke up thinking he was abandoned and continued on. Buxton deserved everything that would be coming his way.

As he strolled down the pathway that led to the smaller temple, he took in the surrounding landscape of rocky, sand-strewn hills. Some of the hills looked like large rounded mounds. Others had definite peaks and were vaguely pyramidal in their shape. Approaching the small temple, he could see that not only did sphinxes line the causeway, but there were two statues of a pharaoh flanking the main entrance. Jorge guessed it might be Ramses the Great, as he was one of the most prolific builders, as well as usurper of temples, but he would have to ask Buxton.

Jorge walked past the entrance and through the sphinx-lined causeway, happy not to see any signs of life in the stone crea-tures. He climbed up the stairs leading to the temple entrance. Once at the top, he turned to take in the vision before him—the sphinxes, the desert, and the lake beyond. The brightening morning sun scattered a sparkle, like diamonds, across Lake Nasser. A green-and-white vessel caught his eye. He pulled his binoculars out of his explorer's bag. It was a cruise boat made to look like a Victorian-era steamboat.

Midway between Jorge and the lakeshore a cluster of people

were strolling toward the temple at a leisurely pace. Judging by their khaki shorts, hiking boots, and sun hats, they appeared to be adventure-seeking tourists. There were only a handful of high-end tour companies that were allowed to cruise this body of water. Jorge's spirits lifted at the thought of not trudging through the desert in search of civilization, now that it was delivered to their door.

He charged forward down the road leading to the temple, eating up the distance between himself and the tour group. They hadn't spotted him yet and probably wouldn't until he was right on top of them. Who would expect to see a random Westerner coming alone from an abandoned temple?

Jorge couldn't let Buxton talk for himself. He would have to control the framing of his relationship with the old man before the group was able to meet him. The last thing Jorge needed was for Buxton to reveal that he was an important head of an agency who needed to be returned to it as soon as possible. No, that wouldn't do. In order to inflict his justice on Buxton, Jorge would have to keep him close and maintain control over him.

Jorge was within shouting distance of the group. He waved his hands dramatically and jumped up and down.

A tall, lean man in a blue T-shirt saw him and waved back. The others took notice and followed him like a group of smiling, sunblocked, behatted lemmings. In almost no time he was encircled by middle-aged travelers.

"Thank god you are here." Jorge heartily shook the presumed leader's hand. "Jorge Trinculo."

A flash of name recognition passed over the leader's face. The man shook Jorge's hand. "Tom Blackburn. Aren't you a little far from your camera crew?"

"Our vehicle broke down quite a ways away from here. We

were down to a few protein bars and some water. I am so glad you are here."

The man's expression turned quizzical as his gaze shifted beyond Jorge. "There are others?"

"My elderly, sun-addled compatriot is resting in the temple up there. He's been amazing trying to keep up with me, given his age, but he has started suffering from delusions. I worry that he might have suffered from sunstroke."

A balding man with a stout beer belly pushed up on his toes. "I'm a doctor. I'd be happy to have a look at your companion."

Jorge's heart sank. It would be much harder to convince a doctor that Buxton was ailing. He turned toward the temple and motioned the others to follow. "What type of medicine do you practice?" Jorge wanted to sound conversational but hoped that the doctor's specialty might give him an angle to work regarding Buxton.

"I am a doctor of chiropractic."

Jorge breathed a sigh of relief. "I don't think what ails him is sunstroke. I think it goes much deeper than that. This experience seems to have been very physically and mentally taxing for us both, but especially him."

Tom, Jorge, and the doctor pulled ahead of the others as they all walked toward the temple where Buxton was. As they came closer, Jorge needed to start scattering the breadcrumbs of his story, and quick. For all he knew, Buxton could be wide awake and on his way down to meet them at any moment. "Last night he was in a corner of the temple rocking back and forth. He was mumbling to himself. When I made my way over to him, he wouldn't even take notice of me. He kept rambling on as if he was in a conversation with some unseen person named Khnum."

Tom's eyebrows knit together. "So, he thinks he is conversing with the ancient Egyptian creator God?"

"Seemed that way last night. Another thing—he keeps referring to himself as Charles Buxton."

"Who is that?"

"I have no idea, but I do know that's not his name. In the midst of his waking dream he kept rambling about someone named Alex and the need to contact her. He was quite adamant. I agreed with him to get him to calm down. I was afraid he was going to have some sort of meltdown if I didn't go along with his fiction. As the night wore on, his rantings became more and more bizarre, something about surviving the twelve gates of the Netherworld. We were planning to leave tonight and trek to Aswan. I don't think either of us really stood a chance to make it, but I really worried about him given his age and mental condition. It is really lucky that you all showed up when you did."

"Has he experienced any blows to the head?"

"Not that I know of."

"It is extremely rare that sunstroke would cause such delusions. It can cause people to be confused or disoriented but rarely to lose complete touch with reality."

"Maybe it is some sort of coping mechanism," interjected Tom.

They crested the hill on which the temple stood. Tom addressed the others in the group. "I think it might be best for you all to stay behind. There is an elderly man resting in the temple. I don't think we want to overwhelm him." The others pulled back and clustered out beyond the pylons that led to the temple entrance.

Tom grabbed Jorge's shoulder. "Don't worry about your old friend. We'll proceed with care."

Buxton was still sleeping soundly. Given what the old man had been through, it really wasn't surprising. Jorge knelt beside him and gently shook his shoulder. "Gerald. Wake up. We've been saved."

Buxton just snored.

"Gerald." Jorge shook Buxton a little harder. The old man's eyelids flew open mid-schnork. His face screwed up in confusion. Probably at being called Gerald, but also at the three heads suddenly staring down at him. He shuffled himself to sitting with his back against the temple wall.

"Who—?"

"It's okay." Jorge sat cross-legged in front of Buxton. "We've been saved."

~᭙~

It didn't take long for Jorge and Buxton to be herded to the awaiting boat. As Jorge predicted, Buxton was emphatically calling himself by name and becoming more and more agitated when people tried to calm him down . . . Jorge's plan of subterfuge worked perfectly. The more the group tried to calm the old man down, the more insistent he became.

The doctor arranged for Buxton to wait in his stateroom while the ever-present tourist police came to pick them up. This unit of the Egyptian police force was tasked with keeping the economic engine of visiting foreigners safe. It was an efficient way for the Egyptian government to utilize the many youths that are conscripted into the country's compulsory military service.

The concerned doctor asked Jorge if he thought it was okay to give the old man a sedative.

Jorge agreed.

Once the rescue boat arrived, the sleeping Buxton was transported onto it. They headed to Aswan, leaving the tour to continue with its itinerary. When the rescuers found out who Jorge was, they brought him up to speed on how much press his disappearance caused. There were many fans who demanded a search party be formed for the pop culture icon. Since Jorge hadn't told anyone where he was going, the authorities had no idea where to start.

Jorge leaned back in his seat as the rescue boat skimmed down the grand Nile. As they neared Aswan, a terra-cotta-colored palace crowned the bluffs ahead. It was the familiar Old Cataract hotel. In the past, Jorge and his film crews spent many a night there and seeing it was almost like coming home. It would be a suitable place to regroup and move forward with his plans.

The famed five-star luxury hotel was built in 1899 to provide lodging to tsars, princesses, presidents, and eventually a world-famous mystery writer. A comfortable place to stay as they explored the temples and treasures of Egypt's southernmost city. At the turn of the twentieth century, Europeans of high standing flocked to exotic Egypt to take in the air and dry out their sodden bones.

Its fortresslike walls and exclusivity would make it a perfect place for Jorge to hide in plain sight. The thick construction kept the Egyptian sun from broiling the well-heeled clientele in the age before air conditioning, but in this case it would do well muffling the sounds. Sounds of interrogation.

The police kindly escorted Jorge and his sleeping companion to the hotel. Jorge felt a comfortable familiarity wash over him as they approached the hotel grounds. Up ahead there was a small crowd huddled at the roundabout that fronted the gated entrance. Jorge squinted at the odd congregation. Was it a tour group patiently awaiting their coach? As the vehicle pulled closer, he could pick out lanyards with press credentials that hung around their necks.

The press. How he loved the press. His not-so-subtle hints to his rescue crew paid off in spades. He'd never met a news reporter he didn't like. Even those so-called experts who went out of their way to try and debunk his theories. Jorge loved a good challenge and adhered to the idea that there was no such thing as bad press. All those who doubted him only strengthened his will to prove he was right.

As the SUV came to a halt, Jorge squinted to see if he recognized any of them. Among the gaggle of men there stood one woman. Gwen.

Jorge stepped out of the car. It took every bit of control he could muster to not run over to her and scoop her up in his arms and breathe in her heady perfume of sandalwood and frankincense. Did she still use that same scent? He guessed he would probably never get close enough to know. He reached in his explorer's jacket and retrieved his polarizing sunglasses, not to block out the sun, but the blinding glare that came from her direction. After all this time, how could he ever make things right with her?

She was still beautiful, but something was different about her. She used to sparkle like an enchanted crystal, auburn hennaed hair that flowed over her shoulders, her neck adorned with jewelry befitting an ancient priestess. Standing before him, she looked like an everyday out-of-the-box Jane with a bobbed haircut, plain gold rope chain, and pantsuit. Had he done this to her? Did he unknowingly snuff out her previous glorious and illuminated self?

As he neared, the tangle of reporters clad in tan and holding mics out toward him resembled a khaki-colored squid. Questions were thrown at him in an unintelligible blizzard of words.

Jorge held out his hands, halting the hubbub. "I know you have been waiting for a long time to see my handsome face again." He flashed his most brilliant for-the-press smile. "Before we get started, I want to thank my amazing fans for standing behind me and for shaking up the authorities to demand a search for me. I have some things I want to share with you, and then I will retire to my room for much-needed rest from my long and arduous journey."

The mics edged in closer. He looked directly at Gwen. He was glad that his sunglasses shielded the effect of her hateful gaze.

"I had a revelatory experience out in the desert like none before. I looked out into the vast desert that spread out before me, and what did I see? I saw my own demise, the end of my great adventure. In that barren landscape, I searched the universe within. I stand before you now a changed man."

Gwen's expression softened ever so slightly.

He removed his sunglasses. He looked directly into her eyes. It felt like his soul leapt over the expectant reporters and landed home. "From this day forward, I will no longer search for the intangible of the universe, but for the universe which resides in here." He tapped at his chest. He could see tears welling up in Gwen's eyes. "That is all."

He nodded at the tourist police who surrounded him. At the signal they maneuvered through the crowd of reporters, who were shouting a barrage of questions at him. What about the show? The magazine? Was he really done? Jorge put on a steely expression as he pushed through the gate and into the extensive garden that led up to the hotel entrance.

He glanced back at Gwen, hoping against all hope that she would follow.

Jorge felt relieved as he passed by the massive fresh-flower arrangement that stood as a fragrant guard to the Moorish-inspired interior of the grand hotel. Abdul-ah, his favorite concierge, was at the check-in desk instead of his usual station near the door. He was thumbing through a book of Egyptian poetry. Glancing at his name tag, Jorge realized he had been promoted to the day manager. Abdul-ah glanced up from his computer screen with a happy spark of recognition that changed to concern as he noticed the police escort.

Jorge shot an easy smile at Abdul-ah. "Hala and congratulations, my friend, I see you've been promoted."

"It is a good thing. Would you want your usual suite? Just about the entire place is at your command. Business is not as it used to be."

"The old suite would be good."

The police officer to Jorge's right spoke up. "What room number? We'll bring your friend up."

Abdul-ah's eyebrows curved up in question. "Is this a friend I am acquainted with?"

Jorge often suspected his stylist had an ongoing and opportunistic tryst with Abdul-ah whenever they stayed at the Old Cataract hotel. "I don't think you've met this colleague of mine. He is old and very tired. He won't be hanging out with me at the veranda bar anytime soon."

The veranda bar was one of Jorge's favorite places in all of Aswan. He looked forward to reacquainting himself with its delightful ambiance imbued with the genteel grace of an earlier era. He loved to sit in the luxurious space reserved for hotel guests, take in the majesty of the Nile and the symphony of sails that danced upon its waters, all while sipping a perfectly made Tom Collins.

Abdul-ah handed him the room's keycard.

Jorge started to head to his room, trailed by his police saviors. "Thank you, gentlemen, I think I can handle it from here on out."

The lead police officer's eyes went wide. "Oh, sir. We wouldn't think of leaving you. We want to ensure journalists or hangers-on aren't waiting at your door. If everything is clear, we will retrieve your friend and leave you to your own devices."

They moved from the polished marble floor of the lobby area to a wide corridor carpeted in rich maroon with gold stripes leading the way, and then turned a corner. Gwen stood in the diffuse light from the ornate brass and glass lanterns hanging from the ceiling.

As he neared her, Jorge inhaled the musty, magical scent of sandalwood and frankincense. It comforted him to know there was one thing that hadn't changed. He was drawn to her like Odysseus's need to return to Penelope.

"I'm glad you made it back, Jorge. I really am. Even after everything."

Jorge fought the urge to blurt out "I love you." He knew those were the last words Gwen would want to hear from him.

A cloud passed over her face as if she read his mind. An uncomfortable silence grew around them, suffocating Jorge's ability to think. His thoughts ricocheted through his head, about how things used to be. His mouth opened, his words filling the void between them with garbage. "At least you won't have to worry about spending the inheritance." He instantly wished he was back in the Netherworld crawling under a large orange boulder.

"What?"

It was something she never knew, something he was only recently allowed to remember when his memories were restored. After they set a date for their wedding, he had changed his will to leave every dime to her, his one true love.

Nervous, he looked away from her questioning eyes.

His gaze landed on a bright glint of diamond on her ring finger, and it wasn't the one he'd bought for her years ago. Of course it wasn't. Jorge left her standing at the altar. He silently berated himself for thinking that she had waited for him in the hallway. It was merely a coincidence. She must have been in search of a quiet place to call in her report to the paper. "Ah, nothing. Really. Please excuse the crazy ramblings of a man who just barely survived certain death. I might be suffering from sun exposure. It's been a while, Gwen. It's good to see you again."

"It's not been that long. I see you all the time." She looked down at her phone and turned it off before dropping it in her purse. "I've got to go."

How he wished there weren't a contingent of tourist police surrounding them, but he realized this might be his only chance. "Don't go. Let's talk. Standing on the brink of death can change a man."

"Change is something I never saw coming for you, Jorge. In a way I'm glad it's found its way to you. I've got to get back to the paper." She brushed past him. His security detail parted to let her pass. The scent of her cologne wafted past him. He couldn't just let her walk away.

"Gwen." His voice cracked. The police around him looked down at the ground, uncomfortable witnessing the personal exchange, but not leaving.

"I'll be at the veranda bar later on." He almost slapped his hand on his head, not believing that was the best he could come up with.

She shook her head as if she'd expected him to say something very different.

"I'm terribly busy, Jorge. I—"

"I understand. I don't mean to take much of your time. I had a lot of time to think about my life out there in the Red Land. There are things I've never been able to tell you that I would like to explain to you."

"I don't have time for your excuses, Jorge."

"That's not what I want to give you. I want to give you answers." Jorge caught the guard nearest to him rolling his eyes. He could feel her pulling away from him. "I will be there at seven."

She had already turned and walked away.

"I know things that could interest you, and your newspaper. I'll give you the exclusive." He knew it was a desperate attempt, but he needed to try.

Gwen turned to look at him.

"Please come."

She smiled, then walked away, her expression unreadable.

Jorge swiped his key card and opened the door. "Looks like we are all clear."

"We will bring your friend." The officers were speaking rapidly to one another as they walked down the hall. Jorge assumed they were gossiping in Arabic about what they'd just witnessed.

Jorge stepped into the darkened room and waited for them to bring Buxton.

Jorge jammed a chair up against the door to Buxton's bedroom. Then he settled into his own bed to get some much-needed rest. Jorge closed the heavy blackout curtains against the afternoon sun.

A crash jolted Jorge out of his sleep. Had the old man woken?

Jorge rushed over and knocked the chair away and opened the door. Buxton was standing next to the nightstand with the phone receiver to his ear. The phone lay on the floor. The old man's knees cracked and popped as he squatted down to pick the phone up. "I woke up and thought I would reach out to some of my colleagues. They are probably worried sick about me."

In four long strides Jorge reached Buxton and grabbed the phone out of his hands. "You need to rest now. You've been through a lot. The doctor instructed you to stay in bed. While we were on the boat, I called KHNM for you."

"KHNM? What's that?"

Jorge couldn't believe that Buxton still wouldn't come clean.

Buxton righted himself. "Give me that phone."

Jorge handed the phone over. While Buxton reached for it, Jorge's fist flew with lightning speed and made contact squarely on the old man's chin. Buxton's eyes went wide with surprise just before he crumpled to the ground.

He heaved the old man's body onto the bed. This wasn't going to work. He must constrain Buxton. Tying him up wouldn't work as that would raise many questions with the housekeeping staff.

He possessed the book of magic, which was great for calling forth Chinese food, but he wasn't sure what else he could do with it. He could try to call forth some drugs. But what if he called forth the wrong drug and killed him? Being elderly, he could have some sort of preexisting condition that could be exacerbated by ingesting the wrong kind of drug. He didn't want to kill him, not yet.

He emerged from Buxton's room and wandered over to one of the chairs where he'd shed his explorer's bag. The book of magic weighed heavily in his hands. If he couldn't sedate Buxton with drugs, what could he do? What could he conjure to really knock him out?

If only he had the small pamphlet-like book of magic spells he'd flipped through in Phillip's bathroom. The small bookcase was right across from the toilet. At the time Jorge thought it was funny Phillip kept it there. Jorge cursed himself for not taking it at the time. Would it be possible to use his book of magic to call things in reverse order, from the Netherworld to the mortal realm?

There was nothing to lose.

Jorge got up and went to the center of the room and sat on the floor. He reverently set the book on the antique Persian rug beneath him. As he'd done before, he stared at the script, clearing his mind of all other matters. He perfected a technique of imagining all the thoughts in his head as ink drawings, then he pictured them swirling together until they became one mass. Then he visualized them streaming out like smoke from a dowsed candle, emanating from the center of his head. It was the spot a yoga instructor he once dated told him was where his third eye was. Once he sensed that the wisps of thoughts contacted the magicked pages, he opened his eyes.

The mirror in the book was now a black void. It was ready to serve.

He closed his eyes, trying to recall the bookshelf in Phillip's bathroom and then the cover of the paperback book itself. The bathroom was now fully formed in his vision. He could feel the tug of a connection form between the realm he presently sat in and the Netherworld.

Luckily, the bathroom was free of occupants, which didn't surprise him. Jorge wondered now as he did then why on earth a dead man had a bathroom in the Netherworld. Was it another way to feel not dead? Recognizing he was becoming distracted, Jorge honed his focus and searched for the small book.

He mouthed the words of the title and could feel the book coming toward him. He opened his eyes and reached into the void to catch the small bound object that raced toward him. He caught it before it made contact with his nose. One of the many things he'd learned so far is that magical things don't necessarily have your best interest in mind.

CHAPTER FOURTEEN

The ancient sleeping spell took much longer to cast than Jorge expected. After finally feeling certain the spell would stick, he removed the phone from Buxton's room and returned the chair to its propped-up position, against the doorknob.

Once on the veranda, Jorge took his favorite seat near the balcony's edge and ordered a Tom Collins. He contemplated the great Nile that flowed past him. Soon the sun would dip below the horizon, painting the sky with a breathtaking symphony of pink, orange, and creamy yellow. Egyptian sunsets were particularly beautiful. Jorge chalked it up to all the desert sand and pollution in the air creating minute prisms reflecting the light of the dying sun.

He lifted the icy delight and smiled as the tart ginny drink traveled down his dust-covered throat. It helped him unwind as he leaned back into the soft cushioned chair, mesmerized by the vista surrounding him.

He rocked his glass back and forth, enjoying the rhythmic clink of the ice cubes against the glass. Would Gwen come? Was it too much to expect from her to show up? He'd spent so much time trying to cast the spell on Buxton. Maybe she'd already come, saw he wasn't there, and left feeling abandoned by him once again.

With his memories restored, it was plain that the time he and Gwen had spent together were the best days of his life. Now she was married. She was somebody else's girl. A dark flame of heartbreak burned within him. Jorge knocked back the rest of his drink. The alcohol coursed through him, amplifying the lust of anger within. Buxton had a lot to atone for.

Light and clear laughter, like a happy wind chime, pulled Jorge's gaze to the maître d' stand. A surge of joy filled Jorge as Gwen's bright green eyes locked on his. In that moment something flashed between them of what they once were, then snapped back to reality.

He delighted in her graceful stride as she neared the table. She wore a guarded expression. He'd have to move in slow and measured steps. He didn't want to frighten her off like a timid song bird, never to return.

"Glad you came," he said. Gwen's eyes flickered at his overloud voice. *Softly, softly,* he told himself.

She smoothed her skirt against her legs as she sat down.

He had a million questions he wanted to ask her. Things he'd been thinking about since the memories started coming back. They had been so natural together. Now it was awkward, like they were complete strangers.

He flagged down the waiter. "You look lovely as always," he said as the waiter neared them. "What would you like to drink?"

Gwen glanced up at the waiter. "Ginger Manhattan." A smile

cloaked with sadness pulled across her face. "You of all people should know that, Jorge."

Her tone sent Mayday warnings through him. Jorge used to love the way she said his name, all soft and honeyed like a warm invitation. "So, what are you doing around here?"

Her eyebrows lifted. "You invited me."

"No. Of course. I meant how did you come to work on the story about my disappearance?" He welcomed the intrusion of the waiter delivering her drink. He lifted his glass. "Cheers, Gwen."

"What are we toasting?"

"A reunion of friends."

"Friends? Is that what we are, Jorge?"

Apparently a toast wasn't in the cards. Jorge took a big gulp of his Tom Collins to steel his nerves. "Well, I'd hoped—"

Her face turned an adorable shade of pink.

"You take the cake. After everything, I still . . ." Her voice trailed off while she stared at her ginger Manhattan.

"Still?" a modicum of hope rose within Jorge.

Her gaze was far away when she tipped her drink back and swallowed it in one giant gulp. "Does it really matter, Jorge? Things have changed. I have changed. Apparently, you've changed. Let's just say I was worried about you. I asked for this assignment when it surfaced that you were missing. Your sudden disappearance dominated the news. I know I shouldn't, but after everything I still care about what happens to you. I thought you died out there." Her glance shifted to her wedding ring. "You said you had something for me."

Gwen fidgeted with the pendant around her neck. He was surprised to see it was the ancient faience eye of Horus he'd bought for her years ago. Jorge purchased it from a grey-market connection that sold items of little historical value that were pocketed from the archaeological digs now and again. Jorge had the amulet encased in a crystal locket.

"That is why I am here now," she said.

Jorge signaled the waiter for another round. "I have so much to tell you." He glanced down at the huge diamond ring on her hand. Anguish filled his heart at the life he should have had with her. Now she belonged to someone else.

The new drinks arrived swiftly; their waiter must have had a keen eye on them. Jorge lifted his glass to toast. "To reacquaintances."

Gwen lifted her glass. "To reacquaintances."

A crash of broken glass from behind the bar followed by Arabic cursing broke through their mutual silence.

Gwen's gaze broke from him and moved to a point beyond Jorge. "So, why did you ask me to come? What are all these things you need to tell me?"

"I have been exposed to things I never would have ever imagined possible even after spending my life searching out the unexplainable."

She looked at him blankly. Jorge wasn't getting to her. Gwen was familiar with his hyperbolic tendencies. His mind spun—how he could make her understand this shift in reality? "Do you remember when I thought I was running out of shows? When the pressure of producing each show raised the bar tenfold, to find something exponentially more sensational?"

Gwen nodded.

"Do you remember how I used to say that it would be the apex of my career to not only find Alexander's tomb, but also find within it a mummified alien?"

Jorge could feel Gwen getting drawn in.

"Or if I were to find the lost city of Atlantis and while excavating, I found a landing pad that was lined with spaceships?" Jorge paused to let those ideas settle in Gwen's memory. "Well, not one of those things can stand up to what I've recently discovered. Something that will blow the hinges off what we humans think we know."

"But . . . I thought you were divesting yourself of all the alien stories." Her mouth turned down into a soft frown as she reached back to her bag. "I thought you'd changed, Jorge." Her expression was somewhere between anger and regret. Gwen stood and locked eyes with him. "Or at least, I hoped you'd changed, but I guess that was another lie."

Jorge gently grabbed her wrist. His heartbeat thumped at the touch of her silky skin. "This is different."

She whipped her hand back and crossed her arms.

"Make a fool of me once. Isn't there some sort of saying like that? I trusted you and where did that get me? All dressed up and standing alone in a Vegas wedding chapel." She shook her head. "You have no idea how long it took me to purge you from my life."

Jorge pushed up from his chair and stood as close as he dared to her. "I know, Gwen. Believe me, I do know. That wasn't my fault."

She slammed her fist on the table. "How dare you. You were a coward to end it the way you did, and I can't imagine anything that will change that fact." Tears welled in her eyes.

Jorge motioned to the chair. "Please, Gwen, just give me five more minutes. That's all I ask. Five more minutes, and I will never bother you again."

To his surprise, she sat down.

"When I said it wasn't my fault, I wasn't being an avoider of blame in an abstract way, but in a very literal way."

Her expression was unreadable.

He checked around him to make sure there weren't any hungry ears close by to hear what he was going to say next. "What would you say if I told you that the reason why I just dropped off and out of your life is that my memory was wiped by a secret organization?"

Gwen closed her eyes and shook her head. "One thing I always loved about you was your vivid imagination. But really, Jorge, you just don't know when to stop. I thought you really had something to say. That you could finally give me some sort of closure."

"Gwen, you have to believe me. Something happened recently, something that I can't go into right now, that restored my memories. I never stopped loving you." He reached over and laid his hands onto one of hers. "I just didn't know I knew you for the longest time. There was always something about you, though, something I couldn't quite shake. As soon as the memories came rushing back, I was devastated to know what I'd lost in you." He glanced down at their joined hands. "The countless memories that have repopulated my mind over time have made me realize that they'd probably wiped my mind numerous times. I don't think my mind is quite altogether right, and may never be, but know that I would never in a million years purposely hurt you."

She pulled away from him and leaned back in her seat. "If that is true, how did they do it? You have to be able to explain it in more detail. Or else I am going to leave this bar and never speak to you again."

"I have no idea how they did it. Yet, I know they did."

"I need something more substantive than your words. I need proof."

Suddenly inspiration hit him. "I've got something that will prove it to you. In fact, it is something that will alter your view of the reality we live in forever."

"Lead me to it."

"It is in my room."

Her left eyebrow arched.

He stood up and rounded the table.

"No funny business?" She swayed a little when she stood, and leaned into him.

Jorge breathed in her scent of her long auburn hair. "Scout's honor."

As they walked to his room, two ideas occupied his mind. One, what her expression would be when she saw the book of magic, and two, that he was never a scout.

CHAPTER FIFTEEN

S cuse me." Gwen tipped into Jorge as they walked down the hallway to his suite of rooms. He resisted the instinct to pull her closer to him.

He leaned against the wall and swiped his keycard. He opened the door. "Entrez-vous, Mademoiselle."

She glanced up at him with a sly smile. He knew she always loved it when he spoke French to her. It wasn't because he spoke it beautifully, quite the opposite. Jorge loved to make her laugh.

Gwen walked straight past the living room area to the floor-to-ceiling balcony doors. She swooped them open and twirled around with an impish grin. "Man, this place brings back a lot of memories." She walked out into the dusky night and leaned onto the railing.

Jorge closed the space between them, standing behind her, watching her enjoy the view.

"Do you remember the last time we were here?" she asked.

With a light touch Jorge grazed her back. "That night we

shared on this balcony, how we lay here all night long staring up at the stars, thinking of our future together, was the most important night of my life."

"What happened?" She wiped away a tear.

Jorge's hands slid down her arms, feeling goose bumps rise on her skin. "That night was stolen from us."

Gwen spun around, eyes glistening with emotion, her head tilted as if she was about to ask him another question. Jorge leaned in close. As their lips met, he was lost in the sweet universe of her kiss, honeyed by bourbon. A soft groan from Gwen plucked the strings of his desire. He pulled her closer. His hands wandered up and snaked through her hair. Her perfume filled the air around him.

She pushed him back.

She leaned against the balcony rail, lips plumped, and skin flushed. "Jorge, I—"

He softly cupped her chin in his hands. He drew his face close, her breath warm on his lips. "I would move heaven and earth to change things." Jorge wandered back into the room, away from her. "You and I have just been hapless pawns in the plans of others." He picked up the book of magic and sat on the couch. Then he motioned for her to sit across from him. "I'll show you what I promised."

Her eyes were fixated on the book he held. Jorge knew its inlaid cover would catch her eye. "Where do you think I got this book?"

Jorge handed it to her. She set it in her lap and reverently passed her hands over its beautiful cover. Intrigue sparked in her eyes. For a brief moment it was like nothing had changed. Although everything had changed.

She smiled up at him.

"Any guesses?"

She inspected it, turning it on its side, looking at its spine and pulling it close to her, searching for some sort of clue in order to give the best guess possible. She motioned to open it.

"Don't."

"Why not?"

"I need to explain before you open the book. Once the book is opened, we won't be able to go back."

"Like a Pandora's box?"

"Exactly. Any guesses?"

"Can I ask some qualifying questions?"

"I'll give you two questions."

"Three?"

Jorge harrumphed. "Two questions and a statement."

Gwen sat up with renewed vigor for the game. "Did you somehow acquire this book while you were lost in the Western Desert?"

"Yes."

"Was it something given to you or taken?"

"Neither, really, and both."

Gwen screwed up her face as she tried to sort out an answer. "I can't imagine something like this would have been left in a tomb or temple. It looks so . . ."

"Valuable and well cared for?"

"Exactly."

"So how can it be that something like this could just be found in the middle of nowhere?" Her eyes brightened. "Oh my god. Did you find a new tomb?"

"You've already burned your questions."

"But, how did you find out about this book?"

"You don't get another question."

Gwen smirked. "Come on, Jorge."

"I met Phillip Philothea."

"*The* Phillip Philothea?"

"The one and only."

"As he's been dead for about two decades, it would have had to have happened a long time ago."

"It was roughly two weeks ago."

Gwen set the book down on the coffee table, brows furrowed in concentration. "It can't be."

"Just say it."

"Did you somehow go to the afterlife?"

"I've been to and come back from the Netherworld."

She turned away.

"Gwen, I'm not kidding." He reached over and placed his hand over hers. "There really is a Netherworld. And I've been there. You have to believe me." Jorge could see that the longing in her eyes matched what he felt deep down. He leaned in.

Gwen pulled away from him, then sat back and fiddled with her wedding ring. She propped the book up on her knees like a golden boundary between them. "So what's with the book?"

Jorge couldn't help but wonder who stole her heart. What knight in shining armor helped her piece her life back together after Jorge fell out of her life? He wanted to know, and at the same time he didn't. "It's a book of magic."

A fresh wave of disbelief passed over her face.

"Would you like some Veuve?"

"How would champagne prove anything? Other than the limits of how drunk I can get. No, I've had plenty enough already."

"If I successfully call forward a bottle of chilled champagne, will you at least have a toast with me?"

"Just one toast."

Jorge smiled. He took the book from Gwen and opened it, clearing his mind to receive its potential. As soon as the void appeared, Jorge reached down into it. For comic effect, he pantomimed being pulled into the void.

Gwen laughed. The energy between them lifted.

He cleared his mind and focused deeply, imagining the bottle coming gently into his hand, to see if he could master the magic of calling forth with more control. The rough foiled neck of the bottle materialized in his grasp. He hefted it out and onto the table.

Gwen's reaction was a mix of disbelief and wonder.

Jorge slapped the side of his head. "Oh, how could I forget?" He reached in and envisioned a custom pair of champagne flutes he bought for her years ago. They were hand-cut crystal in an art deco design of ancient Egyptian lotuses.

He could feel the presence of the glasses in the void. He turned his palm upward and splayed out his fingers, willing each glass to slide gently into place. Their stems chimed together as he lifted them out and placed them next to the bottle.

"Oh . . . Jorge." Her eyes were soft with emotion.

Jorge went over and sat next to her and leaned in. Their lips collided in a tender willingness. His hands grazed her neck as he drew her in. Their bodies entwined like the Blue Nile and the White Nile tumbling into one another.

Gwen pulled away. Her eyes lit with desire. She stood and cocked her head. A cascade of auburn hair fell across her plump red lips. "There's something I need to tell you, Jorge."

Jorge sighed. "I know. I am too late. Your heart belongs to another."

She twisted the ring from her finger and tossed it across the room.

"What the—?"

"What can I say? It keeps the wolves away." A wicked smile spread across her face as she reached down and pulled him up to her. She kissed him deeply, then led him into the bedroom.

———

Jorge smiled to himself as he listened to Gwen singing in the shower, a sure sign that everything would be okay. When she sang sad country love songs, Gwen was happy. It never occurred to Jorge to ask why she sang tearjerkers when her heart was light. It was stranger still since she was a dyed-in-the-wool city girl. The closest she ever came to a farm was buying cage-free eggs.

Last night they lay in bed and talked until just before dawn broke. Jorge told her about the Netherworld, Buxton, and KHNM. Then they fell asleep in each other's arms.

Jorge hadn't been certain what would happen when they woke. Would she slip away in the quiet of morning, regretful? Would this night be all that they ever had together? Would she see what happened between them as a big mistake?

He was certain there was nothing to worry about when she broke into a rendition of "He Stopped Loving Her Today," probably the saddest song ever written. The sadder the song, the happier she was.

She winked at him as she walked by. A thick Egyptian towel encased her hair and another barely clung to her curves, a tenuous tuck-in barely holding fast against the pressure of her full breasts. His mind raced back to the previous night, her body pressing up against his, how she hungrily tore at his clothes. He walked over and lightly tugged at the back of her towel. Her eyes twinkled playfully.

"Now, Jorge," she purred, "you know I can't stay. I need to get—"

"Home?"

"I've just come home." She kissed him soft and slow, then pulled away. "I need to pick up some things."

"Don't go." He ran his fingers up her arms, making her shiver.

"I have a deadline coming up. I need to gather my notes on an article I've been working on."

Something slammed hard onto the floor. Jorge jerked away from Gwen. Had Buxton woken up? Gwen was about to say something, but Jorge put his finger to her lips. Jorge scanned the room. The book was on the floor, its interior splayed open. How did it get knocked down?

"Strange." Jorge made his way over to the book and leaned down to pick it up.

A voice came from the void. "Hello, Master."

Jorge pulled his hand away quickly, as if avoiding a viper bite.

"Did you hear that?"

Gwen came over. "That wasn't you?"

Then it came again. "Hello, Master, can you hear me?"

Jorge knelt and peered at the book, his hands resting on the soft Oriental rug below. The mirror's finish was covered with a layer of fog.

"Turn on that lamp, Gwen."

The book was illuminated by the soft incandescent glow of the lamplight. As the fog dissipated, a face stared back at him, with the most unusual eyes Jorge had ever seen. They were a curious shade of purple.

"Hello, Master." The dark-haired stranger's head bobbed down as if bowing.

Did the book of magic have its own butler? Why did it wait until now to show up? "Why are you calling me Master?"

"I am a servant of these books."

"You live in the book?" asked Gwen.

"No. I am captive in a faraway land, imprisoned in a bottle eons ago. By activating this magical artifact, you opened this channel for me to find you. If you set me free, your wish will be my command."

"But how do I get you out of this book?"

"All you need is to find me, and to call my name. I am not trapped in this book you possess. I am in a bottle far away from where you are now. Your book serves as a transmitter of sorts that allows me to communicate with you from where I am."

"And where will I find you?"

"Two doors down, to the left."

Gwen looked skeptical. "But that's not at all far away. And it's a broom closet."

"Two doors down." The magician's smile faded.

Jorge leaned in close. "What is your name?"

"Idris Niru," he said, then vanished.

Gwen threw on some clothes, and they ventured out into the hallway. Jorge opened the specified door and stared, dumbfounded, at a vast desert.

CHAPTER SIXTEEN

Warm air cascaded out from the opened broom closet door. An expanse of desert dunes glistened in the distance.

"What the—?" Gwen stepped back.

Jorge reached behind him and grabbed her hand. "Ready?"

"You are going out there? On the request of a disembodied face in a book?" She dropped Jorge's hand.

"Haven't you been yearning for an adventure into the unexplained?"

"But we don't have any water or proper gear to just be plopped in the middle of a sand sea. We don't even know where he would be conjuring us to. For all we know that could be the planet Mars."

"If only."

Gwen rolled her eyes.

"We'll be okay. Look by that outcropping of rocks."

"A large tent?"

"Exactly."

"So?"

"Ever heard of Bedouin hospitality? We'll be treated like kings."

"Or executed for trespassing."

Jorge led her through to the other side and then closed the door behind them. As soon as it shut, the door disappeared. He grabbed Gwen's hand as they walked with the hot, bright sun beating down on them. It was a good thing they didn't have far to walk.

The fabric of the Bedouin-style tent rippled in the breeze. The black fabric of the roof was peaked in the middle. Rectangular curtains of richly colored fabric patterned in horizontal lines of gold, red, and green flowed down to the ground.

Jorge stepped inside. Although the tent was richly appointed, lined with large colorful pillows, an abundance of Oriental rugs, and lanterns that hung from the posts like illuminated jewels, it was devoid of life. Specifically devoid of a magician. In the center of the circle of pillows was an unassuming wooden end table, with a large cut-crystal vessel.

Jorge picked up the crystal decanter and shook it.

"Master. No!" A very small voice emanated from the vessel.

Jorge squinted down its long, narrow neck. At the bottom was a replica of the interior of the tent in which they now stood. Pillows all along the outer edge atop a mosaic of brightly patterned Oriental rugs.

"Hello?" Jorge spoke into the top of the bottle, then looked back into it.

The tiny figure stood with his arms crossed. "Please just talk normal. The magicked crystal pulls whatever you say directly to me, Master. Or at least you will be my master once you free me, and then your wish will be my command."

Gwen grabbed the bottle from Jorge and peered in. "How do we know this isn't a trap? How can we trust you?"

"The fact that you are now in the middle of the Western Desert with no food or water doesn't really give you much of a choice."

Gwen shot Jorge an *I told you so* look.

"Trust me, the only thing I want right now is freedom. I've been in this bottle for hundreds of years. Just say my name and rub the bottle; then I will serve you as repayment."

Gwen was unconvinced. "Why were you put in the bottle, anyway? People aren't usually put in jail for being upstanding."

"I was imprisoned by an evil witch who was jealous of my powers."

Gwen put her hands on her hips. "But how can you truly be free? I thought that jinn were always tied to their home by an object, and that they could only be temporarily freed."

"I am not a true jinn. I am a magician, an immortal magician. Once freed, I will never have to return to this humble vessel."

"In other words, you are not tied to the regular rules of engagement between humans and jinns?" asked Gwen.

Jorge liked that his lady was thinking strategically. "I guess we could negotiate some conditions regarding your release." He smiled at Gwen. Exacting revenge on Buxton and his crew just got a thousand times easier with a magical servant.

"My services are pretty much open ended. Being immortal, I don't abide by the rules of mortals. I exist in a more expansive timeline where such distinctions don't matter. You will find me to be very amenable to whatever your desires might be. I have unlimited powers. Powers that would be yours, until my debt is paid."

"How would the final payment be defined?" asked Gwen.

"How would you like to define it, Master?"

Jorge recognized the anger that flashed in Gwen's expression at Idris's not-so-subtle slight. "How long have you been in there?"

"Time flows differently in the immortal life. I am not sure."

"I would like to set the negotiations at a minimum of one hundred wishes until your debt is paid."

The magician laughed. "You are a greedy one. A normal jinn only gives three, and you want one hundred."

"Let me remind you, in your own words, a jinn you are not."

"A hundred is too much."

Jorge replaced the bottle on the table and grabbed Gwen's hand, then made like he was leaving the tent. "Come on, Gwen. I've survived this desert once. I can do it again." Jorge figured that the magician went to a lot of trouble to get them there and wasn't about to let them leave.

A sharp zap of electricity pricked the back of Jorge's neck like an extremely intense bug bite. He dropped Gwen's hand and slapped at the spot. He spun around to see a tiny bolt of electricity arc out of the bottle. Jorge ducked. It grazed the top of his head. "Changed your mind, magician?"

Jorge ducked as another flash emanated from the bottle.

"Are you quite finished?"

"Are you ready to set me free?"

Jorge went over to the bottle. "A hundred wishes?" He leaned in but not too close.

"A hundred wishes." The magician's dejected answer echoed up the crystal vessel.

"I have one more stipulation. I will make my first wish before I set you free. That wish is that you will swear to transport Gwen and me safely back to the hotel."

"Are you sure you want to burn a wish on that?" asked the magician.

Gwen nodded at Jorge with approval.

"Granted. Now pick this old thing up, give it a rub. Just keep saying my name until I am standing there with you. Again, in case you've forgotten, my name is Idris Niru."

"Okay, brace yourself, because you are about to be freed." Jorge picked up the decanter and rubbed its nubby exterior. He repeated Idris's name as a smoky substance rose out of the neck of the decanter and snaked down to the carpeted floor, moving to the center of the most intricate carpet in the room, and slowly filled out into the form of a man.

When the fog cleared, Jorge found himself facing a tall man with a hooknose and an incredibly precise goatee.

Idris grabbed the crystal decanter, then immediately smashed it to the ground. "I have been dreaming about that for ages." He knelt down in front of Jorge, head bowed.

Jorge was heartened at the blatant show of submission. "You may stand."

Idris rose.

"So, we're heading back now?" Gwen's voice was hopeful.

Since they had this tent and no one around for miles, Jorge figured it might be a good idea to sort some things out first. "I think we should have some conversations in this enclave of privacy."

Idris smiled knowingly. "I take it you know what you want to spend your wishes on?"

"You must also be a mind reader as well as a magician."

A sound, like an aborted chuckle, emanated from the magician. "Have a seat, Master."

Jorge eased himself onto the floor, leaning back against an oversized pillow. Gwen sat down next to him. She was indulging him in staying there, but just barely.

Idris knelt, then waved his hands over the table. A bowl of dates and a sparkling cut-crystal decanter filled with water appeared along with a set of three matching glasses. A glint of mischief sparked in Idris's eyes as he poured water from it. "Not an ounce of magic in this decanter. Other than what it took to transport it here. Enjoy. These are provided free of charge. No wishes spent."

Jorge reached for the glass in front of him. The chilled, weighty crystal glass made him realize just how thirsty he was. The water was light, crisp, and cold. It reminded him of hiking in the Swiss Alps and scooping pristine mountain spring water with his cupped hand. He grabbed a date, his teeth sinking into its soft-sweet flesh. "So, you really aren't sure how long you were in there?"

"Probably a few hundred years."

"How is it that you ended up in that bottle? You said you were the guardian of the books. How exactly would you be carrying out your guardian duties from that bottle, anyway?" asked Gwen.

"Let's just say it stemmed from an unfortunate interaction between myself and a rogue priestess regarding one of the four books of magic, like the one you have."

Jorge sat up to attention. "There are other books?"

"Four, to be exact. They were created in the time before time by the original eight Egyptian Gods of the Ogdoad."

Visions of treasure danced in Jorge's mind as he imagined

what it would be like to possess all four books.

"What is this priestess's name?" asked Gwen.

Idris's expression turned cold. "Meyret."

Jorge stiffened at hearing her name. A few weeks ago, he wouldn't have recognized the name of the one who wiped his memories.

"Master, you know Meyret? How could you?"

"Just suffice it to say, I am familiar with what she is capable of. So after you are free from my wishes, what are your plans?"

Idris looked shocked to be asked. "I will move to exact my own revenge."

"I too seek revenge. It sounds like we might be fishing in the same pond."

"What kind of revenge are you looking for? Ruination? Death? Torture? What flavor suits your tastes?"

"Maybe a smorgasbord."

"Variety is the spice of life." The magician chuckled.

"Okay, boys, it is great that you are getting along, but I've got places to be."

"Of course, dear. Down to business. There are people I have had dealings with. Well, really an organization of people. In the past, I've witnessed things they wanted to keep secret, so they wiped my memories."

"The book, it restored your memories, didn't it?"

"Absolutely, I want revenge. But first, I want to start with their leader, Buxton. I want him to have to witness his world fall apart. I want to ruin everyone and everything that he holds near and dear. I think this plan will be set out in stages. In one stage he will be imprisoned while I ruin those he loves. While he is locked away safely, I plan on building a memory machine to wipe his memories. If the great and mighty KHNM can do it, I am sure

I can figure out how. I am certain it is something your magical powers could help with immensely."

"A memory extractor—I like that idea, but what would you need that for? I can see your desire for poetic justice, but would it be worth the trouble when you can just kill them?"

"It is more than poetic justice. If I possessed all his memories, it would be like having a key to the mysteries of this unseen world of magic. He was the leader of KHNM. Are you familiar with them?"

"Only tangentially. I may have a document that might help you in your crusade for the agency's ruination. It is a covenant that binds the agency to the Gods. It fell into my possession years ago from an old adversary of mine that was held captive quite some time ago. They've been trying to find it for ages, really." Idris took a sip of water. "So, you've had interactions with the Gods?"

"Exactly. That is why they have wiped my memories so often. The more I happened upon them, the more I was attracted to them. There is some sort of cosmic magnetism that was created between us with each interaction, making it happen with more frequency."

Gwen reached over and grabbed a handful of dates and shot Jorge a meaningful glance.

Idris leaned in. "I am so glad to be serving someone like you, Jorge. Someone who is thinking so strategically. But why stop with Buxton and his collection of colleagues? Why think so small?"

"What do you mean?"

"Maybe you could bring humanity together in this newly magical realm of man. Dream big, the sky's the limit. Guide your fellow humans to the powers of magical enlightenment."

Jorge looked out beyond the tent and stared into the vast universe of sand and rocks beyond. All his life he'd been searching for truth. All he ever wanted to do was share that truth with others. Make them understand how amazing our world and the universe we live in is. How game changing would it be to use magic to explore the scientific world? All his life his pie-in-the-sky dream was contact. Alien contact. Maybe Idris's magic could open up the galaxy for humankind.

Jorge was abuzz with the possibilities. "Well, if the sky's the limit, how do you feel about space travel?"

"Now, that is an interesting prospect." Idris's expression went somewhere far away. "I've never contemplated reaching out to other worlds. How do you think we could achieve that?"

"Have you ever heard of SETI?"

"The Egyptian God?"

"No, the institute that has a thousand radio receivers pointed toward space for the past thirty or so years. Together we could make what they are doing look like small potatoes."

"I think that is well within the scope of work for our relationship."

"But it feels disjointed, like we have too much we are trying to do. Ruin Buxton, get the books, signal space . . . enlighten all of humanity. Maybe it's just too much."

"Nothing is too much when you have magic behind you. We could find a way to tie this all together and make a simultaneous impact. By the way, where did you find your book?"

"The Netherworld."

Idris looked shocked. "How did you get in? Or more importantly how did you get back?"

"Through a portal."

"That made things easy for you."

"It was anything but easy."

Idris interjected. "At least you didn't have to hunt down your enemy—he was pretty much delivered right to you. I've spent nearly my entire existence trying to track Meyret down."

"Don't you worry, Idris. I know exactly where she is."

The magician's eyes lit with interest.

A current of excitement charged through Jorge as he realized the staggering potential of joining forces with this powerful magician. This moment could change everything. He could meet his destiny head-on and treat Gwen like the goddess she was. "I'll scratch your back, you scratch mine."

"Once again, Master, you amaze me. How do you, a human, know the resting place of the great and powerful priestess?"

"Escaping to the Netherworld is not my first run-in with this group of magical bureaucrats. There is that small one, Gormund—"

"You've actually met Bes?"

"Bes? He works for KHNM?"

"He was assigned as her protector. As the only God who still roams the realm of humans, he goes by that silly name he chose for himself. I think it means beast or something in French."

"A cruel beast is what he is. After the last time Meyret wiped my memory, Gormund left me out in the middle of a desert at a place frequented by those who want to connect with alien life forms. Now that my memories have been restored, I know that he did this as a joke, certain that the experience would end up showcased on an upcoming episode of my TV show."

"Did it?" asked Gwen.

"Of course. The thought of it still burns my ass."

"Your return to the realm of man was through a ploutonion?"

"Now it is your time to impress me, magician. How do you

know about ploutonions? Most have never heard of that ancient Greek term for sacred portals, some thought to be wormholes allowing for travel back and forth through the universe."

"Would it surprise you to know that I am no less than fifteen centuries old?"

"So, would you be considered an immortal tween?" Gwen was getting punchy. Jorge could tell by her tone that they should wrap this conversation up and head back to the hotel.

"Only Gods are born Immortal. No, this curse was set upon me when I became the guardian for these books."

"Curse? Man, I would relish living forever. Just think of all the amazing adventures one could have if they knew they would never die."

"Master, have you been having any unusual dreams as of late?"

Jorge always had unique nighttime visitations and experienced alien landscapes when sleeping. He accredited it to his vivid imagination. He'd had some strange dreams last night, but nothing of real note. "Not really."

Idris peered out into the desert beyond the tent. "Interesting. You may be semi-immortal already, as you've traveled to and from the Netherworld."

Gwen leaned forward, "Hey, sorry to break up this really interesting conversation between you two, but I've got a deadline to meet, so if we could wrap this up, I would greatly appreciate it."

Gwen rose.

Idris spoke. His expression was grave. "Before we portal back to the hotel, there is something you should consider, Master."

Jorge place his hand over Gwen's and squeezed. He couldn't

help but feel like whatever the magician would say next would alter the course of both of their lives.

"Think about wide possibilities. Possibilities as wide as the universe. You can initiate change that at this moment might be unfathomable. If we could find the wormhole, if we could find the books, if we could make contact, we, I meant you, Master could be the captain at the helm of this strange blue world. Just think of what you could do, the things you could change, how you could influence the future history of humanity. You would be spoken of in the same vein as Adam, as the catalyst into a new epoch for the mortal realm. Don't limit yourself to your petty revenges. Revel in them but also have the big picture in mind. You could do so much more. What would you think about that? Most people run through their day to day trying to convince themselves that the possibilities in their lives are limitless. Yours are." Idris straightened his shoulders. "Master. Only you possess one of the four most powerful books in the realm of man and beyond. You are so close. If only you possessed the most powerful book."

The tent flap snapped in the wind. Gwen squeezed his hand. "We should go now."

"So, what are these other books?"

Idris peered out into the vast desert, dark clouds forming on the horizon. "The book you have is the book of space. The other three are water, hiddenness, and darkness. The only mortals who can use these books are those who are of the ancient lineage of book guardians. The one you found had its locking mechanism disabled years ago by one of the people who stashed it in the Netherworld. That is how you, as a regular-old mortal, were able to retrieve it. It would be easy to think that the path to controlling mortals is through some dark power. People instinctually think they need the book of darkness but actually the most powerful book is that of water. Everything on this planet needs it to survive. The subtler hand is oftentimes the more powerful."

Jorge gazed into Idris's odd-colored eyes.

"I will send us back to the hotel room together. It is easiest if we hold on to one another." Idris grabbed Gwen's hand, then Jorge's.

Idris's hand buzzed with a strange energy. It reminded Jorge of one of those old-style metal vibrating massagers a person would strap onto their hand. It was an intense yet pleasurable sensation. "Where can I find this book?"

"Only one person can call that book forward. Years ago, I built a web in anticipation of her coming. You've found the book, setting it all into motion. All we have to do is wait for her to fall into the trap I've set."

"Who is this person?"

The buzzing continued to travel throughout Jorge's body. Jorge imagined this was what it was like to stand in the middle of a plasma ball. The air around him was charged with the crisp metallic smell of electricity.

Idris smiled. "Alex Philothea."

All at once Jorge's flesh came alive with countless pinpricks as he was catapulted into a sensation of nothingness.

CHAPTER SEVENTEEN

Alex strolled through the New Haven train station. When she woke up that morning, she never would have guessed that her day would wind up in Connecticut. She stopped dead in her tracks as she passed a newsstand. On the cover of Popularazzi, a celebrity gossip rag was a picture of Jorge Trinculo with a big toothy grin. In her battle against Raymond Sol, she had a number of run-ins with Jorge. She felt sorry for him. Alex understood why KHNM needed to wipe his memories over the years, but she wondered if it was justified. Maybe they could have found another way. In the few interactions she had with him, he was a scrambled mess. It was explained to her by Niles that you can only erase information so many times until serious distortions occur. His mind was warped material, like an old cassette tape.

What on earth could that strange man be up to now?

She bought the magazine, then tossed it into her scribe's bag and headed to the taxi stand.

The last time Alex saw Jorge was when he'd rescued her after she'd escaped a tomb deep under an ancient site dedicated to the goddess Hathor. Raymond and Salima, aka the God Re and his daughter Hathor, left her for dead, sealed up in the tomb, fully believing she would be a discovery for some future archaeologists. When she emerged from the tomb, she knew she was in the middle of nowhere, and she was uncertain how to get back to civilization. On the horizon a sandstorm was brewing. She remembered the amused relief she felt when she realized that the swirling sands were not an oncoming weather system, but Jorge and a crew of misfits in a military-grade hovercraft.

When he emerged from the craft, he pronounced Alex as the Goddess Hathor. Alex decided it was in her best interest to go along with the delusion.

Alex never figured out who sent this unlikely hero to her rescue. She grilled Buxton about it, but he said he didn't do it, or wouldn't admit to it. She liked to think that it was Niles. But judging by his reaction to her lately, it was ridiculous to think he would go out of his way to save her.

She hailed a cab and gave the cabbie the address to the Beinecke Library. Then she reached into her scribe's bag to retrieve the tabloid. The headline read, "Survival in the Egyptian Desert."

Jorge Trinculo, host and creator of the wildly popular weekly television series *Unearthing Facts of Outer-Space Origins*—or as the space heads like to call it, UFO^2—was found near death in a remote section of southern Egypt on the shores of Lake Nasser. A tour group from the archaeological travel company Far Horizons found Jorge and his companion severely dehydrated and very near death. The crew of the Victorian-style Empress cruise ship took them onboard, giving them immediate basic medical attention while awaiting an emergency rescue crew.

I interviewed Jorge Trinculo sitting on the airy veranda lounge at the swanky Old Cataract Hotel while sipping ice-cold iced tea. A vastly different environment than he was rescued from.

Mr. Trinculo's companion was unavailable for comment, as he wished to remain anonymous.

A loud bark-like laugh escaped from Alex. She could see the eyes of the taxi driver in the rearview mirror, appraising her stability. It struck her as funny that even someone who almost died with him didn't want to be associated with him.
She continued to read.

Spoiler alert: superfans of his television show should brace yourselves for some disheartening news.

PZ: So you must have been asked this a million times already, but here goes one million and one. What exactly were you doing out in the desert with no supplies or resources? No camels, dune buggies, food, or water. For someone who makes their living being ready for the unexpected, what happened?

JT: We were on the search for some desert opals. My companion and I heard of a large deposit of them, and we were just checking up on the intel. It was only supposed to be a three-hour expedition. Our luck drastically changed during that rare tremor that shook North Africa a week or so ago. Our vehicle was dumped down a steep desert wadi, totaling it.

Eventually I found some shelter, but my companion remained unconscious. There was no way I could leave him there to try and get help. In that state he was completely vulnerable—I'd be leaving him to the mercy of desert carnivores. I rationed our water and drank only enough to sustain myself.

When he finally regained consciousness, we were able to make slow progress to the Temple of Dakka, where I was able to use my iodine tablets to replenish our water until we were rescued.

PZ: So now that you are back, what are your plans? You mentioned some sort of big announcement.

JT: I will no longer make my living seeking adventure.

PZ: So your near-death experience changed your life?

JT: Completely, in fact from this day forward, I will not be producing my television series.

Alex mumbled, "What has gotten into him?"
The rearview mirror reflected the cabbie's confusion at her comment. "We are here."
Alex looked up from the article to the honeycombed exterior

of the Beinecke Library. She paid and hopped out of the car and leaned against a cement ledge to finish the article.

PZ: You do understand that this revelation will not sit well with your fans.

JT: And that is a shame. I have no intention of causing any angst for them. My new life's goal is to only bring joy to others.

Alex rolled her eyes.

PZ: Would it be safe to say this harrowing experience became a spiritual vision quest for you?

JT: I guess you could call it that. I sat up one night looking up at the vast desert sky and the multitude of stars over- head, and I realized that all this time I'd been searching for the wrong things. I used to yearn for the connection of alien life, but completely ignored the beautiful life right in front of me. The life of a human.

PZ: And what do you yearn for now?

JT: Spirituality, a deep connection to Mother Earth and my fellow beings.

PZ: This is a monumental shift for you. Without your adventurer's uniform, how do you intend to make a living? Or is money no longer important to you?

JT: No, I will not be living a monastic life. However, I have decided to share the joy I've found to others.

Oh, here comes the BS.

JT: While my companion was still unconscious, I wandered out of our cave enclosure and pondered many great questions. As I walked in the blaring moonlight under the brilliant sea of stars above, something caught my eye, glimmering in the sand. When I picked it up, it was a glorious and beautiful sand opal.

PZ: Many of our readers may not know what a sand opal is. Could you describe it?

JT: Sand opals are formed when a comet or other heavenly body crashes to Earth and lands in a desert. The space rock is superheated when it enters the Earth's atmosphere. When it hits the sand, it turns into an opaque glass, which is a sand opal. If you are looking for an example of one, there is one inset in the breastplate of Tutankhamen.

I was standing in the desert and happened to look down to see a whole slew of these beautiful gemstones glimmering in the moonlight. I found what I've been searching for. I picked the stone up and was suddenly overwhelmed with a feeling of peace and completeness.

I immediately went to the place where my friend lay oblivious to it all. I knelt by him and was overcome with an instinct to place the stone on his forehead. As soon as it touched his flesh, his eyes fluttered open. It was a miracle. I then realized that these stones were divine and had great powers of healing.

Later, in the temple we sheltered in, I took the opal in my hand. My thoughts wandered to my family and friends, who I imagined must have been worried sick about me. It was then that I saw Tom Blackburn and the other tourists. I now carry that same stone as a saving talisman.

PZ: So, what is next for you?

JT: I have already secured mining rights with the Egyptian government and plan to make these valuable and holy . . .

Alex had read enough. She got up from her makeshift bench and tossed the magazine in a nearby trash can. Jorge traded in one form of snake oil for another. She sighed. *The more things change, the more they stay the same.*

CHAPTER EIGHTEEN

Jorge opened his eyes, curious about what was happening while he, Gwen, and Idris were being transported through space and time, presumably back to the Old Cataract Hotel. It was as if he were standing in the middle of a massive snow globe filled with sparks of light ranging in size from fireflies to dust motes, but at the same time it felt as if reality was being atomically blown apart and inverted upon itself.

Jorge pushed out with his free hand. It was absorbed into the golden particles that swarmed around him. He felt an odd prickling sensation on the hand that he could no longer see and quickly pulled it back.

It was true when scientists say that we are all stardust.

The glimmering flecks were coalescing and speeding up. His suite of rooms came into view. Buxton had managed to escape his room and was heading toward the door.

Buxton turned toward the apparition forming before him. The confusion on his face was priceless.

A loud snap-crack pierced the air, and Jorge fell against the floor. Pain shot up his ankle as it twisted against an object while landing. He checked it and found nothing was broken.

Idris ran toward Buxton. He pulled him away from the door and tackled him to the ground. The old man was struggling underneath him, but to no avail.

Jorge walked over to the pile of old man and magician. Idris pulled a pair of manacles out of thin air and slapped them onto Buxton's wrists. "Can't be too careful. Sorry about the landing, Master. Usually for first timers I do a more graduated landing, but in this case . . ." He pulled the struggling Buxton up to standing. "Sooner seemed better than later."

Jorge appreciated his servant's can-do attitude.

Idris pushed Buxton along to the couch and tossed him down.

Gwen's eyes went wide. "Be careful. He's . . . elderly."

That was one of the things Jorge most loved about her. Gwen's instinct to look out for others, even those who didn't deserve it.

Buxton slammed his head against Idris's midsection, toppling him backward.

Jorge rushed over and shoved him back down. "Stay, old man. I know exactly who you are and what you've done to me."

"Let me go, Jorge. I can make things right. I know what we did to you was wrong, but it was necessary. Let me go, and I will see to it that the agency makes it up to you."

"Nothing you can do can set things right." Jorge restrained himself from pummeling him, reminding himself there is a time and a place for everything, and now was not the time. "There is nowhere for you to go, nowhere to run. I'll make sure you'll have just as much choice as I did in the matter."

Buxton's shoulders slumped as he looked down on his mana-cled hands and shook his head. "I know you think—"

In a flash Idris was next to Jorge. He punched Buxton square in the nose. A dark red stream of blood traced down his upper lip. "Quiet. You have no right to pretend to know what my master thinks."

The old man cupped his nose as the blood trickled down his face. "Master?" The old man chuckled as he reached for his pocket square and wiped his nose. "Never in a million years would I have thought to hear the ever-powerful Idris the magi-cian call anyone—"

A bright light flared from Idris's fingertips and Buxton went limp. Jorge caught him just before he hit the ground.

"Better put him back in his room. I fear he will be out for a while."

"You know Buxton?"

"Let's say we've crossed paths."

Gwen was noticeably upset as she grabbed her keys from out of her purse. "Gotta go."

Jorge threw the key to Buxton's room at Idris. "Lock him up. I'm going to walk Gwen out."

Idris dipped into a shallow bow. "Of course, Master."

Jorge led Gwen out into the hallway. Gwen leaned into Jorge and whispered, "Do you trust him?"

"Yes, I do."

"Something about him just doesn't add up."

"Like?"

They continued down the hallway. "If he was in that bottle for a couple of hundred years, then how could Buxton, a mortal, have known him? How did he interact with him? I got the feeling Buxton was going to say something Idris didn't want us to hear before he shut him down."

"All I can say is that I've experienced a great shift in regarding what is possible and impossible. One thing I do know is that I don't trust Buxton. But if it makes you feel better, I will ask Idris about it. But you should really try to trust him. He is the way to a beautiful future for you and me. . . together. He is a second chance for us. Please, give him a chance."

They walked through the lush hotel gardens on a carpet of brilliantly colored flowers. A marble fountain made light splashing sounds in the distance. He pulled her close. "When I met you, it just felt right. This feels right. I was right then. I believe I am right now."

She leaned in and kissed him.

Jorge swung the door open. Idris stood across the room by the desk. Was it his imagination or did he see a flash of irritation cross Idris's face upon seeing his master? Could Gwen be right, or was she only sowing the seeds of doubt within him? "So I take it you've locked the old man in his room."

"Yes, he should be asleep for quite some time."

"That's too bad."

"What is the matter, Master?"

"I was hoping to get some information from him, but I guess that can wait."

"We should use this time to talk about bigger things."

Jorge didn't like the way Idris was directing him. It was time for Jorge to take the lead and reassert his dominion over his servant. "So, magician, is there any way that you can work with him in this state, extract knowledge from him while he is out?"

Idris bowed his head. "If that is what you desire. I am here to do your bidding. This spell that you request will cost you one of your wishes."

Jorge waved his hand dismissively. "Of course."

Idris crossed the room in a few quick strides and opened the door. "No time like the present."

Jorge followed the magician into the dark room.

Idris pushed back the velvet blackout curtains. Bright golden shafts of daylight cut through the star-shower of tiny dust motes.

"I have to see his face while I am working this magic. Also, you will probably want to read his expressions while you ask him questions. Sometimes, even in a sleeping state, reactions can be very telling."

Jorge looked out of the panoramic windows. "You don't think anyone can see us here?"

"And what if they could? It would only look like you are ministering to your ill friend's needs. I sincerely doubt anyone can see us up here anyway. But if it will make you feel better, I can put a ward on these rooms, a protective spell that will keep away any mortal eyes or ears from our business. Then you will have ninety-five wishes to do with what you please."

"Ninety-six?" Jorge started counting on his fingers. "I started with one hundred. I used one for getting Gwen and me back, one for re-spelling Buxton, and one for the warding. To me that adds up to ninety-seven." Was it just a mistaken tally, or was Idris intentionally trying to cheat him?

Idris folded his arms across his chest. "So right you are, Master. Now back to the task at hand. Most spells have a shelf life of around six to eight hours. After that they start to weaken, and by the next day only a small trace of the magic can be sensed."

"Hold on." Jorge went out of the room to the desk, looking for a pad of paper for his wish tracking. While Jorge shuffled through the desk contents, something struck him as missing, but he couldn't put a finger on it. In the middle drawer he found a thin pad with the hotel logo emblazoned on it.

Jorge flipped to the back and wrote in all caps, WISHES, then noted the four he'd asked for so far. He was write-walking and tripped over one of Buxton's discarded shoes and picked one up.

"What are you doing?" Idris called from the other room.

Jorge looked up from the shoe. Idris was hunched over Buxton with his head craned toward him. Jorge flipped the shoe over and rubbed the hard black rubber sole. His only reward was a few granules of sand and something that was a bit sticky. He rubbed his hand on his pants, then attempted to unscrew the heel. Apparently KHNM did not supply their agents with suicide pills like in the movies.

Jorge dropped the shoe and walked into Buxton's bedroom. Jorge shoved his list of spell requests in front of the magician. "I'll be keeping an accounting of the wishes I've asked for."

"Don't you trust me, Jorge?"

He wondered what happened to his new title of Master. "Of course, Idris. As you've noted earlier, I can be somewhat of a spendthrift. I figured it would be good to start keeping track. I just want to have an idea of where I'm at with the whole wishes thing."

"And you are using a notebook for that?"

"Do you have something magical, like a spell or some ancient counting artifact that might keep track?" Although even if he did, it would probably be good to track things himself on the side. Maybe Gwen had been right, and Idris wasn't on the up and up.

Idris laughed. "No, Master. It just seems funny to me that you, someone who has spent their life looking for extraterrestrials—advanced civilizations beyond anything that humanity has ever seen, wouldn't think to use your phone. I am sure there is an app for that."

Jorge pulled out his phone and swiped it to life. He typed in *apps for counting things on a Droi—*

Idris grabbed his arm. "No time for that now, Master. We should get started. I fear that your lady will return and—"

Jorge bristled. What exactly was he trying to imply about Gwen? "And what?"

"You will want to spend much time with her." Idris shrugged as if that was the only obvious answer to the question.

Jorge looked down at the old man as his chest rose and fell. His expression exuded the bliss of someone in a deep and restorative sleep. "Will he remember that we did this to him after the spell wears off?"

"No, he shouldn't. Does that displease you?"

"Yes, I want him to remember. I want him to know all of the secrets he let loose. I want him to suffer from that knowledge. It will be the first act of his punishment."

"What will be the second?"

"Letting him watch as those he most cares about come to harm." Jorge felt a smile creep over him as he thought of Buxton helplessly watching his beloved Alex writhe in pain.

"And then what, Master?"

"I want the agency destroyed. They will have to abide by the laws set forth in civilized society, not answer to the agenda of a few."

"I think it is important that as you question him, you should have your sights set at what you want to accomplish."

"Let's begin."

The magician splayed his hands above the old man's body.

Jorge grabbed the magician's wrist. "Wait. Would it cost extra to have him remember?"

"I will have to cast three spells simultaneously: one would be the truth-telling spell, the other would be to keep him awake and compliant, and the third will be the remembering spell. It will cost you three wishes, and the spells will only last about an hour, maybe longer if the subject is compliant, much less if the subject has a strong constitution."

"But no matter what it will be three wishes?"

Idris nodded.

Jorge pulled out his explorer's notebook and changed the number to ninety-four. He then made a further notation of three wishes for the interrogation of subject *A*. He liked the idea of using a code instead of Buxton's name. It felt far more spy-like.

Idris once again hovered his hands over Buxton's body. A blue glow surrounded him and the old man.

"Why blue?" asked Jorge.

"Blue is the color of truth. It is also the color of eternity. I need you to be silent as I work the spell." The light was starting to intensify. It wasn't necessarily getting brighter but somehow denser.

Jorge moved closer to the bed and leaned into the mattress.

Buxton's entire body was now encased in a cocoon of swirling blue light. Idris chanted in a language Jorge had never heard before. His voice was low and reverberated like a didgeridoo as he rocked back and forth. Jorge's body vibrated in syncopation with the humming.

A peak of the soft blue fog formed over the mummiform body of Buxton.

Idris clapped his hands, creating small charges of electricity. Buxton's eyes flashed open, then widened with fear. His body jerked about in an attempt to escape the sack of magic that Idris wove around him. "We begin."

Silence filled the air around this odd trio of men. For the first time in a long time, Jorge was at a loss for words. He found himself staring dumbly at the old man. For all the thousands of questions he knew he wanted to ask Buxton, none came forward.

The old man was still struggling against the spell. The fear in his eyes sharpened his determination.

"Don't underestimate him because of his age. He has a powerfully resistant constitution. I may not be able to hold him for long. I guess you could just take your time. It will just cost you another three wishes."

Idris's taunt cleared Jorge's mind, enabling him to focus. He knew exactly what to ask. The question he'd been obsessed with ever since his memories came flooding back—why? "Did you enjoy playing God with my memories?"

Buxton's body twitched with resistance. He blurted it out. "It was the most humane choice."

"Humane? Your actions would make a tyrant blush."

"There were those in the room who thought you should be eliminated, erased from the annals of humanity. I fought for you. Wiping your memory was a compromise."

"Who would want me dead?"

"The Gods."

"What sort of crime did I commit that would justify a penalty of death?"

"You happened to be at the wrong place at the wrong time.

You saw things no mortal was ever supposed to see. The secret that the Gods walked among us was kept from mortals for close to three thousand years. If it got out, there might have been riots in the street, civil chaos. Humans rely on the basic constructs of what they perceive to be reality, their expected world. The skin that divides the expected world and all the other realms is a delicate membrane. Like an egg yolk, once its surface has been punctured there is no putting the yolk back. Most humans don't have the capacity to imagine the infinite, to ponder questions of unending dimensions."

"But that is all speculation."

"Can you imagine magic in the hands of mortals? What would become of society under the influence of magic? It is human nature to seek out that which is powerful."

"You should be ashamed of yourself, Buxton. You hold the reins of power in an organization who is there to protect humans. Aren't you selling your species a little short? I don't know how many times mainstream archaeologists have ridiculed me about my unorthodox theories. You have placed me squarely in their crosshairs as a lunatic, but at the same time you have always known the Gods and their magic exist. Isn't it a bit hypocritical for you, a mortal, to be on such an ideological high horse?"

"Before KHNM was founded and before the Gods chose to walk among man, magic was in the realm of man. Guided by a few powerful magician families. That is what kept it all in check. Once the Gods stopped receiving sacrifice, once their names were no longer being spoken, their power was diminished. It would have been a danger to let them dwindle down to nothing, stopping the natural balance in our world. They decided to bank their powers and walk among men."

Now they were starting to get into something interesting. "What do you mean, banked their powers?"

Buxton's head twitched back and forth as he struggled to keep his mouth clamped shut. He finally gave in; his expression reflected an unwilling defeat as the secrets spilled out of him. "They created a container to hold all of their powers."

"So where is this container now?"

Idris's hands were moving slowly over the fog-like cocoon of the spell. "He sure can struggle for an old man. I can feel the spell weakening. We need to wrap this up."

"So, again, where is this God container located?"

"At KHNM headquarters under the Met. It needs to be dismantled."

"Why on earth would you do that?"

"Now that the Gods have returned to the Field of Reeds, to their Immortal palaces, it is an empty vessel." Buxton was talking in a measured way. Was he trying to skate the fine line between truth and lie? Was he trying to outthink the spell Idris put on him?

"I don't believe him, Master. They are trying to dismantle it because they fear its power. You can't have something holding the power of eight or so Gods for two thousand years and not have some magical residue."

Jorge stroked his chin, wondering at the power that vessel might still hold. "Remember that memory machine I wanted to build? The one that would extract all of Buxton's knowledge? Do you think this vessel, this God machine, if we were able to procure it, could play a part in its construction? Do you think the magical residue could aid in that endeavor?"

"You have a keen mind, Master."

"Let me go, Jorge. You have no idea what misery that kind of power can bring." Buxton's shoulders jumped in place as if he were a bound mummy trying to escape from his wrappings.

"Old man, I don't think you have any idea what sort of misery is in store for you." Jorge stood and walked over to Idris. "Change of plans. I think retrieving that God containment vessel should definitely be added to our list."

"Of course Master, as soon as my associate takes care of Ms. Philothea."

"No. You can't . . ." Buxton struggled harder than ever to escape his magical bindings.

Jorge turned to leave the room. Once he got to the door, he looked back at his servant hovering over the old man, the blue magic-fog starting to fade. "Idris, revive that sleeping spell. We've got work to do."

CHAPTER NINETEEN

A small grey stone skittered across the large open plaza in front of the Beinecke Library as Alex made her way to the entrance. The massive building looked like a large stone sarcophagus for a modern-minimalist pharaoh. Its honeycomb-like exterior was made with a grid of Vermont granite inset with squares of marble. Slabs of marble that were cut a quarter-inch thick allowed natural light to permeate the building and protected Yale's unparalleled rare book collection.

Alex neared the main entrance and reached down to pick up the stone that she kicked away. It was a pale grey color, much like the library. She placed it in the secret compartment in her scribe's bag. It would be a small memento of this amazing building.

As she passed through the glass doors, a familiar flutter of excitement stirred within her. As far back as she could remember, Alex always experienced a delightful giddiness at being surrounded by so many books. In this respect, she was certainly her father's daughter.

Alex admired the library's interior, surrounded by the green-grey ethereal light that passed through the marble slabs. The soft illumination revealed swirls and stripes in the living stone. The color gradations of the organic patterns made her think of the alabaster lamps sold in Egyptian souks. She felt like a jinn willingly captured in a magical vessel.

In front of her stood a glass tower that encased some of the rarest books in North America. Five stories filled with a vast universe of informational delights. At the base of this Rubik's Cube-like structure and between two sleek grand staircases lay Alex's destination, the reception desk.

The desk attendant looked up at Alex. She looked tired, making Alex think it must be midterms. "I am Alex Philothea from the Oriental Institute. I am here to see Dr. Albright Knox."

"He was called away on an urgent matter and hopes to catch up with you later. His assistant, Dr. Lindsey, can help you. He is unavailable for the next two hours and can call you when he is free."

She was disheartened that she might have come all the way up here for nothing, being certain that this Dr. Lindsey wouldn't have the info she needed. Alex wrote down her number and handed it to the receptionist. "I guess I will wander around until he calls. I can't imagine a better place to have to kill some time. Maybe I'll even get a little research done." She hoped she could figure out what the number meant on the back of Dr. Knox's card.

"If you head upstairs, any one of our librarians can assist you in finding whatever it is that you are looking for."

It didn't take long to locate the book attached to the reference number on the back of Knox's business card. It wasn't located in the rare books collection. In fact, it was shelved in a completely different library on campus.

Another surprise was that the book had nothing to do with ancient Egypt, other than it was about one of its conquerors and Alex's ancestor, Alexander the Great. The book was not extraordinary in any way. By all appearances it was a general studies book.

She flipped through it, but nothing stood out to her. Why would Dr. Knox direct attention to this book? It was yet another dead end. At the rate she was going, she had little chance of either figuring out how to dismantle the God machine or finding those books of magic.

Was this book some sort of message to her father from Knox? Alex hoped that she would be able to ask him later on. Attempting the obvious, she flipped to the index. Marked out in bright neon pink was Macedon, Philip of, pgs. 321, 322. Was it some sort of code? She grabbed her phone and quickly took pictures of the pages.

Alex slipped the book back on its shelf and made her way out of the library.

Once outside, she heard her name being called. Alex turned toward the voice. A tall, handsome man with jet-black hair and blue eyes walked toward her. Her breath caught. Although he really looked nothing like Niles, there was something about this man that held an uncanny resemblance to him. Alex immediately felt drawn to him, but the unthinking immediacy of it sent alarm bells ringing through her. She wasn't certain if the resistance to her attraction to him came from some residue of her remaining feelings for Niles, or something else entirely.

He reached out and shook her hand. His fingers were cold. Was it a sign of a warm heart? "Rendell Lindsey. Glad I caught up with you, Ms. Philothea."

"You can call me Alex."

"I'm sorry that Dr. Knox is unable to meet with you at the moment. Dr. Knox asked that I invite you to his residence for a light dinner tonight. He instructed me to entertain you until then." A small smile broke across his face, warming his ice-blue eyes for a brief second.

"I'd love to. Thank you for the offer, but it's been a long day. I think I might head to my hotel and take a moment or two to rest and get ready for dinner."

"How about I have a car pick you up at the New Haven Hotel at seven to bring you to the residence?"

Alex was taken aback. "How did you know I was staying there?"

He laughed stiffly. "Seems like that is where everyone stays."

⌇

Before she knew it, it was time to be picked up for her dinner date with Rendell and Dr. Knox. She hoped to get some answers. When the driver pulled up to the residence, it looked like a respectable and moderately fancy house, appropriate to the director of one of the finest libraries in the nation.

Rendell opened the door. As she walked through the threshold, the scent of baking lasagna filled the air, making her realize how hungry she was.

"The cook is running a bit late, and so is Knox. He hopes to be here within the hour." He slipped her coat off and hung it in the closet. "How about we have a quick drink in the salon."

"Do you live here too?"

"No, but we work so closely together that it would almost make sense for us to be roommates."

Alex followed Rendell into the salon. He motioned for her to sit in one of the armchairs. It was a small but well-appointed room with rich wood tones and floral brocade furnishings. A small drink cart was near a cozy brick fireplace beyond the sitting area. Stashed in the corner was a small desk. Alex wondered if that was where Dr. Knox did his work.

Much like the KHNM residency the furniture looked as if it had been in situ for quite some time and would be there to welcome the next library director, whoever that might be. Some of the items looked more recently purchased, but within keeping of the original antique style.

"What would you like?" Rendell made his way to the drink cart.

"How about a vodka and tonic?" Since she didn't like it very much, vodka tended to be her drink of choice for social situations where she could benefit from the conversational lubricant but wanted to keep her head straight.

"Got it." The crystal glasses rang out as the large square ice cubes fell into them.

Rendell pointed up to an oil painting hanging above the mantle. "Believe it or not, that is a portrait of the very first director of the Yale libraries. At the time they called him the proctor of knowledge." He laughed. "I think it has a little more character than 'director.' Maybe we should go retro."

"Well, I guess that would mean that Knox would need to get used to wearing a powdered wig."

He chuckled. "You should look at it up close. The brushwork is amazing."

Alex walked over to the portrait. The man in the presumably powdered wig looked perpetually bored. The artist's skill at making the subject's boredom palpable and ever-so-slightly humorous was great.

Alex glanced over at Rendell. He quickly stuffed something into his pocket, then grabbed their drinks.

Rendell handed Alex her drink and then stood next to her. Both beverages sported a wedge of lime on the lip of the glass. "I find the lime adds a nice light note. I hope you like it." He motioned to the artwork in front of them. "This painting could be one of the best-kept secrets here on campus. If the curator of the collection realized it was here, I think he would find it better placed in one of the galleries."

"It's awfully nice." Alex sipped her drink. It tasted a little odd, maybe a little stronger than normal, or maybe it was the lime. "What vodka is this? I rather like it."

Rendell coughed into a cuffed hand. "Oh nothing fancy, just a little Ketel One."

Alex took another sip. "Are there any other artworks of note in the house?"

"There are a couple lovely landscapes in the master bedroom, but I don't want to be accused of luring you up to see my etchings."

Alex wasn't sure what she thought of Rendell's new flirty side. "How about any other rooms that won't incur a blemish on our reputations."

"Follow me to the library, or what I like to call the office, but don't let the Proctor of Knowledge hear it."

As Alex fell in behind Rendell she realized she'd forgotten to have lunch, and the vodka was hitting her harder than normal. "May I use the restroom?"

"Of course, it's right down the hall and to the left, just past that knockoff Ming dynasty vase."

Alex headed down the hallway and glanced down at the vase. She was no expert, but if it was a fake, it was a darned good one.

Once she was in the bathroom, she dumped out half of the vodka, flushed the toilet, then added some water to make up the difference. She never liked to make the host feel awkward and that their hospitality wasn't to her liking.

Rendell was waiting for her at the end of the corridor. "All right, next stop, the gallery of landscapes."

Rendell slid open two large pocket doors, revealing a large room encased by bookshelves. Two paintings filled the only spaces that were void of books. Rendell walked over to one of them. It was a depiction of rolling golden fields of shorn hay with a dusky blue sky and a puff of clouds.

Alex sipped her drink.

Rendell pointed at the painting. "Knox purchased both of the landscapes in this room. He loves to spend his off time scouring tag sales and auctions. I can't recall the name of the artist, but Knox assured me that the artist was very popular in the 1880s in the Midwest."

Alex took another sip of her drink. She couldn't believe how light-headed she felt. She made her way to a sizable leather chair facing the large wooden desk and sat down. "I don't know what has come over me suddenly, but I think I need to head back to my hotel. I am feeling a bit faint." She staggered forward as she tried to stand up.

Rendell stood and blocked her way. He grasped her shoulders. His eyes were oddly desperate. "You aren't going anywhere."

She sagged back into the seat under the gentle pressure of his hands.

His expression was probably meant to be comforting. It was anything but. "He told me you wouldn't be hurt. Just try and relax."

"Who—?" Was it Knox? Alex's vision faded into a blur like a camera unable to find its focus. She could feel herself retreating into a hazy fog.

Rendell crossed the room and was talking on the phone. She could only assume he was talking to the "him" that promised she wouldn't get hurt.

She tried to focus on what Rendell was saying.

"She's out." Rendell shifted his weight from side to side. Alex opened her eyes just a hair but closed them as he turned to face her. "No, she didn't drink it all, about half, so I am guessing she should be out cold for about four hours or so. I'm going to wait until dark to remove her—the less chance of a neighbor seeing her the better."

Rendell pulled the phone away from his ear as if the person on the other side was yelling very loudly.

"This ends with her," Rendell said. "I know I owe you a lot, but killing my mentor should clear the slate."

Rendell had killed Knox. Her heart thumped in her chest. She was trapped in a house with a killer.

"Yes, Idris." Rendell slipped his phone in his pocket, then headed down the corridor.

She was alone, but for how long? She must escape. She pushed herself from the chair as her body moved like a water-logged sack of sand. Her head spun. She leaned back against the cushion to fortify her equilibrium. A new wave of panic raced through her as she thought about what Rendell might have in store for her.

The adrenaline coursing through her body helped clear her mind. She slowly leaned out of the chair, willing the dizziness down. She stagger-stepped away from the chair. She needed to take it slow and easy.

The house was large, but not palatial. She hoped Rendell was caught up in some task that would at least give her enough time to get through the front door.

Alex slowly made her way down the hallway, dancing a delicate line between steadying herself as she progressed and trying not to knock over any of the knickknacks, announcing her attempted escape. A swell of dizziness overtook her. Her shoulder slammed into the wall, knocking a picture to the floor.

Footsteps thumped toward her. There wasn't much time. She looked around for a weapon. She spotted the non-Ming vase. It looked heavy enough to possibly do some damage.

She hefted it up just as Rendell's shoulder contacted her ribs, sending them both tumbling down. Her vision swirled at the fast motion. She blinked at the two faces of Rendell below her. The vase rolled away, unbroken.

His arms shot up and encircled her. He flipped her on her back and pinned her down. "Stop struggling. I was told you won't get hurt."

Alex let herself go limp and half closed her eyes.

"Atta girl." He reached into his pocket and pulled out a syringe. "Didn't think I'd need this, but—"

In an instant she thrust her knee up as hard as she could.

The syringe fell as his hands reached to his crotch.

Alex thrust her pelvis up, bucking him off her. She kicked him away.

She pushed herself up then grabbed the vase. Lifting it high above her, she brought it down hard on his head. There was a sick thud when the vase made contact and shattered into a million pieces.

He looked to be out cold, but Alex didn't want to take any chances. She picked up the syringe. *What's good for the goose is good for the gander.*

CHAPTER TWENTY

J orge scanned the vast desert landscape as they drove to
the new lair Idris magically built. The magician was
particularly pleased with himself. Jorge couldn't wait to
see what awaited them. He glanced back at Gwen. She
was staring out into the distance. The unconscious Buxton was
strapped in next to her. It was clear by the look on her face that
she wasn't thrilled with the seating arrangement. Jorge hoped
that he would be able to make everything up to her soon. Once
things got rolling, he planned to shower her with so much treasure it would have made Cleopatra blush.

When Jorge and Idris explored the idea of this new center of
operations, Idris suggested that the remote desert would be the
best location, away from prying eyes. It made sense to build it
over the portal that Jorge and Buxton returned from the Netherworld through. If Idris could open it back up, they could do some
unscheduled treasure hunting.

Idris had wanted Jorge to come along with him to conjure the new opal mining headquarters. After the magician had cast a spell over the phone on the Egyptian minister of petroleum and mineral resources about digging rights, Jorge sent Idris on his way to build their new digs. He had complete faith that Idris would know what magic would be required to build it. Jorge told the magician that he needed to stay and keep an eye on Buxton, but in reality, the reason he wanted to stay behind was to be around when Gwen came back.

They were driving in the desert for quite some time. As Jorge started to recognize landmarks around them, it was apparent that they should be close to the portal, but all he could see was a dilapidated shack in the far distance. They pulled toward the structure and came to a stop. Jorge was confused. "Do you want me to drive for a while?"

Idris opened the car door and hopped down to the desert floor. "We are here."

Jorge made his way over to Idris.

At closer inspection the ramshackle building was larger than Jorge anticipated. It stretched out into the distance. "How is this our headquarters? It looks like it is only just barely winning the fight to stay upright."

Idris swept his hands upward, the air above him distorted like thermal waves. "The mine is a front. Something to be seen and instantly forgotten. But the rest—I think you will be impressed."

"The rest?"

"I can't wait for you to see it all." A sly smile pulled across his face as Idris opened the door and ushered them in.

Inside, walkways crisscrossed each other like a wood-slatted plaid. Jorge inspected the earth that was excavated to a depth of about three feet. A miniature railroad ran on both sides of each walkway, sporting tiny mining carts. "Those are for the miners to collect the desert opals once they are recovered from the earth."

"We're going to hire miners?"

"Only when we have visitors." Idris snapped his fingers, and in a blink of an eye the shed came to life. Each excavated section had a person digging, equipped with a bright headlamp and a small garden trowel. The small rail bins rested nearby with varying amounts of desert opal within. "The performance these hologram-like beings put on is quite exceptional. As you can see, there is a cart system that brings the stones to the line supervisor." Idris pointed to the far end of the shed, where a hologram of an old man in a blue galabeya sat at a desk stroking his long beard as he watched over the workers. "He inspects the opals before they are sent to be washed and packaged up for delivery. Or, that is the story we'll tell people." Idris snapped his fingers and all their employees disappeared instantly. "I'll install an auto-magic switch so you can turn them on and off like lights if needed, just in case I am not here when people come around."

"Excellent work, magician."

"You've only seen the tip of the pyramid, Master." Idris led them down a pathway that ran through the center of the shack. About three-quarters of the way to the end of the shed he changed course, heading into an area shrouded in darkness. "Now this is going to blow your mind."

Idris squatted and pulled up on the wooden slats, revealing a hidden passageway. Jorge knelt down and peered into the dark hole with a ladder propped up within it.

"This entrance has been warded for only the three of us to come and go. I will have to alter the spell if you want anyone else to have access."

"What about Buxton? You're not just going to leave him out in the desert, are you?" asked Gwen.

Jorge put his arm around Gwen and pulled her close. He loved how she couldn't help but let her humanity shine, even when it came to her beloved's nemesis.

"He can come in, but never go out."

Jorge laughed. "Like a roach motel."

"Exactly," affirmed Idris.

Jorge rubbed his hand between Gwen's shoulder blades, hoping his touch might smooth over whatever objections she might have. "What happens if somebody who is not on the VIP list tries to come in?"

"Their body will be subjected to about twenty-five thousand volts of electricity."

"Shocking, isn't it?" Jorge laughed as he leaned into Gwen.

She pulled away.

"So, what is at the bottom of the ladder?" Gwen stepped forward.

"Your private quarters."

"Down there?" Gwen's face flushed. "You expect us to live in a dark cellar? We are humans, Idris, not mushrooms."

Idris motioned toward the ladder. "Ladies first. I think you will be pleasantly surprised."

She glanced at Jorge for reassurance.

"Go ahead." Jorge nudged her. "I will be right after you."

Gwen didn't seem convinced as she carefully made her way down each rung until she disappeared into the darkness. The soft plunking sound of each step she made became harder to hear the further she got. From the depths they heard a sharp intake of breath.

Jorge rushed to the opening.

Her laughter greeted his arrival, echoing up the shaft. "Jorge, you will just die. This is amazing."

"After you, Master." Idris swept his hands over the opening. "Someone who could rule the world has to have a palace that will instill wonder and fear into those who dare to tread near them."

Jorge maneuvered himself down the first rungs of the ladder. "Yeah, but twenty whole wishes?"

"You get what you pay for."

Jorge couldn't quite read the look on Idris's face as he made his way down the ladder.

Gwen's voice reverberated through the shaft. "Jorge. Aren't you coming? I can't see you, and I have no idea how to get back down."

Down?

An unseen force pulled at the lower half of his body as a bone-chilling cold pooled around his calves. It slowly moved up his body. It was like trying to move through cold pudding. Jorge lost his grasp of the ladder as he fell into the darkness. His feet pushed through a membrane; its remnants tickled his face as he passed through. Then he slammed against a hard surface.

Jorge opened his eyes. Blindingly bright light surrounded him. As his vision cleared, all he could see was Gwen's rapturous expression. She ran up to him and hugged him. "Isn't it amazing? It's like a giant aerial terrarium."

They were standing hundreds of feet above the desert on a transparent platform. He clutched at Gwen for dear life as his heart thudded in his chest.

"You're squeezing me too hard." Gwen pried herself away from him.

A shock of adrenaline shot through Jorge. He couldn't

breathe. He fell backwards. His stomach reeled. Instinctively, he reached back to break his fall, and his hand slapped against something cool, smooth, and solid.

Gwen stood above him and held out her hand to help him up. "Are you okay?"

An intense dizziness flooded over him as he reached for her hand. He closed his eyes again. This was just like those dreams. The terrifying dream flickered through his mind like a flash motion animation. This was how they always started. Then the floor would open underneath him, and he would plummet to the ground. Hearing Idris arrive, he forced himself to open his eyes again.

Idris drew him to a bench that stood out against the airy nothingness around them with a pearly opaqueness. Out of thin air he pulled a chain of globular crystals strung together with a tinsel-like substance and yanked it down. A blue opaque gas billowed out, creeping up vertically from all corners of the platform, giving the space a solid shape.

Jorge closed his eyes and breathed deeply, trying to calm himself. Gwen's soft fingertips rubbed his head with gentle strokes.

"What is the matter, Master? Do you not like what I've created?"

Jorge's anxiety poured out of him as the room around him visually solidified. As an adventurer by trade, he'd always prided himself on his daring—no mountain too high, no canyon too deep, no journey too dangerous. That was until he started having those dreams after departing the Netherworld. He would dream about a room eerily like this one, but in its transparent state. It started with him standing solidly on the transparent floor in wonderment as to how it was possible. Then, without warning, the space under him would open up. He would fall, screaming, down and down, until he slammed against the ground with a sickening crunch, as if his entire skeleton shattered. He would wake up sopping wet with sweat.

Jorge opened his eyes. "No, it just threw me for a loop." He didn't want Idris to see any weaknesses in him.

"This is only the entryway, so to speak. There are many floors below us in this sky castle, including chambers for sleeping and recreating, as well as a fully equipped prison." The magician tilted his head at the still-unconscious figure of Buxton that was slumped against the now visible walls. "Every king should be able to survey their kingdom, right? I intended for this fortress to make you feel like an all-powerful being hovering over the earth like a mortal God."

"I appreciate that you are trying to make me feel the part, as if I could rule."

Idris looked cross. "Will rule. For a mortal you have achieved much. If anyone can rule the world, it is you."

Gwen's hands stopped making lazy circles on Jorge's scalp. "The world?"

Jorge leaned back and gazed up at Gwen. Her dismay was evident in her expression. "I couldn't see it myself at first. Maybe I can make the world a better place and bring to light all the information that is being kept from mortals. Just think of the possibilities, love."

She still looked unsure. Jorge stood and then wrapped his arms around her. He whispered into her ear. "Remember all the dreams we had, and how we thought one day we could change the world?"

"Yes, but—"

"This is our chance, babe." He squeezed her tight, and she

relaxed against him. They would talk about this later, but this was not a conversation to have in front of the hired help. "So, just to be clear, the blue walls and blue floors are going to be permanent, right?"

"Well, there could be a problem with that."

"What kind of problem?"

"A cost of magic problem."

"What exactly do you mean, magician?"

"There are two major concerns about keeping the borders of this sky castle in an opaque state. First and foremost, if I attempted to keep the current masking spell going on an ongoing basis, it would drain all of my powers, and the cost to you would be exorbitant. It would pretty quickly deplete your remaining wishes, making you the happy owner of an amazing opaque blue sky-hung palace without the aid of a magical servant. If you just want to live out your life up here with your lady love and forget everything else we've planned, then say yes and set me free of my commitment to you. But if you want to see your true potential bloom and do good for your kind, then no, they cannot stay this way."

"I command you make it right, magician. I charged you to make a headquarters, not some sort of invisible castle in the sky. It is not made right. You must remake it. At no cost to me."

Idris crossed his arms. "I can't. Any sort of delay to our plan could cause great consequences to the outcome. Any moment now, I will receive a call from my servant telling us that he has the girl in hand. Once she is delivered, we must not delay."

"Girl?" Gwen pulled out of Jorge's arms. Jorge recognized the flair of jealousy in Gwen's eyes. He tried not to smile at the thought.

He swept a strand of hair from her face and smoothed it behind her ear. "She is going to get another book for me."

Jorge faced Idris, whose arms were folded over his chest, making him look like a stiffened and mummified pharaoh. Maybe he just needed a bit of flattery to make the medicine go down. "I am sure it would not take you that long, being such a powerful wizard."

Idris harrumphed. "If my memory serves me, you gave me no instruction, no parameters. In fact, your exact words were, 'You know best.' I can change it, but for a cost. If I do change it, not only would your wish reserves be depleted, but it would eliminate the camouflage that comes with the transparency. A consistent solid color would be noticeable with the change of weather from day to day. What exactly bothers you about it? Are you afraid of heights?"

Jorge kicked himself for not being more specific about the build-out, but who in their right mind would think to say, "Oh by the way, if you do build me a lair suspended in the sky, please don't make the rooms all transparent, as I have been having bad dreams lately."

"So, you won't change it?"

"I think I have a solution." Idris snapped his fingers, producing a pair of sunglasses, and handed them to Jorge.

"I don't see how this will help anything." The frames glowed faintly. "What's with the halo of light around them?"

"Interesting, you can actually see the magic in them." Idris continued. "Put them on."

Jorge slipped the sunglasses on. Idris snapped his fingers. Suddenly the space around him was no longer transparent.

As if reading his mind, Idris said, "Tip them down your nose."

Jorge pushed them down a smidgen and looked over the rim of the frames. The area around him was clear again.

"A very wish-efficient solution, I must say. Problem solved, right master?"

"I would have to wear these all the time?"

"I will make your bedroom appear solid during the night hours. That wouldn't be too taxing on my powers. I can only imagine how awkward it would be to try and, uh, sleep in those."

Gwen blushed.

"But other than nighttime, I would always have to wear these?"

"While you are in residence, of course. Or until you are able to conquer your fear." An infinitesimal smile flickered across the magician's face.

"I wouldn't call it fear. I've just been having vivid dreams as of late." The words came out sounding far more defensive than Jorge would have liked.

The magicians bowed deeply. "Sorry if I offended you. I have faith that you will beat it. Just as you have conquered all that has crossed your path, great Master."

Gwen sidled up to Jorge and hooked her arms in his. "Those glasses are quite dashing."

Buoyed by Gwen's comment, Jorge suggested exploring the rest of the sky castle.

Idris gave them the full tour. The room that they had arrived in was a widow's walk of sorts at the very top of the sky castle. Idris explained that its purpose was mostly for relaxation and contemplation. He built it mainly for Gwen, as he and Jorge would be spending most of their time working in the laboratory. The magician had envisioned it as a scenic place where she could put her feet up and read.

It was plain to see that Gwen didn't take kindly to being relegated to a sunroom. Although, as the magician revealed the large hidden bookcases containing an abundance of jewel-toned books of every shape and size, her mood lightened palpably.

What seemed to impress Gwen the most was their private suite. All of the furnishings shimmered with the magic that created them, as if diamonds were a readily available material for furniture. In the center of the room was what looked like a large puffy white cloud.

"That must be the bed." Gwen ran to it and threw herself into the fluffiness and instantly disappeared.

Jorge charged toward it. Standing at the fluffy perimeter, he leaned over to see Gwen's blissful expression. "It is divine. Like lying on cotton candy. You've got to give it a try."

He offered his hand to pull her up. "Later dear, we have plenty of time to try it out." She grabbed his hand and extracted herself from the bed. He kept hold of her hand and led her to the farthest reaches of the room. Fortified by her presence, he slipped the sunglasses down his nose.

"It's gorgeous, isn't it?" she asked.

Jorge squeezed her hand.

Idris joined them at the edge of the room. "I hope you are pleased with it, Master. As you can see, down below is what I like to call the infinite pool. You can literally swim in the sky. If you look closely, you can pick out the pearlescent outline marking the full wet bar, tables, sunshades, and loungers. There is a staircase that leads down to it." Idris pointed in that direction. "Your suite of rooms comes equipped with a library retrieval system from the bookshelves located in the widow's walk. It can retrieve books that will suit your mood perfectly. If you desire something specific, just call it out. I will leave the two of you now to explore your quarters while I go deal with our guest and bring up your luggage. Maybe we could all meet down in the dungeon in twenty minutes or so?"

"That's one room we've not gone to. How do we get there?" asked Gwen.

Idris went to a luminescent gold arch in the middle of the room. "This will take you to any part of the castle." He swiped his hand over a control panel in the wall. A small, bright bluish-white light flashed as it was activated. "Come closer."

The panel was nicely labeled—*Dungeon, Pool, Dining Room, Work Room*. What was lacking was a label that said *Magician's Room*. "Where will you be staying?"

"My rooms are not a part of this system."

"But I am assuming that you will be able to pop in here at any time. That doesn't seem right."

"I am here to serve day and night no matter the time. Just call for me, and I will be there. As a magician, I have certain secret rites and rituals I have to perform that cannot be seen with mortal eyes." The tone in Idris's voice was final.

Jorge didn't like it, but now didn't seem the time to argue with Idris.

Idris pressed the button, and a door slid open from the gold-trimmed arch.

The blue light labeled *Widow's Walk* started flashing white. "It looks like it is time." He stepped inside. The magician was sucked upward like he was in a human-sized pneumonic tube.

"Gone in a flash." Gwen's voice telegraphed relief that Idris left them alone. "I don't think he has your best interests in mind."

"Oh, I don't know, Gwen. He seems to be treating me in a manner that I think a powerful wizard would treat someone if they were bound by magic to serve them. He is an immortal creature with vast powers. It must be a little demeaning to be tethered to the whims of a mortal."

"But don't you find it odd that he switches back and forth between helping you meet your destiny and nickel-and-diming you in your spell allowance? It's like he is pushing you in an entirely different direction that you never intended. All you wanted was revenge, and now he has visions of world domination swimming around in your head."

"Maybe he sees great potential in me. He has seen a lot of things. Maybe he wants to partner in making the world a better place without all this secrecy and underhanded deals. We do have common enemies."

Jorge wrapped his arms around her.

"I don't know." She pulled away, then turned to face him. "I think he is hiding something from you. Just promise you'll stay alert for anything that feels off. Against the odds, we've found each other again. I don't want to lose you."

"You have my word."

"Good." She peered down at the sparkling pool. "I need a dip."

Jorge watched Gwen as she strode confidently down the nearly invisible stairs. Off in the distance a large hawk or some other bird of prey was flying toward the sky castle. When it came close, it slowly looped around in wide arcs near the castle. It was almost as if it was looking for something. Or, maybe it was only perplexed at seeing humans wandering around at this altitude. It swooped just over Gwen's head.

She stood by the edge of the pool. Gwen reached behind and unzipped her dress; she shimmied out of it, letting the fabric pool around her ankles. She stepped over the pile of linen and slipped off her heels. Jorge was filled with a voyeuristic lust at seeing her nearly naked, exposed to the bright light of day.

Gwen dipped her toes into the water. Reaching back, she unsnapped her bra and slid her panties down. She turned back at Jorge and allowed him to adore her as he gazed down at her naked beauty. She dove into the pool; her look was an invitation. An invitation he would have to ignore. Until he could get a handle on the height thing, no matter how tempting, Jorge would have to forgo any water sports.

⌇

After swimming Gwen took a shower. When she emerged from the bathroom, she was wearing something he would never have imagined her picking out. It was a tailored dress with pastel pink and green roses covering every inch of the fabric. It looked like something the perfect nineteen fifties housewife would wear. Her feet were adorned with a very nonsensible pair of mint green high heels. The dress was snug and hugged her curves. "Where'd you get that?"

Gwen sauntered over and swiped her hand over a surface with a shimmering border. "Check it out."

A small cupboard opened up, large enough for one person to stand in. It was like a department store dressing room, except on the floor was a small round stand. Gwen stepped onto the stand. She smiled at Jorge as it twirled around. Lines of magic collected around her as if she were the cardboard core in a human-sized cotton candy maker. The wheel stopped. Gwen was wearing a lion tamer outfit, whip and all.

She smacked the whip against her hand. "Been a bad boy, Jorgie?" She smiled wickedly and jumped off the pedestal. "It's a gas. All you have to do is think of what you want to wear, and before you know it, you are."

He jumped in.

When the spinning stopped, Gwen burst out laughing. "Rawr, baby."

Jorge swatted his plushly pawed hand at her and stepped out of the closet. "Ready to tame this wildcat?"

She picked up her whip and grabbed his tail, pulling him to the bed.

Idris could wait.

⤳⤳

It took Jorge and Gwen a while to get themselves back in order. They had lain in the cloud bed for quite some time before they attempted the dressing machine. They both managed to change into something somewhat more reasonable. Jorge chose a fresh set of explorer-wear. Gwen pulled out all the stops with a delightful gold silk sheath that was covered with a spray of tiny gemlike sequins of purple, blue, and green.

They stood before the metallic panel listing all the rooms.

"Feeling like a visit to the dungeon?"

She smiled up at him radiantly. "I thought you'd never ask."

Jorge stepped into the small space that was about the size of a stand-up shower. The floor vibrated under his feet. He smiled confidently at Gwen and pushed the glowing button labeled *Dungeon*. A light flashed overhead. The space below him gave way. A surprised gasp escaped him as he fell downward. His hands flew out to stop the unexpected movement, but his only reward was slamming his knuckles on the hard transparent tube as he was swooshed downward. His body spiraled down and around as if he were sliding through a corkscrew-shaped water-slide. He was picking up speed until his body was ejected onto a cloudlike puff. He could hear Gwen squealing with joy as she slid toward him. Jorge extracted himself from the fluffy mass. He made his way over to Idris. "That isn't exactly what I was expecting."

"You must have enjoyed it, yes?"

"I think *enjoy* might not be the word I would use."

Gwen landed in the cloud-stopper in a flurry of exhilarated laughter, as if she'd just ridden the most incredible roller coaster. "Now that was amazing. I've been to many amusement parks, but their loops aren't nearly as tight as those ones." She slapped Idris on the back. "Great job on that. Just enough *g*'s to get a person giggling all the way down."

Jorge was glad that she liked it so well. "So moving up you have the vacuum effect, and down is the trapdoor/twisty-slide option?"

Idris nodded.

"If the up part is half as fun as down, I'm gonna just love it!"

Idris beamed at her praise.

Jorge swung around at a sputtering sound coming from behind him. He was surprised he hadn't noticed the large gilded cage that hung from the ceiling with a sagging Buxton leaning up against the bars.

The cage swayed as the old man awoke. "Where am I?" He pulled himself up by grasping the bars. Confusion spread across his face as he came to realize he was standing in a cage suspended hundreds of feet above the desert floor.

Idris answered. "You are exactly where you think you are."

Buxton's eyes slammed shut, and he leaned heavily against the bars. "Am I still in Egypt?"

"Open your eyes, take a long look." Idris sneered at the old man.

It didn't sit right that Idris was taunting Buxton. Not out of sympathy, but more like the irritation of having someone else open the present that was meant for you. Jorge strode over to the cage and pushed it, making it swing. Buxton lost his balance and toppled to the bottom of the cage. His head slammed against the solid-gold base. Buxton slowly sat up. A small rivulet of blood ran from his nose to the tip of his mouth.

"You had to know this was coming, old man. You had to know that you were going to reap what you sowed one day. I know exactly who you are and what you did to me." Jorge shoved at the stilled cage, making it sway again. "And to think, I risked my life to save you."

"I will always be in your—"

"Shut up, old man." Idris glared at Buxton.

"Magician, I was thinking our friend here might like to have some company."

Idris cocked his head. Then inspiration dawned. "Ah, yes. Ms. Philothea. Once she is taken, I can hang another right next to him. I think we can expect her soon, and I don't think she'll be too damaged."

"Leave her alone. She had nothing to do with what happened to you, Jorge. She is innocent."

"Nobody associated with you is innocent. You'll all get what you deserve." Jorge pushed the cage hard, making it swing like a massive pendulum.

"How would you like to start wrangling the truth out of him? What methods would you like me to employ?"

"How about birds?"

"Birds?"

"Countless birds flying around in that cage, landing on him, shitting on him, and pecking him all over."

Idris rubbed his hands. "Very cruel. You surprise me, Master —but in a good way."

Gwen caught Jorge's eye. Her expression was laced with disapproval. "Do you really think that is such a great idea? Do you really want that weighing on your conscience? He may not be innocent, but he is still a human being. I can't believe this is you, Jorge."

Jorge shook the cage. "This is the man who tore us apart. You think I am doing something bad? Just think of all the things he did to me . . . to us. He may be human, but he played at acting like a God."

"Jorge, please, if only for my sake . . . please show pity."

There was something in her eyes that made him worry that if he didn't show more restraint, he might lose her altogether. "Of course—anything for you, my love. No pecking. Idris, just have the birds fly around at odd intervals, shower him with shit, and then disappear and return, like a poor man's Prometheus. Just to make it a little more fun, it would be good to have the birds arrive when he contemplates escaping. It could be our own little Pavlovian experiment. Maybe over time he will be subdued to stay in his cage with the repetition. Is that humane enough to pass the Gentle Gwen test?"

Gwen walked over to the cage and gazed at the old man. "So, what you are saying is that if he never thinks of escaping, it will just be him sitting in a cage, right?"

"Of course, my love. He will be responsible for his own level of torture, if any."

Gwen pushed up on her tiptoes and kissed Jorge on the cheek.

"Linking the punishment to his thoughts will be costly."

Jorge waved the comment away, basking in Gwen's adoration. "Just do it."

Idris walked over to the hanging jail cell and clutched at the bars. He closed his eyes in deep concentration. His voice went low with the recognizable hum of casting a spell.

Jorge watched as the magician swayed forward and backward. A chime sounded from somewhere in the room, snapping Idris out of his trance. The sound got louder with each progression. The magician reached into his pants pocket and retrieved his phone, its screen flashing bright. Idris's face lit up at the number displayed on the screen, and he swiped to answer. "Rendell, so good to hear from you. We've been waiting anxiously for our new arrival." Idris flashed a smile at Jorge which dulled almost immediately. "What do you mean?" Idris's eyebrows furrowed together.

Jorge tried to catch his eye, to read what might be happening. Idris lowered his head and walked out of the room.

Gwen nodded toward the disappearing magician. "That can't be good."

A happy sigh escaped from Buxton. "Alex must have escaped." The old man's eyes shone with emotion.

Jorge grabbed the cage and swung it violently. "Maybe. But, if so, it won't last. She has a lot of your sins to pay for."

Buxton's smile disappeared.

Idris bustled into the room. "I can guess you've already figured out that it's not good news. She escaped my servant. He thinks she has made her way back to KHNM headquarters."

"Great. Now they will have their guard up."

"But, Master, we have time. We can wait for the perfect time to strike. Don't worry. We will capture her."

Jorge needed clarification but didn't want to speak plainly in front of their captive. "And what you said was true?"

Idris tilted his head. "About?"

Jorge huffed. "About what makes Alex special?"

Understanding dawned on the magician. "That she is the only one who can call the book forth?"

The satisfied smile on Buxton's face fell into dismay. "You are searching for the books of the Ogdoad? Idris, you have to know that it is useless to search for them. Only certain people can access them and use them."

"Do you think it is such a good idea to let the prisoner overhear our plans?"

Idris waved away the idea. "I wouldn't worry about him. You can be certain that there is no way for him to escape. And even if he did manage to flee his gilded cage, the twenty-five thousand volts of electricity that would jolt his body would definitely halt his progress to the outside world."

Suddenly small birds appeared out of nowhere and were flitting around Buxton like a swarm of large feathered bees.

Jorge was impressed. "It only took a few words to prompt his desire for leaving."

Idris basked in the compliment.

"Can't you somehow magically call her here? What is having all that power for if you can't cut some corners here and there?"

Idris looked crestfallen as his moment of glory went by the wayside. "You'd think. But there are rules, and that won't work. I need to know exactly where someone is at the moment I execute the spell."

Gwen put her hands on her hips and cocked her head. "Why don't you have one of your people follow her and then tell you where she is? Then you can just snap her up."

"It is more complex than that. It is not in any way similar to the magic you've seen Jorge perform. It requires me to create a portal to where the person is and bodily remove them. Which, depending on where they happen to be, could cause quite a stir."

Buxton swatted at the birds flying close to his face. "You aren't going to get her. There are too many people watching out for her now that you've shown your hand."

"If only there was someone else." Gwen's soft voice was almost indiscernible over the bird-sound.

Jorge shouted over the din. "Idris has made it very clear that she is the only one."

The magician snapped his fingers, making the birds disappear. Silence filled the room. "Meyret."

Buxton went white as a sheet.

Idris continued as if talking to himself. "If we knew where she was, it is possible she could call the book forth. She is an ancestor of Alex. They come from the same line. The priestess is her great-great-great-great-grandmother or something like that." He turned to face Buxton. "I bet we can get the location out of him, with the right amount of torture."

"Meyret? The priestess of Maat?" Jorge asked.

Idris looked shocked. "How do you know of her?"

"You forget, I've had many dealings with KHNM. She is the very one who wiped my memories countless times. I know exactly where her tomb is."

A swirl of birds flashed into Buxton's cage.

"Well that suits my, I mean our, plan perfectly." Idris rubbed his hands together.

Jorge was feeling far less confident in what the magician really wanted and if he had Jorge's best interests in mind. Maybe he should think about bringing someone in he could trust.

Someone who was squarely on his side. "I want to add someone to our team. I need an assistant to take care of things that I can't."

"But what about your lady love? She could serve in that capacity."

Gwen glared at Idris with a stare that bordered on violence. She had zero tolerance for sexist remarks.

Jorge stepped in between them. "No, I need someone else." Jorge thought a change of subject might do all of them some good. "So, have you had any luck so far with the memory machine?"

Buxton tried to clear a path through the birds swarming around him. "Memory machine?"

"There is a rather large globe-like artifact that is currently in KHNM's basement. Idris is going to mold it to our ends."

The tornado of small birds disappeared around Buxton. "The God machine. You couldn't possibly have a use for that."

Idris laughed. "We will retrieve it easily from its now unprotected headquarters and see what we can do with it. It has a thick and powerful layer of magic residue for us to harvest. Our intention is to harness its power to create a machine. One that will extract and hold every thought and experience you've ever lived until you are an empty vessel."

"You are going to try to wipe my memories?"

"Of course, old man, poetic justice. An eye for an eye. Now you will know the pain I have felt. I will know every secret you've ever known. I am certain I will find a myriad of uses for all the facts bouncing around inside that head of yours." Suddenly the birds appeared again, making Jorge laugh.

Idris clapped his hands together. "Now that we've gotten that all squared away, we should head to the laboratory. Before we retrieve Meyret, I'd like to do a trial run on the portal I created to make sure it's in working order. The friend you requested might be a good option."

Jorge grabbed Gwen's hand and made his way to the transport tunnel. "He is more like a colleague. What will happen if the portal is not up to par?"

"He'll most likely die. If he is lucky."

Gwen turned to look at Idris. "Lucky?"

"Being teleported through time and space is not a simple thing. If everything isn't aligned just perfectly, let's just say Jorge's friend could end up a gelatinous mass of goo, with a few bones sticking out here and there."

"Who are you thinking of, Jorge?" asked Gwen.

"Edmund."

"Isn't he more like a hanger-on than a colleague?"

"I prefer the word *fan*. He is pretty hard-core. I will need someone with sticking power. Someone who will not only be thrilled to be a part of what we are doing and amazed that they were brought into the inner circle but who will do just about anything I ask. Also, Edmund has been successful in public relations, which could be handy." Jorge stepped into the transporter and pushed the laboratory button. "He will be over the moon to join our little party."

CHAPTER TWENTY-ONE

A fter shooting up Rendell with the drug he'd intended for her, Alex grabbed the car keys out of his hand and searched for the garage. She tiptoed through the house on high alert for the cook he'd mentioned, but never saw any evidence of them. In the kitchen, the oven held a bubbled-over store-bought lasagna. She was a little impressed with the lengths that Rendell went to in staging the dinner story so it would play as real. It didn't seem like he was a professional kidnapper or killer. It made her wonder what this Idris person held over him that would make him do these things.

She got in the black sedan and turned on the ignition, and the engine purred to life. The backward glance to make sure the driveway was clear made her head spin. The drugs were still coursing through her system. She knew it was a bad idea to drive in this state, but what was she going to do, wait for a cab? She had to get out of there, having no idea how long Rendell would be out.

Aside from feeling woozy, she was surprisingly alert. However, after a lifetime of living with her mother's continuous and fluctuating addictions, she realized she probably wasn't the best judge of her own altered state at the moment.

Out on the open road, the dashed line and the flow of black asphalt were conspiring to pull her into sleep. Alex fingered the window levers, rolling all the windows down. The cold night air willed her into wakefulness. She breathed in deep. The soft and gauzy fog that filled her head was thinning, allowing a plan to weave disparate threads into something tangible. She wouldn't go back to her hotel—who knows who might be waiting for her there. She would ditch what meager things she brought with her and drive directly to the train station.

~~~

Once on the train and seated in her private compartment, Alex slid the door shut and hooked the heavy metal interior lock over its bar. The privacy and feeling of security of booking the sleeper was well worth the extra cost. She pulled the curtains together and secured them with the thick industrial Velcro sewn at its edges. Safe and alone, she sagged into the navy-blue seat and pulled out her phone. Who to call? Thorne might be the most appropriate choice, but the thought of dealing with her in a muddled state was less than optimal. Alex had a hard enough time communicating with Thorne without traces of knockout drugs in her system. She flipped through her contacts. A pang of sorrow ran through her as she swiped past Buxton's contact information. She scrolled back up, landed on Luke, and hit the green call icon.

The phone rang for a considerable amount of time. Her eyes

burned with fatigue as she struggled to focus in on the face of her watch. Maybe he'd already gone to bed. Maybe he was out with friends or maybe on a date. A tinge of guilt ran through her. She really didn't know much at all about Luke, nor had she really tried to find out.

Alex was just about to disconnect when he picked up.

"Hey?" His voice was rough with sleep.

The low huskiness of his voice made her flush. She reached up and turned the air nozzle above her on and pushed away the scratchy blanket she'd thrown over her lap. She was suddenly self-conscious of calling him, during his personal time, and more specifically while he was in bed. "Early to bed, and early to rise." She blurted out the first thing that came to mind, making her feel ridiculous.

"Alex?" There was a soft fumbling as if he was sitting up. He sighed. "Long day with Thorne." She imagined him sweeping his hand through his sleep-rumpled hair. Her flush deepened, and she tried to turn up the vent further, but noticed it was as high as it could go. She grabbed a pamphlet in a basket under the window and fanned herself.

"Sorry you got stuck with her."

"You'd think I'd be used to it by now. What's up?"

"The librarian tried to kidnap me."

"Knox? That old man?"

"Knox is dead. It was his assistant Rendell who did it."

"Wait a minute, killed Knox or kidnapped you?"

"Both."

"Are you all right? How'd you get away? Do I need to call the cops?"

"No, I—"

"Are you wounded? Where are you?"

"There is no need to call the police. Take a breath, Luke. I am fine, just suffering from a little drug haze. Rendell, Knox's assistant, drugged me and threatened to roll me up in a carpet for a Cleopatra-style delivery to his boss."

"Great, a psychopath with a historical sense of humor. Who is his boss? I can come get you. Stay where you are. I'll take the agency car. I can get to Conn—"

"I've got it handled, Luke. I'm on a train to Penn Station. It should be leaving shortly. I'll be there in a couple of hours." She pulled the curtains aside to look out at the empty train platform. She'd been keeping an eye open for Rendell, or anyone else looking suspicious, just in case he or his boss sorted out she might be there. "Albright Knox was dead when I got here. Luckily, I dumped out some of the drug Rendell gave me. He called his boss and admitted to killing his mentor, while I pretended to be out of it."

"Knox was the boss's mentor?"

"No, Rendell's." Her voice became clipped. Explaining it all was so overwhelming. All she wanted to do was curl up in a ball and sleep off what was left of the Mickey.

"Oh."

She softened her tone. "Does the name Idris ring any bells for you? Maybe something Buxton might have mentioned over the years?"

"No. But before I pick you up, I'll give a quick look in the archive room. Maybe there is something about him there." Luke's bed creaked and his voice was clear then far away as his phone was propped up between his ear and shoulder as he searched for something. "I just need to find my key. I know it's here somewhere."

Alex's eyelids were drooping. "As soon as this train leaves the station, I'm gonna sleep hard. I've been through the wringer."

"Is that a good idea? That Rendell character is probably still after you." There was an edge of protectiveness in Luke's voice.

"I've been keeping an eye out, and haven't seen him. The door to my roomette has an interior lock."

"I'll pick you up from the station. And Alex . . ."

"Yes?"

There was an empty pause on Luke's end. "Er, nothing. Just stay safe."

Alex slipped her phone into her scribe's bag as the train tugged forward to leave New Haven behind. She pushed her head into the pillow that she'd jammed into the back support and stretched her legs across to the seat in front of her. She retrieved the blue blanket and pulled it up to her neck. Almost instantaneously she threw it back off as a new burn of heat washed over her, not from the rough blanket, but the thought of Luke.

The regular clack-clack of the train pulled her toward a deep and dreamless sleep.

~~~

It felt good to be back at the residency. Alex was surprised how much the place felt like home. When she first came there, she'd felt lost in its opulent beauty, like a wayward street urchin welcomed into a sacred space among temple elite. She was constantly wondering when they would come to realize that she was merely an interloper.

The familiar foyer welcomed her with the grand upsweep of its marble staircase framed by rich mahogany handrails. The soft glow from the Louis Comfort Tiffany art nouveau chandelier suspended from the atrium warmed her heart like an old friend's hug.

She and Luke whispered good night so as not to wake up Jeeves. The steep price of waking him was paid not only by the offender, but the entire house. It was a great way to get on everyone's bad side. The little schnauzer would bark for what felt like an eternity. It wasn't the reaction of a loyal protector, but more along the lines of a grumpy prince, complaining that his clumsy servants disturbed him from the delights of dreamland.

Luke made his way up the stairs, and Alex crossed the foyer to the door that secreted her private elevator. Stepping inside she pushed the button. The ancient mechanism made the expected small tug upward before lifting her to her bedroom.

The lift door slid open, and she stepped into her darkened room. Moonlight cascaded in from the glass doors of her balcony, cutting across the Oriental rug in the middle of the room. Her four-poster bed and the sitting area were draped in shadow.

Something moved in one of the high-backed tapestry chairs. She froze in place. Her ears pricked up. The form slipped out of the chair and stepped into the moonshine. His wide smile showed off his pointed teeth in the silvery light.

"Gormund!" It always struck her as odd that the protector God of home and hearth had such a bestial appearance.

"Did I scare you?" Gormund sounded hopeful at the prospect.

"Of course you did." Alex's heart was racing. "I just about jumped out of my own skin."

"That sounds painful."

"What happened to 'How have you been?' or 'Sorry I've not managed to return any of your calls for the past few months or so'." Alex flicked on the lights. Gormund's large head hung down as he stared at his feet. She wasn't certain if he was truly ashamed or just trying to avoid her gaze so she wouldn't see the mirth in his expression.

Alex shook her head. "So, what are you doing here? More specifically why are you sitting in the dark, in my room?"

"Thorne said I should wait for you here."

"Really?" Alex doubted it but wouldn't put anything past Thorne.

"So here I am, finding myself at loose ends."

"You completely ghost me and then just pop by when you are bored. Where is Meyret anyway? I always thought you two came as a set." Gormund watched over the immortal priestess of Maat while she slept in a tomb buried deep under a cafe in the scrubland of New Mexico.

An expression flashed over Gormund's face that Alex couldn't entirely read. "Let's just say I needed to get some fresh air. Both Meyret and I were called back to the Field of Reeds for a deposition regarding the incident with Raymond. They are none too happy with my involvement with you and how all that played out. I was angry at how they treated us and was getting a little stir crazy. So, I figured it was time to turn on my warded security system, leave the priestess sleeping comfortably, and stretch my legs a bit, have some fun."

"So what exactly does Bes do for fun? Why come here? Why not go visit some of your family in the Field of Reeds? Maybe Salima—I mean Hathor—would like to see you."

"Or Niles?" The knowing look on Gormund's face infuriated Alex.

"I couldn't care less about Niles."

"Oh, the lady doth protest too much."

"I'm dead serious."

"Yes, you are. And it seems that is all you are. What

happened to you, Alex? Now your sense of humor is apocryphal at best, lost for all time like the never-to-be-found tomb of Alexander the Great."

"Gor, you can't ignore someone for ages and expect instant witty banter from them. Also, you are being a smart-ass and you scared the living daylights out of me, not to mention I am drop-dead tired."

"Well at least there is hope."

"Why do you say that?"

He clasped his hands behind his back and smiled. "You called me Gor."

"Really, why are you here and not in the Field of Reeds?"

"I guess some of the recent past events have put me in an awkward position with some. Let's leave it at that. So enough about me, what have you been up to? I mean other than watching the agency fall to pieces under your leadership."

"Very funny." Alex motioned to the chairs in front of the fireplace. "Should we at least have a seat if we are going to be chatting for a while? It feels awkward just standing here so close to them."

"And you are tired."

"That too." Alex sat down, and Gormund took the seat across from her.

Something on the fireplace mantle caught her eye. The artwork was different. Luke must have made the time to move the illustration and the Joseph Campbell book to her room. "So what are your plans with all this 'time off'?" She made air quotes around the last two words.

"That is why I am here to talk to you. And really, we don't have to go over it all tonight. I should probably let you get some sleep. But I definitely wanted to put a bug in your ear."

"Always thoughtful, you are. What kind of bug, by chance? Hopefully not one of those parasitic type that enter through your ear and make themselves at home in your brain."

"Dark thought, Alex. No, I was sitting in my diner bored out of my mind and thought about grabbing a book to read."

"You read?"

"Always funny, you are," he shot back at her. "Anyhow, I couldn't find anything that piqued my interest, so I was staring out the window, longing for a book, and then the idea hit me. I couldn't believe I hadn't thought of it before. Have you thought again of looking for those books of magic?"

"Well I—"

"Don't answer too fast. Just hear me out. I know right now this may not seem like the best time to look for those books. You've got all this malarkey going on with the agency, the lawsuit, packing things up, shutting down the God machine. All that stuff, and I get it." He rested his hands on his knees and leaned forward. "But I have to tell you, there are a number of things that I think support doing this now. First and foremost, I have a lead as to where the books might be. Secondly, if you find the books, maybe they will tell you how to turn that damn God machine off. And thirdly, now you would have someone to go on a little adventure with. I need something going on. I just can't rattle around while others do my work."

"I'll give it a think." She needed some time to sort out how she really felt about this. It was strange to say the least for Gormund to just pop in out of the blue and suggest they go on another adventure given the virtual radio silence he'd thrown her way since their last tour of duty. The fact that he was suggesting finding the lost books of magic only amplified the weirdness. What was he really up to?

"Really?"

"Can I go to bed now? We'll talk more about it in the morning."

Gormund nodded toward the stiff tapestried love seat between them. "Can I crash here?"

"How about you take Buxton's old room. It's all made up and ready to go." There was a time when having him near while she slept wouldn't cause her a second thought, and would have actually made her feel safe, but the fact that he just dropped their friendship so soundly made her question whether or not they ever really were friends. Regardless, tonight she wanted her room to herself and a good night's sleep.

The little Immortal looked crestfallen. He slipped off the chair. "Good night, then." He mumbled as he walked by to the elevator. She heard the elevator door slide shut and he was gone.

Luke hadn't been able to find anything about Idris in the archive room before heading out to pick Alex up. She looked up at the illustration. If she weren't so tired, she would love to step into the archive room before heading off to sleep. But now was not the time.

She slipped into the silk nightgown Salima bought for her on her very first night at the residency, back when all of this was new to her. It hit her how her life had changed so drastically in such a short amount of time. Alex climbed up to the downy softness of her bed and then drew the privacy curtains shut. As she buried herself underneath the heavy comforter, a thought trickled through her mind as she drifted off to sleep. Why was Gormund really here?

She was gliding through the air, but with no fear. Her feathered body was made to soar easily over land and water. Alex dipped and skimmed over the blood-red river of the Netherworld. It felt oddly natural to be back in this realm. She ascended, cruising up to the red-orange mountains that framed the valley. As she got higher and higher, a force pulled her down, as if she'd gotten off track from a predetermined destination.

She swooped past an outcropping of rocks on the edge of a cliff and was drawn to the river. The more she tried to shrug it off, the stronger the force became. Her wings burned as she struggled against it. She let go and shifted into cruise control as she glided toward the river.

Up ahead, she could see a change in the color scheme of the landscape. The varying shades of magenta, red, and orange were gradually washing out to white, and just beyond that lay a land that looked like a version of the verdant Nile valley. Her Ba had flown from her sleeping form.

Her vision was sharp. She could see for miles. In the far distance, she could pick out a small village filled with mud-brick buildings. Even the river transitioned from blood red to the grey-green of the Nile.

Her flight speed increased as she glided toward land. She banked downward and skimmed sparkling water. She could see her form for the first time. Her body was that of a falcon, but her face remained human.

She neared the small village and was drawn toward a particular household. It was quite grand and probably belonged to a noble. Alex perched on a second-story window. Something told her she was close to whatever it was that brought her here.

She pushed up from the window and circled the location looking for something, something she would know. In the front courtyard stood a man feeding ducks. Alex landed on a retaining wall that surrounded the rectangular space. He looked up at her, and their eyes locked. His smile was tinged with sadness as he waved to her.

It was her dad.

Alex woke and tossed the sweat-soaked sheets off her. She pulled the velvet curtains open and made her way to the balcony, opening the doors. Goose bumps erupted on her arms as the night air whispered against her skin.

Alex leaned against the balcony and gazed out to the depths of Central Park that lay just across the street and beyond the Met. The city was still deep in the trance of sleep. It was that time between twilight and dawn, too late for nightlife and too early for the first shift of day life. One thing she knew—that was the last of sleep for her that night. These dreams had been plaguing her ever since she returned from the Netherworld.

They'd started off slowly. At first they appeared to be run-of-the-mill stress-induced flying dreams. But as time wore on they'd become longer and more detailed. The feeling of belonging was the oddest part.

Seeing her dad in this dream was a wonderful thing and a troubling thing. It seemed so real. Did she really see him? Was she really flying through the Netherworld? Or was it just a mash-up of her memories and emotional trauma?

Alex closed the balcony door. Maybe it was a good time to see what she could find in the archive room. Maybe she'd find something on this Idris person.

~~~

Alex searched high and low throughout the archive room and couldn't find a thing about Idris. Eventually her stomach growled, making her look down at her watch. It was already time for breakfast. She returned to her room and threw on some clothes, then headed downstairs.

The small elevator door closed. She shut her eyes, remembering the dream from last night. It was so vivid like the others, but the location was different. Usually she was flying over the city, traversing Central Park, dipping and playing with the air swells. In them, her soul felt open, boundless. She would crest the crown of a large, proud sycamore tree, when a Cooper's hawk would fly beside her. The entire dream was the two of them flying in perfect synchronization through the park, skimming ponds and catching currents that playfully twisted and turned their path as they remained side by side. In the dream, there was this feeling of knowing that this bird was not simply an overfriendly hawk, but Niles.

Although those dreams were enjoyable, the Freudian interpretation of them irritated the heck out of her. Why couldn't she purge Niles from her heart? The dreams made it painfully obvious that after everything that happened, and his blatant avoidance of her, she still wanted nothing more than to be with him again.

When she arrived at the dining room, she was glad to see that breakfast was still laid out. Taking the first meal of the day at the residency always felt a little special with the silver chafing dishes all in a row filled with eggs, bacon, hash browns, fresh fruit, and toast.

Luke was sitting at the far end of the table while Thorne was on the other, like angry emotional bookends. They toyed with their food with an anemic interest.

Alex scooped up some scrambled eggs and bacon, then sat facing Luke. "Have you seen Gormund this morning?"

Luke broke his laser focus from his food. "Gormund's here?"

"I told him he could sleep in Buxton's room. He was waiting for me in my room last night. He mentioned that—"

Gormund swept into the room. "Greetings, KHNM agents. It's been far too long." He made his way to the sideboard and loaded his plate up. He plopped down at Alex's right, across from Thorne.

Thorne sneered at Gormund. Everyone around the table knew she found him to be about as palatable as a flea-infested rat. "What brings you here?"

Gormund smiled, intentionally showing off his razor-sharp pointy teeth. "Haven't seen Alex for ages and thought I'd just stop in."

"That's not what you said last night," said Alex.

Gormund's smile faded as Alex reached over to a small silver tray of mail. It lay just to the right of her place setting. Alex grabbed a piece of mail and worked at its lip with the sterling silver letter opener. "We're all friends here, Gormund, so why don't you share the real reason you came. You were proposing another adventure into the supernatural."

"Don't make it sound like such a dirty thing. Who doesn't need a little fun now and again?"

"The last time you and I had some so-called fun, we almost got killed."

"This will be different, more like a treasure hunt than a battle. Not only will I get to stretch my legs, but it will also benefit the agency in trying to connect the dots on that God machine or whatever you are calling it these days."

Gormund's voice faded into the background as the letter she

held grabbed every ounce of attention she had. It was from Albright Knox's attorney.

"What's up, Alex?" asked Luke. "You look like you've seen a ghost."

"It's from Albright Knox's lawyer." The room went silent. She picked up the envelope that she'd discarded onto the platter and shook it. A small gold key hit the surface with a light clank. She held it close to read the small inscription on its head. It looked like a faint symbol that was almost rubbed flat. It resembled a zero. "The letter states that Mr. Knox requested that this be delivered here at the time of his death. Do you know where the Bowery Bank is?"

Thorne assumed her usual smug look of all knowingness. "That bank has been closed for years. As a matter of fact, the only thing in that space now are very exclusive charity fundraisers and high-end over-the-top corporate Christmas parties and weddings. It's a shame he went to the trouble to have someone send you a key to a bank that no longer exists."

Alex set the key down. "How long since the building was used as a bank?"

"I don't know exactly, seems to me the bank vacated that building sometime in the eighties. It was totally refurbished and renovated. I would guess that any sort of safe deposit boxes would have been emptied years ago, even if they still physically existed."

"But why would he have it sent here?" asked Alex.

Thorne shrugged. "It could have been something he did years ago and forgot about it. Knox wasn't exactly a spring chicken."

Alex held the letter in front of Thorne's nose. "Then why is it addressed to me?"

Luke's eyes brightened. "I guess we know what we are doing after breakfast."

Alex eyed Gormund. "Not heading to Egypt."

Gormund crossed his arms in a huff. "You're not going now?"

"Depends on what we find. Your main enticement last night was the lure that the books of magic would have all the answers to our God machine questions. Now it is very possible this timely delivery might very well be the key to that problem, pun intended."

"But Alex—"

Alex grabbed the key and letter. "Gor, there are just too many things up in the air right now. I think this is an important lead for us to follow. Thorne, have you heard anything more about the lawsuit or found any information about the covenant? They were supposed to be in touch in a week."

"Nothing yet." Her words were as sour as her expression.

"Maybe you should look into that while Luke and I find the safe deposit box that belongs to this key."

"And Gormund?" The Immortal rubbed his hands together.

"This is agency business. No Immortals needed."

"The more hands the better." Gormund gazed up at her with hope.

"Two's company, three's a crowd, Gormund." Luke had an unusual look of self-satisfaction on his face.

Thorne turned around before leaving the room. "Good luck with all that."

Alex took the bait. "What?"

"The bank building. The parties there are very exclusive. They're not going to let you two just wander around."

"Thorne, how would you know? It's not like you are invited

to these things. I could dust off my tux and see where the night takes us." Luke was a little too excited about this venture.

Thorne smiled as she looked from Luke to Alex. "You are right about that, Luke. I've never been invited to a party there. There was an article about a recent fundraiser Elton John was throwing for AIDS research. The interviewer asked how the venue handled events like that with a lot of high-target VIPs on the invite list. Apparently, they headhunt their security detail from intelligence agencies. I am guessing if you are going to crash one of their parties, you need a secret weapon—either that or a connection into the hidden life of the super-rich."

"Or magic." Gormund brightened.

CHAPTER TWENTY-TWO

Alex stepped out of the agency's limo and toward the up-lit white Corinthian columns fronting the Bowery Savings Bank. The massive arched entryway of this modern temple to the American greenback was designed to telegraph its power. The high priests of ancient Egypt with their control over land, treasure, and resources weren't all that different from the modern-day robber barons. They too understood the value of monumental architecture to keep the riffraff in their place.

Beyond the twin life-sized lion sculptures at the top of the stairs and a black iron gate with pointed ends stood the security guards. These guys were authentic. Unlike guards with matching sweaters hired by museums, whose great adversary is the occasional tourist getting too close to the artwork, these guards had dark suits, most likely with weapons secreted away within. Each guard sported reflective shades and the telltale plastic swirl of an earpiece that disappeared into their collars.

A nervous energy swept through her. Alex wasn't exactly sure how Gormund was going to get them in, but he was confident he could. She wondered what party they were going to be crashing.

Luke was spot on with his personal assessment that he cleaned up well. His tailored tux made him look like a sexy yet scholarly 007. She cracked a smile as she recalled his reaction when she exited her private elevator. Apparently, he liked what he saw too.

She wore a near-floor-length black stretch velvet dress that hugged her curves. The deep cut neckline and lengthy slit up the back both made her feel delightfully exposed. It was as if the dress was enchanted with a magic glamor woven into its threads that made her feel a little dangerous.

Alex opted to wear some of her grandmother's jewelry for the party. Around her neck she wore a pearl and crystal choker. Pinned over her heart was a vintage brooch of a bird taking flight with a scatter of paste diamonds trailing behind it. Alex imagined that the three of them must have been quite a sight. Gormund, squat and wide but impeccably dressed, an archivist in a tux, and a research archaeologist in starlet drag.

When they got to the door, Gormund handed one of the guards a piece of paper. The man in the suit glanced at it and waved them in.

"What did you give him?" Alex asked as she took in the massive columned space they'd just entered. Her eyes were drawn up from the pillars to the arched ceiling punctuated with bronze rosettes inset in hexagonal plaster shapes. Her gaze followed the rosettes to the center, which was topped with a golden stained glass skylight.

Directly in front of them was a huge dance floor. Scattered about the perimeter were tables of varying sizes and curved leather couches that created niches where people could congregate.

"Just a quick entry spell. We'd better get lost in the crowd before the spell wears off and he realizes that he is holding a gum wrapper."

They pushed through the crowd to the other end of the space where an illuminated clock stood high above everything. When they rounded the structure, Alex realized this was the old bank's vault. Now it served as a karaoke spot for drunken corporate warriors. Unlike the wild and open dance floor, this space was the tidal pool where the non-dancers congregated.

The large area that used to be a vault was gutted and converted into a miniature night club. It boasted a one-person stage with a mic and a few tables scattered about. The vault's thick walls allowed for singing that wouldn't leak out into the massive wall of sound outside. On the stage was a pale man in a mousy beige suit and bad comb-over singing Patsy Cline's "Crazy" with more heart than Alex would have imagined possible.

"How are we going to find anything in this huge space?" yelled Alex, her voice barely audible over the Euro-tech music being played.

"You've got me, boss. I'm just your keycard. What do you need me for, anyway? Maybe I should get some karaoke in." Gormund started walking into the vault.

"Sorry, Gormund." Alex grabbed his arm.

Gormund turned around and cupped his hand to his ear. "What was that? The music is kind of loud here."

Alex was certain he'd heard exactly what she'd said. "I am sorry, Gormund, for having doubted you."

Luke rolled his eyes.

"Thank you, Alex. I will take that as an apology from this heathen too." He winked at her.

It was painfully obvious that if there ever were safe deposit boxes here, they'd been cleared out. It was a dead end.

The man in the mousy suit yielded the small stage to a middle-aged woman with an expanding midriff wearing a brightly patterned floral blouse. She immediately started singing "Wake Me Up Before You Go-Go" by Wham!, doing her uncoordinated best to dance like George Michael.

Alex looked away from the singing train wreck. "Where to next? No boxes."

Gormund nodded to the stage. "Feel like a little song? Maybe the Supremes. I'll be Diana."

Alex laughed. "Maybe later. Let's split up and check out the outer area. Maybe we missed something on the way in." She walked out of the small space with Luke and Gormund trailing behind her. Gormund looked back wistfully at the small performance space. Did he really want to do karaoke?

The dance-floor lights were flashing in sync with the downbeats of the heavily layered music. The crowd of well-dressed middle-aged dancers clumsily fumbled along. Some of them were smiling like this was the apex of their year, and some wore the pained expressions that often went along with mandatory group fun time with coworkers.

In the far distance, the security guard that let them in was trying to make his way through the crowd and toward them. Alex grabbed ahold of Luke and Gormund just as they started off in opposite directions. "Hold up." She nodded toward the guard.

"Oh shit," said Gormund.

"Can't you cast glamour on us, Gor, like you did on the way in?"

"This building is a neutral zone. Once we entered, my powers were blocked."

Alex nodded to the main entrance. "Damn it. Let's get out of here."

Luke glanced at Alex. "Why run? If they catch us, the worst they could do is remove us from the premises. I don't see what we gain by kicking ourselves out."

"Who says they just want to kick us out?"

Gormund's question hit a nerve with Alex. It could be they were being pursued for crashing the party, but it was likely that whoever Rendell worked for had sent some bodies after them.

"I'm out." Alex made her way toward the front entrance. She glanced back behind her to make sure the guys were following, and quickened her pace.

As she neared the entrance, the guards flanking it simultaneously raised their hands to their earpieces. Their heads turned in perfect synchronization toward Alex. She banked right toward the elevator lobby.

There were four elevators on each side, but aside from that, it was a dead end. She rushed toward the furthest one. She knew it was a long shot, but they might be able to evade the guards by going up.

Luke and Gormund caught up to her. Alex pressed the up button, but the elevator door stayed closed. A glimmer from above caught her eye. The vaulted ceiling was a beautiful mosaic of night-blue tiles framing a glittering field of golden crystal stars. Squinting at the ceiling, she could pick out a pattern of stars that burned brighter than all the others. Her gaze followed the heavenly bodies down to the end of the corridor. The marble wall at the dead end slid aside, revealing a gaping black void.

Turning and running, Alex leapt toward the void. Her

stomach dropped as she broke through the plane and landed with a thud on what felt like scratchy industrial-grade carpet. Her left arm and cheek felt a slight burn at impact that increased greatly as Luke and Gormund toppled over her.

The heavy scraping sound of a large slab of stone being moved filled the space. They lay in the dark in an unseen tumble of torsos, arms, and legs.

Alex could feel someone's hand move to her butt and stay there. "Gormund, really?"

"Not me."

The hand immediately retracted. "Sorry, Alex. I didn't realize . . ."

"Well let's just do our best to disentangle ourselves, without too much damage or exploration. All right?"

"I think I'm on top. I'll just climb down to you," said Gormund.

"Ouch! That's my hand!"

"Sorry, Luke, it's not like I can see anything either." There was a hint of mischief in Gormund's voice, making Alex wonder if it really was an accident.

As she waited for them to extract themselves, she blinked to coerce her eyes into adjusting to the lack of light.

"Great, we escaped a few security guards, only to die in a black box. I knew today was going to be a good day." Alex pictured Gormund with his hands on his hips, his face all screwed up, reflecting the sarcasm in his voice.

"Why don't we orient ourselves to one another, then work back to see how large the space is. So we know what we are up against."

"How do you propose we do that?" asked Luke.

"Should we all hold hands and sing "Kumbaya" or something?" asked Gormund.

"Exactly."

"I was being sarcastic."

"You know, I knew that. No really, if we can find each other and lock hands, then we know where we are in relation to each other. Then we can let go and move forward and explore the space in front of us. Hopefully we will run into a solid surface."

"Or a ledge that hangs over a never-ending abyss," added Luke.

"Great positive spin," said Alex. "Let's do this."

She felt a hard slap mid-thigh. Alex reached down and grabbed Gormund's hand and felt that strange electric shock of his immortality. "Okay, I've got Gormund on one side." She reached out with her other hand and whacked what must have been Luke's chest.

"Ouch."

She turned her palm toward his chest. She could tell it was firm even over the soft fine cotton cloth of his dress shirt. She jerked her hand off his chest and found a more reasonable route to his hand, down the thick tux fabric encasing his arm to his dangling fingers.

Her hand reached at his. He grabbed hers and squeezed it softly. Although the room was still completely dark, she would swear he was wearing a smile.

"Okay, I've got you two. Do you have each other in hand?"

"Yes, should we dance about now like Matisse's muses?" asked Luke.

"We'd have to be naked for that." Although factual, Alex automatically wished she hadn't said it out loud.

"Oooooh," said Gormund.

"Okay, guys, the plan is, let's drop our hands, spin around, and walk forward and see what we find." Alex let go and turned to her best approximation of what a half rotation would be. With her arms outstretched she cautiously moved forward. If there happened to be a bottomless abyss, she wanted to do her best to not be fully committed when it appeared.

A thump sounded nearby. "Damn."

"Luke, are you okay?"

"Yeah, just hit a wall." She could hear the sound of Luke's hand gliding against the surface he'd found. "Just seems like a regular old wall. I'm swiping away, trying to gauge its size. If we all come to a wall, we should all move to our left."

"Good idea—that way we won't pile up again."

"Why is that a good idea?" asked Gormund.

Alex chuckled at Gormund's predictable banter. It was nice having him around again.

Her fingers brushed against something solid and cold. A flash of light happened so quickly she barely believed that it happened. "Did you guys see that?"

"So, it wasn't my imagination," said Luke.

Alex pressed her palms against the surface. A bright light glared out, burning her dark-adjusted vision. Pink and blue dots floated across her eyes. She leaned into the wall. She slowly opened her eyes and turned around in amazement. Embedded in the dark black marble walls of the small room were what looked like pink, blue, and white neon tubes. The tubes formed Egyptian hieroglyphs, and images of the Gods.

She slowly turned, taking all the symbols in. "It's beautiful."

"Yes, it is," said Luke a little overenthusiastically.

Alex caught Luke's glance. His eyes widened, then he quickly looked away.

She could see herself in her reflection against the black stone.

She was in an unusual state of dishevelment—her hair had tumbled down around her shoulders, as had her dress, giving her a decidedly vampy strapless look.

A knowing smile pulled across Gormund's face as he looked from her to Luke. "What next, boss?"

Alex rolled the beaded strap of her evening bag off her shoulder. She left her scribe's bag at home, as it would look at odds with her evening attire. She fumbled with the opening and extracted the key. "I think those hiero-lights coming on had something to do with this." Alex held the small key with the age-rubbed symbol. "Let's try and find the hole it belongs to."

Gormund crossed his arms. "Hopefully it will belong to something that will free us from this tiny prison. I like you guys, but don't relish spending an eternity here all alone."

"You've got us," said Luke.

"I'm Immortal." Gormund smirked.

Alex clapped her hands together. "Okay, boys, let the searching begin."

Luke turned toward the wall and mumbled to himself. "Great. Maybe we'll trigger human-sized meat-grinding blades or spikes like in the movies with tomb traps in them."

"Not helping, Luke." Alex stepped back to appraise the glowing hieroglyphs and symbols. She recognized the depictions of the Ogdoad, the eight ancient creation myth deities, but reading hieroglyphs was never her strong point. It appeared that the ancient lettering in this room was mostly just a random bunch of hieroglyphs not attempting to say anything in particular. It was as if it was written in Roman times when the language had been long dead and the priests were just playing at what they wrote in the text.

She squinted at the symbol on the key, tilting it against the bright light so the pattern might stand out more. The shape was less regular than a zero and more oval in shape.

Inspiration hit her. It was the God Amun they needed to find. She spun around to see him picked out in blue fluorescence, which was satisfyingly appropriate, as he is usually depicted with skin of lapis lazuli. He was wearing his flat headdress topped with two tall ostrich feathers.

Alex rushed over. If her hunch was right the symbol was no zero, it was a goose egg. Which to the untrained would seem random and strange, but she knew that one of the titular names for that great creator God was the Great Cackler, who laid the cosmic egg and created the world. The incongruent image of a God and a great goose never faded in her mind like other obscure facts that she crammed in during her undergrad days. She always delighted in the ancient Egyptians love of puns and wordplay. It was plain to see that whoever created this puzzle, security system, or death trap was tipping their hat to that inclination, as Amun was also known as The Hidden One.

She reached down and ruffled Gormund's hair. "Hey, guys, I think I've cracked it. Pun intended."

"What do you mean?" Luke walked over.

Alex pushed up on tiptoes and passed her hands over the God image, starting with his feet and moving slowly and methodically up his legs, trying to find a keyhole. "Hopefully it will be plain as day."

"If you keep rubbing his kilt like that, you might get more than you bargained for. You know he is a fertility God too."

Alex groaned. "Oh, Gor."

Alex was starting to lose hope as the expanse of the God's body didn't have any keyholes. She glanced down to his hand. He was holding the ankh symbol of eternal life. She felt around its top loop. "Bingo, boys, looks like Amun is also the God of Hidden Keyholes."

When she turned the key, a great rumbling sound emanated from behind the wall. Alex and the others stepped back. A green neon border appeared around the depiction of Amun. The large rectangular stone surface pushed out toward them, then slid away, revealing an old-fashioned teller's cage, brass bars and all.

The metal divider in the cage pulled up, revealing a seated person. On the counter in front of them was a shiny plaque that read *teller*. The teller looked to be a fleshy old woman with a very large purple velvet sultan's hat sporting a sizable amethyst brooch. Three streams of gold chain glittered in a wavelike pattern from the stone. Jutting up from the jewel was an impossibly large golden ostrich feather.

As Alex moved closer, the teller seemed more peculiar. Their skin was pale, not in a desirable way, but in a blueish hue that spoke of never being kissed by the sun. The eye makeup was its own statement of an almost clown-like application of turquoise eye shadow and a thick line of dark kohl eyeliner on the bottom lid. The blue-green color made the teller's hazel eyes stand out. Slightly above and in between the eyes was a hastily drawn third eye in the style of an Eye of Horus, with all of its extra scrolly bits.

Alex leaned into the wooden countertop. At a closer view, the teller sported a robust five-o'clock shadow.

Luke stood by Alex as Gormund held back. Alex assumed he was trying to keep a sight line, as there wasn't anything in the room he could stand on.

Luke laughed. "I get it. You're a fortune teller . . . and a teller in an old bank."

"That's rich. Really, I've never heard that before." The teller's voice was gravelly like the chain-smoking delicatessen owner whose shop was just down the street from the residency.

Alex kicked Luke. She wasn't sure what they were dealing with, but she knew it was never a good idea to antagonize the frontline gatekeepers of any organization.

"I'm Harvey, your teller-teller. Key and pass code, please." His tone was banal, like an uninspired bureaucrat who'd already become vested in the pension system.

"Teller-teller?" Harvey's dry delivery was like a death knell to Alex's ability to not react adversely to this already peculiar set of circumstances. Alex bit the inside of her lip.

"I'm contractually bound to refer to myself that way. If you want to call a magic spell a contract." He rolled his eyes. "Now have you got your bona fides?"

"Magic spell?" asked Alex.

"Do you think I'd be here all day everyday if I had a choice?"

"What'd you do?" asked Luke.

"For me to know and you to find out. Or not." Harvey appeared to be searching for something in a lower drawer.

From the back of the room Gormund spoke up. "I knew you looked familiar. You're the one who . . . wait a minute. You are Hebneb."

The teller looked unimpressed at being recognized. "Go by Harvey now."

"I can't believe they still have you imprisoned. I mean, what you did do was pretty heinous, but—"

"A felon bank teller? Now that is rich." Luke chuckled.

"If I leave this magicked existence, I will crumble to dust. It's been so long since my crime. I've been free for a few centuries. I just can never leave. It's pretty lame, but I guess it's better than not existing at all."

Gormund whistled. "I'll say it's been a long time."

"Do you really tell fortunes too?" Luke was finding this all too amusing.

"The Gods, in all their wisdom, thought it would be doubly funny to give the gatekeeper to this shit box the ability to see things. It's nice to know that when I was being doomed to spend eternity here, I could bring some levity to their lives. How about a key and pass code?"

Alex pushed the key onto the countertop. "This is all I have."

The teller smiled sardonically. "That's a big goose egg for you, then. You need a key and a pass code. No show, no go."

Alex looked over at Gormund. He just shrugged his shoulders.

Luke leaned into Alex. "Are you sure that letter from Knox didn't say anything more?"

"Albright Knox?" The teller's eyes went wide. He picked up the key, holding it up to study it closely. "Why do you have his key?"

"Dr. Knox is dead."

The metal divider slammed down. Great sobs emanated from behind the teller cage, culminating in a grandiose snot-filled nose blow.

"Harvey?" Alex knocked on the divider. "Are you okay back there?"

After a number of soft sniffs, the divider came up. "Sorry, that was very unprofessional." Harvey spoke very loudly and clearly, as if an unseen hand were recording his customer service interactions. "Being stuck here, in this unstimulating environment, can tend to make me a little emotional. Albright was a good and decent man. One of the few customers who treated me with dignity." He blew his nose into a large embroidered hankie.

"Sorry, Harvey. It must be a great loss to you."

"Nice people are so few and far between nowadays." Harvey got a far-off look in his eyes, then refocused. The teller tapped his fingers on the counter. "So, since you have his key in particular and as you are of the female persuasion, and as you happen to resemble the guy who Albright told me years ago might show up with this key someday, you must be Alex Philothea."

"That I am."

Harvey grabbed the key and slipped off his stool. "Be back in a shake."

The teller's footfalls got further away until they couldn't hear them at all. "Must be a pretty large space back there." Alex turned to Gormund.

"I've heard about this place but have never been to it before. I never quite made the cut. This is kind of the Switzerland for the top-drawer Gods, direct descendants of the Ogdoad and the like . . . Secret accounts, tax havens, prized family heirlooms hidden from relatives, stolen works of art, you name it."

"But why have a felon manage it?" asked Luke.

"Oh, he's magically stuck here. If he stole something, what would he do with it? Having him here ensures there will be no losses. Also, he's felt the wrath of the Gods once. I would think the last thing he'd ever want to do is incur that on his head again."

"What did he do, anyway, to get thrown behind bars for an eternity?" asked Alex.

"He was Akhenaten's right-hand man. Did all the dirty work in shutting down all the Gods' temples. They didn't appreciate the whole 'everyone needs to be monotheistic' thing. So, here he sits. Forever," said Gormund.

"That means he is over three thousand years old." Luke looked thunderstruck.

"Three thousand three hundred and forty-nine, to be exact." Harvey was back at his window and shoved a long, sleek brushed-silver box through the cage opening.

"Looking good," said Luke.

"Whatever." Harvey's eyes looked somewhere over Alex's head, making her think maybe he was being monitored. He slid the key back to Alex. "You should be all set to open it."

Alex shifted the metal box so it lay horizontal to the teller cage, enabling it to rest on the countertop.

Luke stood close to her. "Isn't the norm for some privacy here?"

Harvey looked peeved. "Of course. Just knock three times when you are ready for me to further assist you." The divider slammed down.

Alex opened the box. The only thing in it was a timeworn book. She gently lifted it up and flipped through it. "Hieratic. It's all written in hieratic." If hieroglyphs were her weakness, the shorthand cursive style that was hieratic was the bane of her existence. Hieroglyphs were the language of temples and tombs, of holy places, and magic. Ancient Egyptian is a complex language. When trying to learn it, Alex found it more intuitive to relate the symbols to their meanings to remember them, but hieratic was an everyday script that she could never quite get the hang of.

"May I?" Luke glanced at the cover and slowly reviewed some of the pages as he paced the small room. "This will take some time to translate. But from what little I've been able to suss out, this is some sort of manual for the God machine."

Alex closed the box and rapped on the divider. Harvey came and pulled the box into his side of the cage. "Anything else?"

She wondered just how many safe deposits this magical bank held. If it really was a Switzerland for the Gods, she could only imagine what sorts of secrets were held behind the teller cage. "Yes, as a matter of fact, there is." She couldn't believe she hadn't thought to ask before now. "There is a covenant between—"

Harvey's face sagged with disappointment. "Oh, darling, even if I knew where it was, I am expressly forbidden to disclose any information regarding an account without the depositor's permission. And I happen to know that one in particular would never give it."

"So you know who has it?" asked Luke.

"Yes, and I know enough to stay far away from being on their bad side. I've got some paperwork to do. Head over where you entered and put the key in that little hole. And you are done for." He covered a smirk with his hand. "I mean, you can leave. . . you're done here."

Alex glanced behind her and for the first time noticed a very small brass keyhole in the shape of an eye. The Gods were really playing the seer reference hard. There was something about Harvey's plight that made her sympathetic to him. Maybe it was her own experience being toyed with by the Gods. She looked up at his garish eternal costume and thought what a horrible bore his existence must be. She leaned near to the window and gazed into his old hazel eyes swimming in the strange concoction of wrinkles and makeup.

He looked from Luke to Alex, then to Gormund. Then his bright eyes connected with Alex. "Be careful. Call it a psychic freebie." The divider slammed shut.

CHAPTER TWENTY-THREE

Treasure in hand, Alex, Luke, and Gormund exited the void. They peeked from the elevator corridor and into the main party area. The air had been sucked out of the party. Alex pulled her phone out of her evening bag; it was nearly one o'clock. Whatever dimension they shared with the teller must move on a different pace than human time. Although many hours passed in the bank, it felt like they'd only been gone for a half hour or so. The DJ played a cheesy slow dance while those who were left searched for signs of love, or at least the drunken approximation of it. Even the security guards who were chasing them were not to be seen. They hastily left the building and called for the car.

When they got to the residency, Thorne answered the door and acted as if she'd been waiting up for them.

Alex was beat. All she wanted to do was head upstairs and crawl into bed. After saying good night to all, Alex made her way to the elevator as Luke and Thorne headed to the staircase.

Gormund, still standing by the front door, cleared his throat. "Thorne, Alex is going to need you to book two tickets to Luxor tomorrow. And to let the house staff there know they need to get it ready for us to arrive."

Alex spun around, more than a little perturbed at Gormund for attempting to step on her authority. The only person to order Thorne around was herself. In addition, Alex had changed her mind about going with Gormund—finding the God machine book changed everything. That would be her number one priority. Even if translation wasn't her strong point, she could oversee the process and get the ball rolling in dismantling the machine. "Scratch that, Thorne. I'm not going."

Now all eyes were on Gormund.

"You promised." Gormund was doing his best to pout, but that was a facial expression his face wasn't very amenable to, making him look more sinister than playful.

"I never did anything of the sort. First things first. We need to dismantle the God machine. I need to stay here and see that through. It's not the time for me to go gallivanting off to Egypt on some wild goose chase."

Luke looked crestfallen. "I think we can manage a simple translation without you."

"I have no doubt in that. But then we'll need to figure out next steps."

"There are phones, you know. Maybe it turns out we need the books of magic anyway. What if this translation is a dud?"

Luke had a point. There was something unreadable in his eyes, as if he wanted to say something, but just not in front of the others.

Before Alex could speak, Thorne butted in. "You know, it

might be good for you to get out of the city for a while. It might throw your pursuers off."

Luke's expression relaxed. "For once, I have to say I agree with Thorne."

"Let's talk about it in the morning. I've got a terrible case of portal fatigue." Alex headed toward the elevator.

~~~

Alex was soaring over Central Park, dipping and diving in free-flight joy. The urban grit of the city was changed into a fantastic world of deep shadows and treetops with skyscrapers as land-bound constellations. She swooped down to a large open grassy plane and skimmed it at a high speed.

At the edge of the grassy area, she landed on a high branch of a stately tree. Her heart swelled with joy when the familiar Cooper's hawk flew toward her, landing on a branch just above. He called to her, then craned his head upward and pushed off toward the sky.

She followed as he led her higher and higher, past the trees and buildings and up toward the heavens.

Once she caught up with him, the falcon banked to the side instead of flying in perfect unison and extended his talons, reaching out for hers. Caught off guard, Alex tried to pull away, but it was too late. He firmly locked his talons on hers. They spun toward the ground.

Alex's heart raced. Was the bird trying to mate with her? Or kill her? As they plummeted she tried to shake her limbs free, but the more she struggled, the tighter his grip was. The grassy field was coming quickly. He released her from his grip as she hit the ground.

A bright light flashed, and Alex was somehow flying again next to him, but instead of cool green grass misted with midnight dew below her, the ground was a vast desert.

The hawk called to her again, and they ascended into the sky.

This time it felt like he was taking her somewhere. Somewhere specific. She somehow knew the land below was Egypt.

He pulled ahead and dipped down into a deep wadi. The rock and sand canyon was created from eons of seasonal rainfall that cut its way into the soft ground. Through the wadi they soared near a lake.

Alex spotted what looked like a rather large shack near its shores.

He climbed again.

As she gained altitude there was something peculiar about the air ahead. It appeared to be both solid and reflective. In the distance tiny objects moved about. The movement did not resemble the graceful movement of birds in flight, but was more akin to the graceless loping about of humans.

They zoomed closer still. She sped toward the objects to get a better view. She hit something solid.

Her eyes flew open, her heart pounded as she stared up at the bed's canopy. Buxton. He was there, plain as day. He was in a gilded cage. If that wasn't strange enough, they were somehow imprisoned in a transparent structure in the sky.

~~~

Alex tossed off her sweat-dampened sheets and marveled at the field day a psychoanalyst would have with the dreams. She swung her legs over the mattress edge and climbed down to the silky Persian rug.

This last dream really threw her for a loop.

The flossy balcony curtains billowed into the room in generous curves. Alex shivered against the pre-dawn breeze, certain that she'd closed the balcony doors before going to bed. Or maybe she'd forgotten. When she closed the doors, her foot thumped against something solid, knocking it across the carpet and under one of the tapestry chairs. She peered under the chair. The object emitted bright prismed color, even in the sheltered moonlight.

She reached under the chair and grabbed it. The luminous crystal was given to her by Akh-Hehet. She paused before restoring the fiery stone to the secret-treasure compartment in the bottom of her scribe's bag. It was in her scribe's bag last night. *How did it end up on the floor?* She must have toppled it last night without realizing she'd done so. Alex returned her bag to the chair.

It had been a while since she'd thought of Akh-Hehet. Seeing her at the mediation was unexpected. Alex wasn't aware that the seer had any formalized connections to the agency. It was her impression that aside from her friendship with Alex's father, she was a civilian and not tied up in the workings of KHNM. But now it was as if she was assisting the Gods in their case against the agency.

Akh-Hehet's attitude at the mediation seemed to suggest that she was there somewhat under protest. What sort of carrot did the Gods use to pry the seer from her chandelier shop in the outskirts of the Luxorian souk? Sometimes disgruntled employees could be a great resource for information. Maybe a trip to Egypt wasn't such a bad idea after all.

CHAPTER TWENTY-FOUR

Getting sucked up the pneumatic tube was far less startling the second time. Jorge was the first to arrive in the R&D room. He killed some time wandering the sparsely furnished space while he awaited the others.

Across the room was a large circular platform. Jorge wondered what its function was. Something in the distance, beyond the platform, caught his eye. He wandered over to it.

It was a very small structure about the size of a large Nativity scene. It reminded him of those ancient Egyptian models of small houses, like those he'd seen at the Met. This one was constructed of tiny mud bricks. It even had a courtyard boasting a reflecting pool with a working fountain at its center.

The incongruence of this folksy relic existing in the sleek room made Jorge laugh. He had no idea what Idris would need with it. Did the magician use it as an altar for magic or sacrifices?

Jorge could have sworn he saw something moving within the small house. Were his eyes playing tricks on him?

The room was suddenly filled with Gwen's laughter as she tumbled out of the tube. Idris followed close behind.

"I could do that every day for the rest of my life and never tire of it." Gwen straightened her bejeweled shift and headed toward Jorge. Her eyes twinkled.

"I'm glad you like it." Jorge planted a kiss on her smiling lips, pleased that Gwen was so taken by the sky castle, but he had reservations of his own, beyond the whole transparency issues. To him it was like a glorified hamster cage equipped with all the necessary chutes and tunnels; the only thing missing was a wheel. Jorge half wondered if there was one waiting for him in the gymnasium.

Jorge pointed at the large vacant circular platform. "Are you planning on putting on some Vegas-style shows for us here?"

Idris jumped onto it. "No, this is where the God machine will live, once we get it here."

"What on earth is a God machine?" asked Gwen.

Jorge put his arm around her. "It was a vessel that, up until very recently, held the God's powers while they walked among humankind as Immortals. Since the Gods were returned to the Field of Reeds by Ms. Philothea, the globe has been languishing at the KHNM headquarters. It contained the powers of the Gods for close to twenty-five hundred years."

Idris rubbed his hands together. "And as far as we are concerned, it could be a valuable asset in our arsenal of tools. It was a magical containment system for centuries. It has a powerful layer of magical residue, like the nutrient-rich strata of Nile silt that built the black land of Egypt over the centuries."

"What does this sediment, or whatever you want to call it, have to do with your plans?" Gwen asked.

"If extracted as a complete unit, the God machine could

make a perfect vessel for my master's memory machine. I hope we will be able to attain it, but I won't be more certain until we can do a test run or two. That is where bringing forth Jorge's assistant plays a part. But if it turns out we can't retrieve it, the substance within would provide potent magical energy. Which will be very useful to us as we move forward in our endeavors."

Jorge nodded over in the direction of the miniature clay house. "Is that a mini prison for Buxton? Is he going to be shrunk down somehow and stowed away in there?"

Idris laughed, but his eyes remained cold.

If Idris hadn't been so accommodating and seemingly interested in looking out for Jorge's best interests, he would probably think that the immortal was laughing at him behind his expressionless eyes.

"Oh no, Master. That house belongs to a helper of mine. His name is Aah-Ha. My family has used his services for years. I keep this with me so I will have a place for him to stay if I have need of him. I believe in keeping my subordinates comfortable."

Jorge was pleased that they shared the same management philosophy. "A happy employee is a productive employee."

Idris arched his brow. "Of course, Master."

Gwen pushed forward to look at the tiny house. "Oh, it's so adorable. When you mentioned his being called to duty, did you mean that he is a ushabti?"

"The very same."

Jorge was perplexed. "How can that be? Ushabtis are in service to the dead. Is it because you are immortal?"

"Being immortal does have its privileges, but no, that is not why I have a ushabti servant."

"What about the dead person who Aah-Ha should be serving

in the afterlife? Aren't they a little pissed that you've nabbed their worker?"

Idris cleared his throat. "He belonged to Pharaoh Akhenaten. His rule was like nothing Egypt had ever seen. In ancient times he was thought of as a heretic. Now some envision him as a poet and the inventor of monotheism. He was neither. He was a puppet, a puppet for the Gods. Or at least one God in particular, Re. Together they worked toward turning Re into the Aten, otherwise known as 'The One True God,' in an unsuccessful power grab. Now both Akhenaten and Re pay the price in the Field of Reeds. Akhenaten is more a servant than a king, and his ushabtis are called to serve others from time to time as part of a recompense agreement.

"Well, I think it is time now for us to test out our ability to call forth your friend." Idris pointed to what looked like a massive screen. Jorge hadn't noticed it until that moment. "Remember, this could all go sideways."

"Edmund will be our guinea pig, so to speak?"

Idris nodded in assent.

"Are you absolutely certain about this, Jorge? Do you really want to have this on your conscience if it does go sideways?" asked Gwen.

Jorge didn't want anything to happen to Edmund. He'd been a loyal follower for so long. However, Jorge knew deep down this had to happen. "You know Edmund, Gwen. I think you would agree, if something goes wrong and we are not successful, he would have been honored that we included him as one of our team. Don't you think?"

"I hate to say it, but he idolizes you so much. You are probably right."

Jorge walked over to the massive screen. Under close inspection, he saw that what he'd thought of as a screen was a black void filled with minuscule particles. It looked as if someone had shaken out a cosmic rug in the moonlight. Jorge reached in.

"Don't!" Idris rushed over and pushed him away.

Jorge shot Idris a sharp look.

The magician switched to a more deferential tone. "What I mean, Master, is it is probably not smart to interfere with technologies we are unsure of."

"Of course, let's bring Edmund in."

—✓—

It took some time for Jorge to get ahold of Edmund and get him up to speed. Edmund was in a closed-door meeting with the higher ups of NASA, trying to get some solid information about recent sightings in the New Mexico desert. But as typical bureaucrats, they scheduled a meeting with him to tell him they couldn't tell him anything.

Years ago, Edmund sold his successful marketing company for bundles of cash, giving him the perfect opportunity to pursue his interest in the extraterrestrial. He'd been a strong ally and backer for Jorge in the early years when Jorge was living on a shoestring budget while hunting down stories of the fantastic and unknown.

When Edmund stepped out of the portal, Jorge ran over and slapped him on the back. "Welcome, friend. I am glad you could make it." Jorge read the look of wonder on his friend's face. "Can you believe it? We are hundreds of feet above the desert."

"Astounding! This is nothing short of amazing! Thank you, Jorge, for thinking of including me in your latest, and I must say greatest, out-of-this-world adventure." Edmund did a 360, taking it all in, then stamped his foot against the transparent floor.

"If you were going to plummet to the ground, it would have already happened." Idris's patience seemed to be wearing a bit thin. "Now that we are all here, can we move forward?"

"Are we going to bring forth the God machine so you can put it on its pretty pedestal?" asked Jorge.

"That is impossible now. The portal is not perfected yet. At the moment I can only call sentient beings that are willing, like your friend here. I will need to work on calling forward inanimate objects."

"My book can call objects forth. Wouldn't it be like that but on a grander scale?"

"Your understanding of magic is most limited. Your book is more like a parlor trick compared to what I am trying to do. You are trying to call forward a small stone; I am trying to transport the entire mountain. If we can harvest some of the God residue from the God machine, its powers will get me further faster. Do you think your assistant is ready for another ride?"

Traveling through portals was exhausting. Jorge knew it first-hand. Although Edmund appeared to be on board with the idea, Jorge thought otherwise. "I don't want to wear him out too much at the outset. How about your servant Aah-Ha?"

"Good idea, Master. I think it might be safer for him to handle the matter, being a magical entity."

Edmund looked relieved. "Thanks, Jorge. You know I am always up for unique adventures, but I think that portal took it out of me." He hooked his thumbs in his pockets and nodded toward Idris. "So, this guy is a magician? Where is his cape and wand?"

Idris blatantly ignored Edmund's question. "One thing to

keep in mind when you first meet Aah-Ha is that he was created as a courtier ushabti for Akhenaten's tomb. Akhenaten was still known as Amenhotep IV before he got wrapped up in the power grab with Re. Aah-Ha's function was to help the pharaoh in the courtly afterlife, to be a companion, a helper with a hint of court jester. So that can make him a continual kiss ass that more than likely has alternative motives. So be careful of your interactions with him. He must serve you, but he may not have your best interests in mind."

Idris looked pointedly at Edmund, then Edmund waved his hands over the miniature house. "Abracadabra and hocus-pocus." Nothing happened.

"Edmund Skipton, you know nothing of magic. I would appreciate it if you would keep your ignorance to yourself. Now, I will work real magic." He squatted to eye level with the small house and rapped quickly three times on the front door with his knuckle. "Oh come, servant of Akhenaten, lying in wait to be put to work. Heed my call and come, for I have honest toil for you." He knocked three more times then stood.

"Does the work always have to be honest?" asked Jorge.

"Oh, trust me, it's a game of semantics."

Jorge squatted down and peered into the small house. "Did it not work?"

"It never fails. A ushabti can't refuse a call to duty by someone he is magically bound to. It can take a few minutes for him to travel to these lodgings from the tomb where he is normally housed."

Edmund's eyes widened. "There is an undiscovered tomb of Akhenaten out there somewhere?"

"Of course." He turned to Jorge. "Is your friend always so slow to grasp things?"

"Go easy, Idris. All of this is new to Edmund." Jorge decided it was time to change the subject. "So how did Aah-Ha get bound to you?"

"It is similar to an inheritance that passed down from one generation to another."

"What do you mean 'passed down'?" A small but indignant voice came from below. "How dare you, a lowly magician. I am Aah-Ha, royal courtier to the great pharaoh Akhenaten—shame on you for treating me like a common hand-me-down like Aunt Neferura's scarab brooch or Grannie's old beaded linen dress."

"I like the ancient sass." The little ushabti grinned up at Gwen's comment. Jorge had a feeling the two would hit it off.

Aah-Ha stood about six inches in height. He wore a linen kilt and a broad collared necklace studded with turquoise, carnelian, and onyx. "What is it you need, magician? For what did you call me out of my great slumber? And who is this overzealous mortal staring down at me who has one foot in both realms?"

The ushabti was obviously speaking of Jorge. "One foot . . . ?"

A look of annoyance passed over Idris's face. "You have a glow about you, Jorge. A touch of the immortal."

Jorge looked at his hands. They didn't look any different to him.

"Only those who are immortal can see it. The glow appears to us like a golden shimmer. I assume it is magical residue from your time in the Netherworld."

Edmund looked taken aback. "Netherworld?"

"I'll explain everything to you later, after we retrieve the God goo."

"Goo retrieval?" asked Aah-Ha. "That sounds disgusting, but I would think it is safe to bet that is the reason you called me."

"I need to send you into a magical orb from that portal over there and have you scoop up a test sample."

"Easy, right?" Aah-Ha sounded dubious. "Nothing you ever send me on is easy."

Idris snapped his fingers, and a small crystal-clear test tube appeared topped with a rubber stopper. "Here is your vessel for the sample."

Idris handed it to Aah-Ha. The small man had to wrap his arms completely around it to hold it. "Couldn't it be a little smaller?"

"No, we need to gather as much of the substance as possible."

"We? Is someone else going to join me?"

"You will go alone."

"You were using the royal we?"

Idris continued. "You will need to fill it up completely. That tube looks like glass, but it is shear-cut diamond. Its razor-sharp edge will assist you in your sample collection." Idris held his hand out, rubbing his thumb and index finger together. Smoke rose in between his flesh. He unpinched his fingers and a small red-hot object fell into the palm of his other hand. He blew on it, and his breath chilled the air around them as if someone opened up a freezer nearby. The object cooled to a golden hue. It was a tiny shovel. "You'll need one of these too."

"Gold? Idris, you have to know that there are stronger metals than that."

"Keen observation, Master, but this is electrum. It is much stronger magically than just plain gold."

"Flesh of the Gods, right?" Edmund blurted out, like a student that couldn't help but try to impress the teacher.

"Correct. Electrum is a sacred metal, and it is the only metal we can use to extract or manipulate the magical residue."

Aah-Ha took the small shovel from Idris and clasped it along with the tube. "Let's get going. I'm getting weary of holding all of this."

"One thing I don't quite understand, now that you've called Aah-Ha, is how do you intend on retrieving the God residue? I don't think any of us have visited where this God machine is held. If we don't know where it is, how will we get Aah-Ha there?"

"While you and Gwen were getting reacquainted earlier, I took a little mind walk with Buxton. It was relatively easy for me to get what I needed. With all he'd been through, his weary mind opened right up for me." Idris smiled brightly.

With a flash of light and a small puff of smoke, Aah-Ha moved to Idris's shoulder. "Come on, let's get this show on the road."

"Hey, guys, as much as I'd like to hang around and watch a second retrieval, I've got some research to do for an article. Deadlines, you know." Gwen kissed Jorge on the cheek and headed toward the transport niche.

Idris went to the portal and set Aah-Ha on the lip of its opening. Jorge and Edmund joined him, standing on either side. "I am going to need complete silence. This attempt is going to be harder than what passed before, as this will be a round trip instead of one way."

Aah-Ha shifted his weight from side to side. "Get on with it."

Idris raised his arms in the air and closed his eyes, starting the spell-chant. Jorge guessed that the language was more than likely ancient Egyptian. Jorge studied the magician's face as it slackened when he slipped into a trance. He stared at his sharp profile punctuated by his large but oddly proportional hooked nose. There were no wrinkles on his face, making it hard to believe he was hundreds of years old.

The magician opened his eyes. They were filled with countess golden flecks of light as if his sockets each contained a star-filled galaxy.

Jorge looked away from the magician to the portal. Similar specks of gold were swirling throughout the portal. As they grew in number, their movement slowed and then pooled together into small clusters. The glittering masses began to knit together until they almost completely covered the surface of the portal. They swirled in a clockwise fashion until they stopped, and the portal was a continuous brilliant curtain of shimmering light. The golden material shifted to a silver tone until it resembled a very large mirror, looking almost like liquid mercury. In the center of the portal was a massive crystal ball with an opalescent sheen.

"Aah-Ha, servant to the house of Amenhotep, entrusted for centuries under the stewardship of my ancestors, I command you to do my bidding."

The ushabti stiffened to attention. "The law of the eternal ones commands me to ensure the work you give me is given with a full and true heart." Aah-Ha knelt down on the portal frame. His hands raised in the air then down onto the black material in prostration. "For this I swear on the house of the eternals and the Great Goddess of Truth and Justice, Maat."

Idris's eyes matched the mirror surface now. As he spoke, the room reverberated with the strange metallic vibrations of magic. "You may serve me by entering the sphere before you. Use the tools I supplied to extract as much of the material as possible. When you are done, call my name, and I will draw you back.

When you are in the sphere, you will look, and I will see. We will work as one. You will be my hands, my eternal servant."

"By the power of Re, I will do your bidding." Aah-Ha jumped into the portal.

It was disorienting to watch the ushabti travel between the two realities. It was like watching a stop-motion animation or an illustrated flip book. It was hard to see what he was doing, as his small body was easily lost within the large plasma ball. Jorge inched toward the portal to get a better look.

Aah-Ha was having difficulty getting purchase in the rounded object. Jorge squinted, wishing he could better see what progress the ushabti was making. He mentally slapped himself on the forehead, then reached into his explorer's jacket and pulled out his trusty binoculars. He lifted them up to his nose and attempted to twist them into focus. It was harder than he ever remembered to focus them, but then again, he'd never peered into an interdimensional portal before.

The combination of adjusting the lenses and trying to see through the unsteady portal material made his stomach turn. He lowered the goggles for a moment and closed his eyes. The nausea abated somewhat. He opened his eyes and looked through the void again. Aah-Ha was waving his arms frantically as he scrambled toward the portal.

The portal surface was changing from smooth waves to a choppy motion of stormy seas. Jorge's head spun again and nausea rose up. He dropped the binoculars, and they clanked to the floor. Jorge fell to his knees and grasped at the edge of the void to steady himself as his world was spinning. His body convulsed forward, and he vomited into the void.

A bright explosion of light knocked Jorge backward. His head hit the hard floor with a solid crack. Jorge lay there, assessing the damage, his world oddly stationary and spinning at the same time. From his vantage point, he could see that the portal was shutting down as the God machine looked like a faraway ghost.

"You fool!" Idris rushed over to him. His enraged eyes returned to their normal shade of purple. "Do you have any idea what you've done?" Idris was so close Jorge could smell the magician's clove-scented breath. "You have abandoned my faithful servant to the enemy."

Jorge propped himself up and shook his head, trying to clear it. "Can't we open up the portal again and retrieve him?"

Idris dramatically flung himself to standing and walked over to the portal that had gone black. He stood staring at the portal as if willing Aah-Ha back.

Edmund came to Jorge's aide, helping him up. "What happened?"

"Because of the distortion, I couldn't see what was going on. I could only vaguely make out what Aah-Ha was doing. I was hoping if I looked through my binoculars, I could not only get a better idea of what the ushabti was doing, but also get a sense for the room beyond the God machine. It was like trying to see through a three-dimensional kaleidoscope on the high seas." Jorge flicked away a few remaining stray bits of vomit from his explorer's jacket.

Idris turned to face them. The electric spark of rage in his expression muted to condescension as he pulled out a pocket square and handed it over to Jorge. "I won't want it back, thank you. There is a trash can over there."

Jorge grabbed the silk handkerchief and walked to the garbage can and attempted to brush off what vomit he could. "We can't open the portal again and bring him back?"

"In short, no. He is now irretrievable, at least for the

moment. Even if I were to call him, he would put our plans in jeopardy. KHNM would be able to chart the magical trace of my calling to our headquarters, and we aren't ready for that. He is now in enemy territory and has been seen."

Edmund looked skeptical. "But I saw it plain as day. Aah-Ha was alone in the sphere."

"The spell I cast on him allowed me to see what he saw. The reason Aah-Ha was running toward us was because someone had seen him. Someone was in the room that contained the God machine. I will have to figure out another way to rescue my servant from the hands of the agency. But on the bright side, our venture was not a complete failure. Idris held up the small cut diamond flask between his thumb and forefinger. "Ever the good servant, Aah-Ha was able to throw the vial of God essence to me before the portal closed. But I fear the electrum shovel is gone for good."

"So will we be able to take the priestess Meyret from her tomb?"

Idris walked back to the portal, staring once again into the void. "For all we know, that explosion killed Aah-Ha. It looks like your friend will have to take his place."

Jorge patted Edmund on the back. "You game?"

"On it, boss."

CHAPTER TWENTY-FIVE

After the rush to the airport and the ensuing lengthy flights, Alex was glad to pull into the long drive of Chicago House in Luxor. It was the residence that became the home for Egyptologists, linguists, illustrators, and support staff for the Oriental Institute during the archaeological season. During the cooler months of the Egyptian year, they worked on many projects that ranged from the detailed epigraphic survey of the entire temple of Medinet Habu to conserving Greek frescoes at Luxor Temple and curating the large brickyard of discarded temple parts to be pieced together like a massive, ancient three-dimensional jigsaw puzzle.

KHNM enjoyed a long-standing relationship with the Oriental Institute and Chicago House. The general staff was kept unaware of the organization. In an agreement made years ago, the story that the employees of the Oriental Institute were told was that the agents who came and went freely were great benefactors, which was not far from the truth as KHNM paid a

princely sum for this arrangement. The agency had been part-
nering with Chicago House as an operational base since it was
constructed in 1924.

There was only one person from KHNM who was stationed at
the Chicago House year after year. In fact, it was literally the
same person who acted as the continuous agency liaison, their
service stretching back to the time when the agency was formed
many centuries ago.

This one person, or, to be more correct, magical being,
currently went by the name Gini T. Being of jinn heritage, they
naturally switched back and forth over the years from male to
female at will. In this current iteration of themselves, Gini could
be described as the House's campy librarian, whose bold prints
and long dark eyelashes belied the fact that they earned four
master's degrees: one in Egyptian history, one in art, one in liter-
ature, and one in Victorian poetry.

As the director of KHNM, Alex was aware of this cover. It
amused her to wonder how the scholars at Chicago House would
react if they had any idea that Gini was older than many of the
relics they spent their time fussing over. What would they think
if they knew all of their scholarly questions could be answered
quickly and efficiently by the lived experience of their own librarian? Alex guessed that their minds would surely implode.

To keep the lie alive, every few years the jinn put in their
notice to return the next season with a completely different
persona. It was Alex's understanding that back in the 1960s
Chicago House experienced a period of great turnover where
they went through a different librarian each season.

Gini greeted Alex with their arms stretched out in welcome.
Before she knew what hit her, Alex was enveloped in one of their
bear hugs. For a tiny person, they were not lacking in upper body

strength. Alex attributed it to the fact that Gini was a magical being. However, Gini's ability to crush mere mortals in a single hug was not the only overpowering thing about them. Their perfume was wildly known to be applied with the distinct strength of a scent-filled nuclear bomb. Alex's nose flesh burned a little as the gust of their scent puffed up as they hugged.

Gini patted Alex on her back. "Glad to see you, dear." They disengaged from the hug. Gini's eyes grew large. "Oh, and you too."

Gormund half smiled.

Alex couldn't quite read what was between the two of them. At times they appeared to be intentionally oblivious to one another, which made Alex think there might be something between the two divine creatures. Alex smiled at the thought.

One benefit to Gini's scent was that you always knew when they were approaching. As luck would have it, the agency had not yet hired any staff with a sensitivity to it.

When Alex first met Gini, the librarian explained their intentional use of heavy fragrances. Over the course of many lifetimes, they learned that a heavily applied perfume would throw people off the scent of their magical origins.

Alex wondered if it wasn't just that Gini liked throwing people off.

Gini led her into the foyer of the building's entrance. The librarian's tone became formal as they entered the professional space where they might run into Oriental Institute staff.

"Glad to have you back, Ms. Philothea." Gini went to great lengths to speak in an extremely professional manner to Alex, which verged on the comical.

Gini paused at the hallway that led up to Alex's room. "Your room is ready. How long do you think you will be staying this time?" There was a glimmer in the librarian's eyes. Alex wondered if their curiosity had something to do with the squat Immortal intently staring at a potted palm in the distance.

"At this time, I am uncertain."

As Gini leaned in and whispered, "Are you okay?" The concern in their voice was touching, but confusing. Alex wasn't sure what they'd meant. Were they referring to the loss of Buxton? Alex brushed the idea away, as that was heartbreaking, but also in a way old news. It must be the court battle.

"I have every confidence that we will be able to defeat this lawsuit," said Alex.

Gini's eyes narrowed. "It all must have happened while you were in flight."

Alex's heart sank as she gazed into Gini's gold-ringed irises. "What happened?"

"Let's go to your room. Gormund, why don't you join us?"

Gormund rubbed his hands together. "It's not often that two lovely—"

Gini gave him a look that stopped him in his tracks.

Alex paused before entering the room. This was the first time she would stay in Buxton's old room. A wave of loss washed over her as she stepped inside. It was exactly how he'd left it.

All of the furniture at Chicago House dated back to when it was built in the 1920s, and every director over time added to the furnishings and decorative elements of the room. Buxton left his mark by adding a number of art deco pieces. Alex was drawn toward Buxton's favorite desk. If anything was a touchstone of the soul of her mentor, this was it. He would get all puffed up when telling the detailed story of how he managed to purchase the amazing specimen, and how it almost ended up at the bottom of the Mediterranean Sea.

She rubbed her hands over the polished two-toned wood. If only this desk were like a bottle holding a desert jinn. One that she could rub and bring her mentor back. She slipped into the sleek leather chair and faced Gini.

Gormund made himself comfortable at the bench that footed the large bed.

Gini looked every bit the bearer of bad news. "There was an incident with the God machine. I only know scant details. You may need to call Thorne for the latest." They paused as if to collect themselves. "There was an explosion, and Luke suffered the brunt of it."

Alex's mind spun with all kinds of horrible scenarios—she knew what power that containment orb held over the centuries. "Is he okay?"

"He has stabilized. The hospital sent him home after treating him for some minor burns."

"What happened? How did the God machine explode?"

"They aren't quite sure what happened. Luke and Thorne had just arrived, book in hand, and the thing just exploded."

"It can't have just exploded." Alex shook her head in disbelief. "How could something that was built of strong and ancient magic to hold the immortal powers of Gods . . . how on earth could something that indestructible just explode?" She got up and paced the room.

"Well, there is one theory, but I wasn't quite sure if Thorne was joking or not."

"Thorne almost never jokes. What did she say?"

"She heard someone retching just before the explosion."

Gormund laughed. "Retching? Really?"

"Barfing is more like it."

"Thorne really used the word *barfing*?" asked Alex.

"Actually, she did."

Gormund burst into another round of laughter.

Alex shot Gormund a searing look. "It must have been something else. Maybe there was an energy surge or something that she mistook for the sound of vomiting."

"Or, maybe Salima hacked up a fur ball." Gormund fell off his bench and was now rolling around on the floor laughing.

Alex had to admit that imagining the always proper Thorne uttering the word *barf* or any of its variants was quite humorous. "I am choosing to ignore you, Gormund."

"Thorne said it happened just before the explosion. Apparently Luke looked at her with a strange expression, and said, 'Do you hear that? It sounds like someone puking.' Before she could reply, an explosion knocked them back. But that's not the strangest thing. Once the smoke cleared, there was a little man running around the room."

Gormund's laughing stopped abruptly. "A little man? Next you are going to call him probably something equally inappropriate like—"

Gini put their hands on their hips. "Gormund, I am very well familiar that you prefer to be called a dwarf. But in this case the little man that was running around the room was a ushabti."

Alex gasped. "A ushabti?"

Gormund settled back onto his bench. "Well, in that case . . ." His voice trailed off as if he wasn't certain how to end what he was going to say.

"What was a ushabti doing in the God machine? How could it have made its way into a closed sphere?"

"It had to be magic," said Gormund.

"But why in there? Was it the ushabti that threw up?"

"You'd have to talk to Thorne about that. I wasn't there.

Apparently, when they entered the room, they noticed some sort of anomaly within the sphere. As they got closer, Luke exclaimed, 'Is that Gormund?' Thorne did laugh at that point of the recalling."

"Glass houses," Gormund mumbled.

"She said it looked like he carried a little bucket and was washing the interior of the globe or scraping possibly something off it. It took the little man a few clicks to see them walking toward him. He immediately stopped what he was doing and started running away from them toward a swirling void in the distance. Then came the sound of powerful retching."

"But why didn't they think the sound came from the ushabti? He is small, but he is a magical creature—they usually have all sorts of big surprises tucked away."

Gini raised their eyebrows and winked at Gormund. "So true."

Gormund shifted in his seat.

Alex was not used to seeing Gormund squirm as a flush of red crept up his face. The power dynamic between them crackled through the air. Was Gini the one person that Gormund was happily submissive to? Was there a crop and a whip hidden somewhere in the librarian's room at Chicago House? Alex guessed if you lived forever, it could be easy to pick up a fetish here and there.

"After the barfing, there was a great rumbling sound. Then both she and Luke were blasted backward. Luckily, the velocity was strong enough to blast them onto their backs and across the floor and away from most of the shards of magical glass. As soon as Luke's backward motion halted, he jumped up and—"

"It wasn't the explosion that harmed him?"

"No, his injuries came mostly from reaching into the flaming remnants of the God machine."

"Why on earth would Luke do that?"

"To save the ushabti. Once Luke was able to stand, he realized that the ushabti was having a hard time escaping. The explosion created an odd-shaped opening on the God machine's surface. The newly made opening was not only ringed with flames, but the edges were far from smooth. It must have looked like an exceptionally large mouth with angry glass teeth lining it. The ushabti's size was making it impossible for him to get up and over either barrier, and there was no way he could make purchase on the edge without slicing off one of his hands. The little creature scrambled out of sheer panic, but was not able to get anywhere. Luke ran toward the God machine and reached through the fire to extract him. Luke suffered great burns along his arms and abdomen, heavy-duty abrasions over his body, and a smattering of puncture wounds. Even with all of those injuries, he was able to keep hold of the ushabti who was struggling with blind determination to get away from him. Luke insisted that Thorne secure the ushabti before calling for an ambulance."

Alex's mind spun. "So where is the ushabti now?"

"Thorne locked him up in Buxton's old desk in his office."

Alex was floored. "His desk?"

"He is really small, and that ancient desk, as you know, has some pretty deep file drawers. He will be okay. Remember, he is a magical creature."

The discomfort Alex felt must have been telegraphed in her facial expression.

"I am sure his regular enclosure is much smaller than one of those drawers."

"Enclosure? That sounds a little zoo-animally."

Gormund crossed his arms. "Trust me. He will be okay in there. Remember, the purpose he was made for was to be leaned up against a wall in a dark tomb for eternity, just waiting to be called to do some errand for his master. Ushabtis are not creatures of comfort. They are created to create comfort for others. To him, being locked in a small dark desk drawer might be the kindest thing that could be done for him to calm his nerves."

Gini's eyes twinkled as they smiled at Gormund. "I had no idea you possessed such compassion. Yes, Alex, think of what you might do if a small bird was injured and frightened."

"I'll give Thorne a call and find out how Luke is doing. Thanks for the update. Tomorrow is going to be a big day."

"What will you be up to?" asked Gini.

"I'm going to pay a visit to my old friend the seer."

CHAPTER TWENTY-SIX

Jorge stood at the lip of the portal with Edmund, each suited up in their explorer's gear. He turned at hearing the pneumatic tube spitting Gwen out. His breath caught at the sight of her. She pushed from her landing and charged toward him. "Must you go? Can't Edmund do this on his own?"

"I must brave the danger."

Edmund's large eyebrows drew together. "I thought you said it was going to be a no-brainer."

"It's a simple extraction." Jorge nudged Edmund then stepped down from the edge of the portal and hooked his arm with Gwen's. He led her over to where Idris stood to cast the spell. "Edmund and I will enter the tomb, extract the sleeping priestess, and be back here in no time. I have already been there, so it won't take nearly as much out of Idris to transport us there. Then it will be in and out as fast as we can."

Jorge felt bad for immediately enlisting Edmund for interdi-

mensional travel. He was a businessman and part-time adventurer. He had no experience dealing with other realms. To date
his adventures were strictly terrestrial. The worst he needed to
worry about was the possibility of running out of water while
searching for signs of an alien past. "We will just have to deal
with whatever happens on the fly. There are things in life you
just cannot prepare for." Jorge looked into Gwen's brilliant green
eyes. "I will do what I must, whatever it takes to return to the
arms of the woman I love." Jorge kissed her softly and walked
back to the portal.

Idris cleared his throat. "I think it is time we get started. I
don't know what forces of protection might be activated in her
tomb. We may have only seconds to extract her. The God essence
Aah-Ha secured will help ensure your success, as it holds
immense powers." Idris pulled two ornate bowls out of his
smoking jacket and handed one to each of them. "I have placed a
small amount of what was retrieved in these."

The God residue was a gel-like liquid that sparkled like a rain-
bow-hued oil slick. Jorge sniffed it. The scent was a bouquet of
smells that was both attractive and repulsive at the same time.
He inhaled deeply, trying to figure out what exactly it smelled
like. One fragrance was honey and roses combined with the
smell of charred meat and a hint of turpentine.

"Please, both of you pull your faces away from the bowls. I
understand the scent is quite compelling. We have to get
moving."

Edmund continued sniffing at the scent of the Gods. Jorge
kicked his shin. Edmund lowered his bowl.

"Now, drink it. All of it."

Jorge was thunderstruck. "You've got to be kidding.
Drink it?"

Gwen faced Idris. "We don't know anything about that stuff."

"I am not kidding. I don't think that drinking the remnants of the Gods will do you any harm, and should actually protect you as it is circulating through your system. You could slather it on like some sort of magical sunscreen, but I think this will give you better coverage."

"Thinking and knowing are two different things, Jorge. He is being reckless with your lives. Don't do it."

"I must. There are always unknowns involved when you attempt things that have never been done before."

"I don't know, Jorge. I'm with Gwen. Believing and knowing are two different things. It doesn't pass the smell test to me." Edmund set his bowl down and stepped off the portal's edge.

Jorge grabbed his arm. "Can't you see what a great opportunity this is? How many mortals can say that they have ingested the vitals of the Gods?"

Edmund turned to face Jorge. He could see in Edmund's expression that deep down he wanted to be convinced, to have his nerves steeled in the brotherhood and camaraderie of the adventurer's spirit. "As you know, I have traveled to the Netherworld. I have solved a riddle from the great sphinx. I have brought back a book of magic. I have joined forces with a great wizard. These are things that no human has ever done. And now, I glow like the Eternals." He placed his hands on Edmund's shoulders. "Join me, take a chance on the magical. Your life will never be the same. After today, you will view your life in the context of before magic and after magic. Take hold of your bowl, take hold of your destiny."

Edmund retrieved the bowl.

Jorge winked and raised his bowl as if making a celebratory toast. "I'll go first. Down the hatch." Jorge gently tipped the vessel to his mouth. He tried to knock it back quickly like a shot. However, the thick goo pooled at the back of his throat, making him gag. He didn't want to freak out Edmund more, so he willed his body to swallow the magical goop. As it trailed down his throat, there was an unexpected effervescence that fizzed. He tossed his bowl aside, sending it clanking across the R&D room floor.

"Well at least that is done. I misjudged its viscosity, so be aware of that. Think about it like an odd-tasting sticky oyster." Jorge nudged Edmund with his elbow. "Your turn."

Edmund sniffed at the bowl.

"Also, there is a strong fizz at the finish. I am guessing that the Gods' powers must embed the molecules of the substance with energy that gets stored up as bubbles. Either way, it is an odd sensation." Jorge stumbled, feeling somewhat dizzy. The sensation of the tiny bubbles from the God essence coursing through his body threw him off.

Edmund's eyes suddenly went wide. "Why Jorge, you are turning gold."

Jorge spun around to see himself in the blank mirrored surface of the portal. Swirling around him like a cloud of atoms was a silver-gold haze. A surge of strength passed through him. It was as if his body was re-knitting itself together in an unbreakable weave.

Idris broke into the silence. "Edmund, drink your drink. I don't know how long the essence will last to protect either of you."

Edmund lifted his bowl and drank enthusiastically, then wiped his mouth off with his sleeve. "Let's go find us a priestess!"

"Hear, hear!" roared Jorge.

Idris walked over to the portal and pointed at two spots on the ledge. "Here and here."

Jorge laughed at the magician's attempt at humor and stood at the spot Idris designated on the right side of the portal.

Idris looked over at Gwen. "Are you going to stay for the proceedings? If you are, I need to have your promise that you will be still in sound and in movement. I cannot have you interrupting my trance. No disruptions."

"I promise."

"It looks like we are all in our places. Now we begin. Jorge, I will need you to hold in your mind whatever memories you have of Meyret's tomb. Once you do that, I will use it as a magical rope tow, so to speak, and I will follow your memory into the tomb. Oh, I almost forgot these." Idris reached into his smoking jacket and pulled out two large blades that resembled machetes, except these blades were curved and their hilts were encrusted with jewels.

Jorge's grip was a stylized head of Thoth. Edmund's was a crescent moon. "These swords have served me well over time. They were a gift from my long-departed father."

Jorge tossed the sword from one hand to the other. It was surprisingly light for all the precious metals and gemstones. He sliced it through the air. The blade moved effortlessly as though a magical hand assisted him.

Idris handed both of them a sheath for the blades and returned to the spot where he would cast the spell.

"I am ready, Idris. I am going to focus my thoughts on the tomb." The first thing that came to mind was the impossibly beautiful ceiling. It was a half-barrel arch tiled night-sky blue, embedded with enchanted golden stars above. The space was lit with torches, making the stars twinkle like a thousand celestial sequins that surrounded a representation of the pale, naked body of the Goddess Nut, who swallowed the sun each night and gave birth to it at dawn.

He was envisioning the raised sarcophagus in the middle of the tomb that held the priestess with its intricate bas-relief carvings of Nephthys and Isis when Idris yelled, "Jump now!"

Without hesitation Jorge leapt through the portal into the tomb. When his feet hit the ground, he checked to make sure that Edmund had followed suit.

Edmund stood, mouth agape at the ethereal beauty around him. Jorge grabbed his arm, pulling him to the sarcophagus where the priestess lay sleeping. He knew that they were on borrowed time and that Bes, her protector, was probably close at hand.

The limestone sarcophagus towered above them. Jorge knew that the top was open so she could gaze up at the stars above while she was under the magic sleeping spell. All they needed to do was get up there and pull her out.

Jorge carefully climbed up to the sarcophagus's head and peered down at the sleeping priestess. Edmund was soon at the other end, by her feet.

"I guess we will just reach down and lift her up gently, then carry her through the portal." Jorge leaned down and slid his hands under her shoulder blades. As he lifted her up, Jorge wished they would have brought a stretcher or something to carry her on.

They gingerly pulled the priestess out and rested her on the edge of the sarcophagus so they could switch her orientation from horizontal to vertical. Jorge held her upper body with his hands in her armpits as Edmund carefully moved her feet downward. Suddenly, her feet slid out of his hands. Jorge swayed as he tried to steady her. His sword slipped out of its sheath and clanked onto the tomb floor.

Jorge and Edmund locked eyes.

As he held her still, Jorge strained his ears for the sound of alarms or rushing feet. He was surprised to hear nothing. Edmund jumped and wrapped his arms around her. "I would have thought that this of all places would be heavily alarmed."

Jorge jumped down to join Edmund, who was holding the priestess. Jorge slipped his hands in between her arms and let her weight fall against him. Edmund grabbed her feet and hefted her up, and then they made their way to the portal. Jorge was shocked that they hadn't run into any interference.

Up ahead the light from the R&D room cast the interior of the tomb with a strange filtered glow. Jorge imagined this would be what it would look like if you were able to walk behind a television screen. The light glinted off Edmund's sword.

"Hey, wait a minute. Let's set her down. I should grab Idris's sword. It seemed important to him."

They lowered the priestess to the stone floor.

Jorge was just about to grab the sword when a loud crack and a flash of light filled the room. He grabbed the sword in one fluid motion. Out of his peripheral vision, a short, wide man charged toward him, yelling. His razor-sharp teeth glinted. It was Bes, the strange-looking dwarf God of home and hearth, Meyret's protector.

Jorge ran to the portal, glad to see that Edmund was already dragging the priestess through it. Bes was on his heels, but he certainly couldn't stop and see exactly how close. Jorge charged toward Edmund and grabbed the priestess's feet, lifting her up so they could carry her over the portal's threshold. "We're coming in hot!" he yelled.

Edmund backed through the portal with Jorge following close behind.

Jorge jumped from the portal's edge and glanced back. He escaped, just in the nick of time. He could see the God's face pressed up against the portal as it started to close.

"You. Will. Die." A threatening smile pulled across the God's wide face, so that every one of his razor-sharp teeth could be seen.

CHAPTER TWENTY-SEVEN

The phone call with Thorne took longer than Alex expected. Her assistant confirmed the ushabti story but not much more. The only additional information she was able to provide was that the ushabti was from the tomb of Akhenaten and that it managed to escape from where it was being held. Thorne suggested that Alex call back once Luke woke from his drug-induced haze, implying that he might have more insights on the incident. The doctor had given him a strong sedative to allow him to sleep. Before hanging up, Alex tasked Thorne with finding out who sent the little guy. She was quite certain the old dead pharaoh didn't have a beef with her.

Thorne mentioned having an inkling that Jorge Trinculo had something to do with the ushabti. She could have sworn that she saw his crazy hairdo through the interdimensional portal. Alex found it hard to believe that he would be in possession of that type of magical equipment, but she knew nothing was utterly impossible.

The dining room was absent of both Gor and Gini as well as all the Chicago House staff. Alex forgot how early they usually cleared out in the morning. She understood the logic, though. While doing physical work in the hot climate of Egypt, it was good to get as much done in the early hours of the day before the direct assault of the afternoon sun.

It felt good to be back in Egypt. She walked through the lush grounds of the residency and out to the busy Corniche, in the direction of Akh-Hehet's chandelier shop. Although her destination was on this side of the busy roadway, she was compelled to cross and properly greet the great and mighty Nile. All down the road was a line of tour buses awaiting their freshly breakfasted passengers.

A morning breeze ruffled the palm fronds lining the boardwalk, and a cacophony of birdsong filled the air around her. The early-morning sunlight made the river shimmer as if it were adorned with delicate gold leaf.

Her heart was light as she strolled down the boardwalk, making her way to Luxor Temple. The sandstone structure almost glowing under the soft sunlight drew her to it. The souk she was going to was a number of streets behind the temple, but she was glad to have taken the scenic route.

Gathering in front of the great pylon walls of the temple was a small tour group. Aside from them, the entire site appeared to be empty, much like that night not so long ago.

Memories flooded back to her. That night under a full moon, everything felt possible. But now, everything felt impossible.

The temple drew her in, like a voyeur to her own emotional baggage. As she passed through the great sandstone statues of Ramses the Great that fronted the pylons, the memories flowed through her of the time before everything changed.

A shiver passed through Alex as she walked by the niche where Niles kissed her for the first time. She closed her eyes, remembering how softly and tentatively he kissed her. How his eyes looked when he gently pushed away from her. The golden specks that danced around his irises were bright with desire. He explained how it wasn't right for him to want her. He was an Immortal. She drew him close, and they twined together, losing themselves. The impossibility of them was shed as the promise of tomorrow bloomed.

Now that promise had died on the vine. Maybe it never existed.

Alex tilted her head up at the crescent moon still hovering in the silver-blue morning sky. The day was young. That long-ago night with Niles, under the full moon, they meant to go to the shrine that her ancestor Alexander the Great restored. It lay deep in the heart of the temple. She needed to see Akh-Hehet, but it wouldn't hurt to see if that ancient warrior might have left a clue about the books of magic. She figured it was a long shot, but she was so close she might as well check it out. She continued on deeper into the temple.

Alex was filled with awe as she made her way through the last colonnade, into the great hypostyle hall where the Romans added their frescoes, and then into the furthest and most sacred part of the temple.

Most ancient Egyptian temples had three sections. The first would be the most open, usually with huge statues and reliefs of the pharaohs, and sometimes the queens paying obeisance to the Gods. This was the part of the temple where a common person could come on festival days and experience the grandeur of the Gods. The temple's middle section was reserved for the priestly class. In the third and furthest reaches of the temple complex, where the sacred and hidden mysteries of the Gods took place, only high priests and royals could walk.

She passed from the soft light of the courtyard and into the dark inner sanctum. It took a moment for her eyes to adjust. Alex stood in the darkness of the enclosed space and wondered at the fact that the ancient people of Egypt believed that the temple she was standing in was built on the very mound where Amun—the Great Cackler, the Hidden One—was born.

She carefully scanned the depictions her ancestor commissioned to pay homage to the great and powerful God. After making a complete circuit, she looked down at her watch. Time had flown by. She'd been searching the surface of this great stone palace for over a half hour, but sadly had found no ancient missives from her long-departed ancestor.

Then it hit her. She was coming at the problem the wrong way. Unless she happened to come across a necromancer, which was unlikely at best, she was never going to be able to speak to Alexander the Great. But she did know someone who was very much living who knew him intimately—Meyret. And it just so happened Alex was traveling with her Immortal security guard and BFF. Maybe she could pry some information from her still-living ancestor.

But, first things first, she needed to check in with the seer.

The sounds and the smells of the bazaar invigorated Alex. It was a showplace of color and brilliance, with rich and jewel-toned rugs, bright patterned scarves blowing in the wind, and metalworkers' shops of silver, brass, and gold glowing against the bright lights within the shops. Each one was like a different petaled exotic flower luring in the curious shopper as they hunted for the perfect memento of the great and mighty Nile.

She moved deeper into the narrowing alleyways of the souk where the locals mainly shopped. This area tended to be less colorful but filled with more useful items such as spices, fruits, vegetables, meat, and sandals.

She stood at the end of a dark and narrow alley. Although it was almost midday, the sun was unable to penetrate the space. In the distance she could see the brightly lit landmark that was Akh-Hehet's shop.

The storefront dazzled Alex as she stood in front of the main window marveling at the beautiful and otherworldly vision the seer created. Hundreds of chandeliers hung throughout the huge storefront, massed together like a canopy of a large cut-glass old-growth forest. Alex could have sworn that there were a third more chandeliers than the last time she visited.

The crystals were not only an aesthetic choice. As the seer aged and her powers of foretelling diminished, she found that the high concentration of crystals helped boost her powers. She was continually adding to her store's inventory.

Arriving unexpectedly, Alex hoped that Akh-Hehet would be at home and not off somewhere working on the lawsuit or some other errand. It smarted a little that the old woman was on the side of the Gods.

Akh-Hehet had been close to her father. Phillip had first met the seer as a homeless and discounted woman. She was rambling through the alleyways like a stray Caironese dog, begging for scraps and for someone to listen to her. He took her under his wing, found her housing, and got her back on her feet.

Alex tried the door, and it was locked. Usually Akh-Hehet kept it open during business hours. She rapped on the door.

From inside came a soft tinkling sound. Alex guessed it was the seer's bald head brushing up against some of the lower hanging crystals.

The dazzling array of chandeliers parted to reveal Akh-Hehet, wearing a severe black wig with a plait of turquoise and carnelian beads playfully dangling to one side. Apparently, she found one of her dress wigs. A deep frown pulled across her face. "What are you doing here, Alex?"

"I have some questions for you."

Akh-Hehet peered over Alex's shoulders as if searching for something. Her expression relaxed into a soft frown. "You know I can't help you with the lawsuit. I've been conscripted in aiding the Gods. There are no answers here for you. You should have stayed away." Her gold rings glinted light as she moved to close the door.

There was something strangely constrained in Akh-Hehet's demeanor. Alex knew her to have a light playfulness about her.

Feeling bold, Alex shoved her foot forward, blocking the doorway. "Auntie, we don't need to talk about the legal issues, can't we just catch up? It has been ages since we've had a chance to chat."

Akh-Hehet pushed the door. The wood bit into Alex's foot.

Alex leaned in and whispered, "There is something else I need to ask you about. Something has changed in me since I returned from the Netherworld."

The old woman squinted as she let the door pressure slacken. "What kind of things?"

"Dreams. I have been having the strangest dreams."

The color drained out of Akh-Hehet's face.

"What kind of dreams?" The old woman glanced beyond Alex again, her eyes scanning the alley as if expecting someone to be lurking in the shadows. "Oh, never mind, just come in." Akh-Hehet yanked her into the chandelier shop with an unusual strength.

Akh-Hehet closed and locked the door to the shop. "There are some things that shouldn't be spoken of out of doors. How about a spot of tea?" Without waiting for a response, the seer cut a path through the twinkling cloud of crystals.

Alex wordlessly followed the seer, ducking here and there to miss the dangling crystals overhead as they headed toward the plain black curtain that partitioned the area between the shop and Akh-Hehet's Spartan living quarters. Alex's head grazed a cluster of crystals, making them cascade into a tinkling melody.

Alex pushed back the thick black curtain. Akh-Hehet stood in her tiny kitchenette getting the tea things ready. Alex sat down at the small Formica table.

The seer was a jumble of contradictions. Her almost monastic style of her living space was in direct opposition to the more opulent items Akh-Hehet owned. She possessed beautifully crafted wigs draped with gold and precious stones. She had long, flowing embroidered gowns with jewels that would rival the ancient tomb goods of any royal or courtier. And her exquisite wafer-thin bone china tea set was hand decorated with an abundance of gold trim and hand-painted blue roses.

According to Akh-Hehet, she lived her past life many centuries ago as a high priestess during the Amarna period. Were her expensive tastes an echo of this past life?

"Cream or sugar?"

"Both." Alex smiled up at the seer, who was now holding the sugar tongs. "Three, please." The old woman's eyebrow raised as she plopped the cubes one at a time with dramatic effect, then poured the black steaming liquid into the cup, adding a slurry of cream. "I remember now, you like it sweet and creamy, just like your dad."

Alex raised the cup to her nose, breathing in the lovely malty smell of the black tea.

"So what about these dreams?" Concern colored Akh-Hehet's words.

"They feel familiar and at the same time strange. There is something about them that makes me think of you."

"Not surprising; I hear that a lot."

Alex tilted her head.

"Familiar yet strange."

They both laughed a little. The air between them became far less dense.

Alex took a sip of the tea. Its warmth spread through her, reminding her how chilled the old woman's living space was.

"Are you finding the dreams to be more or less symbolic? Or does it feel like you are experiencing real things?"

"They seem more real to me somehow, but most of the things I saw were impossible."

"But haven't you already experienced the impossible? You've battled Immortals and sent them back to the realm of the Gods and ventured into the Netherworld. Why do you still see things as being impossible?"

"I saw my dad."

"What is strange about that? You were in the Netherworld flying around and saw your dad. Isn't that exactly where you would expect him to be?"

"So how did you know I'd been flying? I hadn't told you that part yet."

"Because that is what happens when I am visiting my Hormey."

"Hormey?"

"There are times when Horemheb appears to me as a bird, and we fly together in the deep expanse of the sky. Is there anything else you've been experiencing?"

"I don't think so, why?"

The old woman looked thoughtful as she sipped her tea. "There is a belief that if you go to the Netherworld and you survive, you might emerge with supernatural powers."

"Like some sort of comic book hero?"

"Something like that. But other than the dreams you haven't noticed anything?"

"I can't say that I have. So the dreams you have when you go and visit Hormey. How did you come by those?"

"I too have ventured into the Netherworld and returned unscathed."

"When was this?"

"When I was a priestess of the Great Goddess Hehet, back when I first met Horemheb. We had some adventures, he and I." A warm smile spread across the old woman's face.

"But that was thousands of years ago. How is it that you can remember it?"

"When a mortal spends time in the Netherworld, it strengthens their Ba in a way that makes them almost semi-immortal. I was held captive in the Netherworld for many years, making my Ba almost indestructible."

"Do you think the same will happen to me, that I will be reborn over and over in a never-ending cycle?"

"I don't know for sure, but I doubt it."

"But the dreams, are they here to stay?"

"I am afraid so. With all the uncertainty right now, it might be best to keep it all under your hat."

"Who would care about my random dreams?"

"I can't say. But take it as a word to the wise."

"Taken. I won't mention it. Do you happen to know anything about the books of magic Buxton used to talk about?"

"Why do you ask?"

"I know you can't talk about the litigation proceedings, but I had hoped finding those books might help me with that. Times are uncertain, not only for the agency but for humans. They aren't aware of all the magic that is now swirling around them and will have no idea how to cope with it once they discover it. I hope that KHNM can help the Gods by finding these magical artifacts and keeping them out of the hands of mortals. Starting with the books."

"Honestly, I think the Gods couldn't care less about that. They have other concerns. But like you said, I have nothing more I can add." Akh-Hehet's expression changed from friendly to cross.

"I am sorry, Auntie. I meant no offense. I am just worried about all of the people I am responsible for."

"How about sitting under the crystals for a visioning? It might be helpful to sort out some of your concerns, and I've not had a willing victim in quite some time."

It could be useful to indulge Akh-Hehet. And maybe she would get some helpful information out of the exercise. "Let's do it."

"We might even be able to get some insights into your dreams. If we are able to travel together, I might be able to help you sort it out. Or I could probably take you back to where you saw your dad."

Alex sat back down. "You could do that?"

"It is entirely possible."

"Show me the way."

Akh-Hehet picked up the tea things and set them near the sink, then led Alex through the black curtain and into the sea of twinkling crystals.

Alex walked onto the carpet that lay at the center of the canopy of chandeliers. Last time she was here, Akh-Hehet told her that its intricate pattern was specially woven with magical threads.

They sat across from one another on the carpet. Looming overhead was the massive upside-down crystal triangle. Akh-Hehet had explained that this large four-pointed pyramid served as a focal point for the psychic energy that flowed through the surrounding network of crystals.

Akh-Hehet held out her hands. "Are you ready, dear one?"

Alex clasped the seer's soft, crepe-like hands, the small bones within feeling fragile, almost birdlike.

"Calm your mind, Alex." The old woman squeezed Alex's hand, once again with a surprisingly resolute grip.

Alex took a deep breath, then exhaled, imagining her cluttered thoughts falling away.

"Good, now we can start. I don't know how much you remember from the last time that we did this, but you will need to stay completely silent. I will need you to resign yourself to the fact that you are only a participant in this moment and not an actor. During this visioning, I will attempt to take you to the Netherworld dwelling of your father. I have been there many times, but I have never tried to take anyone with me. I am not at all sure how this will go."

"Is there anything I need to be aware of?"

"You are the first mortal that I will try this with. We are cutting a new path. If we are successful, we will know."

"Know?"

"If the magical threads that run through this carpet are now woven through you."

"Sometimes it is better to not know things."

"You are your father's daughter. I've seen it in you. It is not in your genetic makeup to gloss over or ignore the facts. Let's get started. Whatever you do, remember I am your guide. If you sense that you can act on your own, don't. Even if magical threads are running through you, there is a great learning curve that comes with those powers. There can be disastrous consequences, for both of us."

"All right, I will be seen and not heard, like a good child."

"Good. Now close your eyes and remember, do nothing."

Akh-Hehet started chanting, and as her voice grew louder, a breeze kicked up in the room, making the crystals chime loudly. Her voice rose over the cacophony of sound. "Oh mighty Hehet, Great Goddess of the Immeasurable, please hear the voices of those who come to ask."

Alex opened her eyes as the walls around them disappeared. She allowed herself to be drawn away. Feeling light as a feather, she flew through what looked like a million small twinkling universes. She half wondered if each of the chandeliers were their own galaxy within the universe of cut glass. The thought flew from her mind as the world dropped away and she flew ever higher. She moved with a feeling of lightness and freedom.

The pinpoints of light began to swirl as if she were cast down upon a heavenly potter's wheel. It moved faster until the points of light became streaks as they spun together. She felt herself being pulled toward this celestial bullseye of light and energy.

When her body breached the surface, she braced herself, expecting to feel the heat from the light, only to find that the sensation was more like breaking through a fine mist of ice crystals.

She was flying in a midnight-black sky hung with millions of stars that scattered far into the horizon. It was similar to some of her previous dreamscapes. She turned her head to her right and saw a small starling flying next to her, instead of the falcon that usually accompanied her. The thought of Akh-Hehet as a noisy little common-yet-iridescent bird made her smile.

Akh-Hehet pulled in front of Alex, guiding her downward toward a village that looked like the one she saw her dad in. She was excited and a little anxious at the prospect of seeing him again.

They landed on the wall that surrounded the courtyard. In its center was a large reflecting pool with purple-pink Egyptian lotus flowers floating atop the calm water. The sound of frogs and the rustle of palm fronds filled the night air.

The courtyard was empty. Had they made their way there for nothing?

Returning without seeing her father would be a complete letdown. Alex looked over to the starling standing next to her. Akh-Hehet's attention was pointed at a far corner of the courtyard. Stepping out from the dark shadow and walking toward one of the flickering torches was her dad. He looked concerned as he stood over the pool, gazing intently at its surface. She'd seen that sort of stare before when he was trying to sort out a problem.

He moved away from the pool and sat down on one of the stone benches that surrounded the courtyard. He was waiting as if he was expecting someone.

He looked exactly as she remembered him, although there was something different, something she couldn't quite put a finger on. It was surprising to her how solid and real he looked. She assumed he would have more of a ghostlike transparency.

Akh-Hehet was motioning with her beak toward the sky, then pushed off.

Niles walked into the courtyard.

Alex knew the seer expected her to follow her into the skies, but Alex kept herself firmly rooted to the wall.

Akh-Hehet was circling above.

Unlike her father, Niles burned brightly, with the golden-silvery halo of immortality.

Akh-Hehet landed next to her with a dramatic thump. The starling nudged Alex and dramatically pointed at the sky with her beak.

Phillip stood and walked over to Niles. "What has been taking you so long? You understand what is at stake here, I hope."

Alex shook her feathered head. The seer had to know that Alex needed to see whatever was taking place between Niles and her father.

Niles stood above Phillip with his hands on his hips. "I know better than anyone what's at stake. Don't think I don't know how important her safety is to you. But know this, to see her harmed would crush whatever still remains good and hopeful in me."

A bright joy filled Alex. He did still care for her. She looked over at the starling with hopeful eyes, but all she got was a glare and a swift turn of the head motioning upward.

Alex stood her ground. If they were going to talk about her, she had every right to hear it.

Phillip stood and put his hand on Niles's shoulder. "I really do appreciate all that you've done for her. I know that you were the lone God who argued against her being killed."

Alex's spindly bird legs buckled. Killed?

"Yes, and now I get the delightful distinction of playing invisible jailer between the realms. But I guess given the alternative, I'm glad to do it."

"You won't be so glad if it turns out that—"

"Don't." Niles shuddered. "Have you heard anything more from Horemheb?"

What did Horemheb, a long-dead ancient Egyptian pharaoh, have to do with Alex's continued existence? She tried to speak. An awkward cheep came from her tiny bill. Both men looked in her direction, then back at each other.

Akh-Hehet's sharp beak pecked hard into Alex's neck.

Alex did her best to ignore the angry starling's stare that was blazing into her.

"I know that Horemheb is on the way to find Akhenaten, to bargain with him."

Phillip was a little less tense than when Niles first arrived.

"I am sure he will be more than happy to cooperate. He's got it pretty bad right now since we've returned to the Field of Reeds."

Phillip chuckled. "I can only imagine how it would feel to go from pharaoh to servant."

"Since we've returned to the Field of Reeds, things in our realm aren't what they used to be. The realm was allowed to go to seed after centuries of neglect, and the cracks are definitely showing."

"Maybe you should all call PBS and pitch a show called *This Old Realm*."

"I like to see your humor coming back, Phil."

"Are you certain this will work?"

"Nothing is certain. But it is our best chance."

"But you realize the consequences if it doesn't work."

"Even if it does work, it will cost me in ways that you could never imagine. As I have told you many times before, I will do anything to protect Alex. Anything. I am fully aware of what the price will be for me if we fail."

What was Niles talking about? What sort of peril was he in? She glanced over to Akh-Hehet and a cloud of fatigue swept in, dulling the starling's eyes. Making her stay this long must be taking a toll on the old woman.

Alex nudged Akh-Hehet and motioned upward. The starling took to the air as Alex took one last look at her father and Niles. Her heart was light as she took to the sky.

~~~

Alex's eyes flew open as her rump hit the ground. She and Akh-Hehet must have levitated above the magic carpet. The crystals above them were still.

Splayed across the floor was Akh-Hehet. Alex rushed over on her hands and knees. She was surprised at how the ancient carpet burned her palms. The pain was so striking she had to stop and inspect her hands. No burns or scratches were evident. An electrical heat was radiating up through the knees of her pants. It was so odd because previously the rug was as soft as velvet. Was something going wrong with the magic they used? Could the threads be overheating from their excursion to the Netherworld?

Alex gently turned the seer's head toward hers. Her complexion looked greyer than its usual robust rosiness. Her eyes moved beneath their lids as if she was in the deepest of REM sleep. Alex slipped her hands under Akh-Hehet and lifted her to take her to bed.

Regret spun through Alex as she carried the old woman back to her sleeping quarters in the rear of the shop. Akh-Hehet made her promise that she would just watch and follow the seer's lead, and now the old woman was out cold.

Alex knew this was her fault but couldn't imagine doing anything different. Not only did she get to see her father and Niles, but she also learned some very startling information. Why would the Gods want her dead, anyway?

She nudged her way past the black curtain and laid the seer down on her bed. As Akh-Hehet's head hit the pillow, her wig became slightly askew. Alex lifted her head to reposition the wig properly. She had no idea how long Akh-Hehet would be out. Should she try to call for help or an ambulance? Alex didn't think that the local doctors would know how to alleviate a case of magical fatigue. Maybe it would be best to stay with her for a while. Maybe she would regain consciousness soon. If not, Alex might have to call Gini for an extraction.

A shiver ran up Alex's spine, and she suddenly felt alone in the strange dark space. She scanned the sparse furnishings around her. They were all well made. Alex always wondered if Akh-Hehet, or Emily Loren as she was born, came from a well-off family, but chose to live the life of a modern-day monk.

Near the bed was the only thing of beauty. It was an antique wooden writing desk, and sitting on it was a jewelry box with geometric patterns of mother-of-pearl, onyx, and carnelian inlay. It was nothing short of a master work.

Alex pulled open the long, thin drawer just under the desk-top. The drawer was lined with velvet and within were several necklaces, bangles, and rings that would make any collector of antiquities drool. How had she come by these beautiful pieces?

A moan came from the old woman. Alex rushed to her side. "Are you all right?"

Akh-Hehet's eyes were still firmly closed. The old woman grabbed Alex's wrist. "Meyret, what are you doing here?" Akh-Hehet must have been in the middle of a dream.

"It's me, Auntie. It's Alex. Meyret isn't here."

"It is a good thing, Meyret, that we are talking about Alex. She is in grave danger. The Gods want her dead, you know."

It was shocking to hear Akh-Hehet reaffirming what Niles had said. "But, why would they want Alex dead?"

"You know why. I don't need to explain it to you. It has to do with the same issue I have. The one you've been so kind to help me with over the years."

"They think she might be changed by her time in the Netherworld?"

The old woman laughed so loud Alex checked to see if she was still in the dream state. Akh-Hehet's eyes were still closed. "Don't forget that she also sent them back to their realm, sent their Ba-souls back to where they belonged, didn't she? Showing them a thing or two. I'd say it is nothing short of surprising that she isn't already dead. If it weren't for Niles, she'd—"

The sound of broken glass from the front of the chandelier shop startled the old woman awake. "What the—"

Alex's hands shook with adrenaline. An intruder was in the shop. She motioned to Akh-Hehet to stay put, then crept to the curtain.

As she passed by the table, she grabbed the Monet-printed umbrella from its stand. It wasn't much against a thief, but it was all she had. She was searching the glimmering darkness of the crystal cloud beyond the curtain when a body pushed into her.

She whacked the umbrella hard on her attacker, and they fell backward.

Alex whipped the curtain sideways.

Gormund was sitting on the floor, rubbing his head.

"What are you doing here?"

He stood. "What are you doing hitting somebody on the head, with what I must say is the most lethal umbrella I've ever run across?"

"You broke in. What was I supposed to think?"

"It was an emergency."

"We are fine. I don't get why you broke the glass door. Now I'll have to arrange for a new one to be installed." Alex crossed her arms and gave Gormund what she hoped to be a searing look.

Akh-Hehet swung her legs over the side of the bed with a silly grin on her face. "I knew it would work. I never had the opportunity to test it out, though."

"What?" Alex looked over at the old woman.

"The umbrella. Its core is made of steel."

Gormund rubbed his head some more and mumbled, "Yeah, that sounds right."

"What was the emergency, if it wasn't us?"

"Meyret is gone."

CHAPTER TWENTY-EIGHT

Alex sat in the courtyard of Chicago House, staring up at the palm fronds that swayed in the breeze over-head. She took a sip of the bourbon old-fashioned Gini had made to calm her nerves. She couldn't believe that Meyret was captured. Taken from her own sleeping tomb located in the New Mexico desert.

Gormund was beside himself. He was tasked with watching over her for centuries, and now she was unaccounted for. Whoever took her managed to bypass the magical security system he set in place. It had never failed him before. By the time the alarm sounded and Gormund was able to portal into the tomb, he just barely caught a glimpse of the interlopers as they dragged her through a large portal to some unknown location.

Thorne was right about Jorge Trinculo. He was most defi-nitely part of Meyret's abduction. So, it was likely he also had something to do with the ushabti incursion into the God machine.

When they arrived at Chicago House, they made sure that Akh-Hehet was taken to one of the staff rooms to sleep off her magical visioning fatigue. Before leaving the seer's shop in the souk, they were able to secure the window Gormund shattered. Akh-Hehet was a beloved figure in that neighborhood. Some of the other shop owners pitched in to quickly board it up. The last thing Alex wanted was the old woman to be worried about her possessions while she healed.

Gormund walked through the courtyard and sat in the wrought iron chair across from Alex. He worried the jasper pendant of Isis around his neck. It had been a constant adornment of Meyret's. He'd found it cast upon the floor after the priestess's abductors dragged her through the portal. He'd been wearing it since then. Holding it must have made him feel more connected to her. "What's next?"

Alex took another large sip of her old-fashioned. "I guess we should figure out where they took Meyret. One thing puzzles me. Other than the fact that she is magically awesome, why would they take her? What do they need her for?"

Gormund looked at her drink with envy. He motioned to Gini, who was still at the bar meticulously making themselves a gin and tonic. A mischievous smile pulled across their face as they lifted a bottle filled with the amber liquid and winked at him.

His smile faded. "I have an awfully bad feeling who might be behind this other than our pal Mr. Trinculo. There are some stories in Meyret's life that are only hers to tell. I don't feel right going into detail, but I am concerned that a powerful magician might be at the root of this." Gini set his old-fashioned in front of him. He raised it up to Gini before taking a long pull from it.

"He succeeded in taking her once before, and he is a violent and cruel captor who delights in torture."

"So time is of the essence?"

"I know Meyret. She will not give him what he wants. She has a strong will and a vast pain tolerance. But being an immortal, the torture could go on for eternity."

Gini sat next to Gormund. Their face reflected back the concern he held for Meyret. They patted his stumpy hand.

"So yes, time is of the essence."

That was one thing that Alex never considered. If you were immortal, someone could have quite a field day hurting you repeatedly. "What is the name of this magician?"

"Idris Niru."

A dark charge of fear shot through her. That was the very man who hired Rendell to kidnap her. Before Alex could form her words, she looked up just in time to see Luke nonchalantly striding toward her as if it were completely expected for him to be in Egypt and not New York. The legs of her wrought iron chair screeched against the cement patio as she stood. "Why the hell are you here, Luke? You should be back at the residency recovering."

He had a large bandage across his forehead, and others on his forearms, making him look like a haphazardly bandaged mummy. "Thorne was overly dramatic in her rendition of my condition. I'm all right. Since the God machine has been broken, it seems like the project is more of a cleanup than a dismantling. I thought I could be more help here."

"That was reckless, Luke. You have directly ignored what I asked you to do. If you are well enough to come down here, you are well enough to keep an eye on the God machine and work on its containment. Just because the God machine has been damaged doesn't mean there aren't any issues with it. The disposal of magical materials is a tricky thing."

"Thorne is working on it. As you know, she is thorough to the point of compulsion. I came because I thought you could use more allies here. And now that Meyret has been taken, I would have to guess your need is stronger than ever." Luke took the last chair beside Alex.

"I fear you may be right, Luke. It can't be a coincidence that the very magician who kidnapped Meyret all those years ago is the same one who hired Rendell to deliver me to him."

Gormund let the pendant thump against his chest. "It was him?"

"The very same."

They all sat in an ominous silence. Out of nowhere a large black feather floated down and landed on the middle of the table. Dangling at the end of it was something that glittered like a large black diamond. Alex retrieved the feather. When the stone touched her flesh, it sparked and blue smoke emanated from its top. When the smoke cleared, both feather and gem were gone and in her palm lay a small folded piece of paper.

Alex carefully opened it up and read the message inside.

Take the carriage that awaits you, just outside on the corniche. The horse has been magically induced to deliver you to a place where we can discuss the return of your beloveds.
Idris Niru.

Beloveds. Alex carefully studied the text. It wasn't a typo—the message definitely signaled that Idris held more than one captive. The vision she had at the residency in New York flashed through her mind. Could it be that Buxton was still alive? "Well, I guess it couldn't be any clearer what the next step is."

Luke's eyes went wild. "You've got to be kidding me. Can't you see that is most likely a trap?"

"It's the only lead we have right now. I think Gormund and I can handle whatever comes our way."

Gormund smiled.

"I want to come too," interjected Luke.

Alex still chafed at how he ignored her direct orders to stay home and recover. However, now that he was here and willing to report for duty, the extra muscle might come in handy. "Sure, why not, the more the merrier."

Gini stood. "Me too. It wouldn't be the worst thing in the world for you to have some more magical firepower on your side."

The librarian was surprisingly energized by the thought of getting in the mix, but Alex had to refuse them. "Somebody has to stay here and keep an eye on Akh-Hehet. If she wakes, she might need someone to take care of her."

Alex grabbed her scribe's bag and placed the unfolded paper into the compartment at the bottom of it, then slung it over her shoulder. "No time like the present. Come on, boys."

She led the way through the building and to the front door. As she walked through the threshold, she stopped in her tracks. She couldn't believe what stood before her. It was a beautiful grey horse, but like none she'd ever seen before. Throughout its body were dark grey, almost charcoal-hued smudges, like large globules of ink spattered onto wet paper. But that wasn't what marked the horse out as different. It shimmered with a thin veil, as if glitter was sprinkled about the horse over an invisible force field. Attached to his headgear was the most magnificent black and spangled plumage Alex had ever seen.

The black carriage was nondescript and looked as if it was pulled from a movie set in the 1800s, with an ornate gold handle and velvet curtains covering the windows.

Sitting atop the driver's bench was a very dignified-looking Egyptian man wearing a highly decorated long robe-like galabeya.

Luke reached over Gormund's head and pulled the carriage door open.

"Do you mind?" Gormund looked peeved.

Alex stepped past both and climbed into the carriage.

Luke sat across from Alex. "Are you really okay with this? The three musketeers getting into an unmarked carriage to points unknown?"

"You guys can stay behind if you want. I need to do whatever I can to get Meyret back."

Gormund was still fuming at Luke as he entered the carriage and plopped down next to Alex. "I am Meyret's guardian; I must go."

"I suppose I need to come to make sure neither of you do anything rash." Alex glared at Luke as the black lacquered door slammed shut and the carriage started to move.

The interior of the cabin was covered from top to bottom with dark-purple velvet. She attempted to pull the curtains back, but they were immovable. It would seem that their host didn't want them to see where they were going.

"But what if something happens to you?" Luke asked, looking at Alex.

"Well, I guess you and Thorne will have to battle it out for top dog."

A wide grin pulled across Gormund's face. "My bet is on the skinny, angry woman."

They rode in silence until the carriage came to a stop and gently jostled from side to side. The driver opened the door and pulled down the small retractable stairs.

She scanned the landscape that stretched out before her while climbing down the stairs. They were now somewhere out in the countryside. Down on the riverbank was a large private mooring, and attached to it was a large, boxy Egyptian-style river cruise boat.

Alex remembered the first time she'd seen this type of boat. They looked like large shoe boxes festooned with balconies and strung with lights on their uppermost decks. Their shape was odd for a sailing vessel, but they were perfect for stacking up against one another to optimize the number of operational cruise boats.

This boat was shaded by a grove of lush palm trees.

Alex, Gormund, and Luke made their way to the boat. As they neared the small pier, an ordinary-looking man stepped out of the ship. "I am Edmund, Jorge and Idris's assistant. You may come in."

All three made their way toward the entrance. The man held up his hands. "She is the only one who can come. You will need to wait outside."

Alex stepped forward. "My friends go where I go."

Gormund went red in the face and pushed past Alex. "Do you know who I am? How dare you forbid entry to an Immortal." Gormund's forward progress was halted by some unseen barrier that Alex already passed through. His face bloomed a deeper red. "Bring me to Meyret."

From somewhere within the boat a bloodcurdling scream

resounded. Alex had never before heard Meyret scream but was certain it came from her.

Fury burned in Gormund's eyes. His hands were tight fists at his side.

"My bosses were plainly clear that they only want to meet with Alex. The others must stay."

Another scream sounded.

"Or you could all just return to the carriage. It'll take you back to the residency."

"Just wait out here, guys." Alex was anxious to get to Meyret.

Luke put his hands on the invisible barrier that separated them from Alex. "I don't like it either, but they hold all the cards right now. Let Alex find out what's going on."

The Immortal glared at Edmund. "I never forget a face. I will find you."

Edmund held the door open for Alex. "Ladies first."

Another scream rang out.

Alex halted next to Edmund. "Tell them to stop. Now, or I don't step any further into this boat."

"No can do. I have no way of talking to them at the moment. Trust me, we only have a little further to go. As soon as they see you, they will stop torturing her. Jorge and Idris wanted to ensure that you knew exactly how serious they were."

He led her down a grand staircase to a wide hallway lit with upturned sconces that flickered with flame light. In the middle of the hallway was a massive opening that was probably once a large dining room. They walked under its ornate squared archway that was lined with gilded hieroglyphs.

In the center of the room was a platform which boasted a large throne. Surrounding the throne were massive limestone depictions of each of the Gods who once walked the earth as

Immortals. Alex's eye was drawn to the carving of Thoth with its Ibis head and long curved beak, holding a writing brush in one hand and a papyrus scroll in the other.

The room was empty.

Edmund led her to the ornate throne which was made of midnight-black obsidian trimmed with rich red-orange carnelian. Under closer inspection, the obsidian could be mistaken for ornate wrought iron work if it weren't for its shiny-sharp appearance. The seat and backrest were covered in a mosaic of carnelian tiles in varying tones of yellows, oranges, and reds. "Have a seat."

There was something rather foreboding about the large carved throne. "I'd rather stand."

"Have it your way." Edmund disappeared into the main hall and returned with a large mirror that was set into an ornate gilded frame. He placed it directly in front of Alex, then left the room.

Alex stared into the mirror. Gold specks swirled around inside it. Their speed picked up until it looked like a glitter tornado. The flakes consolidated and covered the entire surface. The surface rippled like molten silvery gold, then flattened out and became transparent, revealing two figures standing within the golden frame. One was most definitely Jorge, and the other was a smug-looking man with a hook nose and a smoking jacket. Behind them was a long table with Meyret strapped to it.

Anger flared in her as she rushed toward the mirror. "Remove her from that table. Now."

The man in the smoking jacket stepped forward. "I am Idris. A very powerful magician, among other things. In the moment, you are not the one in control." The magician pushed a button and Meyret screamed.

Meyret's body twitched and jerked as if she were actively being electrocuted. "Don't do anything he asks, Alex." Meyret grabbed the edge of the table as her body convulsed again.

"Haven't you learned yet, priestess? No speaking unless you are spoken to." He motioned with his hand and the table wheeled out of view. "I don't want any further interference."

Idris cleared his throat to get Alex's attention. "As you are aware, she is immortal."

"Of course."

"You know this can go on for an excruciatingly long time, for her."

Jorge pushed past Idris. "And he is going to enjoy every minute of working her over if you don't do what we ask."

Another wail of pain echoed through the room Jorge and the magician were in.

Jorge continued, "So I bet you are wondering how it is that I know your name, Hathor . . . I mean Alex. And I am willing to guess that as the new director of KHNM, you are wondering how can it be that this guy, who you and your cronies have wiped memories from over and over again . . . how does he know all of this? Well, just know I remember everything. And I mean everything."

"Did Idris restore your memory?" Alex honestly didn't care in the least how Jorge regained his memory, but she was trying to buy some time to pin down where they might be located.

"No. But I do have a powerful magician at my side who I've enlisted to exact my revenge on you and on KHNM."

Idris put his hand on Jorge's shoulder. "I think we should end all this chitchat and get down to business. I have some things you would like to have back, and you can retrieve something I would like."

"What are your terms?"

"I'd like to show you something first."

Both Idris and Jorge stepped back. "Gwen, bring him in."

The auburn-haired woman was tugging someone along into view. As they neared, Alex's heart skipped a beat. It was Buxton. "How can it be? I saw you fall." She stumbled forward toward the mirror as she tried to assemble the fractured reality. The joy of seeing him faded as the seriousness of the situation and the peril he was in settled over her.

Buxton strained against the rope that held him. "Alex, whatever they say. Don't do it."

Idris snapped his fingers. Buxton's eyes slammed shut, and he fell to the floor.

Jorge puffed up. "I saved him. Had I known then what I know now, had my memories been restored, believe me, that outcome would have been very different."

"How did you do that? He was in the Netherworld."

"I saved the old man before I knew who he was. If I knew who he was, you can be certain I would have left him to the hawk-headed creatures."

"How did you get into the Netherworld?"

"I followed you, Buxton, and that little one through that portal. A blue-eyed stranger, who I now know to be Niles Greene, a KHNM colluder, told me to retrieve you from the desert. He told me that you were the Goddess Hathor." Jorge shook his head. "Unbelievable. He said if I continued to follow you, I would be led to great treasure. I jumped through the portal you created just before it closed."

Idris was becoming visibly agitated. "We are not here to relive the past. We are here to move on to the future."

During Alex's last run-in with the ancient Egyptian Immortals, Raymond, the anthropomorphic form of Re, was attempting to kill all of his immediate family to attain the Aten-hood, or one true god. Alex stood in his way. He and his daughter Salima, the actual Goddess Hathor, sealed Alex in an ancient tomb and left her for dead. Alex narrowly escaped with her life. When she emerged from the stone enclosure and into the desolate rock-strewn landscape, Jorge and a troupe of his hangers-on were awaiting to whisk her away in that outlandish sand chariot. Had that really been Niles's doing? Alex tucked the thought away. Maybe Gormund would know.

Alex touched the mirror, hoping she could penetrate its magic. Its cold surface didn't give way. Disappointed, she pulled her hand back. "Let's get down to why you called me here. I must have something you want in exchange for Meyret and Buxton."

Idris stepped in front of Jorge, taking up most of the mirror. "I need something only you can get for me. I even have an idea where it is. But the sad thing for you is that once you retrieve it, you will have to hand it over to me."

"You are looking for the books of magic. If you know where they are, why can't you get them yourself?"

"There are four primordial books of the Ogdoad. The books needed to be separated from each other because for them to exist together would be far too dangerous. Each book was assigned a specific lineage of humans that would be its keepers and would hand down the responsibility from generation to generation. The book in question is part of your ancestry through the priestess, but you are the only one with the unique ability to retrieve it. I know roughly where it might be, but I cannot claim it. Once you find the book, you must willingly give it to me, which will relinquish your hold over it. Then, of course, the book will be mine. Then and only then will you get your beloveds back."

Alex didn't like the sound of it. As much as it broke her heart to think of leaving Buxton and Meyret to the whims of Idris, she couldn't justify handing that sort of power over to the immortal magician. On the other side of the coin, there was a growing part within her that dearly wanted to deliver the book to Idris. The possibility of bringing her beloveds home was tantalizing fruit dangled in front of her. Try as she might, she just couldn't see a way around the danger. "My answer is no."

"That is more than disappointing. Bring him here." Idris yelled to someone outside the mirror frame.

Idris walked to the table behind him. Jorge and the redhead struggled to get the still knocked-out Buxton onto it.

"Are you sure about this? I may not be able to kill Meyret, but I certainly can kill this frail mortal. Jorge, prop the man up. I want her to see his face as he breathes his last breath." Jorge held a knife to Buxton's throat.

Her gut twisted at having Buxton at the mercy of these two miscreants. "How do I even know that is really Buxton? You are a magician; you could be casting a spell over some golem to make me think it is him."

Idris snapped his fingers in front of Buxton. His eyes flew open, wide and awake.

"Ask him something only he would know."

Alex felt a poke of sharp steel against her back. She turned back to see Edmund was holding a knife against her. She cursed under her breath. She'd been so focused on what was going on in the mirror, she had completely forgotten about Edmund.

"I need some insurance that the old man will speak sensibly." Idris waved his hands in front of Buxton's mouth. "Captive, speak and answer this one question true. If you do not speak or if you lie, I will know, and Alex will die."

Alex thought of the first time she'd met Buxton. When he magically transported her down into the cavernous space where the God machine was held. How he led her to a comfy spot where there was a table, and two comfy chairs appeared out of nowhere. She recalled how tired she was and the concern that riddled his face. "The first time we met, you offered me something to drink. What did you bring to me?"

The old man screwed up his face. For a moment Alex wondered if he might be some sort of hologram.

"Coffee. Although it wasn't me who brought it to you. I called Luke, and he brought some for both of us."

Alex's gaze connected with Buxton's warm brown eyes. Did Alex have the heart to watch Buxton slaughtered in front of her? Or, should she agree to the terms in the hope that it bought her some time to figure a way out of this? Deep down she knew that neither Buxton nor Meyret would support putting the agency, or for that matter the world, in danger to save them. Giving a powerful primordial book of magic to an immortal magician who was willing to do anything to possess it would never be worth the risk to them. The destruction he could inflict upon the mortal realm would be tremendous.

Alex cleared her throat. "Still, I will have to say no."

"Are you absolutely sure, Alex? This time he will be dead forever." Jorge seemed to take a lot of pleasure in that thought.

The mischief in Buxton's eyes telegraphed he was going to do something unwise. "Ask Idris about the covenant between the Gods and KHNM. He gave it to Jorge."

Jorge slapped Buxton's face hard, knocking his head backward. An angry red mark came forward on his skin. "Shut up, old man."

To see even the smallest amount of violence done to her mentor shook her to the core. She couldn't imagine seeing him killed in cold blood in front of her. "You have the covenant?"

Jorge looked adamant. "No."

Idris rubbed his chin. "If we did, would that change your mind?"

Buxton shook his head. "Alex, don't."

This time Idris slapped him. "You are not an active part of these negotiations. Why did you bring it up if you didn't want to save your own skin? Don't play the false hero, old man. Gwen, gag the geezer." The auburn-haired woman stepped forward and with great hesitation tied a strip of material around Buxton's mouth.

There was something in the woman's eyes that made Alex think that she might not be one hundred percent on board with what was going on. She could have sworn that she'd seen her somewhere before but couldn't quite place her.

Idris asked again. "So, if we did, would it change your mind?"

Alex put her hands on her hips. "Your partner over there says you don't have it anyway."

Jorge suddenly became antsy.

"My question stands. Would that change your position? If you were able to not only save your friends but gain the covenant you've been searching for? The very document you need to understand the archaic language that binds your agency to the Gods?"

Hope rose in Alex. This could be the silver-platter excuse to agree. She had no intention of giving Idris and Jorge anything they asked for but hoped this would buy her some time. "In a word, yes."

"No. Idris. I will not give it up," Jorge asserted.

The magician leaned over and whispered something in Jorge's ear, and a look of understanding dawned. "Okay, you can have it if you give us what we ask for."

"It looks like you have a bargain," said Idris, and the mirror went blank.

—⁓—

Once they were back in the carriage and heading back to Chicago House, it didn't take long for Alex to get Luke and Gormund caught up about the deal she made with Idris and Jorge.

Although they were both still put out at being left behind at the boat, Gormund was explicitly pleased with the plan and eager to save Meyret. Luke, on the other hand, was peeved. In his opinion, it was downright dangerous to give such a powerful book of magic to someone like Idris, especially at a time when the Gods had returned to their realm, leaving magic lingering in the realm of man.

Before they got into the carriage, Edmund gave them their one meager clue from the great magician. The only thing he knew about the location of the book of magic was that it was stowed away in one of the Egyptian oases, which narrowed the field somewhat. It was more of a bread crumb than a clue. Now they needed to figure out which of the many oases scattered through Egypt they should start with.

It made sense to Alex that the book could be hidden in the Siwa Oasis, where Meyret once lived and Alexander the Great had traveled to. It jibed with both sides of Alex's ancient lineage.

Gormund disagreed passionately. He suggested they try to find the lost oasis of Zerzura. His suggestion confounded Alex. If nobody had ever found this fabled desert oasis, how would they?

As soon as they arrived back at the residency, the three of them decided to meet up in an hour in the courtyard for a council of war. Hopefully a broader conversation would bring forward a plan of action. Instincts aside, most likely it would make sense to start with the oasis closest to them and work their way north to the others.

Alex had started packing things for their journey when a scream tore through the air. It sounded like it came from Akh-Hehet's room.

When Alex got there, Gormund and Luke were kneeling by the seer's bed. They were struggling to hold her down as she tried to get up.

Luke had a pained look on his face. "Steady. You are here with friends."

Alex approached the bed. Akh-Hehet's eyes were wide open with fear.

"Where am I? Please don't tell me you've brought me to Chicago House."

Alex crossed her arms against her chest. "Of course we did. We weren't about to leave you in your shop vulnerable like that."

"Nobody in that neighborhood would have harmed me." The old woman's face was red with rage. "Do you have any idea what you've done?" She shrugged her way out of Luke's and Gormund's grasp.

"We can have somebody bring you back to your shop right away."

"You don't understand. It is too late. I can't believe you can't see it."

"It's okay. You are safe here."

"Safe. You call this safe? I don't know what sort of retribution there will be, but can't you see? You have thrown the lawsuit into jeopardy."

All the cards fell into place. Akh-Hehet was part of the Gods' prosecution team. Alex and Gormund brought her to enemy ground zero. It could only look bad for the seer, like either she switched sides or was playing both sides against each other.

"Oh, man."

Understanding dawned on the faces of Gormund and Luke almost simultaneously.

Luke leaned toward the old woman. "I am guessing they would have no idea that you were here. You've not been here even for a full day. We can take you back discreetly."

Akh-Hehet sat up and cradled her forehead in her hands. "No, they will know, and they'll be sure to question me. I hoped that the time between now and my next reincarnation wouldn't happen for a few more years. But it is truly in the hands of the Gods now."

"What on earth are you talking about? Even if they are mad at you, surely they won't kill you." Once the words came out of Alex's mouth she realized how naïve she sounded. She knew better than most how feckless the Gods could be.

Gormund nodded. "In my experience, questioning of humans doesn't generally go so well. We Gods don't understand how frail you are."

"We'll just keep you here. You can stay as long as you want. At least here you aren't all alone. I can't imagine they would have the gall to come forcibly take you away from the residence." Alex hoped her voice sounded far more assured than she felt.

"I wouldn't put it past them. And what do you propose, keeping me under house arrest forever?"

"There is a lot going on right now that might nix the lawsuit altogether. There is a magician named Idris, who kidnapped Meyret from her tomb, and you may want to sit down for this one, but Buxton is alive, and they have him as a prisoner as well." Alex wanted to stick to the basics. She wasn't quite sure how much she wanted to go into it with the seer.

"Buxton is alive?"

"Jorge Trinculo saved him."

"The aliens guy? What was he doing down in the Netherworld?"

"It is quite a long story, and we need to get going to deliver on our part of this new deal. But if we deliver, we can recover the missing covenant between KHNM and the Gods."

"What will you have to give for these things?"

"A book of magic."

Akh-Hehet looked beside herself. "The books of magic? The ones from the Ogdoad?"

"Exactly. What do you know about them?" asked Alex.

"You are crazy to think of giving one of them to Idris. They contain powerful primordial magic. How can you do it, Alex? The danger here is so great. If he is able to access it, he may be able to physically become one with it and the magic within."

"Is that similar to what you and I did with the visioning to the Netherworld?"

"No, this is quite different. In this case, he would physically go into the book. I think it is called book walking. Whoever does this book walking is in grave danger of never getting out. Especially a nonmagical mortal."

"But what would be the point of going into the book? How would that be able to effect a change in our situation?"

"The story is that each of the books of magic has a hidden place within them. It is like a lockbox of sorts that the person who is of the lineage can alter. If that were true, you could alter the book somehow before giving it to him, and then you might avert any problems this magician might cause. But no living person has ever done this, so all of this may very well be anecdotal."

"You are saying I should try and trick the magician?"

"Exactly."

Luke looked cross. "I don't like it. It seems less of a strategy and more like a Hail Mary. Our biggest liability is our own ignorance. Even if you are able to enter into the book, how would you find the lockbox and how would you know how to dismantle it? And by doing so without any knowledge of how to do it, you could effectively lock yourself in."

The thought of being trapped in a magical book forever did not exactly appeal to Alex.

"Forever." A sorrowful look passed over Luke's face.

Akh-Hehet slipped off the bed and was pacing the floor. Suddenly, she looked up with a gleam of excitement. "I've got an idea. If I could get to my shop and retrieve a crystal from my network, I could try to do some visionings while you all travel to the oasis. I could sort through the possible futures to try to give you the information you need. It wouldn't be perfect, but it would be better than a wild guess."

Akh-Hehet must have read the lack of buy-in on Alex's face, because she continued on. "It is something that could help in making your long shot far less long."

Alex walked over to the old woman. She appreciated the fact

that in spite of the danger they put her in, she was invested in helping them. "It is a sad day when a million-to-one chance looks like the best option. We'd have to send someone over to retrieve a crystal. I am guessing the Gods have eyes on your shop. I can't put you in harm's way again."

"I must pick the crystal myself. It can't be done by anyone else. It has to be me."

"We'll just have to do without it. Like you said, it was a long shot anyway."

Luke stepped forward. "I can take her. I will make sure nothing happens to Akh-Hehet. Even the smallest bit of hope is worthwhile—even Pandora's box possessed a tiny bit of it."

Alex smiled at his lame attempt at a joke. "So true, but it just feels too risky to me. Does the crystal have to be harvested today, or would one that you plucked many months ago work?"

A smile brightened the old woman's face. "You still have it?"

"It saved my bacon in the Netherworld when Gormund and I were trying to find Raymond's lair."

Akh-Hehet sagged. "A good idea, but it may not be enough. Having more crystals around me really amps up my visioning ability."

"How about that chandelier in the dining room? Would that be enough for you? I know it isn't nearly enough to match the many you have in your space, but maybe it could just be enough."

Akh-Hehet looked dubious and shook her head.

Alex caught her reflection in the large floor-to-ceiling mirror across from her. The very same one that was in each of the bedrooms of the entire residency. "I've got an idea that just might work, Akh-Hehet. I am going to get you the crystals you need. Leave it to me. I need you to sit tight in here. The boys and

I are going to do some remodeling work in the dining room. We will make an acceptable space for you to do some visionings while we are gone."

Alex felt a surge of hopefulness rise within her. She knew that sometimes hope could be found in the smallest of places. Even if you were almost certain to fail, the process of doing something could at least keep those fears at bay while you worked steadily toward your end goal, whether you made it or not.

—᭙—

After leaving Akh-Hehet in her room, Alex let both Gormund and Luke know that she was going to start with the oasis that was closest to Luxor and then hit all the other major ones until they found what they were looking for. They would start at the Kharga Oasis, then hit Dakhla, Farafra, and then lastly, if they still hadn't found what they were searching for, they would make their way to Siwa. Alex hoped that they would find what they were looking for sooner than later. Time was running out with the dual forces running against her: angry Gods hungry for revenge, and two of her beloveds in the hands of a man with a well-defined chip on his shoulders and his powerful magician. Meyret's screams repeated themselves like a sharp-toothed earworm.

Alex sent Luke away to pick up a large Range Rover, with lots of backup fuel. Although the vehicle's capacity is pretty long range, it was better to be safe than sorry. If they were lost in the desert with no gas for miles, it would be deadly.

While Luke was on his errand, Alex, Gormund, and Gini worked on reconstructing Akh-Hehet's shop in the dining room. Alex was starting to feel doubtful that her plan would work, but the last thing she wanted to worry about was the old woman going rogue and deciding to return to her shop while she and the boys were out traipsing about the Western Desert looking for the book.

Once Alex explained the idea, they moved all of the furniture out and stuffed it into Gini's office. It just barely fit. After stacking it all up, the office now resembled the burial chamber of Tutankhamen's tomb when it was discovered by Howard Carter, with tables, chairs, and sideboards all stacked willy-nilly.

While they were clearing out the room, Gini asked the maintenance man to retrieve all the floor-to-ceiling mirrors from each bedroom. Alex wondered if the staff would notice, but they were so obsessed with their work, none of them had the time for vanity.

Gini also asked him to post a sign that the dining room would be closed until further notice, blaming a burst pipe in the room above.

Once the room was cleared out and all the artwork taken down, Alex and Gormund set to creating a small room of mirrors within the space of the dining room. The mirrors would be facing inward toward each other with the chandelier in the middle.

The inspiration for this idea came from an exhibition Alex visited recently. It was a retrospective of the work from the Japanese artist Yayoi Kusama's *Infinity Mirrors*. These installations were small mirrored rooms. Hundreds of small abstract sculptures filled the floor, creating a surreal environment that seemed to go on forever.

Alex's favorite room was one with small flickering LED lanterns that were hung from the ceiling. When the door was shut behind her, it felt like she was truly looking into infinity.

Alex wanted to do the same thing with the chandelier, at least giving Akh-Hehet the illusion of a room filled with crystals.

Gini was able to find some large black cloths up in the attic that would aid in sealing off any errant light that tried to come through the edges, marring the intended effect. Among some of the older possessions of the residency, Gini found some old crystal stemware and candle holders. They strung them with some clear fishing wire from the chandelier. Gini even added a few pieces of her chunky jewelry as well.

Daylight was streaming through the dining room windows as Alex flipped the switch to turn on the dining room chandelier underneath its large dark covering.

"Here goes nothing." Alex made her way inside the DIY infinity room. Absolutely no daylight showed through. The only thing that was distracting from the visuals were the cinder blocks at the base of each mirror. Alex decided they should cover them with colorful throw pillows before bringing the seer in. Other than that tweak, she was pretty impressed with their efforts. Would Akh-Hehet feel the same way?

CHAPTER TWENTY-NINE

The mirror went blank and the connection to Alex was cut off. A white-hot fury coursed through Jorge. It was clear that Idris forgot his place as Jorge's servant. Not only did he overstep his role in the negotiations with Alex, but he promised away Jorge's prize possession—the covenant between the Gods and KHNM. Idris gave it to him as a sacred token of their partnership. Tossing it away was like spitting in the face of their agreement.

Idris sneered back at Jorge.

It was time to reset the balance. Jorge slammed his fist into the magician's stomach.

Idris looked startled as he staggered back and hit the floor.

Gwen stood behind Jorge, stock-still. Her eyes shone with pride laced with fear. Did she think he'd gone too far? Had she been right all along about the magician? Was he working toward his own enrichment and not serving Jorge as he professed?

Edmund returned from his errand of escorting Alex back to

her carriage. He strode into the room and toward Jorge, alert to the new and intense energy in the room.

Idris stood. His eyes lit with fury.

Jorge crossed his arms and met Idris's stare. "Why on earth did you think you had the authority to give my covenant away?"

"It must be. What else did we have to entice her to retrieve the book of magic? It was the only ace we held. It was palpable how badly she wanted to get the book to save her two friends, but she couldn't. As the leader of KHNM, it would be a completely selfish move that would put the whole agency at risk. By throwing the covenant into the deal, it put a tasty morsel out, the exact bait she would need to get us our book. You'd be a fool if you didn't see it."

"It wasn't yours to give."

"Don't you worry, little man. Just because I promised it to her doesn't mean she will ever get it."

"How dare you—" In a flash Edmund was nose to nose with Idris. Suddenly Edmund's hands flew up to his own neck as his fingers worked frantically at an unseen noose. His eyes were wide with terror as he staggered backwards.

"How dare you, mortal." Idris raised his arm and flicked his wrist toward Edmund. Edmund fell to the floor, his body twisting with convulsions as he struggled to breathe.

"Make it stop, Idris!" Jorge's voice reverberated through the large room.

Edmund's complexion was turning from red to purple.

Jorge knocked the magician's hand down, but it didn't break the spell.

Edmund's hands flew to his neck as a sickening sucking sound came from him as he struggled to breathe.

"Die, you cretin!" the magician yelled.

"I command you to stop this." Jorge crouched near Edmund and was frantically searching for the unseen force that was choking his friend. Frantic, Jorge leapt to his feet. "This is insane. Edmund has done nothing to you."

A self-satisfied look settled over the magician. "One less idiot is always better."

Edmund's movements were slowing.

"You are going to kill him!" Gwen flung herself toward Idris.

Idris held his other hand out, magically stopping her in place, holding her captive.

Her arms flailed and her legs pumped through the air, but her body stayed in place like a puppet with unseen strings.

"Dear girl, of course I am going to kill him. It is time for your man to understand who really holds the cards in this game." He snapped his fingers. The smoke-filled floor cleared away revealing the desert hundreds of feet below.

An acute dizziness overtook Jorge as the desert scrub far below looked like tiny bits of lint. He closed his eyes and pleaded with the magician. "Please stop. Edmund doesn't have to die."

Jorge needed to save Edmund. Despite the chaotic anxiety that flooded him, he forced his eyes open and made his way to the magician.

Gwen gasped.

Jorge returned to Edmund. He lifted his hand, but there was no pulse. Guilt and grief overwhelmed him as he held the dead hand of the man who always was an energetic supporter of his. Almost as if on a faraway plane, Jorge noticed that Idris had been talking.

"I've been eagerly anticipating this next level of our relationship. I know you've been carefully keeping track of every wish you've made against the hundred I granted you. Right now, you are probably greatly confused as to how your servant could possibly act against you while he is still deep within his term of servitude."

The magician towered above him.

"The accountings of your wishes were meaningless."

"But you bound yourself to me so you could get free from the bottle you were imprisoned in."

"You assumed many things and wanted to see only what was presented to you. I am an immortal magician who put myself in a bottle, setting the stage for you to assume a certain cultural narrative. I will use you to acquire what I've been searching for over the course of many centuries. In short, you are my servant now. I only involved you because you possessed what I wanted. You retrieved the book of magic that once belonged to my lineage. Many lifetimes ago, before I became immortal, my father banned me from the book with a powerful spell and hid it away. Once I knew you'd found it, and I realized who your traveling companion was, it was a perfect alignment to lure Alex in. I needed her to find another book of magic for me. Once she willingly handed it over to me, I was going to make you do the same with yours. Looks like that will be happening sooner than later."

In the distance Gwen howled. Her face contorted in pain. Her body was still oddly suspended in space.

Jorge tamped down his rage and focused on getting Gwen safe. She suffered so much because of him and now . . . "Please, whatever you do, don't hurt her."

Idris walked toward Gwen and leaned forward as if to check that the temperature level of her pain was satisfactory. "I can hurt her in ways you could never imagine. You will now answer to me, man-sized ushabti. She will be my prisoner, to ensure that you do everything I ask of you. You will give me your book. You were a fool, and today is your day of reckoning. Affirm that you understand, or I will kill her right here and now."

Idris twirled his index finger at Gwen, every twitch sending a new wave of pain through her. Her eyes rolled back in her head as tears streamed down her cheeks.

The magician tilted his head. "Well, Jorge. What do you think? I never saw you as a person who would get a kick out of seeing the ones you love in pain, but maybe I misjudged you."

Jorge had no room to negotiate. He would leave the fight for another day. "Make it stop."

"Will you kneel before me and prostrate yourself before me?"

"Let go of your hold on her, and I will."

Gwen crumpled to the floor. She pulled herself up to sitting and sobbed into her hands.

"Come forward, mortal, and kiss the feet of your master."

Jorge ignored the desert below him and forced his way to the magician. He knelt down and kissed the purple velvet slippers. The sharp electrical scent of magic wafted up from Idris's feet. The fragrance was both prohibitive and inviting, like cool night air charged by an electrical storm. He had to do whatever he could to make this right for Gwen, even if it meant complete submission, or at least the appearance of it. "I am the will of my master."

"Stand, servant."

When Jorge stood, the blue-colored smoke rolled into the floor, obliterating the desert scene far below.

Gwen was shaking as if she were standing naked in a cold rain. Suddenly, a thick, soft blanket appeared out of nowhere on Gwen's shoulders. "As you can see, I am not a cruel master. Do what I ask, all that I ask, and I will consider allowing you both to leave unharmed. Go against me, and you will see suffering far more brutal than you can imagine. You will not go quickly like your friend over there." Idris snapped his fingers and a trap door opened under Edmund, unceremoniously sending his body plummeting down to the desert floor as if he were rubbish.

With another snap of the magician's fingers, Gwen disappeared in a flash of crackling magic. The entire room smelled electric.

"Hostages have their place. You and I have much to discuss."

Jorge followed Idris out of the room, knowing two things: Gwen was right all along, and that he would move heaven and earth to get her out of this situation.

CHAPTER THIRTY

The search for the book had already gone on for four days, and they'd ticked two oases off their list. After driving through a surreal moonscape desert, with its snow-white chalk formations, they arrived at the Farafra Oasis. As they did in the other oasis towns, they decided to split up. It was better to have three independent searchers than to stick together. Alex commandeered the car to head to the Roman spring of Ain Bishay. She felt she could use some time away from the guys, and she had always wanted to visit this spring.

Luke didn't like the idea of splitting up. Apparently, he thought it was his job to look out for her. Alex could take care of herself.

Alex drove through the groves of date palms, citrus, and olive trees as she made her way to the Roman spring on the northwest edge of town.

As she climbed the mound from which the ancient spring gurgled forth, she wondered why so few tourists visited the oases. There was so much to their desolate beauty. It surprised her that they hadn't been built up with luxurious resorts. Oases were rich with history, and, at least to Alex, held a certain romance.

Once she reached the spring, she searched the area and found nothing. Alex made her way back to the Range Rover empty handed.

She heard a crackle-pop coming from behind her. The hair on her arms stood on end at the magical electricity that surrounded her. The air was filled with the sharp-clean scent of magic. She turned around, wondering if Idris or Jorge might be checking up on her, but she was even more surprised by what she saw. There was a tiny man, about the size of a ushabti, standing on the top of the mound she'd come from.

The little man walked toward her. "I've been sent here to help you."

Did Idris and Jorge actually send her help? It seemed very unlikely. Idris didn't strike her as a team player. "Who sent you?"

"My master wishes to stay in the shadows."

It felt wrong, but the evidence was standing before her. Maybe it was really sent to spy on her. That made a little more sense. If anything, Luke could probably ID the ushabti to sort out whether it was the very same one that he saved.

"I am Aah-Ha and I am here at your command."

Alex walked over to the car. "Well, I command you to hop on board. It looks like you and I are heading into town."

⁓

It didn't take Alex and Aah-Ha long to get back into town. When she met up with Luke and Gormund at the rendezvous spot, it was interesting to see their expressions upon seeing the ushabti. Luke looked suspicious, and Gormund looked concerned.

"Well, I never thought I'd see you again. I never did catch your name."

"Aah-Ha is the name."

"Aah-Ha?" Gormund laughed a little.

"Yes?"

"Nothing, just testing it out."

Luke crossed his arms. "How'd you get from a drawer in New York all the way to a remote location like this?"

"I have been sent to serve Ms. Philothea."

"By who?" asked Luke.

"Someone who will stay anonymous."

Luke reached down and grabbed the ushabti. He held him up to his face. "You're going to tell us right now, little man."

Gormund smiled. "So glad that wonderful epithet has now been pawned off on somebody else."

Alex could see that this might get a little out of hand. She really didn't want this ushabti to have much material to report back to Idris and Jorge. She wanted to sound upbeat in case he was their eyes and ears. "We'll have plenty of time to get his story. We should hit the road. Judging by the lack of magic books in either of your possession, I'm guessing neither of you had any luck." Alex couldn't wait to get both of them alone to find out what they thought about this mysterious new team member showing up at the eleventh hour.

Once they resupplied and got all their gear together, it was time for them all to pile back into the main vehicle and head out toward the next oasis. They would take turns driving through the night, to get an early start in the morning.

Alex was starting to feel a little glass-half-empty at the

prospect of finding this book. The next oasis was the fourth of the five they planned to check.

Alex didn't know much about the Bahariya Oasis other than the fourteen tombs holding numerous Greco-Roman mummies that were unearthed about a decade earlier.

The ushabti was trying to sort out the best way for him to sit in the large back area of the SUV. The sight of it made her chuckle. It was as if someone left their Egyptian-style dolly on the Range Rover's seat.

Alex pulled out the book on the oases she'd been reading to try and get up to speed on what sites to check at the next one. By the time they'd pulled out of town, the sun had set, and they were surrounded by the deep curtain of darkness that exists in remote landscapes. The bright headlights beamed into the darkness, showcasing the vast landscape of sand and rocks that stretched out as far as the eye could see.

Luke switched on the radio to a station that was—oddly—playing American country music. He smiled back at Alex. "Now, that is what I call good karma."

Alex found it odd that Luke was a fan of country music, being a city boy. And what sort of strange cosmic synchronism allowed him to find that very station on the first try?

Luke smirked into the rearview mirror at Alex as he cranked the volume and sang along with the Hank Williams Jr. song about tears and beers. Somehow Gormund even got caught up in the song, and although it was obvious he didn't know the words, he was excelling at joining in with a close approximation.

Alex smiled at the fact that the team was starting to come together. There was some sort of deep magic that took place during road trips. They somehow managed to bring people together in unexpected ways. She glanced down at the ushabti who had an odd smile on his face.

The effect was contagious, and soon the entire car was filled with four country crooners.

A sudden gust of wind hit the vehicle. It was so strong Luke swerved abruptly to correct their course.

The radio station switched to a slow country ballad which was interrupted with an announcement. The disc jockey spoke rapidly in Arabic, then in English, with a warning that a strong sandstorm of epic proportions was blowing in from Libya. The first waves of the storm were pummeling areas of the Western Desert, and everyone in the vicinity was to take cover.

Another gust hit the car as sand blasted across the hood.

"I've never seen anything like this before." Luke struggled to keep the vehicle moving in a straight line as he battled the wind gusts.

"And this looks like the mother of them all," Gormund added.

"Luke, do you know how much further we have to go before we make the oasis?"

"I doubt we are anywhere near halfway there."

"Gormund, are you familiar at all with this area?"

"Can't say that I am."

Luke switched off the radio and turned on the overhead spotlights. The additional brightness did little to reveal the landscape. It only brought into visual reality just how much sand was swirling around them.

"Should we just stop and see if we can wait the storm out? I am guessing all this sand can't be good for the intake system. If we damage the engine, we'll be stuck here in the middle of nowhere."

"What about air? What if we are completely covered with sand?" Aah-Ha asked, piping up with a quiver in his voice.

"What do you care? You are a magical creature who not only was created to live in a tomb, but you really don't have a need for air," said Gormund.

"I don't relish the thought of being trapped in a car under thousands of pounds of sand and spending an indeterminate amount of time watching you all die then decompose, until some wayward person in some distant future digs me out."

"Couldn't your master just call you back to him?"

"If I fail, there will be no calling back for me."

Luke drove over the large stones that lined the road. "I guess if we are going to stop, we should get off the road. I don't think we want to become an obstacle smack-dab in the middle of it."

"Good idea." Alex peered out the window at the swirling sands. Something in the headlights caught her eye. Was it her imagination or was there a large bluff in the distance?

"Hey, Luke, I think there is something over that way." Alex leaned into the cab and pointed in the direction where she saw it. "It looks like a hillside or something over there. Maybe we can find shelter against it."

The wind picked up and was pushing against the vehicle. Luke slowed down and crawled toward the landmass.

As they neared it, Alex could see what looked like a small cave at the base of a cliff face. "Let's park in front of it, and we can all shelter in the cave."

"Great minds think alike, Alex." Luke smiled back at her, then carefully maneuvered the large vehicle in front of the cleft in the rock.

"How do we know that there aren't any animals in that cave?

Wouldn't they all be looking for shelter too?" Aah-Ha's voice was very tentative.

The cave slanted downward from the opening. Or at least it appeared to—it was too dark in there to tell anything for sure. Alex looked down at the ushabti. "Sounds like a perfect first job for you, my fine magical friend."

"Really?"

"No wild creatures would have any interest in your stony ass," Gormund said, turning to the back seat.

Alex dug in her scribe's bag and found a tiny flashlight that was attached to her key chain, which was the perfect size for him. She opened the door on her side, which opened into the cave. "Go on."

"We'll leave the door open for you, in case you have to run back." Gormund sported an evil grin.

Aah-Ha stood up in the seat and walked over Alex's knees. He turned and gave them a loathing look before clicking on the flashlight and jumping down into the depths to explore the cave.

They followed his progress until they could no longer see his light.

"The cave seems to be fairly deep. That could be good," said Luke.

"Yes, his screams should echo nicely if he is attacked." Gormund rubbed his hands together.

Alex rolled her eyes. She leaned forward and spoke in a muffled tone. Although she knew the little man was far away, she was feeling a little paranoid about magical creatures as of late. "I don't know that I completely trust this thing. I think he was probably sent here by Jorge and Idris to keep an eye on us all."

"He could have been sent by someone else," said Gormund.

"Like who? Meyret? She's not in a place to send rein-
forcements."

"Niles, possibly?" Gormund's voice went comically dreamy.
He held his hands up to his chest and tilted his head as if he
were a lovestruck girl.

"Knock it off, Gor."

"But didn't you say that when you were with Akh-Hehet—"

"Trust me, it isn't Niles."

Luke was stony faced. It was like he wanted to say something
but then thought better of it and decided to stay out of the
conversation altogether.

"Well, what should we do with him? Should we keep him
around, or do you think he is a liability?"

Luke looked pensive. "It's hard to say, but it wouldn't hurt to
keep him around. Regardless of why he is here. He's already
come in handy."

"Why don't you order him to go into your coffin pendant and
stay there. You could hold him there and call him out if you
needed him."

"I don't know, Gor. That would mean he would always be
with me, always be near me and could hear whatever I say."

"You could order him to go to his inanimate state until you
call him forward."

"I don't know."

"What is the saying, keep your friends close and your
enemies closer?"

"I guess there is that. At least I would always know where he
was."

"Who?" The little man was approaching the car.

"Any beasts?" asked Gormund.

The ushabti got a funny look on his face and made direct eye contact with Gormund. "Other than the one I am looking at?" He tilted his head and laughed a little at his own joke against the silence of the others. "Man, tough crowd. The coast is clear."

"Aah-Ha, I command you to resize yourself to fit within my coffin pendant." Alex pulled the out the pin and separated the two halves and held it open. "There you will wait until I call you to duty once again. Once you are in the pendant, you will return to your nonsentient stone form."

"Do you really think that is a good idea? How would I be able to protect you from in there?"

"If I need you, I will call for you. You were ordered to obey me, so you must do so now."

He looked as if he was trying to quickly come up with another reason not to go into the pendant.

Alex shook the pendant at him.

"Man, first a drawer, now a pendant." He shook his head. A sharp snap-crack of magic sounded, and he was gone.

Alex looked down at the once-empty coffin and saw a tiny version of Aah-Ha nestled within its metallic borders. She brought the two halves together, shutting him in. "Well that's settled. I think we'll be here for a while. Since we are stuck here, we might as well get some rest. Let's pull out some of our supplies and make camp."

As the storm raged outside, they rolled out their sleeping bags in a circle and lit a fire. Once the storm was over, they would need all their energy to dig themselves out. They all agreed it would be good to get some shut-eye. Hopefully the storm wouldn't do any real damage to the vehicle.

It didn't take long before Alex could hear the soft snores of both Luke and Gormund. The sound was oddly peaceful against the blowing winds outside. Alex was too wound up to sleep. She stared up at the cave ceiling in the soft light of the lantern they'd left on. Although Aah-Ha had cleared the area, she knew there still might be surprises hidden in its dark corners.

As she tried to coax herself to sleep, she noticed a faint sound coming from the furthest reaches of the cave. It sounded like a small flowing brook. She sat up and listened closely. Was her mind playing tricks on her, or was there a freshwater source within the cave?

Alex unzipped her bag, grabbed her flashlight and then made her way toward the back of the cave. She fumbled the flashlight, and it landed near Luke's head. Curiously, the noise didn't wake either him or Gormund.

Alex retrieved the torch and made her way to the tight opening at the back of the cave. It was so narrow that she would have to crawl on her hands and knees. Wishing she'd brought a headlamp, she put the butt of the flashlight in her mouth. As she moved inward, the light of her torch caught the shimmering motion of water up ahead. How was it that she didn't hear the water from the main cave when they first arrived? And for that matter, why hadn't Aah-Ha mentioned it?

A sharp cry of a bird echoed through the tight space. Her body jerked up in reflex. Expecting the sharp rock of the low ceiling to dig into her back, she was surprised to feel no resistance. Alex pushed herself up to standing. The rock that had previously hemmed her in gave way like a weak fog. It was strange to stand to full height surrounded by a three-dimensional ghost illusion of solid rock.

The bird called again in the distance. Worried, Alex wondered if it had been wounded by the storm and came to the cave for shelter.

She emerged from the rock-like fog to find herself in a deep ravine next to a small stream. Grabbing the flashlight, she flicked its beam at the walls around her which were filled with intricate bas-reliefs depicting an Egyptian creation myth. She was intrigued by the discovery since it didn't resemble any as of yet known ancient Egyptian sacred spaces she was familiar with. When this was all over, she would love to return and document the site.

If she was going to venture further into the ravine, she would need to mark her spot so she would know how to get back to Luke and Gormund. She grabbed some loose stones and created a small cairn.

In the distance, she could hear the flutter of wings.

As she followed the sound, a bright light came from just beyond a wide bend in the stream. When she turned the corner, what she saw took her breath away.

The stream cascaded down a lush hillside and into a valley below. The stream's path was lined with tall grasses that flowed in the wind. Date palms were dotted along its grassy banks, their fronds rustling in that same sweet breeze. The bird flew over-head. It wasn't wounded at all. In fact, it danced in the sky as it played in the swells in the air.

It was as if she stepped into a perfect day—warm tempera-tures, slight breeze—yet there was no sun. The sky above was a bright robin's-egg blue. Down in the valley was a temple. It looked to be made of white stone, but on closer inspection there was a rich and creamy luster of rainbow colors, making her think of mother-of-pearl.

A pathway of shimmering sand followed the stream to the temple. The sand was luminous, as if it were made of tiny grains of diamonds. She knelt and dug her hands into it, feeling its mellow warmth against her skin. She was tempted to throw off her shoes and walk to the temple barefoot.

The bird led her all the way to the temple doors, which appeared to be made of two gigantic abalone shells. She looked for a knocker or door handle, but there wasn't one. Thinking there might be a secret latch amid the iridescent color pools of pink and green, she felt all around the silky-smooth doors but found nothing.

The small white bird dropped out of the sky and flew around Alex in circles. With each pass it came closer to her, as if looking for a place to land. She held out her hand. The little bird landed on her upturned palm. Its tiny feet tickled her skin. It cocked its head sideways and then morphed into a bird made of ivory with eyes that sparkled like tiny black diamonds. A golden loop crowned it, enabling the bird to be strung on a chain.

Alex held the small amulet and noticed a small keyhole in the abalone doors. She rubbed it with her finger to feel the depression, then squatted by it. She peered through the holes and saw a hypostyle hall filled with large black guardian statues, each crowned with massive turquoise and carnelian lotus flowers.

The bird in her hand emanated a dull heat. Its legs transformed into a shape resembling a skeleton key. Alex lifted the small bird to the hole and slid it in. A loud clank came from within the locking mechanism. Alex jumped back as the doors swung outward. The small ivory key transformed back into the small white bird and flew up over Alex's head and away.

Alex walked through the threshold of the temple. It was filled with an eerie silence. She couldn't shake the feeling that she wasn't alone. She glanced up at the dozen shiny black statues, each wearing a full kit of an ancient Egyptian warrior, including the large curved khopesh, or sickle-sword, clutched in

one of their hands. The statues leaned against the massive stylized papyrus bundles that were the support columns for the
temple.

She walked through the hypostyle hall. Her ears pricked for
any signs of life. The forest of imposing statues made her think
of the hawk-headed defenders of Re that she, Gormund, and
Buxton accidentally woke when they were looking for Raymond's
Netherworld lair. A shiver ran down her spine, as she knew she
would be no match for these giants.

Beyond the massive statues was a large reflecting pool in an
open courtyard. A lazy splashing sound came from the pool as if
a large body was trying to extricate itself from an overfull tub.

Alex slipped into the courtyard. The surface of the pool was
carpeted with the purple and blue Egyptian lotus flowers that at
one time graced the shallow inlets of the Nile. She leaned in and
looked into the pool's depths. She could see that something was
swimming in the water. Suddenly, a large hippopotamus head
broke through, making the water spill out over the edge of the
pool.

Another hippo head emerged from the crystal-clear waters;
both hippos' eyes were trained on Alex from the center of the
pool.

She was inexplicably drawn to them. If everything Idris had
said about her lineage being linked to the book was true, maybe
they were. Alex sat on the edge of the pool. The first hippo to
emerge swam toward her, stopping close enough for Alex to
place her hands on its head. Its sad brown eyes looked up to her,
pleading for something.

It broke away from her touch and swam back to its mate.
They both opened their massive jaws and made an epic howl,
shaking the temple. Then they both swam to the far end of the

pool, and looked back at her. It was as if they were calling her to follow them.

Beyond the pool was a small dark room.

As she walked down the length of the pool, the hippos bobbed their massive heads in and out of the water as if encouraging her to continue on. It could have been her imagination, but she could have sworn they were smiling.

In the small room, a barque shrine commanded the space, marking it as the holy of holies, the heart of the temple. Alex grabbed her flashlight and clicked it on, revealing a long golden boat inlaid with lapis, turquoise, and carnelian. The sacred boat was approximately six feet in length and rested upon a dais. Gracing the top deck of the sacred boat was a box-shaped shrine where an effigy of a God would be kept.

She shined the light up into the gilded box. Her heart soared when she saw that there was a book instead of a small golden statue of a god. The beauty of the book was staggering. Its pearlescence shone in its pink-, white-, and blue-hued glory. Could this be the very book that she was looking for?

Standing on each side of the book's protective chamber was a small figure. Alex guessed they were the guardian figures of the treasure. On one side was a male figure with the head of a frog, and the other was wearing a sheath dress with the head of a snake.

Alex knew that they were Nun and his wife Naunet. They were two of the eight of the Ogdoad, the primordial ones. But why would they be guarding this book?

The Gods were a part of the creation story, but not a part of the day-to-day Egyptian myths. In the Egyptian pantheon, once these Gods of creation did their jobs at creating all from nothing and giving form to the universe, they were put on a shelf and forgotten about.

The book itself was tantalizingly out of reach. She looked around for something to stand on but did not see a single thing in sight. The dais was slightly larger than the boat. Alex gingerly lifted herself up to it—all the while the Egyptologist within her experienced apoplectic shock at her willingness to climb onto an ancient artifact. She was hyperaware of her own movement as she made her way to the book.

Alex reached it and easily opened its protective case. Her fingers brushed against the smooth silkiness of the book. She gazed down at its pearlescent beauty.

Suddenly the ground shook violently. She grabbed the book and secured it against her chest and made her way off the barque. She thudded onto the floor. A great light broke through the darkness as a large rent in the wall behind the barque opened into a rough-hewn threshold. Beyond it was a brightly lit chamber.

The shaking stopped. Alex walked over to the newly created threshold and was surprised to find a sumptuous reading room. It contained oversized chairs with an abundance of plush, velvety cushions. Radiating from the reading chairs were five long tables that stood at bar height. Their surfaces gleamed in the brilliant light that filled the room. Circling the room were large bookcases filled with jewel-toned treasures.

Capping the room was a large white dome with thousands of small cubbies that were inset with countless papyri scrolls. It wasn't clear at all what force kept them from falling to the ground. A small colored tag hung from each scroll. They looked like they made up a reference system. The gold and silver tags twinkled like a sea of constellations. Hugging the curved ceiling was a ladder like nothing Alex had ever seen before. The shape of it made Alex think of the great sky Goddess Nut arched across the night sky.

Alex clutched the book of magic close to her chest, as if somehow it would attempt to fly away from her to some corner of the enchanted jewel box of knowledge. It made her sad to think of leaving this magical place forever, but her time was running thin. She needed to get this book back to her crew, so they could figure out what to do next.

But things were looking up. She'd found the book of magic.

~~~

Alex spun around at the sound of footsteps behind her. Dripping wet and walking toward her was a handsome shirtless man wearing a linen kilt with a large bejeweled belt that dangled strategically to hide what would be seen through the now-transparent material. Walking next to him was a woman of unparalleled beauty, and all around them radiated the essence of the Immortal, which Alex was now accustomed to.

The woman's expression was soft, almost familiar as she glided forward, adjusting her sheer linen sheath. The abalone shells that dangled from her headdress tinkled like delicate glass ornaments. Her dress was completely transparent, but unlike the male there was nothing covering her epically beautiful form. She was unbothered at someone seeing her in this state of implied nudity.

The woman smiled radiantly as she grasped Alex's hands. "Welcome, dear one. So glad you have finally come to us. It is a curse to be eternally tied to water. Some days I fancy I would like to trade places with Kek and Keket."

The man slipped his arm around the woman's waist. "Oh, I know you are exaggerating for our company. You, my dear one, could never dwell in darkness. And the primordial waters keep you looking ever so young."

The woman gave him a peck on the cheek. "After thousands of years, you still know how to treat a lady." She smiled indulgently. "Although, you do realize we are Gods and therefore by nature are forever young."

"Touché, my love. Ever lovely, that is what you are."

Everything fell together in a flash. The two beings that stood before her gushing at one another were Nun and Naunet, part of the Ogdoad.

Naunet beamed at Alex. "It is so rare we get visitors. How long will you be staying with us? I see you have retrieved the book of your ancestors."

Nun frowned. "You know, my dear, that can only mean two things."

Alex tilted her head, uncertain of what the God was implying.

"You are in grave danger, and you have some figuring out to do." He motioned into the reading room. "Have a seat, make yourself comfortable, and stay as long as you need."

Naunet hooked her arm in Alex's and led her into the domed room. "Are you hungry? I could bring up some ambrosia from the cellar."

"Darling, you know that ambrosia is not for humans."

A faraway look passed across the Goddess's face. "How could I forget? We lost our dear servants." She motioned for Alex to sit on one of the cushioned chairs.

"I'm really not hungry."

"I'll just bring you some honeyed cakes and tea. You may not realize it, but traveling across to this realm takes a toll on your mortal bodies. It will help sustain you as you read. Sit. Make yourself at home."

No matter how attractive the offer, there was no time to leisurely sip tea and read. It was time to get back to the cave. "Thank you for your kind invitation, but I won't be staying."

"But you came all this way. Why would you come to only see and hold the book? Don't you want to read it?"

"I have come to take the book. I have a need for it in the realm of mortals."

Nun crossed his arms. "That is impossible. You cannot leave with the book. It must forever stay here."

The mood in the room shifted from something like a homecoming to a confrontation. Both Gods now gazed at her with hard eyes.

"But you said this book was of my ancestors. How can you stop me from taking it? It should be mine by rights."

"Don't you understand that the books that surround you contain the words of life and chaos? My wife and I are their sacred guardians. Not a page, not a scrap will leave."

Alex's heart sank. How could it be that she was unable to take the book? Jorge claimed to already have a book. How did his book leave whatever realm it came from? "But this book I hold wasn't kept with the rest. It was outside of them. I would guess that makes it outside of your guardianship." Alex was scrambling to think of an argument or magical loophole that would convince them to let her take it.

"That book was held in a most sacred place. You will not take it." Anger flashed across Nun's face.

A large cracking sound came from the hypostyle hall. It sounded as if a massive rock face cleaved from a cliff and fell to the ground. From where she stood, Alex could see nothing.

Naunet rang her hands. "Don't, Nun. There is no need for that kind of force. I am sure we can convince her to stay."

"That wasn't me." Both Gods looked at each other and hurried toward the hypostyle hall.

Alex followed close behind.

The large black carved warriors detached themselves from the columns, their lotus flower headdresses now turned into battle helmets. They were standing in a tight circle with one of them standing in front of the strange huddle.

When the Gods entered, the warriors all managed to bow deeply as one. "Oh Immortal Gods of the waters of chaos, from which Atum emerged onto the primeval mound before heaven and earth were separated. Great ancestors to the ancient Gods of earth and sky, and great-great ancestors to the Heliopolis Ennead." The leader's booming voice echoed through the hall. As if given an unspoken order, the others unfurled from their tight circle, revealing Luke.

"We've found an intruder in the sanctuary."

Alex's heart dropped at the sight of him. They plucked him up as if he were a small sock puppet, leaving him dangling before them. He was doing his best to try and wiggle out of their grasp.

Naunet wandered over to him and swept her hand down Luke's chin. "This couldn't happen at a more perfect time. We are in need of a servant." She turned to Alex. "As you know, we recently lost two." She clapped her hands. "Today has certainly been fortuitous, my love."

Nun joined her to appraise the new goods.

"He's no intruder. He is with me."

"We know exactly who he is. And the fact that he is with you changes nothing."

"But—"

Both Gods faced Alex. A small lick of fire around the irises in their violet eyes appeared. "This is a sacred space. This one has defiled it."

"Then how is it that I am here?"

"You are a mortal descendant of the Ogdoad. Others who are not would never be able to enter this realm."

"So he could have retrieved the book?"

"He has a genetic connection, like you, but a different line that is linked to one of the three other books, but not this one," explained Naunet.

Nun clasped his hands behind his back. "And fortunately for us, he belongs to a line that owes us a thing or two. Which makes for a perfect captive."

Luke looked up. "Captive?"

"Yes, we are short two servants. Now we won't have to fetch our own tea any longer, darling." Naunet's eyes brightened.

"No way." Luke struggled against his magical captors.

"It won't be so bad. There are many things worse than living out your days in a magical realm." If that was Naunet's way of comforting Luke, she was way off.

"You keep mentioning these servants as being lost. Did they die?" asked Alex.

"Oh no. They were immortal themselves. It was one of your more troublemaking ancestors." Nun's gaze was filled with fury.

"He talked us into letting him try to—"

Nun interrupted his wife. "Don't."

"Don't what?" Alex continued. "In case you are forgetting, you are my ancestors, and he is my friend. If there is anything you shouldn't do, you shouldn't keep things from me. Maybe there is a suitable way out of this for all of us to be satisfied."

"She sounds just like her father." Naunet's voice held a trace of either sadness or disgust, Alex couldn't quite tell.

Now it was Alex's time to get mad. "Was he the troublemaker?"

The Goddess walked over to Alex. "He needed the book and talked us into doing the one thing that will allow the book to be taken. You were right when you pointed out that this book is different from the others. It can leave this realm for periods of time without wreaking havoc, but there is only one way, and it is very dangerous."

"So dangerous that he talked us into allowing him to take our two servants, Frog and Serpent, with him. We all know how well that turned out."

"How about if I do whatever it is that my dad tried to do, but do it alone? I will do whatever it is that allows the book to leave this temple, and I will find your servants and return them. You will hold Luke as your prize. You win either way."

"No. You are the last of your kind. If you try and fail, you will be lost to us forever. Like our servants." Naunet's eyes teared up.

"I would like to add that you don't even know what is required," said Nun matter-of-factly.

"What is required? A dragon slayed? A potion made? OUCH." Luke whacked at the arm of his captor. "Could you call off your guards here? Their soft obsidian hands are starting to cut off the circulation to my extremities. What good would a handless servant do for you?"

"You may ease your grip, but don't let him go."

The giant guards nodded in unison.

Alex was pleased to see that Luke still had some fight in him.

The Goddess's complexion lost its rosy hue. "You must book walk the sacred book of your ancestors. You must intentionally incarcerate yourself in the book and sort through all the spells to find one that will disable the magical mechanism that doesn't allow it to be taken."

"That doesn't sound too hard," said Alex.

"The book longs for your kind. The book is a magical being. The book will do everything it can to keep you. If you wander through the book, you may never find a way out. Getting in is easy. Getting out, well, that may never happen."

"If you fail, and you more than likely will, your friend will be our servant until his dying day, and you will be locked in a book of magic until your bones turn to dust."

"But if I succeed?"

"You may leave with the book."

"What about Luke?"

"Unless you bring our servants back to us, he will stay."

CHAPTER THIRTY-ONE

J orge followed Idris out of the laboratory, stunned by the
turn of events. The magician was droning on about
something, but Jorge was deep in his own thoughts. He
couldn't believe how the tide had turned from the
elation of his limitless future potential to the shock of finding
himself an unwilling conscript. What had he been thinking in
toying with such powerful magic for his own personal gain?
Edmund was dead, and Gwen captive. How many more casual-
ties would there be because of him? How could he have been
such a fool? Gwen was right about Idris, if only he'd listened to
her. Now he must save her or die trying.

Idris stopped in front of the doorway leading to Jorge and
Gwen's suite of rooms. He hesitated just before opening it. "You
aren't listening to a thing I'm saying, are you? You'd better be
alert, and do everything I ask, to the letter. How well you serve
me will greatly influence Gwen's future or lack thereof. Will she
be set free to live a long and happy life with you, or will you both

be staked out in the desert sun and left as an offering for the creatures of the Red Lands? How would you enjoy watching your beloved be a plump and sunburned jackal snack?"

Deep inside, Jorge seethed at Idris's cavalier attitude, but he managed to dig into his TV show personality tool kit to mask his emotions and let the words roll off him. The magician seemed to take great pleasure in the thought of killing both of them in such a barbaric way, reminding Jorge of serial killers speaking of their kills as if they were masterpieces to be relished. There was a deep and sick evil inside Idris that Jorge had missed altogether. How did he fall so thoroughly for the story Idris spun for him? Did the magician cast a magic veil over Jorge to keep him from seeing the truth, or had Jorge been too enamored with having a powerful magician at his service to notice? Was it ultimately his ego that caused this situation that endangered the woman he loved?

"I understand. I am here to serve your every wish."

Idris's icy fingers gripped the back of Jorge's neck like a vise. "Master," Idris hissed through his teeth.

"Of course, Master." His words squeaked out.

Instantly the pressure was gone, and Jorge gasped air in.

"So long as we are clear on our roles now." Idris pushed Jorge through the threshold. "Until our guests arrive with the new book of magic, you might as well take some time to contemplate your situation." Idris snapped his fingers, and the doorway became a force field.

Jorge reached out to touch it.

"Don't. You will regret it, if you value your hand. That force field is a very strong magical ward that will not allow you to pass through this door until I want you to. Take some time to get yourself ready for the big show. When Alex and her KHNM cronies come here with the book, you will need to pull from your actor's bag of tricks and not let on that anything has changed. You will still be able to reprise your role of boss man. During the exchange, there will be a time for you to act."

"What do you ask of me?"

Idris's hand flew up, and he made a squeezing gesture.

The air caught in Jorge's throat. "Master."

"Good. You are a quick learner. You will kill them, of course."

"But, Master, why not just take the book and be done with it? Why bother killing them?"

"I have what you might call a history that needs to be rectified with them."

When Jorge had regained his memories, he wanted revenge on Buxton and to eventually kill him. Buxton was directly responsible for Jorge's pain and deserved punishment, but the others? He wasn't on board with indiscriminate killing, even if they had ties to KHNM. He planned to ruin them, but kill them? What sort of man did Idris think he was? One thing Jorge was absolutely certain of was what sort of man Gwen would think he was if he went through with it. She would be lost to him, forever.

Jorge needed to bide his time and find out more. He tilted his head down in deference, hoping it would telegraph obedience. "Certainly, this kill isn't one of pleasure. I have known you to be wise and not one to jump the gun. There must be another reason for this kill, Master."

"Alex's death will devastate Meyret. I want to watch her suffer from it. The grand theater of killing Alex in front of her ancestor is merely icing on the cake. When Alex willingly gives me the book and she dies, the book's magic will bind to me forever. Buxton is dead weight both literally and figuratively. Whatever other unlucky souls they may bring along will have to die too. I want no mortal witnesses." He quickly changed tack. "But I will leave that to you."

It was becoming clear that Idris might once again be leading Jorge down a path of lies. He was becoming very leery of the magician actually honoring his promise to let them both leave after the trade was complete. Jorge knew if push came to shove, he would do anything to save Gwen, but killing someone? Jorge needed another survival solution.

Jorge knelt. "I am yours to command, Master."

"When our guests arrive, I will supply you with the killing tool you will need. Once Alex and Buxton are both most certainly dead, and you have given to me your book, I will set you and your lady love free."

"What about the covenant, Master?" Jorge knew he would be lucky to escape with his life, and the ancient scroll didn't measure up, but it would be good to give Idris an inkling that the real Jorge was still lurking somewhere within this obedient servant.

Idris shook his head and looked down at his kneeling servant with a sad condescension. "The only prize you can hope to take from me is both of your lives." He turned on his heels and walked away. A short laugh rang through the hallway. Idris turned around to look at his still-kneeling servant. "Oh, and the clothes on your backs, of course. We can't have you wandering around the desert naked. Especially her, pale complexion and all."

CHAPTER THIRTY-TWO

L uke's gigantic stone captors released him. Immediately after, Nun clamped a bronze cuff around his ankle. "This will stay in place until you return with our servants, Alex. No matter how long that takes."

A look of defiance sparked in Luke's eyes.

"Try to escape, and guardians of the temple will deliver you back. They tend to take exception to mortals going against the will of the Gods. We would hate for a friend of our Alex to become damaged in any way." Nun's words were less a threat than a factual statement of concern.

"I'll be back before you know it." Alex smiled down at Luke, hoping her words conveyed more conviction than she felt.

She clutched the book of magic to her chest as they waited for Naunet to emerge from the temple's reading room. The Goddess had left them to retrieve an artifact that would allow Alex to enter the book of magic. Being an avid reader, Alex knew the feeling of being lost within a book, but the God guardians meant it literally. The thought of being plunged into a bound container of magic was exciting, but the reality of traveling into an inanimate object gave her pause.

Naunet strode into the courtyard. In her hand was what appeared to be a large golden straw topped with a feathery papyrus frond. The air around them was still, but the frond danced with life as if a breeze played it into motion.

Nun held his hands out. "The book, please."

Alex set it on his palms with a gentle reverence.

The Gods walked together to the reflecting pool.

Alex followed. She tried to make eye contact with Luke, but he was pointedly looking away from her. She knew he didn't approve of her bargain with the Gods.

Naunet beckoned Alex to her. "You must come close to me, dear one, to be at the ready if it works."

"If?"

Nun's expression hardened. "Nothing is guaranteed, especially when it comes to the magical. If destiny shines upon us, you will enter the book. If the judgment of Maat sees our motives as unjust, the book may be lost to us forever."

It hadn't been clear to Alex the sacrifice the primordial Gods Nun and Naunet were making for her. They were taking a big chance on Alex being true of heart and being able to succeed in this fool's errand. They could lose their two beloved servants for eternity as well as the primordial book of magic they were tasked with protecting since the dawn of time. While the Gods chanted, spinning the ancient spell, Alex was filled with a new sense of responsibility for their trust in her and the sacrifices they might endure if she failed.

The chanting quickened into an intricate and complex

harmony. Nun grabbed Alex's hand and led her to stand on the pool's rim.

Alex glanced back at Luke. This time she caught his eye. He smiled. It was a warm smile like a welcome hug from an old friend, or a shaft of sunlight on a cold day. If things went south, and she couldn't return, at least she would know they parted on good terms.

Naunet placed the golden reed apparatus in Alex's hand, and Nun unceremoniously dropped the book into the pool. Then both Gods stood behind her and stopped chanting as the book sunk into the water.

Alex leaned over to jump in.

Nun barred her with his arm. "Wait."

Both Gods knelt on the ledge near her and peered into the water as if trying to read the ripple pattern for some sort of sign.

Nun rubbed his chin. "I say she jumps now."

Naunet's voice went soft with disbelief. "I think we've failed. It should have happened by now."

"What should be happening?" Both Gods ignored Alex.

Nun stood. His brows knitted with vexation. "I say she jumps in. It might work still. If nothing else, she might still be able to retrieve the book."

"You and I both know it isn't likely she would survive it."

"She will at least have the breathing reed."

For the first time Alex looked down at the strange object she held. She was getting tired of the back and forth between the Immortals. She moved to jump, and Nun barred her again.

A brilliant smile shone on Naunet's face toward her beloved. "You do care."

As the Gods shared a Hallmark moment, a small shimmer on the surface of the water caught Alex's eye. It turned a pearly white, then spread over the water's surface. Alex tapped Naunet's arm. "Look."

The entire surface now resembled a giant liquid likeness of the abalone-shelled book cover.

"Dive now," shouted Naunet.

Nun shoved Alex forward. She flailed into the water. Her chest and face slapped hard against the surface. Her hands instinctively pushed into the water and dog-paddled. The cool metallic breathing reed slipped out of her hand. She dove down to retrieve it as it twisted away from her. Alex pushed up for a full breath of air, but the surface above her turned opaque. She slammed her hand against it. She pushed off with her feet to propel herself toward the descending reed. Her heart thumped hard in her chest. Her mouth begged to open in search of air. Shutting down the panic, she sped toward the one thing glinting in the distance that could save her.

Two large hippos were swimming toward her like heat-seeking missiles. Their speed belied their size. Their approach was intentional and targeted. Alex was well aware of the deadly dangers of hippos, creatures with behaviors very unlike their goofy-looking appearance.

One of them was holding something in its mouth. It could have been her oxygen-deprived brain, but it appeared to be carrying a knife in its mouth, pirate style.

Her throat was on fire as she held her breath. She changed course, steering away from the hippos, and found herself eye to eye with a massive crocodile. His rough, leathery arms grabbed her. He slammed Alex into his chest, nearly knocking what little breath she had left out of her.

Tiny stars exploded in her eyes as he spun her downward in a death roll.

A large body thumped against them, knocking her out of the crocodile's grip.

One of the hippos chased the large beast away. The other approached Alex, not holding a knife as she earlier imagined, but the breathing reed. It nudged the gold apparatus against her hand. The metal scraped against her palm. Alex grabbed it and shoved it into her mouth. She struggled against her body's instinct to breathe through her nose. Instead, she slowly fed her greedy lungs with the limited intake of the reed. She slung her arm around the hippo's back to steady herself as she pulled in the blessed life-sustaining air.

The croc-chasing hippo returned and swam right up to her. Its warm brown eyes made contact with hers as she pulled long breaths through the tube. It dove under her and held in place. She instinctively knew that this water horse wanted to give her a ride. As it gently rose upward with great precision, she let its meaty neck slip between her legs. Leaning forward, she wrapped her free arm around the animal's chin. Once she was in place, the hippos swam toward a large rectangular shaft of bright white light ahead of them, eventually making their way through the shaft until breaching the surface.

She pulled the reed apparatus from her mouth and detached herself from the hippo. They were in a swimming pool in a very large, stark-white room. She swam to the edge and grabbed onto the lip. At the very far end of the room was a silver waterfall that seemingly fed the pool. Bookending the waterfall were two smaller blue falls that appeared to empty into some unseen place. The color of the small falls cycled through every imaginable tone of blue.

Alex set the reed breather on the perimeter of the pool and pulled herself out. The water tickled her skin as it cascaded down her. She stashed it away in the hidden compartment of her scribe's bag for the return trip.

The room around her wasn't at all what she'd expected. She assumed that a book of magic would be filled with rich and vibrant colors, but the space was Spartan at best.

"Where am I?" Alex asked the hippos.

Their only response was to blow water out of their noses. They silently dipped down into the water and disappeared, leaving Alex completely alone.

She wished she could have brought Luke with her. It would be nice to have someone else around. Then it hit her. She wasn't alone. Alex flipped open the coffin pendant and shook the small ushabti onto the palm of her hand. "Awaken, Aah-Ha, this I command you."

The little man's eyes flew open while his body expanded to his regular size of about six inches. "What is your wish, master-of-mine?"

"I need your help." Alex still didn't trust the ushabti but was banking on the rule of self-preservation. Regardless of who sent him, even if his boss were her, Idris, or Jorge, it would be counterproductive for her or Aah-Ha to be stuck in this book of magic forever.

Aah-Ha took in their surroundings. "Wherever we are is beyond my pay grade. I'm not sure what help I can be. We are surrounded by serious and heavy-duty spells."

"At least I won't be alone in this book of magic."

The little man's face fell. "Oh shit. Really? I'm inside a book of magic?"

Alex nodded her head.

"Why, in the name of the Red Lands, would you physically enter a book of magic?"

"Neither of us would be here if it weren't for your master. That Jorge has gotten us both in a fix."

"But—" The little man stopped himself from going further.

"What was that?" She lifted him to her ear, wanting for all the world for him to give up who his master truly was.

"Oh, nothing. Now that we are both stuck here, you will have an eternity to try and get it out of me."

"At least we'll have each other."

The little man rolled his eyes at Alex. She motioned to her open bag. "Why don't you hop in here? I've got to figure out a way into wherever we are." Alex lowered him down to her open scribe's bag.

Aah-ha continued to mutter to himself as he settled himself into the bag. Alex left the top open so he could ride convertible style.

Alex inspected the waterfall. There was something just behind the curtain of water that she couldn't quite make out. She shimmied her way between the water and the wall behind it. Up ahead, she could see what it was, a recess in the wall.

She slipped inside the small niche and found a ladder that went up many stories. At every sixth rung or so was a nautical-looking portal and a number. Alex counted nine portals in total.

Alex looked down at Aah-Ha. "Up for a climb? I think this might be the table of contents for this book of magic."

"Like I have a choice."

Alex ignored the ushabti's sarcasm and climbed. She glanced into the first portal and saw there was an empty room with lines of text everywhere. The next portal up was filled with a deep blue so dark it bordered on black.

"Brace yourself. I'm going to open it."

"Why am I not surprised?"

The brass-framed portal was adorned with an intricate sea motif of fish and other larger sea creatures rendered in beautiful detail. They were so enchantingly created they danced around the solid surface. Near the portal's identifying number was a large horizontal lever. Alex pulled down to open it, half expecting a deluge of water to come pouring out, but there was nothing, not even a drop.

She poked her head inside and couldn't believe her eyes. The seascape that she saw through the portal was now a collage of different texts on scraps of white paper with black text.

She closed the portal. The interior changed back to its watery hues.

Opening the portal once again, she could read the landscape with lines of text as it flowed by her. Affixed to the large scraps of paper were smaller ones with words like jellyfish, flounder, and seaweed. Alex closed the portal again and saw each of the items depicted in the text move past the window.

Aah-Ha pulled himself out of the bag. "What do you see?"

"Wonderful things."

"Doesn't that joke ever get old for you Egyptologists?"

"Sorry. Force of habit." That reaction had become second nature to Alex as an undergrad. It was the iconic quote from Howard Carter when his benefactor Lord Carnarvon asked him what he saw when he poked his head into the newly opened tomb of Tutankhamen.

"It's pretty amazing. It is one part child's diorama and one part masterpiece."

"That's about as clear as mud."

"It's hard to describe." She peered into the closed portal that now reflected the Technicolor ocean dreamscape she had first seen. Opening the portal once more, she grabbed a small piece of paper with the word *water* on it. It tore away with a slight tug. When it passed through the portal, it changed to a tiny bead of liquid that rolled down her forearm. "It looks like the deep sea from the portal, but when you open and look inside, it is like an unbelievably massive collage of words."

She leaned into the portal, peering down at its interior edge. Rushing by the wall was a channel of dark blue water running toward a faraway tube. Was this one of the water sources for the two multicolored blue waterfalls in the white room?

Alex closed the portal and climbed further, checking out each portal as she did. Each level reacted in a similar fashion—vibrant colors and living motion as viewed from the exterior, and the sea of text in the interior. The exception was the very first one that was only text.

After viewing the fourth portal, Alex came to understand that each level was a representation of the earth's water systems. The second portal was the ocean; next up were rivers, then lakes, streams, glaciers, brooks, mountaintop snowpack; and the very last room represented rain clouds.

As she made it to the top, she was at a loss for what to do next. She'd hoped that a plan of action would become clear once she explored the choices in front of her, but she was at another dead end.

Alex climbed back all the way down. She must have missed something.

As she gazed up at the first portal, it struck her that she hadn't bothered to poke her head in that one yet. Alex opened it. The text that was scattered across the interior of the chamber immediately drew together as if it were lead shards being pulled together by a magnet. She craned her neck but couldn't read it, the font size was too small.

"We're going in."

"What does this one look like?"

"Believe it or not, it looks to be the 'about the author' page of this book."

"Great. I am sure that will be helpful, to learn about the overblown ego of this book's maker. Maybe we should just swim back?"

"Not a chance. We must save Luke and disable the book. You can't make a fortune if you never invest in something."

"I'll remember that when we are stuck here for eternity."

Alex pulled herself up and in. Unlike the others, the room didn't have a channel of water running past its outer edge. She wandered over to the paragraph and read.

About the Author:

This book of magic, The Waters of Chaos, was composed from the Holy Spoken Word of the God Ptah, faithfully transcribed and recorded by the bookkeeper, Hapi Merneptah.

The bookkeeper lives within this book in a lonely cabin up on the mountains. His favorite things to do are make new friends, wander the book, and keep the spells of magic contented. He loves walking on rock-strewn paths and, of course, reading. He is currently branching out from his ghostwriting practice to write a series of historical romances that crosses genres into memoir-fantasy.

"Well it looks like our itinerary now has some substance. We're heading up to this lonely cabin. I would take a wild guess that his cabin is situated on one of the levels, most likely three through five."

"You can't be serious. Are you really going to walk right

straight into the spider's web? Are you hell-bent on being kept within this book forever? We need to do some more recon, get the lay of the land before we try to make contact."

"We need to get the Gods' servants back. It seems most likely that both of them will be in close proximity to this Hapi person."

Aah-Ha rolled his eyes. "Why did I have to get assigned to you?"

"Again with the self-pity. Your master could always call you back."

"As I have explained before, if I fail, my master will leave me to rot."

Alex climbed the ladder. "At least for you there is a chance of being called back someday. I am the last of my kind with connections to this book. If I fall down this rabbit hole, there will be no one to pull me up. Your master might reconsider, you never know. As Naunet said—"

"Eternity is a long time."

"Exactly."

Alex assumed the bookkeeper was from ancient-Egyptian stock. It would make sense that he would choose to live in the river portal, which was a detailed rendering of the Nile valley. No ancient Egyptian ever wanted to stray far from their beloved land. She opened the river-themed hatch and squeezed through. When she landed, the floor of the strange torn-paper text collage of the Nile valley visually shifted to a color-filled diorama of the landscape. Not true to life, but as if she were standing in the middle of a stop-motion movie made with construction paper.

"Aah-Ha, I have a mission for you."

The ushabti hopped about as she rooted around in the scribe's bag trying to locate a small spool of dental floss. The tiny container held a remarkable amount of material that could be put to a lot of uses. It always surprised her how many times having it at her disposal saved the day. The spool she carried with her contained about one hundred and fifteen yards.

Searching for it around Aah-Ha was impossible. Frustrated, she cupped her hand in front of the ushabti.

"Excuse me for being in your way, oh Master." The little man crossed his arms and stomped heavily onto her hand.

She set him on the rim of the portal and shot him an exasperated look, then continued her search. Finally, her fingers grasped the small plastic container. She flipped it open and pulled at the end. "Hold still. I'm going to tie this around your waist. You will be able to fulfill your earlier desire for recon. We need to find the bookkeeper's hut, and I think it's best we don't put all our eggs in one basket."

He stood with his hands on his hips, looking perturbed. "So all I am to you is trap-bait? Are you actually going to wrap me in dental floss?"

"Don't think of it as floss. Think of it as your lifeline." Alex pulled out enough to wrap around the ushabti a couple of times before tugging it into a tight knot.

"Ouch. Could you make it a little snugger?"

"You wouldn't want it slipping off mid-mission. You'd be lost to me forever." A small part of Alex enjoyed giving the ushabti a tough time.

"Awww. You do care."

Alex picked him up and set him on the ground. "Now hop along, like a good soldier. I will be watching you from here."

"Great. So dignified. To survive for centuries in service to the great pharaohs of Egypt only to come to this, exploring some kid's craft project with dental floss tied around my waist."

Alex could hear grumbling continue even when he was quite a distance away.

Eventually she lost sight of him, but could feel the occasional tug on the floss as he moved through the space. At one point there were three or four sharp tugs to the line, making her wonder if he was trying to communicate something to her or if he was being attacked by some unknown paper beast. In hindsight, it would have been a good idea to set up some communication techniques via floss-jerk before he headed out.

After a time his tiny shape was making his way back to her. He'd removed the floss from his waist but was using it to guide his way back to her.

"It looks like we have a way in. This room is comprised of many layers of paper that make up the entire landscape. The floor moves on large metallic disks like massive clockworks, nested inside each other. It makes it hard to keep steady and walk in a determined direction, as it is always shifting, so the rope served as a handy thread of breadcrumbs back to you. Without it I don't know that I would have found my way back."

"You're welcome."

Aah-Ha rolled his eyes. "Once I got deep into what looked like the center, I noticed an anomaly on one of the sheets of paper in the depiction of the Nile. I could see some sort of visual distortion like waves of heat in the distance. I think it might be a portal into where the bookkeeper lives. I tied down the floss near the portal, so we can find our way back."

"Good job. Did you take a peek?"

"Not a chance. I'm leaving that up to you, boss."

"Do you think I can fit in the portal?"

"It was quite large."

If the ushabti weren't so small, she probably would have

taken offense. She cut the end of her floss from the container and attached it to the brass portal door. As the floss became taut, it sent a cascade of movement through the paper landscape. She could hear some of the material tear as it cut through the diorama-scape.

Alex squatted down and put her hand in front of Aah-Ha. "It's time to hit the road."

Once he settled back in her bag, she followed the floss line ahead of her.

It took a while for Alex to get used to walking through the environment. It was as if she was walking through a completely rendered landscape. But depending on the light and shadows, it was as if she were traversing through many delicate layers of theatrical scrims. Even when she thought she could vaguely pick out the framework behind the illusion and feel grounded, the magicked paper allowed her to walk through it. If all of that wasn't disorienting enough, the ever-spinning landscape, controlled by the clockwork below, would have confounded even the greatest of navigators. She was thankful to have the small bit of floss to guide her.

Alex made it to the riverbank of this Nile. It was eerie to be in a place that in the real world teemed with life, but was dead silent here. Absent were the sounds of birds, boats, and people. She stepped into the river, half expecting to feel the water lap against her pant legs, but there was nothing.

She continued into the river toward a small island. In the scrim ahead, she could see a tear that blurred in and out of focus.

Alex poked her head into the hole and was gladdened to hear the call of birds. Craning her neck, she could see them darting about in a midday sky. The bookkeeper had carved out a little slice of reality beyond the diorama.

She stepped through the large gap, feeling the sharp buzz of magical energy as she passed through the conjured membrane and onto soft sand. The mountain seemed more of a mole hill to Alex, but she sensed that the ghostwriting bookkeeper had a flair for overstatement. Ahead lay three paths. Two led around the so-called mountain. The center pathway pushed through a lush grove of date palms and sycamore trees.

She chose the middle path. The other two were more likely to avoid contact, but Alex wasn't sure that was what she needed. Alex followed the path through the grove of trees to the crest of the hill and ended up at a very unimpressive circle of dirt with stones scattered about the perimeter. At the apex of the hill was a very plain bench. It was the sort of place where a person might go to enjoy a sunset.

From the bench she could see all around the mountain. A wax-paper-looking wall surrounded it, vaguely obscuring the spinning diorama outside.

Something snapped in the not-too-far distance.

"We've got company," Aah-Ha exclaimed from her scribe's bag.

"Shhhh." Alex flipped the scribe's bag shut.

"Thanks." A muffled voice came from inside her bag.

She thumped the side of the bag with her finger.

Alex turned around to see a very large man standing before her, blocking her way back down the path. He wasn't big in the storybook villain sort of way, but more in the way of someone who spent most of their time reclining while eating bonbons. His head was shaved clean, and he sported a large potbelly that jutted out and over his pleated linen kilt, while his chest hosted a pair of sagging man-breasts. Aside from his less-than-attractive appearance, his face was lit with the joy of a five-year-old who'd just spotted a unicorn in their backyard.

He moved with unexpected grace and speed toward Alex. Apparently, this bookkeeper shouldn't be completely judged by his cover.

"A guest! Finally, a guest! Let me introduce myself. I am Hapi Merneptah, keeper of this book. Welcome! It has been far too long since I've enjoyed new company." His grin broadened. "Wait a minute. I know who you are. You aren't just any guest. You are one of the book. As a nonmagical creature, there is no other way you could be here. You will be so glad you came. You and I will have a lot of fun together. You'll see."

Alex reached down and held her hand against the top of her scribe's bag. It wouldn't do for Aah-Ha to suddenly decide to pop up and see his shadow. It would probably be good for Hapi to not exactly know how many guests he had.

"Call me Hap. All my friends do."

All the way down to his house, the bookkeeper chattered like a small bird.

They rounded a corner, and Hapi's house came into view. It was rather large and cut from the living rock of the mountain. It reminded Alex of the ancient Anasazi buildings in Arizona. Hapi's house was four stories. It didn't seem to read as a cabin in any way, unless you were accustomed to sprawling mansions.

On the very top level was a large wraparound deck. Leaning against the rail was a man with a wide face and bulging eyes holding an umbrellaed drink. Nearby, reclined on a chaise lounge, was a woman with a long angular face and a fluid sinuous body.

Frog and Serpent.

She'd found Nun and Naunet's servants.

CHAPTER THIRTY-THREE

As Alex stepped into Hapi's house, it looked nothing like she thought it would. She mistakenly assumed that an ancient magical creature would prefer to have their environment echo the times in which they initially lived. In this case, it was everything but. The interior was more high bachelor pad or man cave than anything else.

They entered a large room on the main floor that was taken up almost completely with a humongous burgundy wraparound couch. Across from the large sofa was a massive television. It made Alex wonder. What sort of reception did one get in a book of magic? Did Hapi have a cable bill?

He smiled in response to her apparent confusion. "Think of me as a park ranger in your world. A park ranger located on a high peak of a remote mountain."

Alex successfully resisted rolling her eyes.

Hapi continued on. "A mountain that no one ever visits and a ranger who can never retire. And when I say never, I mean forever-never." He reached down and grabbed a supersized remote control. "Let's just say the Gods favored me with some entertainments. I get all channels here and some you've never seen." He clicked the massive screen to life. As he cruised through the channel guide, Alex caught glimpses of what looked like a home shopping network for magical items, a game of soccer played between a team of unicorns and Pegasus, and a game show hosted by what appeared to be a leprechaun.

While he flipped through more channels, Hapi commented. "The unicorns always lose. In the rock, paper, scissors game of the magical world, wings win over horns. The Horned Ones are always so wrapped up in their need for justice and redemption they constantly call for a rematch. Always, I mean always, there is a game on. Good thing they have an eternity. Humans think unicorns disappeared because the age of innocence died, but it was really just the call of the game."

"What about the game show?"

"That one is pretty boring to watch. Leprechauns, you know."

"Sorry, I don't."

"Not so good at giving away treasure. No one ever wins. Ever."

Hapi landed on a split-screen view that was fed by closed-circuit cameras from various locations around the realm. Alex squinted at the thumbnail of where they crossed into the mountain. She could just barely pick out the dental floss. Hapi didn't seem to notice.

"As you can see, I have many surveillance cameras too. They've come in handy from time to time, but as you can imagine, they are just a little less thrilling than watching tiny green men hoard treasure."

Judging by his expansive belly, the bookkeeper could use a little less couch time.

"Welcome." A baritone voice came from a rather roundish figure on the staircase. "Frog's the name."

The sleek female glided down the staircase next to him. Her golden eyes were cold and hard. "I'm Serpent. I am so glad to finally have something around here other than the masculine perspective."

Her bored tone belied her sentiment.

"Nice to meet you." Alex sized them up as they approached. There wasn't anything in either of their presentation that struck her as being in distress or telegraphing a come-rescue-me vibe. They gave the appearance of being right at home. Her game now became doubly hard. She would not only have to find a way to bring them back under the watchful eye of their host, but would need to coax them into leaving. What if they didn't want to return to their life of servitude? Then what? There was no way Alex could drag them back unwillingly. Both Frog and Serpent were supernatural creatures, not to mention much larger in size than she. Bringing them back could prove to be impossible.

Hapi guided Alex toward them. "These are my roomies. Life is so much better with friends." He shot Alex a glance that sent a chill up her spine. He probably meant it as friendly, but behind it was a kind of possessiveness. Alex remembered her college roommate's possessive boyfriend. Whenever he walked in the room, it was as if her friend's personality went under an invisible lockdown.

Frog stepped forward and shook Alex's hand. "There isn't much chance for adventure here, but Hap has ways of making your stay enjoyable. It'll just take some getting used to." He smiled broadly, but the sentiment died before reaching his eyes.

Maybe there was some discord Alex could play with here. Could it be that they were skillfully playing a part for their captor?

Hapi linked arms with Alex. "Let me take you to your quarters. You've had quite a journey." Frog and Serpent followed close behind.

While she walked through the house, Alex made a mental note of everything around her. It would be necessary when it came time to escape.

The bookkeeper led her to the top of a staircase leading down to a basement den that was dug into the mountain rock. Hapi motioned for her to head down.

Alex turned to look behind her as Frog and Serpent pulled an iron-barred pocket door out from the wall. It slammed shut with a loud clank.

A touch of pity warmed Serpent's golden eyes. "It won't take you long to realize that staying here is what you want."

Frog looked up at Serpent. "For us it took . . . a couple of weeks?"

Hap laughed. "Oh, time, the great changer of memory. If I recall correctly, it was most likely months. But time here is like an endless river. Frog, why don't you rustle up some nachos for our new roommate. She must be starving. I've got my daily rounds to do."

With that, they all left her staring up at the bars of her prison. The den, much like the living room, was furnished with an oversized couch and a huge flat-screen television.

She plopped down on the couch and flipped open her bag. Alex peered down at Aah-Ha. "I think it is time for you to hang out in the pendant again. I'd like to have a few secrets of my own."

His shoulders drooped. "Oh joy. Back in the tiny metal coffin."

It wasn't only the sad look on the ushabti's face that changed her mind, it was the idea that it might not be good to keep all her eggs in one basket. If Hapi had a wild hair to lock up her belongings, that would include her secret weapon. "On second thought, why don't you find a comfortable, but very hidden, place to hang out? If the opportunity comes to steal those keys, take it."

It wasn't long before Alex heard the key turn in the lock upstairs.

Aah-Ha darted behind the couch.

Alex glanced up as Frog and Serpent descended.

With one hand, Frog shoved the keys into his back pocket. In his other he held glass-necked bottles dangling from between his fingers. "I wasn't sure if you were a beer drinker, so I brought some other options."

Serpent was walking behind Frog, holding a heavily cheese-laden plate of nachos. As far as nachos go, these didn't look like any real preparation had gone into them. Absent of any chopped tomatoes, beef, or guacamole, it appeared to be a large glop of that oddly creamy queso that convenience stores run out of on Superbowl Sunday atop a pointy bed of tortilla chips.

"Have you got any ginger beer?" Alex wanted to keep a clear head.

As he handed it to her, an expression of disenchantment washed over his overfriendly countenance. It seemed he might have had his bulging eyes on that beverage for himself.

She screwed the lid off and took a sip.

A gleam of excitement sparked in Serpent's eyes. "Mind if we stay awhile? It has been ages since we've talked to someone from the outside." She set the nachos down on the coffee table in front of Alex and grabbed the beer from Frog.

Alex nodded and, taking a tortilla chip, scooped up a large daub of queso and raised the orange-yellow concoction to her hosts. "I appreciate you bringing me something to eat." She popped it in her mouth and enjoyed the crunchy, creamy saltiness of it.

"Glad to have you here." Frog's eyebrow arched as he reached for a chip. "Do you mind?"

"You just ate. Those are for our guest. Next you'll be wondering yet again why your sweatpants don't fit anymore." Serpent appeared to take her job seriously as Frog's shamer-in-chief.

A deep frown pulled at the wide corners of Frog's face.

"Have a seat." Alex gestured toward the empty cushions.

Frog grumbled. "We'd rather stand."

They both stood awkwardly in front of her. Alex guessed they were instructed to block any point of exit.

Aah-Ha poked his head out from the edge of the wraparound couch. He must have spotted an opportunity to try and swipe the keys, but Alex couldn't figure how he could possibly get into Frog's back pocket. Frog was more stout than tall, but his pocket height was clearly out of the ushabti's reach.

Alex stood and walked over to a credenza by the television on the pretext of retrieving the remote. She hoped that both of her jailers would turn to follow. If things went just right, Frog's butt would be located just above the coffee table where Aah-Ha might have a chance to climb up and grab the keys. She needed a distraction and answers, so why not kill two birds with one

GIFT OF THE SPHINX 407

stone. "I am sure you know that I came here from your home. Your masters, Nun and Naunet, miss you. They sent me here to find you and bring you back."

"How quaint." Frog crossed his arms over his stout chest. "After all these years."

In her peripheral vision, she could see Aah-Ha was on the table and tiptoeing to Frog's back pocket.

She needed to keep their attention focused on her. "They are beside themselves. It isn't just your service they miss. Naunet spoke with great passion about how you were not just helpers, but eternal friends." Aah-Ha was on his very tiptoes swiping madly at the one key that was hanging over the edge of Frog's pocket. She laid it on thick. "They both are devastated by your absence. Quite frankly, when I ran into them, they were both despondent with loss, which has only grown more pronounced over time. I think if you saw them today, you would be shocked to realize that they are just mere shadows of their former selves."

A small tear formed in the corner of Serpent's eye.

The keys clunked onto the table.

Frog spun around. "What's going on?"

Aah-Ha grabbed the keys and ran to the stairs.

Serpent's head reared back. She struck with lightning speed and snapped him up and spit him onto the couch. "And who is this little man?"

Frog, his eyes brimming with tears, grabbed Alex's arm. "You were just buying time for your little friend to try to swipe my keys. Well, I just want you to know that your little charade failed. Nothing you said rang true. At all. Serpent, take this little man upstairs and lock him up in the special cabinet. I am sure Hap will take a keen interest in this new guest."

Frog's icy tone made her shiver. She'd blown her ace in the

hole. Maybe it was time to come clean. "He is a ushabti, in service to me, and his name is Aah-Ha. I have been sent here to take you back. No matter what you think, Nun and Naunet—"

"Come back? I don't know if you've noticed, but we've got it pretty cush here." Frog ignored Serpent's evil glance as he reached over and defiantly grabbed a nacho out of the gooey marshland of cheese.

Serpent slid over to the couch, nudging Aah-Ha over and making herself comfortable. "Admittedly, it is nice not being someone's servant. There is truth in that. But, even if we wanted to leave, and I'm not saying we do, we can't."

Frog's eyes bulged. "Over the years, I could count the oh, *never*times you've mentioned how much you miss being at the beck and call of two very needy Gods. A life of service is nothing short of demeaning, right, little man?"

Aah-ha looked as if he wanted to chime in, but instead twitched awkwardly.

"Say what you will, Frog, have a seat. I've known you since the mound of creation rose from the waters of chaos, and deep down, I know you wish you could leave this place and return home."

Frog made a croaking harrumph that sounded like a cross between a burp and a hiccup and plopped down next to Serpent. Aah-Ha shifted his position on the couch once again. The stout frogman crossed his arms tightly over his chest.

Aah-Ha climbed to the cup holder in the armrest and settled in. Now at a more equal stature to the others, he spoke for the first time. "Why are you still here living with Hapi? As magical creatures, I would think you would be able to leave this realm with no problem."

"Hap. Whatever you do, don't call him Hapi. Got that, little man?" Frog glared over at the ushabti.

Alex would have to find a way to smooth Frog's ruffled feathers.

"What does he do?" asked Alex.

"Well, let's just say he is anything but happy."

"Believe what Frog says. Keeping Hap happy is important for the quality of your time here. Don't ever call him Hapi."

The magical creatures seemed to be avoiding Aah-Ha's question. "Thanks for the tip. So really, why are you still here?"

Serpent's reptilian-shaped mouth turned down even further at its corners. "Hap, being the bookkeeper, knows our true names and was able to cast a spell on us. It makes it so we become vastly disoriented if we break through the membrane to the other side of this level. We have tried many times to escape, but neither of us made it very far. The last time one of us tried, Hap was so angry that he kept us apart for three years."

"That was worse than any torture he could have come up with for two linked celestial beings." Frog laid his hand on Serpent's.

"If I have a way for you to leave, would you come with me?"

"*If* is a word that lacks in certainty," said Frog.

"Hap doesn't strike me as someone who pays attention to small details. When he leaves this level to do his rounds of the book, would he notice a thread of floss running through the outer rim?"

"Of course he would. He may be somewhat dim, but not blind. Come on, Serpent, we've wasted enough time on this pointless chatter. This one comes to us with great-and-mighty dental floss as our savior." Frog leaned his large body off the couch.

"I will just have to come up with a better plan. If the floss is gone, if he removed it when he was leaving to go on his rounds, that plan obviously won't work."

A smile brightened Serpent's expression. "Wait a minute. He hasn't crossed through there in ages. With that body, do you think he really climbs that ladder?"

A buoyant hope rose within Alex. "How does he get to the other levels?"

"A year or so ago, he had the Gods install an elevator."

—~v~—

With Aah-Ha tucked away in the scribe's bag, Alex, Frog, and Serpent made their way off the mountain and through to the river-level portal using the undetected floss. Frog and Serpent leapt out of the portal and ran toward the large pool of water in the white room. As they neared the water their humanlike forms morphed into their animal forms.

"Wait! We have one more thing to do," Alex yelled at them.

Standing at the edge of the pool, the two magical creatures turned their heads. "We?"

"I came here with two missions. One was to save you, and the other was to disable this book of magic."

Frog jumped in the water and quickly resurfaced. "You think we are going to go all the way up to the top floor and help you turn the water off and get caught by Hapi? No way. Please consider your job successfully half done."

Serpent slid into the pool, her head raised high out of the water. "We have two very important Gods waiting for us. Do you really want to risk us getting caught again? See you on the other side."

A smile pulled across Frog's face. "That is, if you make it."

Before Alex could argue with them, both Serpent and Frog disappeared into the waters of chaos. It hadn't occurred to her that they would be able to shift into forms that didn't need a breathing apparatus. Alex chided herself for not thinking fully through their potential shape-shifting abilities.

Aah-Ha popped his head out of Alex's scribe's bag. "Figures. You never can count on magical creatures, unless they are magically forced to do so."

"You are saying you'd do the same if you could."

"Not exactly."

"Only because you couldn't survive the swim for lack of air in your current animated form, unless of course you were stowed away in my coffin charm."

"Let's just say if I could, I would be right behind them." He shuffled within the bag, looking down at his feet. "And by that, I mean nothing personal. As far as masters go, you are pretty nice, but it is like you are a magnet for trouble."

"At least they didn't leave us empty-handed."

"What do you mean?"

Alex made her way to the ladder and started climbing.

"They told us how to disable the book."

~~~

The topmost and ninth portal lay before her. Its frame was different in color from the others. Instead of brass it was cast of electrum. The circlet of metal contained shapes of clouds intermixed with raindrops made of beautifully faceted diamonds. Beyond the glass portal lay a vast expanse of sky.

Alex opened the small door.

The room was massive, bringing to mind a cavernous ware-house holding the servers of the technological cloud, but in this instance, it was literally filled with clouds, or at least the top third was. Every shape and density of cloud a person could imagine stretched out into the seemingly infinite horizon.

There were the puffy white clouds of a spring day. Some clouds were thin streaks of grey and others were dark and stormy. They all mixed together in a lovely mosaic of ephemeral celestial bodies. From these clouds, thousands of gem-sparkle raindrops fell downward until they hit the grey concrete floor. The diamond-like raindrops rolled down the floor in all of their glimmering glory to the canal that flowed by the portal wall. Once the gem-raindrops made their way into the canal, they morphed into the crystal-clear liquid of the central waterfall in the white room.

The twinkling rain was mesmerizing. Alex could have just gazed into the scene before her for countless hours. It was as if the very sky above was raining down diamonds like so many stars. It was nothing short of breathtaking.

"How do you suppose that we are going to get through that? It looks like the worst hailstorm I've ever seen."

"I think it's beautiful." Alex reached out with a cupped hand. A gem-raindrop hit her skin with a soft tickle and then shifted to water as soon as it stilled. "I think we will be fine, so long as I don't end up in a giggle fit. These drops feel amazing once they touch your skin. It feels both warm and cold at the same time, like standing in snowfall while sipping on hot chocolate."

Alex entered the portal and let it rain down on her, reveling in the ecstatic joy of having its magic wash over her.

Aah-Ha cleared his throat. "If we don't get moving, we might run into our not-so-little friend. Also, I seem to be getting a little more than wet in here."

It was odd that the gem-rain that fell on her clothes didn't turn into liquid. It was as if man-made materials didn't trigger the transition from the gem-rain to its liquid form. It struck her that it might not be a bad idea to try and take some of this gem-rain back with her as an ultimate souvenir. "Climb up to my shoulder. I am going to flip up the top of the bag and try and collect some of this material while we are looking for the valve."

"Oh great."

"I could just send you back to the pendant."

Aah-Ha made his way up Alex's arm. "And miss my charming company?"

Once he was situated, Alex walked through the glittering rain. Moving deeper within the space, she noticed that the water was flowing toward her in a number of distinct gem-streams. With no means of finding anything in a room of ever-shifting cloudscape, she decided to walk against the general current. She turned back and spotted the portal glowing in the distance, glad that she could follow the stream back. It wouldn't do to get lost in this chapter.

Alex looked at the clouds overhead, half hoping to spy a pipe system. But no such luck. Her heart sunk at the sheer size of the room. It would take her an eternity to search it. Other than the portal that she came through and its canal, there were no walls or identifying features.

Glancing down at her feet, she could see a pattern in the gem-flow below. Areas of the stream split as if flowing around a small stone. Behind her was a loose pattern all the way to the portal.

She squatted down to the diversion nearest her. The floor where the waters parted didn't have any topography changes that would have the gems react in such a way. Alex placed her hand on the empty area nearest to her. The surface became warm to the touch and glowed as if it were alabaster lit from within. The entire floor surface suddenly changed from the grey concrete to a warm amber stone. A rumbling came from above as if massive clockwork gears were struggling to churn against age-old cogs.

The rumbling came closer. The sound was like the Gods were bowling overhead. Suddenly a bright light flashed before her eyes. A sharp sting erupted on the top of her hand. She jerked her hand away. The lightning flashed again, but this time it landed on the spot where her hand had been.

A golden orb shaped like a light bulb erupted from the floor, glowing softly. Hieroglyphs encircled the bulb.

Aah-Ha read from Alex's shoulder. "Turn bulb in case of emergency."

Alex reached down. It turned with ease.

The rumbling stopped. Through the gentle tinkling of the gem-rain a ding of an elevator sounded, followed by the voice of Hapi. "Stop! You—"

Alex twisted the bulb with all of her might. The rain stopped instantly—only a few errant drops here and there plunked through the large space like an old showerhead.

"Hang on," Alex yelled at Aah-Ha. She jumped up and ran to the portal. Behind her were the labored breath and heavy foot-falls of the bookkeeper giving chase.

"Stop! Now! Or you will be sorry." From what Alex could tell, he'd stopped running and was muttering to himself. The words were indiscernible, but the cadence sounded like a spell.

Alex charged forward.

She jumped over the now bone-dry canal and reached for the portal. As soon as she touched it, the portal disappeared.

He had trapped her. She looked down at the dry canal bed and was struck with inspiration. "Hold on tight, Aah-Ha. If you thought that was a wild ride, you have another thing coming."

Alex dumped her bag full of water-gems. As soon as they hit the canal's smooth, angled surface, they morphed into a gush of semisolid roundels of water. She flung herself onto them, laughing with abandon as she flew down toward the waterfall at top speed. Her stomach lurched as she bumped off its edge and was ejected, falling down toward the pool. Water stung her skin and nostrils as she broke through the surface and torpedoed downward. Alex thrust her arms up in broad strokes and pulled herself up to the surface.

She clung to the pool's edge and looked for the ushabti. He was nowhere to be found. Alex splashed around frantically looking for him. Had he not made it down the waterfall with her? She scanned the surface of the water for any telltale signs of the ushabti. Then it hit her. Alex opened up her coffin pendant. "Aah-Ha, I command you back into my pendant." His small body came flying from somewhere above her toward the open coffin pendant in her grasp.

She clasped it shut, then retrieved the breathing reed from her scribe's bag. She took one last look before diving in the water. She saw a red-faced Hapi, apparently stuck in the chute.

~~~

An unexpected tableau revealed itself when she emerged from the ceremonial pool. Luke was stretched out on a lounger, seemingly unconcerned that she was, up until that very moment, in great peril. He exuded the air of a visiting pasha as Serpent and Frog scurried about. Nun and Naunet were nowhere to be seen.

When Luke spotted her, his eyes went wide and the large brown ceramic tiki-themed vessel he held slipped out of his grasp. It crashed to the floor, breaking into a thousand pieces. Bright Kool-Aid-red liquid pooled like cartoony blood against the soft pastels of the abalone floor. Startled, Luke shot up and knocked over the snack-filled table that was adjacent to him. Three silver trays piled with various nibbles further littered the floor.

A small crusty object, looking suspiciously like a pig in a blanket, rolled and came to a stop by Alex's foot. She stared down at the savory pastry as droplets of water marked the floor around it. She looked back to Luke as he was righting the table. He never struck her as particularly klutzy. Had she startled him, or was there something more behind it? "I see they've been keeping you busy."

Luke flashed her a hurt look, then picked up a silver tray.

Frog and Serpent stopped their frenzied dance of whisking away the collateral damage. Frog stomped over to Luke and yanked the tray from his hands.

Serpent held her head high and defiant. "It is our job to serve."

Frog was shoveling the scattered finger foods into a bucket. "The last thing we need is more trouble."

Luke chuckled. "You two were really in the Frog house when you showed up without The Great One's progeny."

Both Frog and Serpent groaned.

Frog looked up at Alex. "Please make them stop—his jokes, if you can call them that, are killing me. And that is saying a lot coming from a magical creature."

Serpent looked equally pained. "We are built for eternity, but not for this."

Luke shrugged his shoulders, indifferent to the pain he inflicted on the magical creatures. "Seriously, your ancestors were not hoppy with these two."

Serpent and Frog groaned.

Alex rolled her eyes at him and his dweeby attempt at humor, but couldn't help but smile.

Luke caught her eye and held it, then quickly looked away.

The intensity of his gaze sent a small shiver throughout her body. Feeling awkward, Alex looked into the far distance and saw Nun and Naunet as they entered the sanctuary.

Nun strode toward Alex with Naunet close at his side. "What's with all the frog jokes? I think you're going to make Serpent feel unloved."

Naunet rushed toward Alex with open arms. Alex was surprised at the bear-hug embrace. "Thank the stars of Nut, you made it back!" The Goddess shot daggers at Serpent and Frog. "And with absolutely no help from our faithful servants."

Both Serpent and Frog fell to the floor in supplication, then spoke as one. "Oh Father of Gods and his magnificent wife, the two Blessed Ones of the waters of chaos and the waters of life, all-powerful beings of the Divine Eight who brought existence from the void. These humble servants beg forgiveness."

Luke sat down on the lounger with an exasperated air as the two magical creatures rose from kneeling. "Talk about tiresome. You think my jokes are bad. Try living through that a hundred times or so. Couldn't you change up the words they recite every time the f-word comes up?"

Alex drew her eyebrows together. "'f-word'?"

Luke and the Gods answered as one. "Faithful."

Frog and Serpent dropped down once more and started their dirge.

Naunet snapped her fingers. "Enough."

Both Frog and Serpent stopped speaking, then stood.

Naunet continued, "I cannot say that you faithless servants have done enough penance to absolve the atrocity of leaving our dear one behind, but Luke is right, this groveling in unison is getting tiresome."

A sigh of relief came from both servants.

Nun crossed his arms. "Don't think you're off the hook yet. We've got plenty of time to continue your punishment after our guests depart."

Naunet sat on the edge of the pool and ran her fingers across its surface. "I think it has been ages since the pool has been cleaned."

An odd look passed between Frog and Serpent. Alex wasn't quite sure if it was disgust or just general disgruntlement, but either way she knew it wasn't something they looked forward to.

Nun walked over to Naunet and placed his hands on her shoulders. "My beloved and I have come up with one lasting punishment that I think is in line with your crime."

Naunet reached up and clasped one of Nun's hands. "We are going to tell our dear one both of your true names. You will then be her servant too for as long as she lives."

The servants' faces went stone white.

Alex was shocked that her ancestors would do such a thing. And apparently both ancient magical creatures were too. Knowing someone's true name allowed you great power over that individual. In ancient Egypt, all mothers would give their children two names, the one that everyone knew, and a secret name that only the mother would know, deflecting any harm someone might want to magically inflict on their children.

Naunet stood and beckoned Alex to come to her.

They each leaned into one of Alex's ears and whispered the names.

~~~

With the book of magic tucked away in the scribe's bag, Alex and Luke didn't make long goodbyes. Nun and Naunet informed Alex that she needed to return the book by the next full moon. They were very clear that she was not taking the book, but merely checking it out. If the book was not returned in that time, it would be her ancestors who would pay the price. The lost oasis, all the knowledge it contained, and the Gods who protected it would become inaccessible to her linage and the human realm for eternity. Nun and Naunet would become imprisoned within their temple forever.

Before passing through the large pearl-white gateway of the temple, she gazed back at its opulent beauty. Both Gods and their servants watched them leave as the doors closed behind Luke and Alex.

As she stepped onto the pathway that cut through the verdant land ahead, she felt a slight tug at her neck. The bird pendant came to life, leading her and Luke along the stream toward the cave and her sleeping companions. When they entered the tunnel, the bird flew onto Alex's hand and returned to pendant form. Alex slid it back onto her chain.

They ducked into the tunnel that led to the cave, walking side by side. "I guess you can thank me now."

Luke stopped walking. "Thank you?"

"For saving your ass. It's a lucky thing they wanted their servants returned. If that hadn't played out to our advantage, I have no idea what I could have bargained with to free you. I think imprisonment by them would have been the least of your worries had everything not worked the way it did. Why on earth did you follow me in the first place?"

"I happened to wake up and thought you might need some help. Excuse me for being concerned with your safety. Your pal, Gormund, is probably snoozing away blissfully in the cave at this moment."

"Well I guess we both owe each other some thanks."

Luke shuffled forward, his head down. "I was just trying to help."

"The weird thing is, how did you get to the oasis anyway? From what Nun and Naunet said, it is only accessible to myself and those from my family tree."

"Did the guardian statues try and capture you?"

"You have a point Luke, but maybe you only have guest privileges of sorts to that oasis. Why didn't Gormund follow? I know he isn't that hard of a sleeper. Who knows, maybe there is an oasis realm that you can access, and I can't. When we get back to headquarters, we should check in the archive and see if we can find anything in your family history."

"Like what?"

"Magic."

"I sincerely doubt that. I come from a long line of very practical doctors. I was the black sheep that broke the generational secession of medical practitioners."

"I would argue that the fact that you come from generations of doctors actually makes it highly likely your family has a magical line. Wasn't magic and medicine all the same thing in ancient Egypt?"

"Have it your way, Alex. Just don't be disappointed when you find out I am anything but magical." Luke dug out his flashlight and turned it on. He stopped walking immediately.

Alex halted next to him, staring out at the brilliant rock formations that stretched ahead of them. When Alex first wandered through the tunnel in the dark, she assumed that it was nothing but mountain rocks. The small beam of light revealed billions of sparkling crystals. It was as if they stepped inside a massive blue-hued geode.

He cast the light about. The walls sparkled. "Speaking of the magical . . ."

"It's beautiful."

He moved the beam to the floor, catching bright flashes as the light played along the ground plane. Strewn across the tunnel floor were hundreds of crystalline pebbles that danced with brilliant color. The streambed was lined with the glimmering gravel.

Alex kicked at the small stones. As they skittered away, it was as if she'd kicked a handful of stars across the night sky. She squatted down and made a small pile of the rocks, then scooped them up. "Could you shine your light on these?"

Under closer study Alex saw that within each crystal was an unmistakable flame at its center.

With her free hand, she flipped open her scribe's bag and grabbed the book of magic and handed it over to Luke. "Don't get any ideas."

"Like?"

"Given your ability to find trouble, I would hate to fill your head with a list of possibilities."

He let out a small laugh.

She searched around in her scribe's bag for a small pouch that was usually there. As she rooted around, her heart sank. All the water-gems from the book of magic had tumbled out of her bag in her great escape from Hapi. She was lucky that they enabled her quick escape. However, it would have been nice to have a souvenir from the book of magic. Had the pouch fallen out as well?

Her fingertips finally grazed the pouch's velvet fabric. She pulled it out and poured the small stones into it. "These could come in handy. You never know. Considering the fire within them, maybe they hold some sort of power. Probably not as much as the ones from the book of magic, though."

Luke was watching her put the stones away. His eyes lit with amusement when she looked up at him. "I can see the agency gossip is true."

"How do you mean?"

"Your mom calls you Magpie, for all the random treasures you collect." He bumped into her playfully.

She bumped him back. Her gaze connected with his brilliant green eyes which softened as he leaned in even closer. Something within her tugged her toward him. Her mind was invaded with the uninvited thought of how good it would feel to be pulled into his embrace. She stepped back.

They stood apart from one another like two magnets suddenly flipped with their northern poles facing each other. "Luke you are a wonderful guy, but—"

He kicked his foot out, sending a few of the glimmering stones skittering away. "We should get back to the others. I know, you don't have to say it, Alex. I completely understand."

"Say what?"

"You are still stuck on Niles."

"Luke, whatever may or may not be going on in my personal life, I am your boss . . . and you and I just can't happen." However, the idea of it sent a hot flush up her neck and into her face, making her cheeks burn. She was thankful for the semi-darkness of the tunnel.

He looked like he wanted to say something but thought better of it. He brushed past her and turned back. "Let's get this show on the road."

Alex was certain he didn't one hundred percent believe that was Alex's only reason, and she wasn't convinced either.

They walked in awkward silence until they got to the crack that led to the cave and their sleeping friend.

Luke motioned for her to slide under before him. "Ladies first."

She scooted under the crack and shimmied her way back until she could fully stand.

Gormund was pacing back and forth through the cave. He looked up at her and a broad smile pulled across his face in apparent relief. In his usual style, his sharp, pointed teeth telegraphed a mixed and disconcerting message—happy face, pointy teeth. He ran over to Alex and hugged her. "So glad you've come back. Where have you two been?" They broke apart just as Luke was making his way through the crack. Gormund rubbed his chin. "Looks like you two were up to no good. Emerging all tousled and flushed, rolling out from under a rock after being gone for ages."

"Whatever, Gormund." Luke was brushing the sparkling rock residue from his pants.

Gormund walked over to the crack that they came from. It had turned into a solid rock wall. He rubbed where the crack was seconds ago.

"I found the lost oasis, and the book of magic."

"We."

"I found it. Luke, you were following in my wake. I never

thought to ask you, but why didn't you wake Gormund and bring him with you?"

"I really tried."

Gormund placed his hands on his hips. "That's the weird thing."

"That you are a super hard sleeper?"

"No, Luke. The thing that is weird is that you were able to follow her at all. It seems this cave, the storm that raged outside . . . all of those things were orchestrated to get Alex here. Alex is the only one who should have been able to cross over into the oasis. Even I, a God, was incapacitated. Only the strongest of magic can bar Immortals like me. But you are regular old flesh and bone, a run-of-the-mill ordinary man. It makes no sense."

"Unless?" asked Alex.

Luke harrumphed. "Okay, Alex, you win. Unless my family has magic lineage."

"There are two distinct possibilities. That your family does come from one of the four tribes of the book. Or more likely, being the average Joe you seem to be, it could be that someone has put a spell on you to act as a magical protector of Alex."

Luke puffed up at the suggestion. "Magical protector. I like the sound of that."

Gormund glanced up with a twinkle of mischief in his eyes. "Or you two are related somehow. Which would make your quick and rumpled lovers' getaway all the more scandalous."

Alex coughed into her hand and quickly changed the subject. "Whatever, boys. Time to get moving. We need to get back to headquarters, but before we reach out to Jorge and Idris, there is something I'd like to do."

"Crawl back into the cave with your protector?" Gormund wiggled his eyebrows.

"Gor, get your mind out of the gutter. I want to give that enclosed crystal room we made for Akh-Hehet a try. On the chance she can forecast some possible futures for us before we engage with those who want the book."

Gormund let out a short grumble. "I can't believe you are going to give that book to that imbecile."

Alex walked toward the mouth of the cave. She glanced back at Gormund. "You know, I honestly wonder what part Jorge is playing in all of this. All of it seems beyond the scope of his abilities or intellect. I think the one who really wants this book is that magician. Jorge is probably just his mark."

Alex threw the keys at Gormund. "Why don't you drive, since you slept through everything else."

Luke laughed at the jab at Gormund. "How are we going to get the vehicle out from under the sand? It'll take forever to push all of it away."

Alex opened the door behind the driver's seat and slid in. "Our driver can back into the cave and let the sand fall into it. Then we will drive right over it. The beauty of having a Land Rover."

Gormund started the car, notched it into reverse, and then shot backward, freeing it from the sand that piled up during the storm. The large dune poured into the mouth of the cave.

Alex drew her seat belt across her chest. "Buckle up, boys. I have a feeling it's going to be a bumpy ride."

CHAPTER THIRTY-FOUR

J orge paced back and forth in his room. He needed to
figure a way out of the mess he'd gotten himself and
Gwen into. He stared at the magical force field that
blocked him from leaving. The waving fields of magic
were mesmerizing. He studied it closely, hoping to find an
anomaly or chink in its armor. In his limited experience with
magic in the recent months, he'd come to realize that similar to
Japanese artworks, magic almost always held an imperfection
within. It was just a matter of finding it. But in magic these
imperfections related to the spell that was cast. Idris, in a
moment of great hubris, once explained that every magician had
an Achilles' heel of sorts. Each spell-making voice held specific
flaws or tells unique to it.

When Jorge gazed into the force field, he didn't see any such
chinks in this armor. He surveyed the room. When his eyes
rested on the pneumatic tube, he was struck with an idea. Could
he be so lucky that Idris, in the moment of creating the force-

field jail for his prisoner, forgot to make the pneumatic tube unusable to Jorge?

He rushed over to it and jumped inside, giddy at the thought of finding such a simple answer.

Jorge pushed the button that would take him directly to the dungeon. When his finger touched it, a jolt of electricity charged through his body, throwing him against the wall of the translucent tube.

A crackling noise sounded in the small space, like a PA system coming to life, followed by a familiar laughter. "Tsk-tsk, Jorgie. And here I thought you were going to be a good boy. I will give you this one for free, but try again, and I will start making your girl just slightly less attractive. I am not playing a game, mortal." The speaker clicked off.

He peeled himself off the floor. Maybe the only way out was to give Idris what he wanted and hope that Jorge misjudged the magician's intentions, but deep down he knew the only real chance out of this situation was to figure out a way to get Gwen and himself out of the sky castle before the shit hit the fan.

He tucked his hands behind his back and wandered over to the balcony. As he leaned into it, the low wall pressed into his thighs. Out in the distance lay the patio with the infinite infinity pool that hung over the expansive beige desert below.

He remembered how excited Gwen was regarding the suite of rooms Idris created for them. As soon as they were alone, she immediately ran down to the pool and swam graceful laps as if she was suspended in a liquid cloud. It was painful to not share that moment with her, held back by his newfound paralyzing fear of heights.

Fighting against the anxiety, he leaned forward over the balcony. He jerked back, half expecting a shock from a magicked boundary. Curious, he tried it again. Nothing. He had found his way, if only he could manage to combat his fear. Idris must have thought that this escape route was impossible for Jorge.

It was a smart instinct by the magician, but Jorge recognized this free fall was the only option. Attempting it would call upon every ounce of courage he possessed. He needed to fling himself over the balcony to a transparent terrace that may or may not exist and could send him plummeting hundreds of feet to his death. Even if things went optimally and he did hit the terrace below, he wasn't even certain that the terrace door below would allow him to access the sky castle.

This wasn't a mission he could fail at. She was here because of him. Her life was in danger because of him. He must find her, save her.

Jorge never was a pill popper. He always believed that there wasn't anything that he couldn't power through, until now. One of his film crew suffered from many types of anxiety and possessed a virtual library of medications to make it through each day. Peering down at the desert floor far below, he would give almost anything to have one of those little white wonders right now.

His entire body quaked as he held onto the rail. Jorge tried to calm himself by taking deep breaths, but there was no use. He just had to do this. Jorge hefted himself up, his arms burning as he swung one leg and then the other over to sit on the metal bar. His head spun while his center of gravity felt as if it was being pulled down to the desert floor hundreds of feet below by some unseen force. He closed his eyes and thought of his one true love Gwen, imprisoned and in danger. He must save her. He pushed himself forward. His eyes flew open, adrenaline shooting through his body as if his blood suddenly turned to pepper spray.

Hysterical laughter burst out of him as he plummeted toward the unknown.

His body slammed hard against the transparent terrace, knocking the wind out of him. It took him a few clicks to be able to breathe again. Before trying to stand, he mentally checked for broken bones. Aside from some racking pains in his rib area, he was mostly intact.

It took a minute before he could stand.

Blocking out the vast desert that stretched out far below, he pushed himself to the doorway. If he recalled correctly, it would lead him to the grand foyer.

Jorge slid the glass door open.

Now all he needed to do was find Gwen.

CHAPTER THIRTY-FIVE

When Alex, Luke, and Gormund arrived back at Chicago House, they all converged in Akh-Hehet's room. They recounted their adventures to the still recovering seer and Gini. When Alex revealed a plan that she'd hatched on the way back from the cave, it didn't seem to hold up under group scrutiny. It felt so concrete in her head, but after saying it aloud in front of the others, it became obvious just how many holes it had. Alex's enthusiasm dimmed with the unimpressed faces that surrounded her. Maybe a visioning would clear a path forward.

Akh-Hehet's expression was laced with sadness. The kind of sadness where you realize a person whom you love managed to get you both in great peril. Alex hated that she'd put the sweet old woman in a supremely bad position with the Gods. Alex knew from personal experience how dangerous the Gods were when they were displeased. The seer would be in grave danger if she was found consorting with their enemy. If only she could find a way to make it right. Maybe they all needed some supernatural guidance. The seer was frail and could probably use more rest, but Alex needed to ask. "Do you feel rested enough for a visioning?"

The old woman was recumbent on a purple velvet button-tufted chaise lounge, propped up with half a dozen puffed-up pillows. She shifted her legs over the side of the couch and smiled, but the dark circles under her eyes belied her attempt at projecting enthusiasm. "Of course, Alex, anything I can do."

Gini knelt in front of Akh-Hehet and spoke with great reverence. "Oh great and mighty seer of visions, of things that mere mortals cannot see, please assist in taking us on a visioning journey to witness a possible future."

The old woman visibly brightened at Gini's words. The formality in the gesture of one magical being asking assistance from another touched Alex. She was alarmed to realize that she never approached the seer with the deference she deserved. A sense of mortification dawned within her that she might have been continually committing a faux pas by not observing this nicety. Had the seer made exceptions for her since she was Phillip's daughter? Was she blustering about like a country cousin, not realizing what was expected?

"Of course, my dear." A spark lit in Akh-Hehet's eyes. She whipped off her bejeweled wig and flung it clattering to the floor. The seer strode over to a small bedside table and grabbed a crystal vial filled with a rose-colored liquid. The smell of roses filled the air when she pulled out the stopper. "I need something to lubricate my way into the visioning realm."

A wave of calm and focus washed over Alex as she breathed

in the heady scent. The fragrance was far more complex than she originally thought. In addition to the sweet-fresh smell of a dewy rosebud, there were layers of vanilla and something warm like cinnamon or cayenne oil.

Akh-Hehet emptied the liquid into her cupped hand. She massaged it into her scalp. "Ahhhh, Lilies of the Nile, my favorite and most rare of essential oils. Once, in ancient times, these flowers graced the marshlands of the Nile. Each flower was created by the tears of Isis as she mourned the loss of Osiris. Now they can only be found in the remotest corners of the Netherworld. These flowers are imbued with potent magic—the joy of love, the sorrow of loss, and the anger of betrayal. The only thing that is magically stronger are the tears of a God, which if collected can do most anything you can imagine."

"Tears of the Gods? Now that is rare." Gini smacked Gormund on the back.

He looked up at her. "What do you mean by that?"

"Oh, you know exactly what I mean."

Luke cleared his throat. "So, why the oil? I don't recall you needing it previously."

"Gini and I have tried a few visionings while you were away. Not a lot of successes, spotty really. I think this powerful and magical oil will bring the focus I need, not being in my usual crystal-cloud room."

"Let's head down now." Gini pulled a long swath of golden silk embroidered with tiny starlings from their jacket. The stitching shimmered with a rich iridescence, like sunlight playing against a bird's black feathers. It flashed purple, blue, and green. Gini wrapped the material around the seer's eyes and led her out of the room.

Alex wondered why Akh-Hehet needed to be blindfolded and was about to ask when Gini put a finger to their mouth, making her even more curious.

They made their way to the dining room, where the DIY chandelier shop was. Alex took in the great disparity in attitude between Luke and Gormund. Concern was written all over Luke's face, and Gormund's was bright with excitement. To see them walking side by side, they were strikingly different. One tall, totally human and handsome, the other short and stocky, in a quasi-human form, with a face that was somehow both friendly and disquieting.

Gini led the old woman into the makeshift visioning chamber. Alex held up the heavy drapery that served as a barrier to outside light so the others could pass through. As she sat, Alex was amazed at the visual impact of the mirrors reflecting the warm light from the chandelier a thousand times over. The floor was strewn with colorful rugs and brightly colored pillows. It was like being in a jewel box kaleidoscope of colors and patterns.

Gini whispered into Akh-Hehet's ear, and they sat down.

"Let's all gather into a circle." Gini motioned for them to take their places on the floor.

Luke and Gormund sat on either side of Alex.

Gini untied the silk blindfold. It slid off Akh-Hehet's head. Unlike nonmagicked silk, it glided down to the carpeted floor as if its threads were enchanted with the spirit of a starling. It landed in a soft pile in the center of their circle.

Akh-Hehet spread the scarf flat against the carpet. "This silk was stitched with the power of seeing—of seeing what was not there but what could be. The fabric itself was woven from the same eternal loom that wove the very carpet in my chandelier shop. Some say it is the very loom that Daedalus, who built the great labyrinth for King Minos of Crete, gave to the Greek demi-God Circe. This scarf is one of my more portable visioning tools." She smiled like a doting parent as she lovingly smoothed the fabric. "I don't often get the chance to use it. When I do, I realize I have forgotten how absolutely beautiful it is."

Luke leaned in for a closer look. "But why the starling? I don't recall there being any mention of starlings in ancient Egyptian folklore."

"You may expect an Ibis or maybe an Egyptian waterfowl, like one sees in so many tomb paintings." She gave him and endearing smile. "Not everything has to refer directly back to ancient Egypt. There is a wide world full of magic and possibilities. This cloth was woven for me, in this lifetime, by a strong practitioner of the ancient rites, in a small hamlet outside of London." Akh-Hehet got a faraway look in her eyes. "It was a rainy and cold day when I happened upon her. I always knew that I was different from those that I had grown up with. All my life, I'd been called to her, in my dreams and in my waking life. It was like a constant dull ache for an unknown thing. An unknown thing I knew I was incomplete without."

Tears rimmed the old woman's eyes. Alex couldn't tell if they were of sorrow or joy. It was probably a little of both.

"It took so long to find her. I can only guess that the universe knew when I was ready. I remember like it was yesterday, sitting in her small thatched cottage as the fire in her hearth crackled and popped. I sat there with her for how long, I do not know. She and I traveled this way and that, in an epic visioning, as she taught me how to truly see. On one of these visionings, I saw my reflection in a still pond. I was shocked to see myself not as Emily Loren, the name I was called by then, but as a starling."

Her eyes cleared and she patted Gini's hand. "Are we ready, my lovelies?"

Alex nodded.

"As you must know, I will need silence, and whatever you do, do not break the chain of hands. Most of you will see nothing other than what I experience in my trance. Do not wake me no matter what. The only person who can potentially join me in the visioning is Alex."

Luke looked shocked. "What do you mean?"

"Gini and Gormund are Others. They are not allowed to partake in the gift of mortal visioning. And you, although a unique specimen of a human man, have never been to the Netherworld."

Akh-Hehet closed her eyes and started her chant. Her body swayed from side to side like an entranced cobra dancing to an unseen charmer's pipe. Alex studied the old woman. As she drifted into the trance state, her expression relaxed, making her look decades younger. Alex wondered if it was caused by a joy the seer held for the visioning realm or if it was the cast of magic that emanated from the old woman as she moved between worlds.

Alex focused on the seer's chanting and inhaled the flowery fragrance of the Isis-lily that wafted around the small room. The web of connectedness wove itself between Alex and the seer. It was as if her consciousness became tethered to the energy that spilled out around her in soft waves. In Alex's mind's eye, she was looking down at everyone, even herself as she hovered from above.

A starling darted by her and toward an expanse of light that lay ahead.

Alex flew as fast as she could, trying to catch up to the starling. In this dream realm, the seer was much faster than Alex. The starling flew out of sight. In the great expanse ahead of her, she had to somehow follow a being she could no longer see. If she abruptly did an about-face, would she find her way back, or would she become even more lost in the maze of mirrors? Alex darted straight up, hoping that with a different vantage point, she might catch a glimpse of the starling. She saw nothing. She was all alone.

She focused her thoughts and tried to home in on sensations that might anchor herself back to the realm of the real, but there was nothing. Her heart raced at the thought of her consciousness being stuck forever in this infinite hall of mirrors. Alex's wings were fatigued. She needed to turn back; it was the only way forward She cut back and flew in what she believed was the direction they had come from.

"Alex!" The seer's voice boomed from everywhere and nowhere.

Alex looked behind her and slammed into something. Her eyes flew open. She was, once again, sitting in the mirrored room with the others.

"Thank god! I thought I lost you." The seer crawled over to Alex and crushed her in a surprisingly viselike hug and whispered into her ear. "This plan, the one you hatched, you cannot do. It is certain you will die."

Alex pulled away from the seer. "No, that can't be."

"I know what I saw."

"How did you see anything? All I could see was the vast expanse of mirrors and lights."

The seer leaned back on her heels. "I saw different possibilities in every mirror. I lost you because I became frantic to find another possible ending. In each vision, the only way to success was to follow your plan, but in every case, the one who traveled to the Netherworld will die."

Luke stood and placed his hands on his hips. "So that does it. We will come up with another plan. Maybe Gormund and I are the ones to finish this job."

"I must save them. You heard what she said. The only possible way is through our plan. Those futures are only possible futures. Nothing is set in stone, right?"

Luke looked down at Alex. "You can't do this, Alex."

Alex gazed into Luke's stormy eyes. "I will concede that we are all road weary. Let's take some time to at least put on some clean clothes, and we will regroup refreshed. Maybe we can come up with some backups to our plan. But when push comes to shove, no matter the outcome, I must go. I am the key to making this right, no matter the cost. I am the leader of KHNM and the buck stops here. End of story."

⌇

Once Alex made it back to her room, she stripped off her sweat-stained travel gear and jumped into a blistering-hot shower. As the steam built up, her tension washed away, allowing her to come up with some fresh ideas.

After toweling off, Alex threw on some clothes, then grabbed a few essentials for the adventure ahead of them. When she arrived at the library, Gini was already holding court over one very rapt subject. The cozy vision of Gormund chatting merrily with Gini made her realize how much they all meant to her. Everyone at KHNM was like the extended family she'd never had. They both stopped talking and turned toward Alex as she approached. Luke was nowhere to be seen. He was probably still gathering his gear.

Gormund waved her over.

When she neared them, Gormund was unhooking the leather cord holding Meyret's jasper Isis talisman from around his neck. "You should wear this as we move into battle with Jorge and Idris. I think it will give Meyret strength to see her beloved wearing it."

Alex pushed it away. "I couldn't. You are her protector. You should have the honor of stringing it back around her neck once we rescue her."

"I don't know, Alex. Aside from the sentimentality of it, there was something about the power within it that frightened her. Since you are both from the same bloodline, you might be able to tap into whatever latent magic it might hold, and that could be a great asset to us."

"Frightened her?" Alex couldn't imagine her ancestor being frightened of anything. The story of the amulet was getting more peculiar by the minute.

"It was a totem of sorts for her. She created it after she escaped from Idris years ago and never went a day without wearing it since. It was the one thing that she was strangely protective of."

"Well maybe it is a sign." Luke walked into the room. "A sign of success. Maybe it means that you are to return this trinket to Meyret."

Akh-Hehet followed close behind, shaking her head. "That pendant was born of the pain and deep damage Meyret experienced. I don't see how any situation involving it could ever be a good omen."

"Either way, it feels nice to have something of Meyret's."

Feeling the weight of her ancestor's locket against her skin was a reminder of what was at stake. "Why don't we all have a seat. I think I have come up with a backup plan."

They all made their way to the long worktable at the far end of the room. As they sat, Alex wondered why it was that Gormund and Luke always bookended her like two oddly paired loyal and protective hounds. Across the table sat Gini and the seer.

Alex opened the coffin pendant and shook the ushabti out, standing him upright on the wooden surface. She wasn't a hundred percent sure if this plan of hers would help at all toward not getting her killed, but she figured it was worth a shot. "I think we might need some help from our little friend. Aah-Ha, I call you from slumber. Wake, ushabti, worker bound to my call. I call you to do my bidding."

The spark of animation grew within Aah-Ha until he reached his fully actualized size of six inches. "What is your wish, Master?"

"Under the agreement that binds you to me, you must do all that I command. I reiterate that fact, as your newest task is to tell me the full truth in all I ask."

Aah-Ha crossed his arms, looking put out by the suggestion that he would ever lie to his master. But one thing Alex learned in her dealings with magical beings was that you needed to be explicit with them—otherwise they would find a way to weasel out of any situation that didn't suit them. "Of course, my master. Your humble servant is only here to do your bidding."

Alex found it fishy that Aah-Ha refused to tell her who his master was. She figured it was time to get down to the bottom of that swamp. "Before me you served another. Was your master Jorge Trinculo?"

"No."

"Was that person Idris?"

The small man looked down at his feet. "I was his servant for many years. But I have served many over many years."

"Was he the one who sent you to me?"

"I am bound by my oath. I cannot say his name."

If she wasn't going to get an answer to that question, there had to be another way to get at what she needed from him. That boiled down to trust. "Do you swear and hold true that you are now only loyal to me?"

"Of course, my master."

Gormund rolled his eyes. "Does this game of twenty questions have a point? I thought you had a plan."

Alex ignored him. "Two questions that you must answer true. Did Idris send you? Are you a double agent?"

"The magician did not send me. I can serve only one master at a time, and that is you. I have changed many hands over time as I've been used as chattel in an ancient debt. I was created and magically bound for the eternal house of Pharaoh Akhenaten. In my service to you, I cannot fail you or I will be obliterated, as if no one ever knew my name."

It was likely he was telling the truth. The magic that bound him was powerful. That wasn't the only reason Alex believed him. She knew one of the greatest fears in ancient Egypt was to have your name cease to be spoken. You would live on in the afterlife, so long as your names passed over the lips of the living. To disappear from existence, as if you never were, was a frightening thought to those ancient beings. Alex would be sure to keep an eye on him. Managing magical beings was a tricky skill set. "Okay, Aah-Ha, you are now officially a part of this team."

The little man straightened up. "I will serve you until I can no longer. It is a pleasure to serve such a just and kind master."

"Thank you, Aah-Ha. You will play a key role in our success or failure. I think we need to split into two forces and hit Jorge and Idris from two angles. One party's mission will be to locate and figure out how to release the hostages, while the other will buy time with Jorge and Idris in book negotiations."

Akh-Hehet looked doubtful. "But we don't even know where they are. How would the hostage release team find them?"

"I had a dream many nights ago. Actually, in hindsight it was more like a visioning. In it, I flew across the Egyptian desert with another bird." The memory of how she and the bird danced in the air together made her heart flutter. She shook the thought out of her head. "Anyhow, during this dream, an extremely large castle in the sky was revealed to me. It was something I can't imagine any mortal could have created. Buxton was a captive. Does this sound familiar to you, Aah-Ha?"

"That is the sky castle that Idris conjured for Jorge and Gwen."

"Can you show us where the sky castle is, Aah-Ha?"

"I can do one better. I can magically apparate there. Idris created protections on the castle so only those who have been there already can enter. To his mind that only includes the three of them. Any trespassers will be instantly killed. One thing he didn't consider is that magically calling me to duty there gives me carte blanche. I can be the one to free your friends. But if I am caught, I will never return to your service, even if you call me."

"Why is that?"

"Once retaken by my previous master, the magic that once bound us together will trap me until he sees fit to free me."

"And you are willing to do that?"

"You are a kind master to even ask me. I would gladly serve you to meet your ends."

"Aah-Ha, you have proved to be a most loyal and effective servant. However this turns out, I thank you for all that you have done." Alex's voice was filled with emotion. She hadn't realized how attached she'd grown to the strange little man. "If you don't return with Meyret or Buxton by morning, I will let Jorge and Idris know we have the book and coordinate a time for the exchange to take place. If you have failed, hopefully we can find another way to save our friends. And Aah-Ha, I hope whoever your master is will know that you served me well and not banish you as one who has never been."

He made a small bow. "I must go now, my destiny awaits." With a puff of air the ushabti disappeared.

Alex wiped a small tear from the corner of her eye. "If all goes well with our mini secret agent, Buxton and Meyret may very well be here for breakfast, and there will be no need to ever hand over the book of magic." Alex stood. "I think it is about time that we all get some rest."

Before everyone could make their way out from the library, Alex caught up with Luke. "Do you have a minute?" Alex drew him back into the stacks—she wanted privacy for what she was going to say to him. "I . . . we are at a point in this mission where things could go very wrong. I just wanted to clear the air between us about what happened, or, to be more correct, what *didn't* happen in the cave."

"Really, Alex, you don't have to."

"I just wanted you to know that you were right. It wasn't just because I am your boss. Right or wrong, I still have feelings for Niles. The energy between you and me has been off since then, and I think it could be a distraction from our mission to save Buxton and Meyret. We need to be fully focused on the task at hand."

"I understand." Luke made a silly mock-salute. "Boss lady."

Alex playfully whacked him on his arm. "I'll understand too, so long as you never call me that again."

CHAPTER THIRTY-SIX

It took Jorge longer than he thought it would to get to the sky castle dungeon. As he traveled through the structure, he was hyperaware of his surroundings. He didn't want to hurl himself through the space only to get caught by his "master."

Gwen locked eyes with Jorge as he crossed the dungeon's threshold. Her two roommates were fast asleep.

Jorge pressed his finger to his lips. He hoped to whisk Gwen away without waking the others.

All three prisoners were in gilded cages strung from the ceiling. Gwen's swayed slightly as she rose to stand and grasped the golden bars.

He suddenly realized he might have risked everything for naught. How on earth was he going to free her from this metal prison? He took a mental inventory of the items in his explorer's vest. The small pocketknife he always carried, although its blade was very sharp, was not at all up to the task at hand.

He pressed himself against the metal bars. Gwen leaned in close. A puff of her spicy-exotic perfume gave him comfort, making him wish he could reach through to her, hold her, and never let her go. "I am so sorry, my love. You tried to warn me about Idris and I wouldn't listen. I've put you in grave peril. Will you ever forgive me?"

Her small hands pushed through the cage, and she grabbed the vest of his jacket and pulled him to her. Her lips were soft and yielding. She let go. "You were trying to build a new future for us and lost yourself. I think I understand what happened. I lost you once—I don't want to lose you again."

"Of course." Jorge squatted down to take a gander at the lock. Hopeful that his breaking and entering skills might come in handy, he extracted his explorer's knife and pulled out the toothpick and tweezers. He doubted it would be long enough to reach the mechanism, but he was here to try.

He fumbled the knife, and it clattered to the floor.

Gwen's fellow prisoners stirred.

Meyret rose, wiping sleep from her eyes. "It looks like your knight in shining armor finally arrived."

Jorge ignored the sarcasm in the priestess's voice as he slipped the knife into his jacket pocket minus the toothpick. As a professional adventurer, he knew it was best to immediately stow your gear away. You never knew when a speedy exit was required. He worked at the lock for a few quick moments before he heard the pleasing clunk of an interior latch giving way.

Hope gleamed in Gwen's eyes as he opened the door.

This was going to happen. They were going to escape.

Meyret's voice cut through the blissful moment. "You can't leave."

Jorge grabbed Gwen's hand. "Just watch us."

"No, I mean, I won't let you."

Suddenly Gwen's flesh turned frigid, and it was like he was holding on to a human-shaped ice cube. A sharp chill burned at the palm of his hand. He let go. Gwen's stiff body toppled backward as if she were an ice sculpture knocked from its pedestal at a winter festival. Her still body leaned awkwardly against her suspended cage.

"Stop whatever magic you have hexed Gwen with. If you do, I will free you too and you can come with us."

"Do you think I am that easy, mortal? Do you know why I sit in this cage? Not because I cannot run. I could pick these nonmagicked locks more easily than you with your clumsy human things, but I know there is no use in running. Wherever you go, Idris will find you. Idris will kill you. I am in my cage like a good little girl, waiting for the moment when I can cause him the most damage. I am putting aside my petty wants so that I may save my beloved, my kin, my Alex from his evil plan. Beyond the safety of your girlfriend, don't you see that by running you will be turning your back on your own people?"

"My own people?"

"What do you think will happen when Idris owns all of the books of magic? Can you possibly be so oblivious to the deadly consequences that your little adventure could cause for humanity? You are playing with an immensely powerful lion who has an appetite to take your world and make it his toy."

The truth in Meyret's words cut large chunks out of the flesh of his reality. All this time he was unknowingly playing with the future of humanity for his own reckless gain. How could he have been blind to it? He lived his life to hunt down truths and expose them to the world at large in the hope of making it a better place for all. Never did he ever want to put civilization in jeopardy . . .

He felt a deep shame, like salt poured over the freshly made wounds of his self-image, realizing what harm he had done in pursuit of his own wants and desires. He allowed himself to be lulled into a false sense of power at having an immortal magician at his service. Gwen was right all along. Not only were they scrambling for their lives, but Jorge might have also opened up a deadly Pandora's box for humanity to deal with.

"Don't let this be the moment where you sold your own world down the river for a momentary freedom with her. Believe me, it will be momentary. He will find you, and he will take pleasure in killing you both as slowly as he possibly can."

"She is spot-on." Buxton was awake and pulling himself to standing by using the bars of his cage.

Gwen was propped up against the bars of her cage like an ancient mummy who lost her sarcophagus. The only part of her body that moved was her eyes. They followed the verbal back-and-forth between Jorge and Meyret. As the priestess spoke, Gwen's eyes twitched in frustration at her inability to move.

There was some sense in what Meyret was saying. He knew that Gwen, if she could talk, would be agreeing with the priestess. "Please let Gwen be. If you unfreeze her, I promise to listen to what you have to say."

A whisper of sound, like a scurrying mouse, came from the opposite side of the room.

Jorge's head twitched toward it.

"Don't worry, adventurer. If it was Idris, he wouldn't be hiding in corners. Before I return your girlfriend to her natural state, you have to promise me that you will stay. That you will fight. You must go back to your room like a good little boy and wait for your master. You must decide your path quickly. Mortal bodies can't handle spells for long. The longer she is frozen, the more likely she will be changed forever. Or worse yet, I won't be able to bring her back."

Gwen's eyes darted back and forth.

Buxton chimed in. "What she says is right. The priestess holds powerful magic over life and death. This matter is of great importance to her. It would not bother her to sacrifice your beloved for what she wants."

"I will do anything."

The priestess crossed her arms. "You must call Idris's real magical name and then banish him. Once you know his true name, you will be able to wish him away. That is the only way to end this. And you must promise me that you will do this on the seal of your life."

"I promise. Please set Gwen right. I beg you. Tell me his name, and I will do it."

"There is a problem in that."

"Of course."

Buxton chimed in. "Clock's ticking. He's already agreed. While you are sorting out the details, let the girl go. You don't want to kill her for nothing."

Gwen's eyes filled with terror.

"Jorge, you must lock her back in her cage immediately."

"I promise."

In an instant Gwen's complexion regained its rosy glow. She pushed herself from the cage to standing and held her arm out to Jorge. "Lock me in, dear. We need to make this right."

Gwen climbed back into her prison, and Jorge locked her in.

"So, what is the problem with Idris's name?"

"Years ago I learned his true name. He put a spell on me so that I would never be able to speak it or communicate it in any other fashion."

"Why didn't you tell your fellow prisoner over there the secret? Surely he would be up for banishing the magician."

"As I said I cannot communicate it in any other way, not sign language, not an anagram, not a pictogram. Even if I could speak his name, Buxton doesn't possess a book of magic. Only those who possess one of the books of magic can determine how to use it."

"If it has to be me and you can't say his name, then how are you going to share it with me?" asked Jorge.

Meyret motioned for him to come near. "I have a riddle for you."

He made his way over to the priestess. Jorge leaned in as she whispered the hint into his ear.

"Is it really that simple?"

"When the time comes, call out to Isis, knower of all names; then say his name out loud and command him be banished to your book. If you think all of that is simple to achieve, then you are correct in that."

The slapping sounds of Idris's slippers echoed through the hallway outside the dungeon. Jorge quickly distanced himself from the priestess and made his way to Gwen's cage. It would be bad to give the magician any ideas of cross-collusion between his prisoners.

Idris crossed into the room. "Well, well, well, it looks like you're not all that good at following orders, Jorgie. You couldn't resist trying to play the hero. I will send you back to your room, like the bad little mortal that you are. I warned you, and now your girlfriend will pay the price for your insolence."

Gwen's eyes went wide with fear.

"Leave, lover boy. It will be ten times worse for every minute you tarry."

Jorge wanted to thrash the magician, but knew he was no match for him.

"Did you hear me?"

"Yes, Master." Jorge lowered his head. He could hear the birds swarm into the cage. Gwen's terrified screams rang in his head, making him want to tackle the magician and tear him limb from limb. It took everything he had to keep his head low as he imagined the birds scratching into her flesh. If he looked up and saw what was happening, he would make things worse by doing something stupid. Half measures could get her killed. He had to wait until he could take the magician down completely.

As Jorge exited the dungeon, he spied what looked like a tiny ushabti-sized man emerge from a dark corner. In a flash the little man was gone. Maybe it was just a mouse.

CHAPTER THIRTY-SEVEN

A lex woke to frantic knocking on her bedroom door. She sat up in her bed. The rapping was coming from the lower portion of the door. Aah-Ha must have made it back. She jumped out of bed and opened the door to see the ushabti looking up at her. His shoulders slumped with disappointment.

"Are Buxton and Meyret downstairs?" Alex knew the answer but had to ask anyway.

"If only that were the case. I have failed you."

"I am sure you did your best." Alex stepped out into the hallway and started knocking on the other bedroom doors and shouted, "Council of war in five minutes, in the salon." She looked at her watch. "Four a.m., at least we will get an early start for our date with destiny."

A sleepy-eyed Luke poked his head out of the door, his tousled hair looking somewhat similar to an unintentional impression of Jorge's gel-shellacked whirlwind hairdo. "Man, and I just fell asleep too. I'll be down in two shakes."

Alex could hear movement in the other three rooms, signaling that they all were no longer sleeping. She squatted to the floor and held out a hand for Aah-Ha. When he climbed aboard, she lifted him up to her shoulder and went down to the kitchen to brew some coffee.

They all ended up congregating in the kitchen. The aroma of fresh brewed coffee drew them in like the hypnotic song of a nymph. Alex took in the motley crew standing around the large prep island in the middle of the kitchen, each holding their mug of black magic as if it were a sacred elixir. Gormund kneeled on the seat of his chair to make up for his lack of height, but he was still dwarfed by Gini who was next to him. It appeared that Luke tried to smooth his hair down, but a few random bits jutted out here and there. Poor old Akh-Hehet's complexion was grey with fatigue.

Alex figured now was a good time as any. "As you can plainly see, neither Buxton nor Meyret are here. So we will have to go with plan B and confront Jorge and Idris at their lair. Aah-Ha didn't come home empty-handed, though. He said he got some pretty important intel." Alex lifted her hand to her shoulder and lowered him down to the island surface.

The ushabti puffed up his chest. "I do. I think what I found out might really help us."

It warmed Alex's heart that he now included himself as one of their number.

Gini took a long draw from their coffee. "Do tell, little man."

Gormund shot the librarian an evil look. Gini returned the favor with a devilish smile.

"There has been a definite shift in the power dynamic

between Jorge and Idris. Jorge and his girlfriend, Gwen, are now prisoners of the magician."

Gormund stroked his chin. "Now that is interesting, but I can't say surprising. I wondered why the magician was associating with such a loser, but now it makes sense. Jorge was only a means to an end."

Aah-Ha bristled at the Immortal's interruption. "When I found them, Jorge escaped whatever prison he was in to free Gwen. He was almost successful, but Meyret talked him out of it. Telling him that he needed to stand up and fight Idris. Not only for himself and Gwen, but for the sake of humanity. She said for a mortal like him, there would be no place to hide from the magician."

"She would know."

Aah-Ha put his hands on his hips.

Luke ran his hand through his hair. "Let the ushabti finish. It's late."

"Early really." Gormund flashed a smarty-pants grin.

Akh-Hehet shot them a matriarchal stop-this-nonsense look. Chided, they both crossed their arms and leaned back into their chairs.

"Meyret told Jorge that he needed to stop Idris by calling him by his true name and banishing him into the book of magic that Jorge possesses."

"Jorge possesses one of the four books?"

"Yes, it was the one entrusted to the Gods Hek and Heket. The book is commonly thought of as the book of space."

"So, this doesn't make sense, Akh-Hehet. How can it be that my ancestor knows his true name and has not already used it? Why not cut to the chase and use it herself?"

Gormund's brown eyes softened with sadness. "Many years

ago, Idris put a spell on Meyret that wouldn't allow her to speak it."

Akh-Hehet sighed. "And, Jorge, being a possessor of one of the four books of magic, has the ability to imprison him within the book."

A small spark of hope lit within Alex. "I possess a book. What is his name? I can banish him."

Aah-Ha looked down at his feet. "That is the bad news. She whispered Idris's true name into Jorge's ear. I couldn't hear it."

Gini leaned over the countertop. "Akh-Hehet, in all of your lifetimes have you ever learned what the magician's true name is?"

"Our paths never crossed. I do know certain facts of his life from Meyret, but not something as personal as his true name. He was from an ancient Egyptian lineage that protected one of the books of magic and migrated up to what we now call Iran. He was born during the Sassanid Empire, during a time of a great plague. His hunger for eternity led him to hunt down and capture Meyret years ago. That is all I know of him."

"Wait a minute. He was born a mortal?" asked Alex.

"Yes. He became immortal sometime after he had imprisoned Meyret."

Luke crossed his arms. "Why, then, is he searching for the books of magic?"

"His father banished him from the family business, so to speak, when his desires took a turn for the dark."

Alex sighed and gazed despondently into her coffee mug as if the remaining grounds could foretell the magician's name. Alex hated to ask the seer but could see no other way. "Could you do a visioning and try to find his parents in the Netherworld?"

"Why would they give up his name? That would seem a little harsh," said Gini.

The old seer pursed her lips as her gaze focused on something seemingly far off in the distance. "Maybe the father?"

"Gini, could you dig into the library's collection and see if you can find any details about the time in which Idris was born? If the plague was happening when he was born, I am guessing that his mother would have been looking to use sympathetic magic to save her son. Maybe there is some sort of reference book on hand that would shine some light on the cultural beliefs or superstitions at that time."

Gini rubbed their hands together at the prospect of jumping down the research rabbit hole. "Your wish is my command."

Out of nowhere a large black feather floated down, landing on the middle of the table right next to Aah-Ha. Alex recoiled at the sight of it. Idris must know somehow that they had returned with the book. She retrieved the feather. As she touched it, blue smoke emanated from its top. As the smoke cleared, she could see the expected small folded piece of paper.

Alex carefully opened it and read the message inside aloud. "'A carriage will come at dawn.' It looks like we've been summoned."

Alex peered out of the kitchen window at the silver-blue predawn sky; she could tell it was just before the sun would break the horizon.

"I suggest we all grab our gear." She looked down at her watch. "Meet up in the driveway in twenty."

With a puff of magicked smoke, the die was cast. It was time to prepare for battle.

After the team left the kitchen to retrieve their gear, Alex sent Aah-Ha back to Idris's lair to try to gain a strategic advantage for them, whatever that might be. She wasn't certain what exactly she expected from him, but since he had access to the lair, it would be a good idea to have someone unexpected on the inside.

Alex went to her room. She grabbed her scribe's bag and tucked the book of magic under her arm and headed back downstairs. Both Luke and Gormund were waiting for her by the residence's entrance, standing on either side like an odd pair of door markers. Outside, the same black carriage that took them to the initial meeting with Jorge and Idris awaited them. Luke opened the door and ushered them inside.

As the carriage pulled away, Akh-Hehet ran out from the residence, chasing them down with amazing speed for her age. Gini was following close behind yelling for the driver to stop.

The driver halted the carriage, and the old seer poked her head into the window near Alex. "You can't do this. Your father would never forgive me for letting you walk into this trap. You will not return. That is what all the visions say."

"You know as well as I do your visions are only possible futures. I must honor my father and his memory and go where I am needed."

"That is exactly the same attitude that killed him."

Alex clasped the liver-spotted hand of Akh-Hehet that rested on the carriage door. "There are worse things than dying. Like living with what you could have done or should have done. I must do everything I can to stop this. The regrets you make today only feed your future demons. I would be a fool to say I am not afraid of what is to come. You know as well as I do this has to happen."

Akh-Hehet's eyes welled up with tears as she stood back.

GIFT OF THE SPHINX   459

Gini put their arm around the seer. They both waved as the carriage pulled away. The old woman mouthed the words, "Be safe."

Alex watched the landscape scroll by as the carriage made its way through the center of Luxor to the vast and open countryside. All three of the occupants were silent. No need for rehashing details, especially if the enemy was listening in.

Eventually, the carriage came to a stop at the pier that led to Jorge's converted Nile cruise boat where their initial negotiations were held. Unlike last time, the boat radiated a strange energy. The entrance gaped open, unguarded. None of Jorge's lackeys were playing the role of bouncer.

Gormund hopped out first, landing with a thud on the ground below. Alex followed Luke as the three of them walked to the planked ramp leading into the massive rectangular boat. She was glad Edmund, Idris and Jorge's bouncer, was nowhere to be seen.

As they approached the boat, it looked ghostlike, as if it were a mirage. They stepped through the threshold. The floor was solid enough, but its surroundings looked like a softly imagined graphic novel. The sharp smell of magic surrounded them.

As the three of them moved through the ghost boat, they entered a clearer and more defined copy of the boat than the one they'd come from. It, like the one they entered through, appeared to be completely empty. Alex turned to look behind her at the blurred boat vision they'd left.

Up ahead, she saw a mirror that looked exactly like the one she negotiated with Jorge and Idris in. She expected to see Jorge or Idris's face in the mirror looking back at her. Their being absent made her wonder if this was some sort of trap.

A cracking sound behind her made her jump. Idris's face appeared in the mirror. "Welcome, my guests. You have crossed from a magically created boat mirage in Luxor to one docked near Aswan. Lake Nasser to be specific. Please exit the boat and make your way to the temple on the hill."

"I don't like it," said Luke.

"Me either," grumbled Gormund.

Idris raised an eyebrow. "You have my protection of passage."

"But then how will we get back?" asked Alex.

"You will have that same protection once our transactions are completed."

"I don't like it," Luke restated, but this time his distaste was reflected in the mirror. It looked like he'd just realized he was sucking on an aspirin.

"You don't like anything, Luke," Gormund chided.

Alex could have kicked Gormund. She wasn't crazy about the situation either, but it was unwise to give Idris the impression of a team divided. "Let's go."

The boat was moored on a longish wooden pier. They walked up the dock to a path. Up ahead was a road that led to the temple on a hill. It was the Nubian Temple of Dakka—the very temple Jorge said he'd been rescued from initially. It made her wonder what its significance was to Jorge and Idris. "Come on, guys. It looks like we have a bit of a hike."

Once on the road, Alex felt free to speak. "Why do you think he didn't meet us on the boat and is making us walk to this remote temple?"

"Maybe he wanted to lure us to a place where our bodies would never be found." Luke's tone was anything but enthusiastic.

"But why here? There is a lot of nowhere in and around Luxor. Why use such powerful magic to lead us here?" Gormund asked.

Alex wondered the same thing.

Luke stopped walking. His face went white as a sheet. "That can't be a good omen." He was pointing toward a recumbent human-sized lump with the remnants of what looked like jeans and a white shirt topped with a line of feasting carrion birds.

"I hate to say it, but we better go check it out. Maybe it isn't a person. Maybe it is an impala or some other desert creature." Alex cringed at the thought of inspecting the dead and half-eaten critter no matter what species it hailed from.

"Doubt that. When have you ever seen a deer wearing white cotton after Labor Day?"

"Yeah, vultures really are nature's vacuum cleaners." Gormund half laughed.

"Why don't you check it out. Luke and I will wait for you here."

"If you aren't up to it." Gormund frowned, seemingly disappointed that Alex and Luke weren't going to play the identify-the-dead-thingy game. He trudged off, kicking up dust clouds in his wake.

"This is one of the very rare occasions where it is actually beneficial to have him around." Luke nudged Alex with his shoulder.

Alex reached into her scribe's bag, retrieved her phone, and dialed the residency. Gini picked up the phone after two rings. "Anything?"

"The good news is that Akh-Hehet was successful at finding both of Idris's parents in the Netherworld, but neither would give up the goods. Even his father, who was known to loathe him. Go figure. Akh-Hehet even pulled a few strings to get an audience with Isis, but she is still very pissed at KHNM, so she wasn't exactly willing either. She made a comment that initially felt random, but I don't know . . . something about it seemed really specific."

"What was that?"

"She'd mentioned something about stonewalling us and then broke up in laughter."

"It could be something, but as you know, the Gods are a strange bunch. More than likely Isis was just finding our little plight oh-so-entertaining. Were you able to find anything about the time when Idris was born?"

"Not really. The line of logic you were following around names based on healing or protective practices of the time sounds like a good direction. But so far I'm not able to find anything."

"Damn it. If Akh-Hehet is up to it, ask her to keep trying too. We are heading to our rendezvous spot. If you find anything, text me."

In the distance, Gormund stood over the body and flapped his arms to make the vultures relinquish their prize. "You guys might want to come over here." Although far away, Alex could hear the uncertainty in his words.

Alex said goodbye to Gini and slipped her phone back in her bag. She braced herself for what she was about to see.

"Actually, stay there. I've figured out who this is, or more technically correct, who this was." He hurried over to them.

"Is it Jorge or Idris?" Alex hoped it would be one of them. One less enemy wouldn't be the worst thing ever.

Gormund shook his head. "That vulture country buffet was the poor slob that acted as security in our last meeting."

"Edmund?" asked Alex.

"Was that his name? We never got introduced, as Gormund

and I weren't allowed in on the negotiations." Luke sounded as if his nose was still out of joint about it.

Gormund's gaze fell to the rocky ground below. He kicked a couple of stones into the distance. No matter how tough Gormund played it, when it came down to brass tacks, he was just a softy. "By the looks of the body splatter, our friend Edmund fell from a great distance."

"Body splatter?" Alex felt a hot bile rise up her gullet.

"Judging by the looks of the body, its position, and the trajectory of some of the soft bits and blood spray, I would say that he had quite a fall. I would say that by what remains uneaten, the body has been there at least overnight."

"Thank you, Dr. Grossout." Luke crossed his arms.

Alex touched Gormund's shoulder. "I appreciate that you went and checked it out for us. Let's get moving. Akh-Hehet couldn't get any further information. I told them to keep trying, though." As they made their way to the temple, it occurred to her why Idris chose this pathway. He wanted them to walk past the crumpled mass of dead Edmund. The thought didn't comfort her.

In Ancient Egypt, priests belonged to what was considered the House of Life. They were priests, but they were also magicians. It made all the sense in the world that Idris would want to have this meeting in this house. A place where his powers would be amplified to his greatest benefit, and a place where he would more than likely be victorious.

The front pylon of the temple towered above them. The limestone was harsh against the sun's light beating down on it. The glare burned Alex's eyes. She looked away, blinking to clear away the glare spots. Her body slammed against a solid wall, although the temple was still twenty feet away. In close succession, Luke and Gormund thudded against the same surface.

It was nothing but a thin sheen of magic. Tilting her head to the side, she could see its transparent iridescence. It was like looking at a very large soap bubble. Depending on the angle, she could see purples, blues, and greens swirling on its surface. Idris had put up a magical border fence.

Movement from inside the temple caught her eye as Buxton and then Meyret were being prodded out through the gap between the pylon walls. Buxton's hands were tied behind his back and Meyret's hands were tied to his. Alex's heart lightened at the sight of them.

Buxton yelled out. "Leave this place, Alex. Do not trust—"

Idris emerged tossing what looked like a glittering ball of golden light at Buxton's mouth, instantly shutting it. "If you want the same, priestess, I can accommodate." Idris pointedly stared at Meyret.

Jorge followed Idris. Behind Jorge was a redheaded woman. It must be Gwen, the woman Aah-Ha mentioned. She and Jorge had a fling years ago that ended rather poorly, or at least that was how it played out in the tabloids. Jorge was holding a rolled-up scroll in his hands. Alex guessed it must be the covenant.

Idris and his crew stood together on the other side of the barrier. "Welcome, guests. Are we ready? The sooner we start, the sooner we will be done. Jorge holds the covenant. All I ask is that you hand over that book of magic, and you can have both the covenant and your friends."

There was a scurry of movement in the shadows of the temple. Could it be Aah-Ha lurking and waiting for a moment to snatch up the covenant?

Alex looked Idris straight in the eye. "In a show of good faith,

I ask that you let Buxton go free. That will be the first parley into our negotiations."

"No deal. You give me the book. I will hand over the covenant and the captives."

It was time to bluff hard, and she knew it. "You have broken the pact. You promised an even trade. You lured us out to the middle of nowhere instead of Aswan. Then as we made our way here, we ran across a body of one of your own. Which we take as a veiled threat when you promised us safe passage. And now we discover you have erected a powerful magical force field between us. None of these things speak of good faith."

"In the interest of moving things along, all right. But remember, no funny business. Jorge, untie the old man and send him over to them."

Jorge lay the covenant down on the ground and made his way to the bound captives.

Out of the corner of her eye, Alex spied Aah-Ha tiptoeing toward the scroll. He was slowly making his way out of the shadows. If Gormund and Luke noticed the ushabti move toward the covenant, they didn't let on.

If all went well in the moment that Aah-Ha grabbed the covenant, Buxton would be on their side. She could call the ushabti to her, scroll and all. It wouldn't be a complete success, but she would count herself lucky if they left with the covenant and Buxton. Leaving Meyret with Idris and Jorge wasn't optimal, but they could rally back with another plan to free her. Meyret would likely be tortured, but as an immortal, he couldn't actually kill her. Alex hated what would happen to Meyret, but she hated the idea of giving the magician a powerful book of magic more.

Jorge untied Buxton. "Go, old man."

Luke and Gormund moved to meet Buxton at the crossing-over point.

Aah-Ha reached down to grab the covenant.

Alex held her breath.

The ushabti fumbled the large scroll. Idris's head snapped around at the sound like a cobra tracking prey. His arms shot out, one pointed at Buxton and the other at the cowering ushabti. Sparks flew from his fingertips. "You speak of betrayal, daughter of Phillip Philothea, as if you are innocent." The silver sparks wove into nets that surrounded both Buxton and Aah-Ha. The ushabti lay on the ground, accepting his fate, but Buxton fought against the restraints.

"Oh, I wouldn't do that, old man. Those threads will only get tighter as you struggle. Not that I care really, but you continue to be a bargaining chip." He snapped his fingers, and Buxton's eyes closed as he fell to the ground. "Don't worry, my dear, he is only sleeping. But I have to say that the friendly terms we have been enjoying have changed."

Idris picked up the ushabti and held him to his face. "I'll have some fun with this one later on." Aah-Ha disappeared into the folds of Idris's robes.

After everything Aah-Ha had done for them, Alex hated to think of what Idris would do to him.

"Now, daughter of Phillip, this is what happens to those who deceive me." Idris pushed his palms together. A ball of light appeared in his hands. Idris tossed the shining globe from hand to hand, toying with it as small bolts of lightning shot in all directions as it grew in power.

The electric smell of magic traveled beyond Idris's protective barrier to Alex.

Idris pulled back his arm and hurled the orb at Gwen with the force of an angry god. A stream of energy, like the tail of a comet, trailed in the wake of the orb.

Gwen stiffened, her eyes wide, standing stock-still as if suspended in time as it careened toward her.

Jorge tracked the orb's arc, working out its deadly calculus. He sprung out in front of Gwen.

The bright-sharp power exploded in his chest. As he screamed out, the smell of burning flesh permeated the air. Jorge stood firmly rooted in front of Gwen as he blocked her from the stream of deadly magic still surging from the magician's hand. He shielded her as his mortal flesh burned from within. A brilliant light glowed outward from his eyes as he held his arms outward, looking like a burning flame angel.

Through the flames it looked like he was trying to say something.

Gwen reached out to touch him as the flames licked up his body.

Alex ran to the magic barrier and pushed against it, frustrated that she couldn't pull Gwen away from Jorge's burning body. "You'll burn."

Gwen moved closer to Jorge.

"Don't make his sacrifice for nothing, Gwen."

Idris closed his fist. The magic halted.

Jorge thudded to the ground. Smoke rose from his burned and smoldering body as rivulets of blood streamed out of his eyes, nose, and ears.

Gwen collapsed beside Jorge. "No!" Her hands scrambled over his prone body, searching for signs of life. Her words were punctuated with sobs. "No . . . no . . . no. You can't leave me again."

Idris swept his arms wide. "Now you have witnessed exactly what I can do to your beloved Buxton . . . at any given moment."

Alex clutched the book to her chest, watching as the blood collected under Jorge's body. His sacrifice surprised her. It wasn't what she'd expected from the cartoonish version of the television personality she'd known. If things could have happened differently, if KHNM would have chosen another path, maybe he could have been working for the agency instead of being yet another casualty. This had to end. "Let Buxton come over, and I will give you the book."

"You have lost your claim of fairness. You will hand me the book, and I will give you the scroll. Then we will talk about your friends." A wicked grin slipped over his face. "It is your turn now to give a show of good faith."

She must stand firm. If they traded the book for the covenant, she would have nothing left to bargain for Buxton and Meyret. "No. Buxton, Meyret, and the covenant for the book. Otherwise I walk."

Gwen continued to wail over Jorge's body.

Meyret caught Alex's eye and raised her hand to her neckline. Alex felt the familiar connection between them open up. The first and only time this internal communication happened was when Alex first met Meyret in her sleeping tomb. And this time she heard the message plain as day. *Isis knows all names. Trust in the rock.*

Alex reached up and grabbed hold of the Isis pendant that hung around her neck. Then everything fell into place. Jasper. Idris's name was Jasper. A stone with healing properties. She dropped her book of magic to the ground and flipped it open. Sudden inspiration dawned on her—knowing that magic was an unforgiving and precise beast, she made a last minute alteration to his name and hoped she made the right choice. "I, keeper of this book, call upon Isis, She Who Knows All Names, to banish Gasper Niru, son of the clan of Hek and Heket, to this book The Waters of Chaos. This I command."

Idris's eyes went wide in disbelief. He charged toward Alex, screaming as if he was being burned alive. His body transitioned from solid into a ghostlike holograph, dissipating to vapor as he was sucked into the book like smoke into a filter.

Alex slammed the book shut.

Everyone stood in stunned silence.

Alex snapped to. She should check to see if Jorge was still alive. She made her way over and squatted. His hand was limp as she felt for a pulse. The only movement from his body came from the trembling of Gwen as she clutched his lifeless form.

Alex never knew Gwen but could understand how she must feel. Losing her love, watching him die before her eyes. Alex reached over to touch the woman's back. "I know this must be hard. But there is nothing we can do for him."

Gwen sat back on her heels. Her face was flushed in anger.

"Don't you touch me." Gwen shoved Alex back with surprising force. Her auburn hair fell across her face. She tucked it back as she stood and made a sweeping gesture with her hands. "This is because of you. Jorge died because of you. Because of your organization, I have lost the love of my life, and all for this? For a stupid book he had to die?"

"It wasn't just—"

"Shut up. Just shut up." Gwen's voice was high and tinny.

Alex stood and then stepped back to give Gwen some space. "I know you have no reason to believe me, but I am sorry for your loss. Let me help you take him down to the boat and bring him back to Aswan. Back to where you can honor the hero he was today. We couldn't have defeated Idris without his great sacrifice. Please, let me help you. Once we get to Aswan, you will never need to see any of us again."

Meyret knelt next to Gwen. "Dear Gwen, it would be a great honor for me to carry this brave man and raise up my fellow prisoner."

Gwen nodded in assent.

Meyret and Luke somberly made their way over to Jorge. They lifted his lifeless body and headed toward the boat. Gwen followed close behind.

The sharp call of a falcon rang through the air, pulling Alex's attention to the hillside above the temple.

Buxton grabbed Alex's hands. His eyes were glistening with emotion. "I never thought I would see you again." He swooped in for a hug. "I am so glad you pronounced his name with the Persian inflection. We would have all been doomed with a plain ole Jasper."

"I guess my education counts for something." Alex hugged him tight. "It is so good to see you." Glancing over Buxton's shoulder, Alex saw the falcon swoop by. Her gaze connected with it for a second, but that was all it took to know who it was—her flying companion, Niles.

The falcon changed direction toward the spot where Aah-Ha lay on the desert floor.

Alex flung herself toward Aah-Ha just as the bird of prey clenched the ushabti in its talons.

The falcon cried out as it climbed in the air, then swooped down, passing right in front of Alex's face. The wind off the raptor's wings sent a familiar energy sparking through her body as she watched him soar through the air. Would there ever be a time when they could be together again? Would she ever again feel his embrace?

Buxton nudged Alex. "I guess Aah-Ha is being called forth to be returned to his original master."

"Akhenaten?"

Buxton's expression was purposefully blank, like a witness who would neither confirm nor deny information. He linked arms with her. "Come on, we've got a boat to catch."

"And I have two very anxious Gods waiting to get this book back." As she strolled down to the boat with Buxton, she wondered what Hapi would think of his new roommate.

EPILOGUE

The bland institutional-grey corridor was no match for Alex's mood. If she were a chameleon whose coloring was affected solely by its state of mind, today she would have been a vibrant rainbow shining against the glum hallway. As of late, her musings were as sunny as a perfect spring day with Technicolor blossoms sprouting out in brilliant multitudes. Her giddy outlook was front and center for everyone to plainly see.

Everything was okay. Buxton and Meyret were safe and back in her life, and Buxton was restored as director of KHNM. Although she thought she'd done alright at the helm, it would take years of experience to fill his shoes properly. Maybe someday Alex would once again be the director, but thankfully that day was not today.

Bruce, the maintenance man, hailed Alex with a hearty hello as he popped her nameplate off with ease. "The glue mustn't have had enough time to adhere."

"Thank god for that." She cracked a brilliant smile and swept through the door to Buxton's reclaimed office.

Her joy multiplied as her gaze landed on her cheerful mentor sitting at his desk. On either side of him was a stack of boxes that she and Luke packed not too long ago.

Buxton motioned to the chair directly in front of him. He reached over to a small old-fashioned-looking pencil box. "These are the remnants of the previous occupant." He slid it in front of her as she took her seat in the soft leather chair across from him.

Alex chuckled. "Luckily for the agency, she didn't stick around too long."

"Don't sell yourself short. How do you know that I don't plan to retire soon? You did a bang-up job, Alex. There were some definite risks you took, but as Herodotus said centuries ago, 'Great deeds are usually wrought at great risks.' The way you handled the sudden burden of leadership makes me very proud of you and secure in the thought of passing on the torch."

She sagged into the chair. It wouldn't surprise her if he wanted to spend his golden years doing something entirely different. She should be happy for him.

His eyes twinkled with mischief. ". . . someday. Don't worry my dear, you can wipe away that forced smile. I'm not ready to give up. I just wanted to make sure that I wasn't stepping on your toes. I tried to stop Luke from unpacking until you got here, but he wouldn't hear of it."

Luke looked up at them. "Just trying to get some decent leadership around here."

Alex rolled her eyes at Luke and then turned to Buxton. "What's up? Thorne said you needed to see me urgently."

"When we returned from Egypt, there was a very thick legal brief that was waiting for you. Of course, I opened it since I am now you, or really just me once again. Anyhow, I took it upon myself to read the entire document last night." His hand rested on a stack that was equivalent to a couple of reams of paper.

Alex now knew exactly where the dark smudges under his eyes came from.

Buxton lightly tapped the papers with his hand. "You see, we are in a bit of a pickle. Although we now have the covenant, and that will help our lawyers with some of the original language of the agreement . . . well, the Gods have redoubled their position. They refuse to negotiate and are standing firm in their decision to shut us down."

"But how can they do that? Especially after Jorge's mortal interference with the magical dangers that are now in the human realm, can't they see the worth in KHNM continuing to serve?"

"As you know, since the Gods have been relegated to their realm, they have fallen on hard times. While they walked in the world of the mortals, the Field of Reeds fell into disrepair. To make matters worse, their number of worshippers keeps declining along with their powers. The only stream of divine income for the Gods is for their names to live on in praise. In their weakened state, they are unable to create the reality they want to exist in. In plain terms, they need hard cash."

"The Gods are destitute?"

"Well maybe not quite destitute, but they are in a desperate state. They need to fix up their realm to live in the style that they are accustomed to, but they are weak, and their powers are waning. So far, Thoth is the only one who has come out of this all right because of his import-export business of God fetishes." Buxton's voice trailed off, realizing that he'd brought up a touchy subject.

Luke plugged away at his work, head down.

An uncomfortable silence filled the room.

Buxton cleared his throat. "So, there's the rub and the source of our current issues. The Gods need money, lots of it. They see it as the only way to get back to where they deserve to be. They need some seed money to get things rolling to reclaim their powers."

Luke stopped what he was doing and leaned back on his heels. "Seed money? Where do they expect to get that? Some sort of supernatural loan agency?"

"If only." Buxton shook his head. "Things are much more dire than that."

Her heart sank as the pieces of the puzzle came together. "They want the agency's money. Don't they?"

"They wish to liquidate. Their main argument is that they created this agency. Therefore, the accumulated funds and properties are theirs as the founders."

"That can't be." As soon as the words came out of her mouth, she realized how naive she must have sounded. No matter what the covenant said about the agreement between KHNM and the Gods, this new wrinkle certainly did have some logic behind it. Were they all going to lose the agency? How would mortals defend themselves in this new world of magic?

"I have a temporary ace in my pocket. I'm not sure if it will work out, but I may have found a short-term investor to keep the agency lights on while we struggle to find a resolution. It is someone you know, who has come into a lot of money recently. They should be here any minute."

"Who is it?"

Buxton leaned forward over his clutched hands that rested on the desktop. "Alex, I want you to have an open mind. We don't have many options at the moment. At first I was unsure about her intentions, but I think she really wants to help us, or at least that is what she is being told to do by her beloved through the dreams she's been having."

The way Buxton was acting really threw Alex for a loop. She'd never seen him this solicitous before. "Of course, Buxton. You know I always—"

Thorne swung the door open and marched in the office. "Your two o'clock is here."

Gwen strode into the office with a large ornate book tucked under her arm.

Alex sat in stunned silence as Gwen took the seat next to her.

Before Alex had time to unscramble her brain, Buxton reached over to shake Gwen's hand. "I appreciate your offer of help, given past events. Glad you could make it here on such short notice."

ACKNOWLEDGMENTS

Thank you to everyone who has read *Gift of the Sphinx*. I hope you enjoyed the latest installment of the KHNM series. I really got a kick out of writing and imagining all its magical realms. I hope it was just as much fun for you to read.

A great deal of thanks goes out to my husband Rob, for being there throughout the very long path of this novel, from the first word to publication. Thank you for being a constant soldier in the battlefield, triage unit, and rescue ops in the ongoing campaign of writing, editing, and publication. I am constantly amazed at your willingness to read and reread draft after draft. Thank you for your constant support and for continuing to be my valiant champion and sounding board.

Thank you to my family and friends who have been supportive of me throughout as I hide away on weekends working on edit after edit. I appreciate your continued understanding and support.

Thank you to my supremely talented writers' group: Michael

Gooding, Heidi Hostetter, Bridget Norquist, Ann Reckner, Emma Rockenbeck, Laurie Rockenbeck, Heather Stewart-McCurdy, and Elizabeth Visser. As you all know, the path to writing and publishing this book was filled with countless obstacles. Thank you all for your continued support, insights, and friendship through that long and winding road. Without all of you, *Gift of the Sphinx* would have never seen the light of day. A special shout out to Laurie Rockenbeck for the extra near-the-finish-line time and effort.

Thank you to Melanie Henry whose valuable insights went a long way in making this novel be the absolute best it could be.

Shelitha Blankenship, thank you for your ongoing support of the KHNM series.

To my colleagues at the Seattle Office of Arts & Culture, thank you for your encouragement, support, and kindness in asking, "How is the writing going?" (Even with the knowledge that you might need to buckle in for an over-long and detailed exposition.)

To my Mummies, Bob Brier and Pat Remler, again—thank you for sharing your vast knowledge about ancient Egyptian history, myth, and culture with me and being willing to answer the every-now-and-again oddball question. I continue to learn so much from you both. As with *Daughter of Maat*, Pat's *Egyptian Mythology from A-Z* was a constant companion as I wrote this novel.

Thank you to Kristin Carlsen for your brilliant copy-editing skills, and to Mariah Sinclair for your spectacular cover design.

In this novel, I endeavored to represent the ancient Egyptian pantheon of gods and their myths as accurately as I could. Any missteps were completely my own.